Twisted Knight

Twisted Knight

K. Bromberg

BRAMBLE

TOR PUBLISHING GROUP • NEW YORK

TWISTED KNIGHT

A Bramble Book
Published by Tom Doherty Associates / Tor Publishing Group
120 Broadway
New York, NY 10271

www.torpublishinggroup.com

Bramble™ is a trademark of Macmillan Publishing Group, LLC.

Library of Congress Cataloging-in-Publication Data

Names: Bromberg, K., author.
Title: Twisted knight / K. Bromberg.
Description: First edition. | New York : Bramble, Tor Publishing Group, 2024.
Identifiers: LCCN 2024021597 | ISBN 9781250323408 (trade paperback) | ISBN 9781250323415 (ebook)
Subjects: LCGFT: Romance fiction. | Novels.
Classification: LCC PS3602.R64263 T95 2024 | DDC 813/.6—dc23/eng/20240510
LC record available at https://lccn.loc.gov/2024021597

Our books may be purchased in bulk for promotional, educational, or business use. Please contact your local bookseller or the Macmillan Corporate and Premium Sales Department at 1-800-221-7945, extension 5442, or by email at MacmillanSpecialMarkets@macmillan.com.

First Edition: 2024

Printed in the United States of America

0 9 8 7 6 5 4 3 2 1

To those readers who love their romance
messy, complicated, and undoubtedly
swoon-worthy. Step into the gray with me.
This one is for you. . . .

PROLOGUE

Rowan

I hate this place.

The estate lawyer's office with its sleek, dark wood and navy-blue accents that reminds me of an open casket—polished and with no purpose but for show.

Its owner, Henry Williams, with his stiff upper lip, his clasped hands, and his wire-framed glasses perched on the edge of his nose as he glances up at me.

The way the dust particles dance in the streams of light only to get lost when they find their way to the dark again.

More than anything, I loathe the reason we are all sitting here—the entire Rothschild family—waiting like a pack of rabid wolves. Because if we're here at the estate lawyer's office, then that means I finally have to accept the reality that Gran is gone.

And in losing her, I've lost the only person in my life who truly got me. My biggest cheerleader. The unyielding rule breaker. The woman who has encouraged me to follow in the path she forged even though it's against Westmore societal norms.

My gut twists right along with the heaviness in my heart.

Mr. Williams's sigh is heavy yet sympathetic as he unclasps his hands and flips to the next page from the folder on his desk. "As to the charities. Your grandmother bequeathed—"

"Can we get on with this?" my brother, Rhett, asks. His knee jogs, and his phone vibrates yet again as his impatient huff carries through the room. "It's been a week already. She'd want us to know what she left us."

"Forgive him." My mom's lips pull tight in an apologetic smile with a quick glance to my brother. "Death makes him rather . . . unsettled."

Unsettled? How about just admitting he's an all-around prick in general?

Henry clears his throat. "As I was saying, your grandmother bequeathed a million dollars to the Humane Society. Another one-million-dollar donation to the Fairmont Revitalization Fund. And—"

"Jesus Christ. I don't care what she left to charity." Rhett stands and throws his hands out. "I want to know what she left me so I can get out of this fucking place. So . . . can we just cut to that part?"

My dad shifts uncomfortably and glances at my mom as Rhett's impatience eats up the air in the room—but as usual, no one says anything. The golden child gets to throw his tantrum and the rest of us are just bystanders.

"Sure. Yes." Henry's smile is tight as he slowly flips through the pages of the will. He acts as if he hasn't read it before when we all know damn well he has. "Here it is. 'To Rhett, my grandson. Your last name alone is an inheritance in and of itself. Wield it wisely, for the continuity of the Rothschilds' impact on the town of Westmore rests on your shoulders. In addition, I leave you your grandfather's prized possession—his heirloom watch.'" He looks up, that smile frozen in place now.

"And?" Rhett prompts.

Henry looks down and studies the document again, his lips pinched when he looks back up to meet Rhett's eyes. "She also leaves you your grandfather's collection of golf tees from the courses he's played around the world."

"*And?*" Impatience edged with concern fills Rhett's voice.

"And that's it."

"What?" Rhett explodes. "What the fuck do you mean, *that's it*? I'm a goddamn Rothschild. I'm the lone grandson. I'm . . ."

"Exactly," Henry says softly. "Those two things guarantee you success and status here in Westmore. I believe that was her point."

Rhett seethes. It's in the set of his shoulders, the grit of his jaw, and the flexing of his fists. He turns to face me, his glare malicious, as if I had anything to do with this. "This is fucking ridiculous," he says before storming out.

"Rhett? Honey?" And there goes my mom right after him.

My dad looks at Henry and then me as he stands. Torn between what he wants to do and what he needs to do. He hesitates. "Excuse me, I need to go make sure he's okay."

Of course you do. We wouldn't want Rhett to have a tantrum without an audience, now, would we?

Henry nods as my father hurries out before turning back to me, the only Rothschild left in the room, and lifts his eyebrows. "I think it's best if we table the rest of this for another day. Any protest to that?"

"No. None at all."

And now I can pretend for a bit longer that she's still with us.

Silly, but true.

ONE

Rowan

I tip the wineglass to the sky and empty the shiraz like a dehydrated woman stranded in a desert.

That's how much I'm looking forward to tonight's event—Westmore Country Club's Auction for Change. I have no problem with the charity aspect of it. It's more the watching of Westmore society's who's who strut around in their finest while not actually giving a damn about the charity they are here to support that is my issue.

My glass is promptly snatched from my hand, but before I can protest, my mom holds it out of my reach. "Wine is meant for sipping, Rowan, not for gulping—just as ladies are meant to worry about their place in society rather than which rung of the corporate ladder they're on."

Luckily, her back is turned when I roll my eyes, or I'd get another refrain about how ladies need to act proper or they'll never find a husband.

Which is fine by me.

I can stand on my own two feet. I am self-sufficient. The last thing I need or want is to depend on a man.

Been there. Done that. Bought the T-shirt.

But those are fighting words when it comes to my mother, and a fight isn't exactly what I want right now. Not when in mere minutes I'll be standing in a room full of women with much the same mindset as her. It's either hold my tongue now or speak up. And the latter will no doubt reward me with constant remarks all night long. I can hear them all now.

See? Julie Edgemoor quit her job and look how happy she is being just a mom.

Did you hear Moira was nominated chair for the Westmore Society Women's League? What a dream come true for her. And to think she almost wasted her talent on being a corporate lawyer.

"Yes. Of course," I say and step my bare foot into a high heel. "How could I forget that a life of subservience is all that matters."

"Stop it," she says with a wave of her hand, dismissing my gender equality comments as she always does.

How often does she wish that it was me that night in the car instead of Cassie?

I push down the thought, bury it so the pang dulls and the ache is smothered.

My mom crosses the room and automatically reaches out to tuck the hint of my bra beneath the shoulder strap of my dress. I let her fuss while the wine begins to buzz in my head. It is my mom's birthday after all, which is one of the main reasons—well, the *only* reason I've agreed to do the pre-party thing with her tonight.

But when her fussing stops and her gaze turns scrutinizing, my dread returns. What is she going to pick apart this time?

"I really wish you hadn't done this." She reaches out and toys with one of my curls. A curl that's now a dark caramel color rather than the pale blond I was born with. "You're the face of the company, Rowan. Our brand." Her lips twist in that sour expression every kid hates to see regardless of age. The *tsk* that follows even more so.

"Yes, of course. The face and nothing else." Bitterness tinges my edges.

"What*ever* possessed you to do this?" she asks as if I hadn't commented.

Gran's death? My world turned upside down? Take a guess.

"I needed a change," I say softly.

"A change is choosing red for your toenail polish, not dyeing your hair." The corners of her lips turn down in disapproval. "Well, it's nothing a trip to Trina won't fix," she says of her longtime hairdresser.

A protest would be futile, so I don't give one. Instead, I make a noncommittal sound, eyeing my empty wineglass with envy. "I like it." I shrug.

"*Hmpf.*" Her smile doesn't reach her eyes. "Is it so bad that I want you to settle down and be happy?"

I bark out a very unladylike laugh. "What does my hair color have to do with *settling down*?"

She plucks imaginary lint off my dress. "Men prefer blondes. You and I both know that."

"Ah. Yes. I forgot. I think you left your free will and lack of judgment back at the altar when you married Dad." I roll my eyes and continue before she starts the "you younger kids don't understand" speech. "I've told you: I don't need a man to be happy."

A scowl flickers. "I don't know why you keep fighting it, honey. We've known the Williamses forever. Chad is a good man. He'd be a caring husband and good provider for you."

"Mmm." It's my only response to a conversation I could repeat in my sleep. While there's nothing wrong with Chad . . . he's *Chad*. A second brother of sorts. Kind and gentle and not exactly my type.

She meets my eyes and offers me an encouraging smile as her hand slides down to hold mine. "Excitement and passion ebb in a marriage. What you need is comfort and reliability. Someone who knows your ways and how you were brought up. Someone you don't have to try so hard with. A man who understands our family, our place in this town, and who we are. Chadwick Williams is all that and then some. Plus, he's been in love with you since second grade. That right there saves you the whole having-to-make-someone-love-you part."

Huh. Nice to know it's so hard to love me.

"With all due respect, Mom. We tried the dating thing, remember? He's a good guy—great in fact—but there was absolutely no spark—"

"Sparks burn out. Smolders last longer. You're going to be thirty soon, sweetie. You could just settle into the life you were meant to live—being a good wife, the wonderful mother I know you'll be—and become a committee chair at the Junior League. It could be yours in a heartbeat if that's what you wanted."

Ah yes, the preordained life of a Rothschild woman. Of a Westmore society woman for that matter. The one that I'm told time and again so many are envious of and that I should appreciate.

First my hair. Then Chad. Can't wait to see what she brings up next.

"Enough about that, dear," she says, batting the conversation away like it never happened. "You look absolutely stunning tonight. The picture of perfection—even if you did forget to bring earrings. Do you know what would go perfect with that dress? A pair of ruby pendants." She reaches up and touches my earlobe as she tucks my hair behind my ear.

I roll my eyes. "Rubies?"

"Yes." Another dreamy smile. "Perfectly subtle and ladylike. Such a romantic stone, don't you think?"

"Of course. Ruby earrings." Just like the pair I overheard her and Chadwick's mom talking about a few weeks ago. What a coincidence.

Does she have anything better to do than try to marry me off?

The answer is, *she doesn't.* And she wouldn't be deemed a good Southern mother if she focused her attentions elsewhere.

"Oh, look. Where has the time gone?" Her smile transforms to one of excitement. "We wouldn't want to be late now, would we?"

I stare longingly at the half-empty bottle of wine across the hotel suite and sigh. It might do me a lot of good to drink the rest of it before I go upstairs, where I'll be expected to play the part of the perfect daughter of Emmaline and Rupert Rothschild.

Sister to their prized son and heir to the family *everything*, Rhett Rothschild.

Former debutante and society woman in waiting.

College educated but for no other reason than to be a well-rounded, future contributing member of the Westmore social circle—the unspoken but well-known elites of this town.

The face of our family-run business, TinSpirits. A company created by my great-great-grandfather that started out making signature spirits and that has since reinvented itself with canned cocktails. A place where I had to beg for a *real* position. One that didn't involve my looks or my body. One that had relevance and where I could utilize my intelligence.

Vice president of marketing.

A position I coveted until I finally earned it, only to learn it was merely a placeholder without any real power. Despite that—or maybe because of it—my desire to run the family business only intensified to the point that I've progressively expanded my position, taking on more and more tasks, for no other reason than to learn the company inside and out. To become invaluable.

Silence permeates the elevator as my mother and I stand a foot apart, her adjusting the way her fur coat drapes over her shoulders and me dreaming of all the other places I'd rather be right now.

But duty calls. A duty I'm trying my damnedest to break free from despite all expectations.

The elevator dings as it passes each floor. *A countdown to impending doom.* Said doom being Westmore's biggest social event of the spring. The place to be seen and be noticed.

For me? It's the place to drink too many cocktails and roll my eyes at all the over-the-top ridiculousness.

"Just remember that we have enough gossip going on right now in regards to the family and the business," my mom says in a low, even tone. "The last thing we need is for you to cause more tonight with your nonsense. These people run in our circles, help make deals and connections for us that further our name and its legacy with their patronage. They are the support chain for our business."

My business.

Or at least the one I plan on taking over, come hell or high water.

"Mm-hm," I murmur because if I don't make promises, then I can't break them.

"With Rhett's possible run for city council, we all need to be putting our best foot forward, so make sure to mingle." She adjusts the diamond rings on her fingers. "You never know who might be here."

The elevator dings and the doors slide open. The noise hits us first. The hummed chatter accented by a loud laugh here and there. The room at the top floor of the District Hotel spreads out before us. People mill about with drinks in their hands, smiles on their faces, and adorned in their finest attire. Perfectly tailored tuxedoes. Designer gowns in varying styles. Jewels worn like status symbols by the women who have them on and the men parading those women around.

Scattered around the space in various locations are pieces of art—sculptures, paintings, and a few other items—all placed behind velvet ropes and illuminated with lights. The proceeds from their auction will benefit Carolina Children's Fund, a charity set up to help kids in need who live in cities on the other side of the river—Fairmont, Broadmore, Granville, Livingstone. The places the Westmore elite never dare venture to but that they can tout as recipients of our charity on their social résumés.

The minute my mom is called away by a fake smile and saccharine sweet greeting from one of her fellow Junior League members, a martini is thrust into my hand.

"Thought this might come in handy."

"You're a lifesaver." I kiss the cheek of one of my best friends—and the only person who keeps me sane most days—Caroline. I make a show of looking her up and down. "Look at you."

She curtsies with dramatic flair. Her strawberry-blond hair is swept up and her long black gown is probably worth more than a down payment on a luxury car. I love the woman to death, but her sense of reality is just a tad skewed. "You know us Vandeveres." She rolls her eyes and playfully adopts the matronly tone my mother had seconds before. "Known for dressing the part and *being* the part."

"Ah, yes." We take sips of our martinis and sigh. "If they only knew you like I do."

She bats her lashes and then laughs. "But they don't, so my perfect reputation will remain intact."

"Your secret is safe with me."

She nods and when her eyes meet mine, she tilts her head and pauses. "Talk to me, Row. You hanging in there?"

I close my eyes and fight the swell of emotion that threatens to overtake me. It's odd how a simple question like that brings back the crushing blow of grief. I clear my throat and muster a smile. "I'm okay."

"Okay as in, you're lying and full of shit? Or okay as in, I'm getting there but I need copious amounts of alcohol and laughter tonight?"

"The latter."

"I can most definitely help you with that."

"I knew you could." I smile and tap my glass against hers as Caroline lifts her heels in her Manolos and surveys the crowd.

The room is spacious with open-faced brick walls that show a stylish amount of wear and high ceilings with ducting showing. It's trendy and contemporary while the women in the room appear the exact opposite with their sequined, beaded, or feathered gowns. No doubt many are vying—and hoping—to be deemed best dressed in country club gossip tomorrow. The men stand around in overpriced tuxedoes with their chests puffed and stories ready to exaggerate.

In other words, it's a typical Westmore function. Pretentious and overdone. Flashy and superfluous.

"So, who are we watching tonight? Who would Gran shake her head at while wanting to call them out on their bullshit?"

I can picture Gran's voice saying those exact words. Can see her searching the crowd and sighing.

"Everyone." My remark draws a laugh from her.

"She was the best at that. Putting you in your place with a beguiling smile so you didn't even realize she was doing it."

"She was." My smile is bittersweet.

"Too bad she's not here to manage Chad and how he will no doubt become your shadow at some point tonight as if that's the proper way to charm a woman."

"Him *and* his mother."

"A double shadow."

"Lucky me," I say.

"Yes, it wouldn't be a proper Westmore event if Mrs. Williams didn't pile on the 'you're going to marry my son' pressure. Publicly, I might add. Be warned, though, that Chief Williams might put out an APB for you if she presses him hard enough."

"I'd love to say you're full of shit, but we both know differently." I shrug. "And I can run my own interference on that."

"I know you can, but Gran always added a flair of 'don't fuck with me' to her *suggestion* that people actually listened to."

Here's the thing with Caroline. She's a Southern girl through and through. Cotillion Queen, engaged to a man their families matched her with years ago. A chair in the women's club. A gracious host. She ascribes to everything that my mom wants me to be—and she's perfectly okay with it. In fact, she wants it. And while we are wildly different in that respect, our opposites attract, and years of having grown up together only serve to help us have the best time together.

"Then there's Rhett," she says with a purse of her lips. "No doubt your gran would give him that cold-as-ice stare tonight when he tries to assert himself as being on equal footing with some of the big players in attendance."

"When does he not?" I snort. The image of him throwing a tantrum the other day at the lawyer's office is still fresh in my mind.

"Especially now that he's thinking of running for office . . . he's going to be insufferable."

"You mean more than he already is?" I roll my eyes, hating this new development in Rothschild land. "Is that even possible?"

"What do you want to bet that he's going to make a scene trying to win the featured item tonight? He'll do some kind of bidding war or cause a commotion so that all eyes are on him."

I open my mouth to refute her, to defend my brother, but know she's spot-on. "I'm not taking that bet. We both know that's exactly what's going to happen," I concede as we both glance toward the painting she's referring to. "It's hideous."

"It is." She grins. "It looks like someone swallowed five colors that have no business being together and then sneezed onto the canvas."

"No shit."

"Just think. When he wins it, he'll most likely hang it in the office so everyone can see just how rich and important he is."

"Oh, Jesus."

"Yup. How else is he going to cement his status as the Rothschild in charge now? Poor guy is so sick of everyone telling him how *Daddy* used to run the place when *Daddy* stepped down well over two years ago." She tips her glass in my brother's direction where he just so happens to be standing beside our father—carbon copies of each other right down to the drinks in their hands and the puff to their chests. "In his eyes, though, buying the prized painting might just do that."

"That's a very sad but true observation."

"Then there's you, who could run TinSpirits blindfolded with your hands tied behind your back, and no grandiose statement needed to hide your inadequacies behind because you don't have any." She taps her glass to mine as a warmth of appreciation spreads throughout my body.

"Thank you. That means a lot coming from you." *Is it sad that my close friends recognize my capabilities when my own family doesn't?*

She nods. "You know I believe in you. I'm sorry that belief isn't going to save you from your mom pushing you to stand beside Rhett, though, while he's bidding."

I groan.

"Yep. She'll make sure a photographer is lined up, front and center, to capture your undying love and support for your brother."

She's right, and I hate that she is. *The Rothschilds stand together.* My mom's motto makes an unwelcome appearance in my thoughts.

"I think I'll hide in the corner at that point of the evening."

"At least that will keep you safe from Chad and the APB the chief puts out for you."

I snort. "Always looking for the positive."

"Always."

I catch a glimpse of a feathered dress in the corner and lift my chin, welcoming a change in topic. "Looks like Muffy Johnson is on the hunt again for a new husband."

"Would that be number six—"

"Seven," I correct.

"Seven. Wow. Bless her endurance. Or rather"—she holds a finger up—"bless whoever she snags this time around because they're going to need it."

"No doubt." I laugh. It feels so good to have someone to commiserate with who understands this screwy world we live in.

"I know you're going to argue on this one, but we should probably mingle some before the official auction starts."

"Caroline," I groan.

"I know, but ooohhhh . . ." she purrs. "Who do we have here? *Hello, gorgeous.*"

"Who?" I ask casually because anyone who is new to our society circle garners that response from her. But when I follow her gaze, the martini I'm lifting falters midway to my lips. "*Oh.*"

"*Oh* is most definitely right," she murmurs as I take in the man who has captured not only my but the entire room's attention.

He's tall with broad shoulders, dark hair, and an immaculately tailored suit that stands out in a room full of them. Even at this distance, it's clear he's handsome in every sense of the word, but it's the air about him—brooding, aloof, untouchable, regal—that has me instinctively taking a step closer.

He's standing alone, swirling a glass of amber liquid in his hand, his attention on a scrap metal sculpture that's on the auction block.

He looks like something I'm not supposed to have, and that makes me attracted to him all the more.

A quiet murmur has spread throughout the room as everybody else begins to take notice of the outsider. They feign interest in the auction item he's studying, needing to stare a little longer at the man whose presence is overshadowing it.

"Who is he?" I ask.

"*Damn.* Oh . . . *it's him.*"

"*Him?*" I ask, clueless but unable to take my eyes off him.

Her smile is a slow crawl across her lips. "The man everyone is talking about. Men and women alike. *Holden Knight.* Now I can see why."

As if on cue, the object of our attention looks up and meets my eyes from across the room. I smile reflexively but receive nothing more than a stoic, assessing stare in return.

Well, well, well. I don't think my mom has to worry about me being the center of gossip tonight. It looks like someone else just took that crown for the time being.

TWO

Holden

They all want to know who I am.

This outsider in their otherwise insular world.

It's in their furtive glances. Their whispered murmurs. The subtle lift of their chins in my direction. They're supposed to be paying attention to the auction. To the money being raised for the charity they claim to support.

But mystery sells better.

Intrigue has a stronger pull.

Who is he?

Where is he from?

How'd he get an invitation?

Who does he know to get in here?

No doubt their list of questions and speculations is long, but they'll know soon enough.

I glance around again as bidding begins on the final item of the evening, and my gaze lingers on the woman who caught my eye earlier. She's stunning and I'm more than intrigued. Or maybe my intrigue has to do with the fact that I'm not exactly sure how she fits into all of this just yet.

Soon enough, though, I will.

As the auctioneer begins, I focus my attention where everyone's should be—on the painting displayed at the front of the room.

Much like the people in this room, it's an eyesore of contrasting colors, bright and clashing, flashy but meaningless. The lights shining on it, highlighting it, do it no favors, and it evokes absolutely nothing from me other than revulsion.

The *oohs* and *ahs* cutting through the room around me as paddles are raised to bid on it say otherwise.

It's just like the people here to put a ridiculous value on something that doesn't matter. On something that elevates their social status but does nothing for their moral compass.

Then again, who am I to talk, especially with the events I'm here to set into motion? The events I've been planning for years.

"Two," a man calls out from across the room.

I know who he is. I know *what* he is. He's arrogant, immature, and I know the money he just bid isn't exactly his.

He's already in my sights. Unfortunately for him, he doesn't even know it yet.

But why should he? He's a Rothschild. An untouchable figure in this town.

If anyone knows that, it's me.

Well . . . that's all about to change.

The auctioneer scans the room to see if there are any more bidders for the painting. His gavel lifts. He glances around again, giving one final chance. He begins to lower it as all gazes shift to Rhett Rothschild and his apparent winning bid.

Smug fucker.

"Three million." My voice is clear. Commanding. Unwavering. And offering a million more than the last bid. *Rhett's bid.*

Gasps replace the murmured whispers that have been following me all night.

The glances that were sly for the better part of the evening now become unapologetically blatant.

Rhett glares at me. *That's right. I'm stealing your thunder.*

"Three million?" the auctioneer asks, astonishment painting the edges of his tone.

"Three."

He starts to talk but then looks my way again as if to make sure

I didn't misspeak. I nod to let him know I didn't. "Do I hear three million one thousand?" he asks, his gavel already raised as silence permeates the room. "Sold, to one Mr. . . . ?"

"Holden. Holden Knight."

It's my turn to look now. To ignore the auctioneer's stare and scan the room that is completely focused on me, the new man in town who's made sure his name is already known. The one who's paid top dollar to rent out the penthouse at Indigo Towers, the most exclusive building in town due to its steep price tag, endless views, and prime location. The newest member of the Westmore Country Club. The one who has made a point to be seen dining with every important politician in town.

I meet the eyes of those who I know want to meet mine, waiting for a flicker of recognition on their faces or a pause of hesitancy. Neither comes.

Why would they remember someone like me?

Their lax lips morph into warm smiles. Women's cleavages are adjusted. Men's chests are puffed out. The need to suddenly cozy up to the wealthy outsider paramount.

As I expected.

It's amazing what money can do. How it changes perceptions. How it can open doors. *How it can ruin your life.*

I return the smiles now given openly with nods as I make my way through the crowd that parts for me.

That revenge I've been waiting years to exact?

That starts now.

And the man they're all suddenly wanting to know?

They forget that they already do.

THREE

Holden

It's suffocating.

The room. The pretention. The pandering for my attention that began immediately after my winning bid and the realization that I'm the Holden Knight that I've made sure they've been hearing about in their circles but have never really seen.

My sigh is heavy as I close my eyes and let the aged scotch sit on my tongue. I welcome its burn as it works its way down my throat. As the memories that are always on the periphery move to the forefront of my mind. As the men who cemented them there mill about this room without even knowing it.

A few keystrokes got me into the charity's server. It was child's play after that to make sure my name was on tonight's exclusive guest list. To set the wheels in motion.

Winner takes all.

From here on out, though, it won't be as easy. Far fucking from it. But isn't this the game I've prepared for most of my adult life? The one where failure isn't an option?

"Well, well, well. If it isn't the most talked-about man of the hour."

So caught up in my own thoughts, I didn't realize I had company. Company that's way too close on this expansive balcony.

That means she only wants one thing.

"The circles you want to mingle in? They're inside," I say, prepared to blow the woman off and let her know I'm not interested in whatever it is she's selling—most likely *her*—but when I turn to face her, the remainder of my smartass remark dies a quick, shameless death.

It's her.

And the pieces fall into place.

Rowan Rothschild.

I'm met with a pair of expressive green eyes. They hold mine with a sincerity I don't deserve, and a challenge I don't particularly want.

"Who said I wanted to mingle at all?" she counters with a dismissive laugh before taking a long sip of the martini she holds.

I take her in.

The olive skin. The defined cheekbones. The dark, caramel-colored hair that falls in waves over her shoulders and is tucked behind one ear. The toned arms and more-than-impressive body filling out the elegant and curve-hugging dress.

To be intrigued by her is one thing.

To be attracted to her? That's a whole other Pandora's box I'm not ready to open.

She lifts a lone eyebrow as my eyes come back to hers again. "Like what you see?"

My smile is cold despite my natural reaction to a gorgeous woman. "I don't think it particularly matters what I like."

Her laugh is throaty and rich and begs for my attention. "That's where you're wrong and you know it."

"Is that so?" I murmur, not fully committed to wanting this conversation yet.

"It is." She turns to face me, her hip now leaning against the railing, the emerald of her eyes glinting. "You're a man who knows what he wants, what he likes, and makes no apologies in taking it. Case in point: most men would have tried to hide the fact that they were just checking me out. You on the other hand? It seems that you like doing things and being seen while you do them."

Her smile comes out in full force and would drop a lesser man to his knees. She's stunning, simply stunning, with an elegant beauty that would be hard for anyone to refute.

"Perhaps." I take another sip of my scotch and turn back toward the darkened skyline, all but dismissing her.

Distractions. They're the last thing I need right now. And she— standing here, talking to me, becoming more attractive by the second as she does so—with her sass and lack of intimidation is promising to do just that.

"And the painting?" she asks, not getting the hint.

"I don't believe that's any of your business."

"I'm making it my business."

My chuckle is low and unforgiving. "Clearly you think highly of yourself."

"Then it seems we both do."

A smile toys at the corners of my lips. She's got some fight in her. I respond despite myself. "What about the painting?"

"You just spent a pretty penny on it."

"I think most people here have plenty of pennies available for spending."

"True. We do. And yet the mystery man who no one quite knows just one-upped all of us with that show he put on."

"Hardly." *What's her angle?* There's no way she can know what's going on. *Can she?*

"What do you plan on doing with it?" She ignores my question. Her heels click as she moves closer.

I watch the liquid I'm swirling around in my glass. "Throw it away. Burn it. I haven't decided just yet."

She freezes. "What am I missing here?"

"Nothing. You heard me perfectly fine. Art's just not my thing."

"Then why buy it?"

"I have my reasons." *Anything to prevent* them *from having it.*

"So, buy it then destroy it? Just like that?"

"Hmm. Yes." I lean forward, rest my elbows on the railing, and slide a glance her way. "*Just like that.*"

Out of all the reactions I was expecting, her throwing her head back and laughing is the last of them. But that's exactly what she does.

For a woman I had no interest in talking to, she now has my undivided attention.

"What's so funny?"

"You'll fit in well at Westmore."

"Why's that?"

"You have the 'classic prick' thing down pat."

"If that's supposed to be an insult, you're going to have to work harder."

She snorts and that composure of hers crumbles some with the stumble that follows. Her hand reaches for the railing to steady herself, while mine reflexively grabs her arm to do the same. Her proximity affords me a closer look. The glassiness to her eyes. The ease of her smile. The empty martini glass in her hand that was full only moments before.

Her body. *Christ, her body.*

Her nearness affects the both of us. It's in the hitch of her breath and the sudden jump of my pulse. Her lips part ever so slightly as we stand frozen for the briefest of seconds.

Distractions, Holden. Stay the fuck away from them. Especially in this crowd. Particularly her.

Her lashes flutter before she gives a quick shake of her head and takes a step back. "Sorry." She holds her hands up. "It's been a rough week, and this"—she lifts her glass up—"is how I've chosen to cope tonight."

"Enjoying yourself that much, are you?"

"Yes. Having the time of my life, can't you tell?" She rolls her eyes and huffs out a breath but then she meets my gaze again.

"No," I retort. "Don't you have somewhere else you should be? Someone else you can bore?"

"Nope. I already did my duty for the night."

"And he got rid of you that quickly after? That's . . . embarrassing."

Her glare is lethal. Good. Maybe she'll leave me the fuck alone, because the longer she stands here the easier it is to justify the distraction that is wanting her. Wanting a woman who is most definitely off-fucking-limits.

"This is where I return the jab and say if you're trying to insult me, you're going to have to try harder."

"The difference between you and me is you care. *I don't.*"

"For the record, it was my brother I was talking about. The duty I had was in regards to him."

"How cute. You still have to hold his hand to cross the street."

"No. I have to take up residence anywhere that won't upstage my perfectly positioned sibling. It's every woman's dream, isn't it?" She motions to one of the servers who is walking around with a tray of martinis and trades her empty for a fresh one. She takes a sip, her eyes meeting mine above the rim.

"I don't claim to know what every woman's dream is." *But I can sure as fuck fulfill most of them.*

"You should. Here in Westmore—"

"You keep talking like I care, sweetheart. I'm sure there are plenty of people in this room who'll pat you on the head and give you the attention you're craving. But it's not going to be me."

"Definitely have the classic prick thing down pat."

I nod and take another sip of my drink. "Yep. Sure do."

"What charity are we benefiting tonight?" she asks, throwing me for a loop.

"Why?"

"Just trying to figure you out."

"Figure away." I tip my glass in her direction. "No doubt another martini will help with that."

"Don't mind if I do to both." Her smile has a chill to it, but even its iciness is hot. "Let's see, you spent a ridiculous amount on a painting you're going to destroy. You paid twenty-five thousand for a plate of food from a Michelin-starred chef that you're not eating. And you're standing out here enjoying the fact that everyone is talking about you because you get off on it."

"You don't know the first thing about what I get off on."

And Christ if the little smirk on her lips and challenge in her eyes doesn't reel me in when I need to be taking huge steps back.

"So the question that begs to be answered is: What *are* you doing here, Holden Knight?"

"Raising money for a charity just like everyone else."

She studies me, her eyes narrowed, her lips pursed, as if she's trying to figure out if she believes the facade I'm putting on. "And that's where you're either full of shit or naive as hell if you think anyone here actually cares about the damn charity. They care about themselves. About being seen. About posting on social media that they were here with the who's who of Westmore, making it known they run in the same circles. Perceptions matter. Optics matter. Status matters."

"You're here, aren't you?" I murmur and take a step toward her, the temptation of her way too strong.

"I don't have a choice."

"Then maybe you should grow a backbone so you do have one."

"You don't understand."

"You're right. I don't. Can you leave me be now so I can drink my scotch in peace and enjoy the view?"

I take another sip, welcoming its burn as it works its way down my throat. As the memories that are always on the periphery move to the forefront of my mind. As the men who cemented them there mill about this room without even knowing it.

Are you there, Mason? Are you watching?

I let the ghost of a smile come, even if momentarily, before opening my eyes and looking at the city that took everything from me.

The same city I've returned to, intending to get a piece of it back. The same city I'm now staring at as the auction's after-party carries on behind me.

It feels weird to be back. *And perfectly right.*

"My family has been a pillar in this community forever."

"You're still here?" I lift an eyebrow but don't look her way.

"They are, you know."

"Awesome. Good for them. No doubt you throw your name

around as often as possible to show that too. I, on the other hand, couldn't care less."

"Fuck you."

I look her up and down, surprised by her response and rather liking the grit to it. Pretty and polished but blunt and tenacious all at the same time. "Nah. Not my type. But, uh"—I motion to the room full of people at our backs—"be my guest. Maybe you're one of theirs."

"Charming." She holds her hand out for me to shake. "Rowan Rothschild. I'd say it was a pleasure to meet you, but . . ."

FOUR

Rowan

Yeah, that Rothschild.

There's the slightest hitch in his movement when I say my name. A cough over his sip of scotch to hide his embarrassment that he was talking like that to me. A Rothschild from Westmore.

I may be buzzed, but I saw it.

What did my brother do now?

That's my first and only thought as Holden's glance lingers on my hand before he decides to take it. The shake is slow and thorough, his eyes never leaving mine as he does.

I never throw my name around. I never use it to get access or gain clout, but Mr. Holden Knight needed his ego checked. I knew that would do it.

Is the man gorgeous? Oh my god, yes. In all the best, most mysterious ways.

Is he a prick of epic proportions? So far, it's looking like he is.

He's intriguing but aloof. Reserved but talkative. Enigmatic but—

"Rowan Rothschild," he murmurs as he studies me with that pensive intensity he wears as easily as his tuxedo.

"Perfect daughter and Stepford sister, at your service," I say with blatant sarcasm and a mock curtsy.

"I knew you looked familiar."

"Two seconds ago, you were telling me to take a hike, but now that you know who I am, you're not so eager to see me go."

"Call me curious."

"I think I'd call you opportunistic."

He shrugs. "Always. Is there a problem with that?"

Yes.

No.

At least he's honest.

"That's what I thought," he murmurs in that deep rumble of a voice that sounds like gravel dipped in honey. Smooth with a little grit to it.

"So that's why you're here? *Opportunity?* To throw your money around and let it be known you're here to play?"

"Why are you so concerned with how I throw my money around?" Holden asks but then looks over my shoulder and surveys the crowd. There is something about the look on his face—a bristling, a distaste, a . . . something that I can't quite put my finger on, but it's there when he meets my eyes again. "It's benefiting the charity you're championing, is it not? Or do you not care about the cause and are simply here to see and be seen?" He tilts his head. "My bet's on the latter."

"And your bet would be wrong." I cross my arms over my chest in a defensive position. "The money being raised is pretty much the only positive thing happening tonight."

"And here I thought you were going to say the only positive tonight was meeting me." The dry sarcasm in his voice has a smile tilting up my lips.

"Of course. Forgive me." In a move that even surprises me, I reach out and run a hand down his bicep. His arm tenses beneath the fabric of his jacket. Our eyes hold, challenge, and then that smile playing at the corners of my lips curves wider. "I forgot the proper response to all of your flattery was to fall at your feet."

"There's only one reason I like women at my feet and it's not because they fell." He quirks an eyebrow as his eyes darken and nostrils flare ever so slightly.

The comment is crude and unexpected, but hell if it doesn't have me wondering about the man beneath the suit. It's not like I needed prompting. I've been wondering that since our eyes first met. "I'm sure you get all the women with lines like that."

"You're still standing here, aren't you?" The muscle ticks in his jaw as his challenge settles between us.

"Me being out here has nothing to do with you and everything to do with them." I glance over my shoulder at everyone inside and my head swims. Guess that last martini hit me harder than I thought.

"Them?"

"Do you ever notice you respond to almost every comment with a question?"

"Humor me, Rowan," he says, and there's something about the way my name sounds on his lips—almost an intimacy to it—that has chills chasing over my skin. "What is it about *them* that you're wanting to avoid so badly that you're standing out here with a man you don't know and aren't quite sure you want to?"

He eyes me above his glass as he takes a slow sip. His tongue darts out to lick away an errant drop, and I have to force myself to meet his eyes again. He makes me uncomfortable and turned on at the same time. I've never felt that combination before, and I'm not quite sure that I want to.

"I don't like their rules," I finally say.

"I'm not one for rules much either but I have a feeling we're talking about two completely different sets of them. Care to narrow this down for me?"

"My family's." It's something I shouldn't admit, but god does it feel good to be able to say something to someone who doesn't know us. Who doesn't look at me as a bystander when that's all everyone else in the goddamn town does. Who is new in town and not under the veil of their bullshit yet. A nervous chuckle falls from my lips, but it doesn't stop my admission.

"They have rules?" he scoffs.

"To look pretty and keep my mouth shut."

He's quiet for a beat and then he nods. "From where I stand, I'd say you're successful at the first. Not so much at the second."

Something about his comment bolsters me. The gin probably helps too. "Well, this is as close as I get to being quiet. Take me or leave me."

"Apparently I don't have a choice seeing as you're still standing here, interrupting my scotch with small-town gossip I really don't give two fucks about."

"Oh, you'll fit in just fine around here," I murmur. He makes those comments yet his eyes look like they want to devour me.

"Meaning?"

"Nothing is what it seems in this place. And I have a feeling you are much the same." I shrug. "Like why it is you're here."

"To buy a painting?"

"Bullshit. No one is here to *just* buy a painting. Everyone has another reason. What's yours?"

"My reasons don't matter and frankly are none of your business."

I take a step closer. The scent of his cologne tickles my senses, a drug drawing me in when I don't want to be anywhere near him. And yet I don't step away.

Maybe I like playing with fire—because I have a feeling that is exactly what he is.

"You forget. Everyone's reasons are everyone's business in Westmore."

"Maybe it's as simple as I've recently relocated here. An 'all work and no play' type of thing. Maybe I'm looking for some new friends."

"Friends? In this crowd?" I snort, not buying it for a second. "Be careful what you wish for—you might just become one of us."

He steps even closer to me. Close enough I can feel the warmth of his breath on my cheek. "And who would that be?"

"Pretentious. Incompetent. Self-serving." Laughter erupts from the ballroom, and when I look at the circle of men making the noise—Rhett, Chadwick, Porter—the sneer on my face is as automatic as the derision in my voice. "Like *him*."

"Like *who*?"

"My brother. *Rhett*. I figured you'd already met him seeing as you purposely upstaged him earlier during the auction."

"Rhett. Yes. I haven't had the pleasure . . . or displeasure, it seems, if I were to put any stock in what you're implying."

I chuckle. Of course he's doubting me—I'm a woman with firsthand knowledge of how this town works. Why was I still hoping that he might be somewhat different?

"Implying? Really? Look at him in there puffing his chest like he's the king in his castle, ruling his world, when he's really failing miserably at everything. He's all smoke and mirrors, fooling everyone with his ruse, while everything that matters turns to shit." I take a sip of my martini as I wait for Holden to defend Rhett.

Isn't that how this town works? Men stick together? Women have to kowtow?

"Sounds like he's an incorrigible fuck."

His words surprise me. Egg me on. Make me feel heard when normally my ingrained instinct is to protect my brother. I hate that I want Holden to like me over Rhett, despite not being 100 percent sure I like him.

"At times," I say cautiously but then realize this is my only time to make a first impression—to win Holden over to my side before the rest of Westmore tries to. So I expand. "Rhett acts like a prince when he's really a pauper. It's like no one cares but me that the company is hemorrhaging money and about to default on loans that will surely devastate us and lay even more people off. They're blind to it all because he has a dick—" I stop myself. Eyes wide, lips pursed. Did I really just say that to a stranger?

But that stranger's laugh rumbles through the charged air and hits me harder than expected. "Why stop now? The floor is yours, Miss Rothschild."

"Never mind. It's been a week, month, night . . . take your pick."

"No. I'm invested in this story now. *Please.* Don't stop." He leans against the railing beside me so that his hip brushes against mine. He lifts his chin to the crowd inside that we are both staring at now. "He's the prized possession because he . . . has a dick, as you so politely put it, and . . . what else? You're more qualified, more astute, and more demanding, but no one can see past the fact that you're a woman? Am I reading this right?"

I study him and try to figure out if he's mocking me or agreeing with me.

"Didn't you know in coming to Westmore you've walked back in time? Where my only ambitions as a female should be to serve, support, prop up the prized son, and wear freaking ruby earrings all while smiling big and pretending I'm perfectly content."

"I think you need to work on the perfectly content part."

I level him with a side-eye and then come to my senses. I'm out here venting to a man I don't know about personal shit I'm supposed to just accept. "Look. I apologize for the rant. Let's chalk it up to it being a rough couple of weeks. You didn't deserve to be bombarded with . . . all of that. I barely even know you and here I am—"

"Your secrets are safe with me, Rowan."

"That's not very comforting considering no one knows anything about you."

"If I wanted people to know about me, I'd tell them."

"Again with the dark, dangerous, and mysterious card, huh?" Anything to get the discussion off of me.

"I'm more than certain half this party googled who I am after my winning bid. Should I assume you looked me up too before you decided to come out here and talk to me, or had you already heard the name but didn't know the face?" He sets his glass on the railing before adjusting one of his cuff links. "The internet should tell you all you need to know."

He's right about that. All of it. But I want more. "Facts. Figures. Rumors. Those aren't the types of things that intrigue me."

"Then what does intrigue you, Rowan Rothschild?"

My name rolls off his tongue but it's more than his voice that has my breath hitching. It's him reaching out to wipe a drop of my martini off my bottom lip with his thumb that has my heart thundering in my chest.

It's a simple action on his part and an extremely complicated reaction on mine. A visceral one that has my nipples tightening and a slow simmer of an ache burning. It's confusing and fleeting, and I'm chastising myself the minute I comprehend the reaction.

But he sees it too.

It's in the smirk on his lips and the arrogance in his eyes.

He did that on purpose.

And I gave him exactly the reaction he wanted. *Fuck.*

I step back and shake my head. He thinks I'm going to fall for that? That I want to fall for that?

"What's your story?" I ask, needing to understand this. Understand him. Why I'm still standing here.

"I don't have one."

"Everybody has one." He lifts his eyebrows in response. "C'mon," I say, trying to sound persuasive and not desperate, "I just told you mine."

"No. You told me your brother's."

An exasperated sigh falls from my lips. "His story is mine. Sad, right? We Rothschilds are bound to duties and familial obligations that were predetermined way before we were born."

"But with two sets of rules."

"Yes, with two different sets of rules." I nod, thinking of my brother at the reading of the will the other day. Of his expectation that Gran was going to leave everything to him and then his tantrum when she didn't. What does the fact that this made me happy say about me? "You're deflecting, Holden. I asked you first."

"And yet I don't owe it to you to answer, do I?"

Our eyes hold and for the briefest of moments I think he's going to kiss me. I want him to kiss me.

It's the dark night around us, the gin in my veins, the feeling that someone heard me . . . and more than anything? An undeniably blatant attraction.

"Holden." His name is a whisper I don't even remember saying. Our eyes hold. His Adam's apple bobs.

"Good night, Rowan."

"You're leaving? Are you telling me there's something more important than me?" I tease.

"Don't ask questions you don't want the answers to." His smile is reserved as he takes a few steps back, his gaze roaming over me one last time. "And I'd opt for sapphires over rubies for you. They're powerful. Regal. Confident."

"They'd clash with my dress."

"Then change the dress." His gaze darts down to my parted lips. "Enjoy the rest of your evening," he says and starts to walk away.

"I refuse to believe what they say about you," I blurt out.

He pauses and looks back over his shoulder at me. "Do you think I care what they say?"

"They're all wondering who Holden Knight really is. Who he's going to reel in, chew up, and then spit out."

He chuckles. "Good. Let them keep wondering."

"Nice to have met you, Mr. Knight."

The space between us does nothing to dissipate the electricity of our attraction or my desire for him to stay.

"You might want to reserve that judgment," he says before walking away without another word.

Rowan

"Shit. Shit. Shit."

How did I lose track of time? There's no way I'm going to be on time for cocktail hour with the girls. Here's to being fashionably late.

I hastily gather the stuff up I've spread all over the conference room table. My laptop. Notepads scribbled with my handwriting. Graphs. Financials.

It's everything I've been poring over, trying to decipher and then commit to memory, so I can devise a plan to get TinSpirits out of the hole Rhett is currently driving us into. The same one Rhett doesn't seem to worry much about.

I may be "the face of the company," but lately it feels like I'm the only one who is trying to save it.

TinSpirits is one of the oldest signature spirits companies in the Carolinas. A company whose roots go back to Prohibition but that has adjusted and reinvented itself into what it is today—one of the leading canned cocktail brands in the region. But even with this recent success, why have our profits continued to wane? How do we have enough orders on the books for this year and beyond but are struggling to stay out of the red?

Rhett blames our financial struggles on rising input costs, on global warming and its fallout, on the cost of manufacturing, but I'm not buying it. If that's the case then we assess, adjust, and adapt.

But we're not doing that . . . and why not?

The building is all but vacant as I make my way up to the top floor where my office is. There are a few stragglers here and there, no doubt finishing up some last-minute things before heading out for the weekend, but for the most part everyone has left.

Like I should have hours ago.

But all thoughts of a relaxing night out with my friends fall to the wayside when I pass the main conference room, notice its door shut, its blinds drawn, and hear voices on the other side of both.

I knock and open the door before a response is given.

All conversation stops.

Alarm bells sound in my head as I take in those in the room. My brother, Rhett, the company's CEO, sits at the head of the table. Chadwick Williams, Rhett's best friend, the company's COO, sits beside him, eyes huge and full of apology as they meet mine. His lips part as if he's going to say something, but then snap shut just as quickly.

The men sprinkled about the conference table avert their gazes rather than meet my eyes. Top management. Our lawyers.

And all the board members.

Those alarm bells turn into full-blown sirens.

"What the hell is going on here?" I ask, stepping into the room where I rightfully have a place as TinSpirits' vice president of marketing.

Things that have felt amiss over the past few weeks flood my mind. Meetings held offsite that I learn about after the fact. Hushed conversations between Rhett and Chad in unoccupied offices. Constant appeasement from my brother. *Chill out, Row. Nothing is going on. Quit being such a nag. Everything is under control.*

But this feels like anything but under control. More like a blindside.

But in regards to what?

"Rhett?" I demand.

"I thought you were gone for the day."

Uncertainty tickles at the base of my neck. "I was supposed to be . . . and I have a feeling that's exactly what you were expecting."

"Your car isn't here."

I stare at my brother, hating the lump that's lodged in my throat and the discord his lack of an answer has created. "It's parked out back. I want an explanation as to what this is all about."

"It's just board member stuff," Rhett says.

My spine stiffens immediately. Those are fighting words between us, and he knows it.

"Board member stuff," as in a board I don't have a seat at because I'm not him. *A man.* My last name and the fact that my family founded the company hold no bearing here.

More than aware of how triggering those words are to me, Chad offers me a smile that is a mix of placating and patronizing as he rises from his chair and moves around the table toward me. "It's nothing major, Row. Just a few votes over mundane stuff and a little brainstorming afterwards." I want to believe him—he's never done anything to make me do otherwise. And yet unease tickles its way up my spine. "You know how Rhett and I like to throw ideas against a wall and see what sticks."

"Alone. Over a beer. Not here. Not like this with the company lawyers and the board present." I try to keep the panic from my voice.

"Isn't this what you've been asking for? To shake things up a bit. To make some changes. Something to help increase our cash flow—"

"Interesting way to phrase 'a buyout,'" a voice at my back says. A voice that has me freezing in place. "Now, where were we, gentlemen?" Holden Knight asks as he rounds the conference room table, rolling up the sleeves of his dress shirt as he goes, with a nonchalant glance my way. His presence is a complete shock to my system. His words even more so. *"And Rowan."*

"I'm sorry. What did you say?" I choke over the words.

Buyout?

Bitterness coats my tongue and my body flushes with a heat that makes it hard to draw in a breath.

I take in his dark hair, tanned skin, broad shoulders, and vibrant blue eyes that hold mine as he lifts one eyebrow. "Is there a problem, Miss Rothschild?"

I'm reeling. From seeing him here. From the words he just uttered that I'm still trying to process. From the guilty grimace on Chad's face and the measured look on Rhett's that tell me what I just heard is true.

The smile I offer in return is anything but warm. "Yes, Mr. Knight. A very big one." I plant my hands on the table. Anything to steady my arms, which are shaking violently with the fury coursing through my body. "I would love to know why *you're* standing in *my* boardroom."

"Your boardroom? Cute." He lifts a brow, grinning smugly, before turning to Rhett and completely dismissing me. "Let's continue where we left off, shall we?"

"I was talking," I say.

"And now *I am*," Holden asserts.

He thinks he's going to dismiss me? I glance around the room at people who are supposed to have my back. They all think I'm going to stand here and let this—*whatever this is*—go on? Fire burns up my spine. "Excuse me, but—"

"As I was saying . . ." Holden lifts a hand to quiet me, and it only serves to infuriate me more.

"Look. I'm trying to remain professional," I say, struggling to keep my voice even. "But I'm on the cusp of losing my shit if one of you doesn't tell me what the fuck is going on here."

His chuckle fills the room, doing nothing to ease the atmosphere that's already rife with tension. His eyes meet mine and amusement glints in them. "From where I stand, I'd say you're successful at the first. Not so much at the second."

I glare at him, his words repeated from the balcony that night. His response to my familial duties to "look pretty and keep my mouth shut."

His smile taunts me.

My blood runs hot.

Then cold.

My heart tumbles in my chest as our conversation on the balcony replays through my mind. How he pushed me away. How he was indifferent. How he was a prick . . . right up until I introduced myself.

The coughed choke when he heard my name.

His sudden decision to stay. To talk. To answer my questions with questions.

Dread filters through me.

I did this.

I gave him the info he needed. I led him right to the weak spots so he knew where to hit the hardest—or make the deal sweeter.

Obscenities scream in my head and die on my tongue as he holds my disbelieving stare.

Motherfucker.

They're all wondering who Holden Knight really is. Who he's going to reel in, chew up, and then spit out.

"So it's us, then?" I ask.

The sharpening of his smile tells me he knows exactly what I'm referring to. A private joke that I don't find to be funny at all. His lack of a response is an answer in itself.

Oh. Fuck. *It is.*

Rhett moves in my periphery, and I whirl on him. "*You sold the company?*"

"*Some* of the company. Think of it more like a partnership. We'll be better off with a new—"

"Are you out of your mind?" I shriek.

"If the two of you want to have a sibling spat, the door's right there. Please do it outside," Holden says drolly, only fueling my rage.

"I. Want. Answers."

Holden's unamused sigh weighs down the room. His bored expression complements it. "It's called a business deal. Two sides meet. Two sides negotiate. Two sides agree." The lift of his eyebrows is condescending at best. "Would you like to sit quietly and watch? You might just learn something."

"Oh, fuck you," I grit out.

He smirks. "Go on."

Every part of my body feels like a coil about to snap. "If you'd think for a single goddamn second that you have any valid business dealings with TinSpirits, then you'd be mistaken."

Rhett's chair squeaks as he shifts, but my stare doesn't waver as Holden plants both hands on the conference room table, the veins in his forearms flexing. A flicker of that smirk ghosts over his lips. "You're a bit late for that, Rowan. That negotiation part I just told you about? That's been completed. You're just in time to watch the ink dry on the letter of intent." His eyes twinkle with smugness. "I think the word you're looking for is 'congratulations.' You're looking at the soon-to-be majority owner of TinSpirits."

This isn't real.

Can't be.

There's no way this could be happening.

I look over to Rhett, who's looking down at the pen in his hands.

Oh. My. God.

He did this.

That son of a bitch did this.

"You're so excited you're speechless. I'm flattered," Holden says, pulling my scrambled thoughts back to him and his arrogant smirk.

"If you think I'm giving up my family business without a fight, you're crazy."

The muscle in his jaw pulses as he motions to the papers on the table. It's the only hint of any reaction that he gives. "It doesn't exactly look like you have a say in the matter." He glances at the men around the room and smiles before looking back at me. "Does it, now?"

His words are like acid churning in my gut. How did I not see him for what he was?

"I was right. You *are* a prick."

"Never claimed to be any different, but I don't think that has any bearing on my purchase." He shrugs. "If I had to guess by your reaction, I'd say you're against the deal."

"There isn't going to be a deal."

"Gentlemen? She thinks what she has to say matters." He crosses his arms and doesn't back down from the challenge in my stare. "*It doesn't.*"

My pulse thunders. My head dizzies. "This isn't happening," I say more to myself than to anyone.

"But it is." Holden waves a dismissive hand that has me gritting my teeth and fisting my hands. "The board voted," he states matter-of-factly, as if my whole world—my goals, my dream—hasn't just been yanked out from beneath my feet. "A letter of intent has been signed. Due diligence is up next. Then we'll finalize."

Letter of intent has been signed. Ink drying.

My chest constricts.

"It's not my fault you're the face and not the name. If you were, then you might have had a chance to have your staunch displeasure recorded in the minutes," Holden taunts. My jaw is clenched so hard I wouldn't be surprised if my teeth cracked. "Any complaints should be taken up with current management."

"Meaning you."

"Yes." Sound. Resolute. Unflinching. "Shortly it will be."

"And what do you plan on doing as the majority owner?" I demand.

His shrug is anything but apologetic. "Whatever I deem appropriate to stop this company from dying."

My head spins at the blindside. It takes everything I have not to march over to the table and tear up the documents there. But I don't, can't, because I'm frozen in place with disbelief.

My dream.

To own the company. To take the helm and remake it into the giant it once was. All stripped away without me ever getting the chance.

It's not like Dad or Rhett would have considered me capable, but I still would have fought like hell to prove otherwise. I would have let Rhett screw up enough, put the company in dire enough straits that my dad and the board members would have no choice but to let me swoop in to save the day.

The last thing I anticipated was for Rhett to look at outside investors and capital. To invite the one thing our father said he'd never allow—outside ownership. The one thing Gran would have fought vehemently against.

Fury replaces the disbelief as I turn to my brother with a voice cold enough to cause frostbite. "You're a spineless coward."

His shrug of indifference enrages me. "I'm trying to save the company. I'd think you'd be happy about that."

The company you were running into the ground.

"We've weighed so many options, Row," Chad interrupts, clearly sensing a no-holds-barred fight is about to happen. No doubt he wants to prevent it so we don't put a bad foot forward with our new "partner." "Bringing an outsider in who has a diverse portfolio, a proven track record, and strong capital is our best option."

Everyone shifts uncomfortably in their chairs.

Everyone being the colleagues I look in the eyes on the daily or talk with on the phone regularly. Everyone meaning people who I thought had my back, who would at least have given me a hint at what's been going on.

I scan their faces and the ones who have the guts to meet my eyes do so with pained expressions. But is the pain from screwing me over or because they don't want this deal to happen?

"The board backs this?" I ask.

Rhett nods. "Pretty sure Holden made it clear that they do."

"I want to hear it from your mouth."

He nods. "They do."

Fucking asshole.

"Why wasn't I informed?"

"Because you're not on the board."

The emotions raging through me leave me raw. My hands tremble and my head pounds. "You sold us out," I whisper.

"*I* did what *I* had to do," Rhett says, his voice low and even.

"Of course you did. Taking care of you is what you do best. Did you forget that it's my company too? My family legacy? I could have turned this around myself."

"You're in marketing, Row. The model on the ad campaigns. You don't know what the hell you're doing when it comes to profit margins and bottom lines," Rhett says.

"That's your excuse?" I bite out. He's wrong and he knows it. "Dad?"

Rhett's flicker of a smile says it all. Our dad knows. Approves.

It seems I'm the only one who didn't know.

My heart twists. Gran would be rolling over in her grave knowing he's selling what her grandfather started.

Tears burn in my eyes as my pulse races with fury. I will not show any emotion. I will not give Holden the satisfaction of seeing me break. Of knowing I'm affected in any way, shape, or form.

Your secret's safe with me.

And I will not acknowledge that I gave the asshole directly across from me, the one already dominating this conference room like he owns it, the ammunition he needed to know where to attack.

Rhett may have weakened the company, but I led the wolf right into the henhouse.

A henhouse that, clearly, he was already casing when we talked on the balcony.

"Is the family drama done?" Holden looks from Rhett to Chadwick to me. "I don't like my time wasted. Let's start yet again, shall we?"

"Please," Chad says.

"As the soon-to-be majority-owning entity of TinSpirits, there will be new commands and controls implemented immediately. You will be receiving an email by morning with a detailed list of expectations and pathways on how to move forward."

"What about layoffs?" Marcus asks at the far end of the table, concern etched in his expression. "Employees are going to worry."

It seems details haven't been ironed out yet, and by the uncertainty in Marcus's voice, maybe I was wrong. Maybe this has all been sprung on them as well.

"Entry-level and intermediate employees need not worry. Their paychecks and jobs are secure. As for upper management? *For you?* That remains to be seen." Holden offers a shark's smile. The room does a collective shift of discomfort from effectively being put on notice.

Play the game or you're out.

"I'm quick to pull the trigger on things I don't like. Take that warning however you see fit," he says.

"I propose that you take your finger off the trigger and wait until you officially own the company to make any changes," I say, pushing for a fight.

"Don't you remember the other night? I thought we already established that I don't care what people think. That still stands. And as for what I do or don't do, that's my prerogative." He challenges me with his stare, daring me to push harder. "Changes will start promptly."

"You're making a mistake," I say to everyone in the room.

"You're free to leave so you don't have to watch, then." When I don't move, he turns his attention to the room. "As I was saying, it will be business as usual for all outside of this room. Seamless. That's how I expect this transition to be."

I glare at my brother as Holden drones on about things I currently don't care about. Expectations. New agendas. Site visits. One-on-one meetings with him so he can figure what "fat to cut."

This has to be a dream. *Or a nightmare.* I will Rhett to meet my eyes. For Chad to do the same.

But both are too chickenshit to face me.

"Seamless," Rhett says, standing to assert authority over the company he essentially just gave away. "I hope now that you've all heard Mr. Knight's plans, it's helped to assuage any fears you might have had. While Knight Holdings will own the majority stake in TinSpirits and Mr. Knight here will be integral in making some important changes, I remain the CEO. Chad the COO. Everything will be the same *but different*." He smiles to reinforce the words he just spoke. "We'll be a better company because of this welcome *partnership*."

A man buying the majority of our company is not a partnership. It's a takeover. Plain and simple, and my brother's naive if he thinks that "hostile" and "takeover" don't go hand in hand.

Everyone starts shuffling their papers and laptops click closed as our upper management tries to come to terms with what just happened. No doubt there will be a lot of texting from office to office.

"I need a minute alone with Mr. Knight," I say.

"Wanting to lavish the praise so soon?" Holden quirks an eyebrow.

"I'll stay," Rhett says.

"You'll go," Holden says without any room for interpretation. He's in charge now regardless of the title or company attached to my brother's last name.

Rhett looks at Holden and then at me. *Does he really think I'll have his back right now after he just stabbed the knife in mine?*

More furtive glances are given as the remainder of the people leave the room. Their uneasiness and anxiety permeate the air as they do. Rhett moves cautiously, stopping at the door and hesitating a moment, before walking through and shutting it.

The minute the door is closed, I walk around the table and stand right in front of Holden.

"So this was your game all along? Weasel your way into a Westmore function. Make yourself seen, your name known . . . and then get information out of me?"

"Weasel? I wouldn't say it was that difficult."

"You're an asshole."

"Aren't you a ray of fucking sunshine?"

"You could have told me why you were there."

"And you could've kept your mouth shut. Or left me alone with my scotch on the balcony like I asked you to numerous times. You stayed. You talked. You shared." He shrugs with indifference. "How was I to know that a VP of the company I was looking to buy was going to be at the auction? I'm good, Rowan, but I'm not that good."

"I'm supposed to believe that?"

"Believe what you want."

I hate him. I hate this good-looking prick that apparently blew so much smoke up Rhett's ass he couldn't see through the haze.

But I fucking can.

"Why didn't you tell me your intentions?"

"And ruin the surprise?" He chuckles. "I rather enjoyed seeing your reaction. A bit dramatic but memorable nonetheless."

"You enjoy this, don't you? The flair. The making an entrance. The shock value."

"Don't beat yourself up over it, Sunshine. The outcome would have been the same regardless of if we'd met or not. The only difference is I walked into this knowing you are not particularly fond of your brother."

There's a warning somewhere in his statement, but I can't quite figure out what it is in the moment because my mind is clouded knowing that he's right. One hundred percent right.

"Why us? Why TinSpirits?"

Holden purses his lips, and our stares hold as he leans back in his chair. "For one, their spokesperson is irresistible." The muscle pulses in his jaw but his eyes wait for a reaction from me that I don't give. "And two, I like learning new things. I like turning things upside down and challenging myself to put them back together while improving them."

"We make alcohol."

"I'm more than aware."

"Signature spirits, canned cocktails, microbrews. Do you have any experience in our industry?"

"I don't need to know your industry to be successful."

"So, what? You think you can walk in here with your good looks and blank checkbook and things will happen?"

"Ah, she does think I'm good-looking." His smile deepens. "Thank you. I thought your hatred for me might have dulled my shine. Good to see it hasn't. For the record, failure is never an option in my ventures. Especially this one."

The way he says that phrase, so resolute, so final, gives me pause. "What's your end game?" I cut to the chase.

A ghost of a smile flickers on his lips, almost as if I'm a mouse and he's the cat having fun batting at me, but he doesn't answer.

If I was uneasy before, I'm even more so now.

"Look. I've dreamed of running it since I was a child, and I'm not letting you take that from me."

His sigh is condescending at best, the chuckle that follows even more so. "I admire a woman who knows what she wants . . . but this is my dream too, Miss Rothschild. One I've waited way too long to have. And nothing—*nothing*—will get in my way of having it."

His cryptic response has me taking a step closer. "I'll get in your way, and I'll enjoy every second of it."

"I think you're forgetting that we're on the same team here."

I snort and take a few steps back, our eyes still locked on each other's before I turn on my heel.

"I think what you meant to say was 'thank you,'" he says at my back.

I turn to face him. "Come again?"

"*Thank you.* I believe those were the words waiting to come off your tongue. *Thank you* for saving my family's company. *Thank you* for making sure it doesn't devalue to nothing. *Thank you* for not firing the current management on the spot like they deserve to be."

"I don't need saving. Not by you. Not by anyone."

"What? You were going to single-handedly come in and turn things around yourself when it's clear the golden boy disregards you and your intelligence?"

His words sting but I take the hit on the chin. "Yes. I had a plan.

A proposal drawn up. I was possibly coming into some money. Had planned to buy out—"

"Possibly? A trust fund, I presume, then? How ... *Westmore elite* of you."

I work a swallow down my throat as I force myself to think before I speak. But screw decorum. Screw manners. *Screw him.*

"You get off on this, don't you?"

His eyes scrape up and down my body, doing way more than just unnerving me. "Oh, Sunshine, you have no idea." And when I stalk out of the conference room, ire adding the extra sway to my hips, the chuckle he emits carries down the hall after me.

SIX

Rowan

"Row. Wait up!"

The sound of Chad's voice doesn't cause a break in my stride as I make my way down the empty hallway. It seems everyone who was in the meeting got out of here in a hurry. "Go away," I say over my shoulder.

I need fresh air. I need a second so my skin doesn't feel like it's suffocating me. I need the silence of being locked in my car so I can sit and think and process and . . . scream at the top of my lungs if I want.

"*Please.* Let me explain," he huffs as he jogs to catch up and then falls in step beside me.

"Being blindsided is pretty self-explanatory if you ask me."

He reaches out to grab my arm to stop me, and it takes everything I have not to yank it away and plow it into his stomach.

"Rhett made me promise to keep this under wraps." His eyes search mine. "He's the top dog here. You know that. If I had told you, you would have marched right in there and blasted him, ruined the deal . . . sent all the employees running scared."

"That's bullshit and you know it."

"C'mon. I know you, Rowan. Are you telling me I'm wrong?" He lifts his brows, and I can't deny that he's right.

"I had a right to know, Chad."

He hangs his head for a beat and nods. "You did. Rhett's made

a mess out of this place and when Holden approached us a few
weeks back, it was like his offer was hand-tailored to what we
needed. Capital. Retention of operating control. His experience
navigating various marketplaces."

"A few weeks back? Like how far back?"

"Through lawyers, like six weeks. In person, a few days after
the auction. That's when he came at us, hard, and after seeing how
much he spent on the painting, Rhett knew Knight had money to
burn."

It was me. I gave him all he needed to know. I told him where
the weak spot was, and he exploited it.

"What is it?" Chad asks—he must see the guilt on my face.
"What are you not telling me?"

"Nothing." I roll my shoulders and draw in a deep breath. "You
vetted all this experience he supposedly has?"

His nod followed by a quick swallow doesn't exactly give me
confidence in his response. "Self-made multimillionaire. Sold his
software company years ago and has since used those profits to
dabble in buying fledgling companies."

"Dabble? Because *that* sounds convincing."

"Look. Rhett was hell-bent on making this deal," he whispers
and looks around as if to make sure no one can hear him.

"Just because one of Rhett's ideas panned out in the past doesn't
mean they all will," I say, knowing how ridiculous that sounds
when talking about the man who convinced our dad to transition
TinSpirits from solely making signature spirits five years ago to
making canned mixed cocktails.

It's what gave this company new life. Opened it up to a different, younger demographic when ours was mostly aging, and what
earned him the status of golden child.

Not that he needed any help since he's the only male grandchild
in the Rothschild family. That alone cemented him into anointed
status.

"He wants the deal, Row. I don't know what to tell you." He
scrubs a hand through his normally perfectly styled hair. Right

now it's sticking up at all ends and is a mess. Clearly this whole thing has been hard on him too. "We've done nothing but weigh the pros and cons ad nauseum, and he thinks it makes the most sense for your family legacy, for the company's value, for everyone employed here, to take the deal."

"*He* thinks. Yes. Of course. But what about what *I* think? About what *you* think?" I shake my head in frustration. I hear what he's saying but also reject the idea because we wouldn't be in this position in the first place if Rhett hadn't put us here. "This is bullshit, and you know it."

"I think we're stuck between a rock and a hard place and Knight's offer is a lifeline. The board clearly agrees."

"Fuck the board," I state.

"I don't think that's really an option," he jokes, but it falls flat.

I unclench my jaw and try to sort through my cluttered thoughts. How can I stop this? How can I turn this around? How can I sabotage Holden's due diligence so he walks away? How can I salvage what I've never gotten the chance to save and then run?

Sure, Chad and Rhett are considered part of the good ol' boys club—the blindside only served to prove that—but I know them. I can read them . . . or at least I thought I could. But bringing in somebody new, somebody like Holden Knight? That's a whole different ball game.

It's better to deal with the devil you know.

"We don't have to see this through," I say. "We can void the letter of intent somehow. I'm sure our lawyers would know how to do this. Some legal technicality that Knight overlooked. Bring it to your uncle Henry. Your cousins. You have a family full of fucking lawyers. One of them should be able to tell you how to get out of this or how to bend the rules just enough that we can't get in trouble."

"That's a big ask, Row."

"If Rhett asked, you'd do it, though, wouldn't you?" I hate the pleading in my tone. The weakness it implies when I need to be anything but if I have a chance at fighting this. "If we can break this intent, then we can try and raise the capital ourselves. I've been looking into the benefits of selling off one of our brands. If we did that, we'd be able to keep the company as is while earning enough from the sale to keep moving forward. That would allow the three of us combined to retain the majority ownership. Keep it in the family."

There's a flicker in his eyes. A spark. And I've known him long enough to sense the idea intrigues him.

"Things are more complicated than that," he says.

"How? It's a matter of—"

"I hear what you're saying but that's a huge task to accomplish in a short amount of time."

"Who says there's a time limit? So long as we can tread water until we figure it out, we'll be okay."

"We've been treading water for longer than you know. We need capital to stay afloat. We—"

"But don't we owe it to ourselves to try?"

"You know nothing about doing something like this, Row. The minute you start asking, people will start talking. The wrong kind of talk could yank this deal out from under us before it's finalized."

"Great. Even better. If the deal is going to fail on rumors alone then it isn't a very good deal to begin with. Problem solved."

Chad hangs his head for a beat and draws in a deep breath. "This isn't just a deal you're trying to sabotage. It's the trust of the board too. The last thing you want to do is piss off everyone who's supposed to be in your corner."

I sink my teeth into my bottom lip and give a curt nod. He's right, but this isn't the time or place to hash out something like this. It's not even a discussion I should be having until I can gain my bearings after everything that has just been dumped on me.

There has to be a way to stop this.

"You forget. You were supposed to be in my corner too." I shake my head and then walk away.

"Row. Wait!"

I don't wait. Screw these men who think they can walk all over me.

I have to find a way to fix this. To stop this. To make TinSpirits mine.

If Holden thinks I'm going to let him control my destiny, he has another think coming.

What I'd give to tell them all to fuck off and walk out the door right now.

What I'd give to leave so they could see how valuable I really am.

But I can't.

My heart sinks, threatening to break as the magnitude of this impossible situation weighs on me.

I blink back another shot of tears.

Gran, I promised you that I wouldn't let him throw this company away. I promised and I intend to do anything and everything I can to keep it.

SEVEN

Holden

She's a striking figure. Tall and statuesque. Confident and defiant. Even now, even after finding out about my purchase, she still carries that same posture as she walks toward her car.

She was a good choice for the face of TinSpirits.

The blond version of her anyway. I glance to the left of the window, where a framed poster of a marketing campaign rests against the wall. It's the profile of her face. Her red lips twisted into the slightest of smirks as they toy with a straw between them. The signature white can of TinSpirits in her hand. Her green eyes peering sideways at the camera as if to say, *You know you want to join me.*

Then there are the ads for the signature brands of alcohol. The curves of her body beside a bottle of dark amber. Both shadowed. Both backlit. Both sensual.

And now she, the face of the company, walks all alone in the mostly empty parking lot toward what I can assume is her ride. Her head is still held high despite the crushing blow I dealt her a bit ago.

I study her from the wall of windows on the sixth floor and almost feel bad for her.

Almost.

But just like I was collateral damage all those years ago, she has the same fate now.

She reaches her car and looks back toward the building, almost as if she knows I'm standing here watching her. Judging her. Looking for hints of the pain I know she's feeling inside to cross her pretty face.

I smirk.

If she thinks this is hard to process, she doesn't know what's about to hit her.

Just wait, Sunshine. I'm not done yet.

I slip a hand in my pocket and move out of the conference room. Time to implement round two of "commands and controls" for the day.

God, this feels better than I imagined it would.

The hallway is quiet, most of the staff having gone for the day. The door to the corner executive office is open.

Rhett, the poor excuse for a CEO, has his head down as he searches for something in his desk. Chad, his spineless sidekick, sits in front of the desk, foot resting on his knee, phone in his hand, oblivious to the storm swirling around him.

"Leave your key to your office when you go," I say from the doorway.

Both heads whip in my direction. Their wide eyes stare back at me, their jaws slack—bewilderment in its rawest form.

"Excuse me?" Rhett asks, rising to his feet, dropping a square, silver lighter he was holding onto the desk with a *clank*.

I startle at the sight of it.

Then cover the startle with a baiting smile. "I didn't stutter."

"But this is my office." He looks at Chad for backup.

Kid, Chad couldn't help you find your ass from a hole in the ground. But keep looking at him. No skin off my back. It would be annoying if it weren't so satisfying.

"Everyone needs to make sacrifices," I say, lifting a brow. "Wasn't that the gist of what you said in the conference room earlier?"

Chad looks between us warily. "We have plenty of other offices you can use, Holden."

My look is cold and biting. "It's Mr. Knight to you."

He stares blankly at me.

I hold his gaze long enough to drive my point home. Then I turn back to Rhett. "When I'm talking to you, I expect a response from you. Not him. Clear?"

Rhett throws his hands up. "What's going on here?"

"This is what's called making business decisions. If you would've done more of those prior to this point, maybe I wouldn't be here."

Rhett drops his hands to his sides, anger flashing through his eyes. "My sister did this. Not me."

Fucking Christ. Rhett's really going to stand there and blame her for the mess he made of this company? For the debt he's in up to his eyeballs? From the poor decisions he's made putting himself before the good of the company?

No wonder she despises the prick. He keeps showing me why it's so easy to do.

I step into the room and lean my shoulder against the jamb.

"One minute you're claiming she's part of this triumphant trio. The next you're throwing her to the wolves," I say. "I guess that means I shouldn't trust a word you say."

"There is no triumphant trio," Rhett says, standing taller.

"The two of us make the decisions around here," Chad says, lifting his chin and following Rhett's lead.

"I'm not sure that's something I'd be proud of," I say.

Rhett narrows his eyes. "We've kept this company from drowning. The third part of that trio you're talking about, my sister, was simply here trying to be important. Trying to make herself be more than the face on the billboard. She thinks she has more skin in the game than she actually does."

My sister did this. Not me.

Pick a lane, asshole. You keep weaving to whatever side you think is going to win my favor.

I want to laugh, to call him out—to tell him his sister has more balls than the two of them combined. But I don't. *Why?* Because I don't fucking care.

"Rowan's the weak link," Chad says, feeling the pressure of Rhett's gaze. "That's all she is."

"And yet you chased her down the hall after the board meeting like a lapdog waiting to heel."

Chad's attention switches to his shoes.

I shouldn't get this much pleasure from pushing their buttons. I didn't come in here to drivel back and forth, but watching them squirm—putting them in their place—is too satisfying to pass up.

Rhett sighs. "There's a history there. Between them." He motions to Chad and to the air, making me assume he's talking about Rowan.

I chuckle. "Of course there is."

"He's going to marry her."

Come again? I'm rarely at a loss for words and yet that comment did just that. *Dickless Chad is the last person I'd expect a woman like Rowan to fall for.*

I'm rarely wrong with first impressions. Guess there's a first time for everything.

"Charming," I finally manage, while losing what little respect I had for Rowan and the woman I thought she was. "Gentlemen, if you'll excuse me."

They share a look. *What happens next will tell me how easy or hard the next few months will be.*

Without a word, Rhett collects some of the stuff off his desk while Chad stands and waits for his friend.

"You forgot something," I say, pointing to the lighter.

He falters, looks at it, and mutters something about it being his grandfather's.

Clank. He flicks the lid back. *Click.* He lights the flame. *Clank.* He jerks his hand so the lid closes over the flame and extinguishes it in what looks like a nervous habit.

But the memory those three sounds evoke hits me hard and out of nowhere. *The last time I saw that fucking thing our positions in life were so very different.*

I grit my teeth, contain my anger, and hold my hand out for his key. "Move the rest of your stuff into the office down the hall by Monday."

Rhett meets my eyes and the muscle pulses in his jaw. I dare him to look a little closer.

Do you feel the slightest flicker of recognition when you look at me? Do you question why you're brushing that feeling aside every single fucking time we meet?

A part of me wants to remind them who I am. The other part wants me to wait until they fall and I have my foot on their throats before I jog their memory.

You have time, Holden. Time to bat and tease and play with them before you move in for the kill. Don't deny yourself all you've waited on.

My smile is meager at best when Chad passes by me on the way to a waiting Rhett at the door.

I watch them leave as the realization of what they've done, what they've given up so easily, begins to settle in.

You ignorant fools.

I blow out a breath and take a seat in Rhett's cookie-cutter office. It's straight out of a "how to look the part of CEO" article. Dark greens. Deep mahogany. Nothing inspired or creative or articulate to be seen.

Then again, I shouldn't expect anything less from a man who leveraged his family's wealth and legacy for his own personal benefit.

I strum my bottom lip with my finger as the tiniest bit of stress eases from my shoulders.

This part of the plan is complete. Now on to the next—the one they really don't see coming. It's not surprising, really, that they're so fucking clueless. Those two have no idea the amount of dirt I have on them—or how I plan on burying them with it. Shovelful by shovelful until the pressure is so intense that they can't breathe anymore.

I sigh in satisfaction.

They didn't even expect it. Questioned nothing. They were so goddamn desperate for more that they just held out their hands and ate up every word I told them.

Chad turns and looks back at me before rounding the corner. Despite the distance, the glimmer of irritation in his eyes is undeniable.

What's that about, Chad, you foolish little prick?

I wink at him.

Maybe I'll steal the one thing you apparently love too.

First your company, Rhett. Then the face of it.

Then your woman, Chad.

The face you both need. The woman behind it.

Two birds. One stone.

How sweet would that be?

EIGHT

Rowan

I'm restless.

I've blown off my friend Sloane once again. I've ignored repeated phone calls from Caroline—which means word has spread through the grapevine about Holden Knight and the purchase of TinSpirits.

I left work early and then took a jog on the beach before driving around for what felt like hours. Anything and everything to process the hurt and the betrayal and the disbelief that I can't seem to come to terms with.

Running TinSpirits has been my dream since I was little. When all my friends dressed baby dolls and played country club, while Cassie followed my mother around like a shadow wanting to be just like her someday, I sat and dreamt of being part of the company. Childish drawings of new bottle designs morphed into tagging along to product shoots—and then ultimately messing around during one of those shoots and ending up in the ad myself.

My mother hated it at first. *Rothschild women do not work. They volunteer. They socialize.* She argued with my dad when I begged to tag along with him at work. I may have purposely made myself a pain in the ass so that she let me go, simply to get a break.

But when I asked to work there during my teen years, she put her foot down. That was a man's place. Rhett's place. The family legacy for him as the male heir to carry on.

But when the modeling for TinSpirits accidentally happened, she accepted it. How very Rothschild of her to allow her daughter to be a pretty thing to look at but refuse to acknowledge the substance beneath the exterior.

Gran knew I was unhappy. Pushed me to stand up for myself and fight for more. To demand that if they wanted me to continue to be the face of a campaign that was taking off and reviving the company, I deserved a seat at the proverbial table.

My parents bucked the idea. Rhett was indifferent until he realized that my presence at TinSpirits meant he could do less.

No board seat was offered, but I was able to work there. I was able to take all my childhood dreams of how to sell the family brand and apply them.

But that didn't change the family allocation of duties. Rhett was to be in charge of the Rothschild business legacy while I was to be in charge of our family's continued social standing.

While the designation never deterred my determination, it had me wondering every now and then where things would stand if Cassie were still here.

I watched Rhett tear down the company brick by fucking brick with his poor decisions and selfishness.

And now I'm being told he's not only committed to selling what is partially mine but will be remaining at the company's helm when all is said and done.

Then there are my parents. My dad, who, like his father and his father's father before him, stepped back and cut himself out of the business entirely at age sixty. Is he really willing to let his wealth and his legacy be parceled off and whittled down to all but nothing? To figuratively give up the company his family built?

Sure, he has the family trust and all that's in it, but he's even divorced himself from that by letting Rhett manage it.

Not that I understand that by any means.

My phone buzzes through the car speakers. Caroline. *Again.* The knots in my stomach twist even tighter.

Word spreads faster than lightning in Westmore. I don't know why I thought Holden Knight buying TinSpirits would be any different.

"I don't know what to tell you, Caroline. You're going to have to give me a minute," I say to my empty car. The words fall into the void, making me sound lonelier than I am.

The sand on my calves itches, and when I shift my legs to abate it, I realize just how sore they are from the miles I ran on the beach. My eyes burn from the aimless driving afterward. Anything to process my brother's betrayal.

How could he do this to me?

How did our parents let him? And them knowing and not telling me makes it all hurt that much more.

I turn on my signal and make a right into his gated community. The guard peers into my Range Rover, recognizes me, and with the warmest smile I've had today, allows me through.

My heart thumps and dread sinks into the pit of my stomach. But resolve reigns.

I shouldn't be here. I make a right onto Birdsong Lane. *This isn't going to help.*

Yet, I don't turn back.

"What would you have done, Cassie? Would you take this lying down?" A bittersweet smile ghosts my lips as I picture her frozen in time as her seventeen-year-old self. "Maybe. Probably."

I miss my twin sister. Every minute of every day. Maybe she could have been my ally here. Maybe I wouldn't be alone—a Rothschild in name only, it seems.

As I pull to a stop at the curb, the ninth hole of the Westmore Country Club golf course glows in the golden hour just behind Rhett's house. Logic screams inside my head to give it the weekend before I accost and accuse him—to go home and think this all through and develop a game plan first.

But my heart, and everything inside me, says to charge on. To not spend another minute with this hurt trapped inside.

He opens after my second knock. Rhett stands there with an unapologetic look on his face that I don't miss a beat trying to change. "What kind of chickenshit move was that? You went behind my back like some dickless coward and agreed to sell the majority ownership of our company to some random asshole we don't even know. It's *our* company, Rhett. *Our* livelihoods. *Our* fucking futures."

"It's still ours, Row. There's just less of it now."

"Wow." I just stare at him in his ignorance.

"If you're worried he's going to change the ad campaign, that you won't get to model anymore, I already negotiated that as part of the deal."

I chortle as I stare at him in disbelief. "That's what you think I'm worried about? Remaining the spokesperson?" I snort. "You're the biggest, most selfish bastard I've ever met."

"What's that supposed to mean?" His hand is propped on the door, and he's yet to invite me in.

Does he really not see the problem or is he so blinded by the idea of a bailout and erasing the errors he's made, so focused on the influx of capital, that he doesn't care about anything else?

"It means that you *sold* majority ownership to a man we don't know. A man I don't have a good feeling about. Don't you think I had a right to know?"

"It was on a need-to-know basis. Board stuff." The asshole winks and my fists clench in reaction. I've never thrown a punch at my brother but there's always a first time for everything.

"He'll have total control, Rhett. You just handed him the fucking keys. He can veto anything we want to do and undo anything we've already done." I point at him, my finger shaking in the air. "He'll be in charge. Not you. Not Chad. *He will be.*"

"Knight doesn't know shit about alcohol. Not the distillery side. Not the manufacturing side. Not the marketing side. Other than how to consume it, he's clueless."

"And you don't think that's a problem?" I say the words, but something tells me Holden Knight is far from clueless about any venture he takes on.

"No, more like, it's perfect. He's clean as a fucking whistle and richer than shit, so his lack of knowledge will work to our benefit. He's going to need us as much as we need him."

I snort at his naivety. There is nothing simple or uncalculating about Holden Knight. Call it gut instinct, a hunch, but I doubt he needs anything from anyone. "You're . . ." *Unbelievable. An asshole. Shortsighted.*

"I'm what? You're the one who hooked up with him. Not me." *What the fuck?* "Yep. Your little balcony convo with him didn't go unnoticed. Everyone's talking about how you slipped out early from the auction and they're saying it was with him."

"You're about two seconds away from being kneed in the balls," I grit out as his smirk taunts.

"So it's not true, then? You didn't dig your claws in Westmore's newest eligible bachelor?"

"I'm warning you," I threaten.

"I wasn't the one trying to sleep my way into keeping my job."

"Right. A job I didn't know was in jeopardy on the night of the auction." I roll my eyes. "You are so full of shit. No amount of rumors you push about me will shift everyone's attention off of *your* fuckups."

He shrugs. "The board's not fond of the rumor. Sleeping with the boss would be a very bad look for you. They'd question your judgment first, then your motives. Then discount you from there on out as being like every other woman out there—gold-digging her way to the top." I ball my hand into a fist and cock it back as he barks out a laugh. "Oh relax." He waves a hand as if nothing is amiss. "I'm just fucking with you. Jesus. You're so easy to rile up."

"So glad you think all this is funny. This isn't a joke, Rhett."

"I know. It's pretty damn serious." But the chuckle he emits says he thinks it's anything but. "This is for the best. I promise you. He has big plans for us. He wants to take us from a regional brand to one with national recognition. I know what I'm doing. You don't. That's why you need to stay in your own lane and let me take care of mine."

But that's the thing. He doesn't realize that he doesn't have a lane anymore.

"Stay in my lane?" I raise a brow. "You mean the lane where you disrespect me in front of our employees by pulling the 'you're just the VP of marketing' crap? Or the one where I've been poring over ways to keep the company you drove into the ground in Rothschild hands?" I smirk at him. "No worries there. That lane is gone now, because once Holden signs on the dotted line, no one is going to give a shit what you say, Rhett. You sold the only reason anyone listened to you at all. Great job."

"I'm still relevant."

"You keep thinking that."

"Winning the election for city council will guarantee that."

I snort. "You're so full of yourself you can't see straight."

"I know I'll win and when I do, I'll have a hand in controlling what Holden can and can't do with the company. He wants to expand manufacturing? He'll have to come to me. He wants to finish my idea to build a new distribution center in Fairmont? That'll be all me." His smirk is smug. "I've already been promised a seat on the urban planning committee, so I'll be the one pulling and controlling those strings."

"Just like a Rothschild to buy something instead of earn it fair and square, huh?" I say.

"Now you're just being ridiculous."

"And you're being the condescending prick I've come to expect."

I stand there, dumbfounded, trying to process why I care. Why I still want this company and the chance to run it when no one else does.

My life could be so much easier. I could take the money and vacation with Caroline. A beach in Ibiza could be calling to me to stay for months—and I could without worry. I could visit Cannes and Paris Fashion Week. I could make a thing of visiting and seeing every symphony in the world. Everything—every action, every trip, every reaction—could be on a whim.

But I can't do any of that because I care.

Because I have a heart.

Because I have something he doesn't have—loyalty. To what my great-great-grandfather built and what my gran held tight to.

And that, more than anything, is what has my gut churning.

"So we're good, then?" Rhett asks.

I stare at him and shake my head before turning on my heel and walking away.

No. We are most definitely not good.

NINE

Holden

FIFTEEN YEARS AGO

"God, it's hot in here," Mason says quietly, pulls off his shirt, and tosses it on the couch beside him.

"*Shh.*" I look up from my American History textbook and fire off a warning glance to be quiet.

He's right though. It's as miserable and muggy inside our tiny apartment as it is outside. Feels like hell on earth. The Carolina summer has arrived with a vengeance, and it doesn't look like it's going to be abating anytime soon.

Air so thick you can feel it when you inhale.

But the last thing Mom needs to hear is us saying we're hot. She'll try to pick up an extra shift at the diner or look for an additional house to clean after she gets off work. Even if she earned more, it wouldn't be enough for us to leave the air conditioning on long enough to make a difference.

We have fans. Ancient oscillating fans that blow the hot air around the small space, but it's better than nothing.

"Maybe we can sleep with the windows open," he says, but we both know we can't. We may not have much, but it's more than a lot of other people have around here, and a ground-floor apartment is a blessing and a curse in that respect.

I make a noncommittal noise as I stretch my fingers, cramped from annotating this stupid text. "We'll figure it out. I can sleep on the couch tonight so there's more room in the bed. Now finish your homework."

He groans. "It's boring though."

"That book's not the best. I'll agree with you on that, but you still have to read it."

"Why? When am I ever going to be stuck in the wild with a dog as my only friend and you not around?" Mason asks, brushing his hair off his forehead. He needs a haircut. I'll have to see if I can trade Mr. Dobbins again, mowing his lawn in exchange for a seat in his barber chair.

"Because school is important. It's how we get to the other side of the river someday."

He stops and drops his pencil, his curious eyes holding mine. "Is it really like the movies there?"

I chuckle and play off his curiosity about the country club where I work. The one on the other side of the river where wealth is more common than not, and the residents don't have to leave their windows open at night because they can afford to air-condition their entire larger-than-life estates.

I make a concerted effort not to talk about the things I see and the differences that are blaringly obvious between our life and the lives of the people I serve. I figure if Mason doesn't realize what he's missing, then he can't exactly know how much to miss it. And the last thing I want him to realize is just how drastic those differences are.

Defeat, whether it comes to you later in life or is handed to you at birth, often smothers hope.

But not in this house.

Our mom refuses to allow that to happen.

"Nope. Nothing like the movies," I lie. "They're people just like us."

"Yep. Holden's right," our mom says as she moves into the room from the postage stamp of a back patio where she's been hanging up some laundry to dry. "The only difference is their luck met their opportunity at the right time. We're just waiting for our time."

I smile at her. The years have been hard on her but have not diminished her beauty. She has the same dark hair and light eyes that I do, but there's an innocence to her that makes it hard for people to believe she's in her midthirties.

"You look tired, Momma. Let me go with you tonight and help," I offer. A full eight-plus hours waiting tables at the diner and then off to clean office buildings at night for some extra cash on the side is enough to make anyone look tired.

"Thank you, but no. Schoolwork is more important."

"But we can get it done now and still go with you," Mason says. The office building is like an adventure to him. A foreign world where he can run down halls, pretending he's a corporate bigwig while we clean up after them.

She moves across the cramped space and absently runs a hand down the back of his hair. "Thank you. I appreciate you both, but you need to get that homework done and get a good night's sleep. No one can learn when they're dozing off in class. Besides, we don't need to spend money on three bus fares. That's ridiculous."

"I get paid tomorrow," I say. "That makes us that much closer to getting a car so we don't have to worry about that anymore."

She gives me a look I don't understand and then jumps when a police siren erupts suddenly outside.

Both Mase and my mom hunch down and the sight of it eats at me.

No matter how used to the sounds you get, they still jar you each time they pass by these paper-thin walls.

"Do you think there are sirens like that in California?" Mason asks.

"There are sirens in all cities, baby," Mom murmurs but has a soft smile on her face.

California. Her dream. For her. For us. To save enough money to get us the hell out of here and move to where her brother lives. To the land of possibility, no matter where you're from, where dreams come true, and where sunshine—without humidity—persists.

"Yeah, but there seem to be a lot here."

"They're just passing through from one city to the next is all. We should be lucky we hear them. That just means they're keeping us safe," she says with a knowing glance my way before moving toward the small dinette in our "kitchen."

She busies herself and just as I'm getting fully back into my *riveting* chapter on the Articles of Confederation, Mason's laugh causes me to look up.

I'm met with my mom's wide smile and face illuminated by the candles burning on the small cake she's holding as she walks toward me.

She and Mason start in on singing "Happy Birthday."

Emotion swells in my throat and I blink back tears that threaten to spill over. I thought she'd forgotten. Hell, I'd even forgotten most of the day, but when your mother constantly burns the candle at both ends to provide everything she can for you, the last thing you do is expect more from her.

And this? Her finding time to make me a cake at some point in her crazy day is that *more.*

The song finishes. "Happy seventeenth, Holden. Make your wish."

I look from her to Mase, close my eyes, and make my wish. *I wish that someday I will get us out and to a place where sirens mean ambulances and not crime. Where we can leave windows open to sleep. Where we can have our own bedrooms. Where laundry is dried in a machine and not on a line. Where Mom can sit in the sun while I provide all the things she deserves.*

When I open them and blow the candles out, my mom claps her hands, nothing but love reflected in her eyes when she looks at me. "Let me go get some plates," she says.

"What did you wish for?" Mason asks, the promise of cake way more important than homework.

"I can't tell you or else it won't come true," I say and knock my knee against his.

"I know what I'd wish for," he says as dishes clatter in the kitchen.

"What's that?" I expect the twelve-year-old in him to say a Play-Station or an iPhone. Things his peers have that we don't.

"For us to have the same last name," he says, eyes down, voice hushed.

I open my mouth to say something and then close it. *How did I not know this bugged him?* "Mase. Dude. Just because you're a Simpson and I'm a Knight doesn't mean anything. We're still brothers. Still best friends."

He nods. "I know, but Mom's a Simpson too."

I wrap my arm around his shoulder and pull him against my side. "If it makes you feel any better, I'll be a Simpson from here on out." *What the fuck, right? It's not like my deadbeat of a father's name means anything to me.* "Who's going to know any different?"

"How could you do that?"

"Simple. Just say that's my last name. It's not like people check. Would that make you feel better?" I remember what it felt like at that age to be lost and confused. To not have a dad and to need more of an identity. But I thought I was doing that for him. Clearly, I'm not. If doing this is all it takes to give him that security, that identity, not a problem.

"Really?"

"Really."

"Before we have cake, there's one more thing," Mom says, moving back across the small space with her hands behind her back.

"Holden said he's a Simpson now," Mase blurts out.

My mom eyes me and raises an eyebrow. "He did, did he?"

"I did." I nod, leaving no room for interpretation. Mase sits a bit taller beside me. "What do you mean there's one more thing? The cake is more than enough."

Her eyes well with pride as she holds out a present to me. "Happy birthday."

"Mom. We can't aff—"

"Hush." Her smile is as sentimental as her voice. "Open it."

It takes me a few seconds to remove the paper and open the generic brown box, but when I do, it doesn't matter how hard I try to act cool, the tears fucking come. Especially when I'm looking at something I've wanted desperately for years but have never asked for.

Our money is meant to go to bills.

It's for saving for a car so my mom doesn't have to get on the bus after work in the middle of the night when it's not exactly safe.

It isn't for a laptop computer. I stare at the refurbished Mac-Book through blurred tears, wanting it so badly but knowing how selfish it would be to keep it. To put my wants above the needs of our family.

In disbelief, I shake my head. Schools on the other side of the river assign laptops to all of their students for the entirety of the school year. It's not even a privilege, but rather the norm. But not at the school I go to. At mine, your only chance to use a school laptop is to go to the computer lab and do your homework there.

But I'm never able to because I have to watch Mase after school.

So I turn in handwritten homework—a modern-day scarlet letter that tells everyone my family is too poor to own a computer.

I blink the tears away and look up to my mom. "So what if it'll take a little longer to buy a car." She shrugs, a smile toying at the corners of her mouth.

"I can't accept this, Mom." Those are the hardest words I think I've ever had to say. "We've been saving for a car for forever and—"

"Shush. I won't hear any of that." She puts her hand on my arm and squeezes. "I'll gladly leave early to get a bus ride. What's most important is that you have every chance, every advantage I can give you, for you not to be like me."

I hang my head as guilt and excitement wash through me. "There's nothing wrong with you."

"It's hard wanting to give you the world and only being able to give you a sliver. You'll understand that someday. This is some of the sliver."

"Thank you." I choke the words out.

"No need to thank me. You do more than enough for our family, Holden. School, watching Mase for me, helping me, working . . ." She shakes her head. "Thank you for being such a good kid. I'm so very proud of you."

Her words mean more to me than the computer and that says a whole hell of a lot.

Overwhelmed by the turn of tonight's events, all I can do is nod and stare through eyes blurred with tears at my gateway to the world.

At my chance to be something more.

TEN

Rowan

Fires.

I've done nothing all week but put them out. Little ones. Big ones. Smoldering ones that had the potential to become out-of-control wildfires. If it wasn't one thing at the office, it was another. And if it wasn't another, it was calming the nerves of employees who were silently freaking out about this "transition."

It doesn't help that random people with stern faces and crisp suits have been behind the closed doors of the conference room for the better part of the week. Hell, every time one of them walks down the hall past my office, I stop what I'm doing and worry they are going to ask me questions I don't know the answers to. Questions that prove or disprove my worthiness to this company.

It doesn't help that Holden has barely appeared all week. He uprooted Rhett from his office—my brother still hasn't stopped bitching about that—but hasn't been here to use it. And when he does make his presence known, he has the phone to his ear or is behind the closed doors with the rest of the people he brought in.

To say anxiety is at an all-time high is an understatement, regardless of how much we managers try to smooth over those nerves.

As for me? I'm still wading in an ocean of uncertainty. The days that have passed have done little to abate my hostility and disbelief while fueling my skepticism on how exactly this is all going to work.

While I'd searched for information on Holden Knight after the auction, I renewed my efforts this past week. To my dismay, I haven't found anything about him, his company, or his past that I can use to further fuel my dislike.

The problem is I've found quite the opposite. The more I've read and researched, the more I admire the man who made himself into a multimillionaire out of nothing. From unspecified humble beginnings to self-taught computer programming to creating software for the banking sector that he then sold for a ridiculous amount of money.

The fact that I've come to admire that about him pisses me off. I don't want to respect what he's made out of himself.

And then there are my peripheral searches on him. His social circles. The charities he's donated to. The women who have been seen on his arm. His life in Silicon Valley.

He's never been married despite the various beauties that have been photographed with him at events. Flawless women with curves and grace. I've even dug into the rumors captioned beneath their pictures only to find nothing salacious or out of the ordinary that I could use to my advantage.

The question still remains. *Why us? Why now? Why an industry that is uncharted territory for him?*

"Miss Rothschild?"

I look up to find a woman standing in my doorway. Her presence in this office has been a constant as she has followed Holden like a shadow, but she has yet to be introduced to any of us. She's petite with beautiful silvery-gray hair in a pixie cut, a cream-colored pantsuit, and an efficient smile.

"Yes?"

She nods curtly. "I'm Audrey, Mr. Knight's personal secretary. He'd like a moment of your time."

No "nice to meet you." No "I've seen you around the office." Just a summons to go see the King Asshole.

Lovely.

"Nice to meet you too," I say with a tinge of sarcasm. "I wasn't aware he was in the office."

"He has a habit of being everywhere and nowhere all at once. You'll get used to it."

Unfortunately. "Sure. Yes." I glance at my desk and then back up. "Let me finish what I'm doing, and I'll be there in a few minutes."

She lifts her eyebrows. *"Now, please."*

Seriously?

I grit my teeth as I stand and make my way down the hall to my brother's *old* office.

When I walk in, my feet falter. He's rearranged the furniture.

A subtle hint, no doubt, that change is coming. Or just a plain, old-fashioned power play.

And there Holden is, sitting behind the lavish desk, head down with the sleeves of his dress shirt rolled up. He's scribbling something on the pad in front of him while I silently seethe from being ordered like my only purpose is to be at his beck and call.

I wait.

And then I wait some more.

He clearly knows I'm here as Audrey shut the door when I walked in. Is this yet another power play to let me know where I stand? To let me know who's boss?

Fuck that.

"Nice of you to finally show up to work," I say.

Holden sets his pen down, leans back in his chair, and his gaze all but bores right through me when our eyes meet. He purses his lips and nods very slowly. "So that's how you want this to go, Sunshine?"

I shrug, ignoring his little nickname for me. *Aren't we a ray of sunshine?* "If you plan on ordering me around, then expect to be treated accordingly."

He chuckles. It's a low rumble in the quiet room. "This is where you're under the impression that we're on equal footing. We're not, Rowan. Rest assured, *we are not.*"

I take a step forward, run my finger over the credenza against the wall, and don't acknowledge his remark. "It was a nice touch taking this office. Petty to say the least."

"From your comments the first night we met, I'd think you'd appreciate Rhett being put in his place."

"Things have changed considerably since then," I say.

"Not from where I stand. Rhett's still Rhett, you're still you, and everybody wants to be me."

"And the company is still going to be yours."

"Glad we have that clear," he murmurs as he tracks my movement about the room. A room I've been in countless times before but that suddenly feels so very different. "You're a complicated one to figure out."

"Depends on your definition of complicated."

"You dislike your brother and yet you stand here defending him."

"As family does. Do you not have any siblings?" I ask, the muscle in his jaw ticking. "Do you—"

"Then there's Chad. I can't quite figure out what your relationship is with him, but it's more than clear by how many times he goes in and out of your office all day that it's a close one."

Ah, so he is watching and assessing after all. No doubt Audrey might have a hand in that too. What he doesn't know is that I refuse to talk to Rhett right now. His betrayal still sits front and center for me, so Chad has been given the unfortunate task of being the go-between.

Do I despise my brother right now? Of course I do. But the last thing I want Holden Knight to know is that there is a fissure between us. Fissures can be exploited. Taken advantage of. Used against you.

I've already given him the advantage once. I won't make that mistake again.

"You're not responding." Irritation peppers his tone. No doubt he's used to people being intimidated by him.

"Here's what I don't get." I stop at the window and look his way, still not giving him what he wants. "What's a man with your background, your expertise in computer software, want with a company that sells alcohol. Spirits?"

"*Vices.*"

"So you like to exploit things. People. Norms."

His chuckle is a low rumble that reverberates through the room. "That was quite the leap, Rowan. Congratulations on going off the deep end as is expected."

"As is expected? You don't know a thing about me."

"*Hmm,*" he says and the sound—judgment tinged with suggestion—tells me he thinks otherwise.

"Keep playing your games. They won't work on me."

"And yet you walked in here wanting to do just that. Play a game. Get the upper hand. Put me in my place," he murmurs with a knowing arrogance that has me clenching my jaw. "You're going to have to try a little harder if you plan to outsmart me. I'll always be one step ahead of you." He leans back in his chair, the squeak of it filling the silence. "Now, should we get back to the topic at hand? Your question about vices, in particular?"

"Be my guest." *Asshole.*

"TinSpirits sells a good time—*you*, being the face of it, sell the idea. It also sells to the flip side. Those who use *our* product to escape their every day. To plug a void they need filled. *Vices.*"

"That word has a negative connotation to it."

"There's a light and a dark side to everything. You just have to look hard enough to find both."

"Wow. Bravo." I make a show of clapping my hands. "Quite the show and yet you still didn't answer the question. Why TinSpirits? Why the Rothschild brands?"

The twist of his lips says he's less than amused with me. Good. I'm not impressed with him either. But our eyes hold, and I take some pride that he's the first to break.

"I'm an entrepreneur at heart."

"Uh-huh." I cross my arms over my chest and lean my ass against the windowsill. "An entrepreneur who picked up and moved across the country out of the blue."

He nods. "Ah. Yes. Well, you'll learn I like to keep things close to the vest. I'll leave the spilling of family secrets and the hitting on random strangers when tipsy to you."

My temper fires. "You're an asshole. Trust me when I say I wasn't hitting on you. If I'd known the real you—*this* you standing in front of me right now—I wouldn't have been in the same room let alone breathing the same air as you."

He lifts a brow. I can't quite read his expression, but I know I don't like it.

"You're just as much of a coward as my brother."

He presses his hands against the table and stands abruptly, sending his chair rolling back into the cabinet behind him.

"It would behoove you to remember who you're talking to," he says.

I smirk. "Oh, I know exactly *who* and *what* I'm talking to."

He stands tall, looming over me from what must be a six-foot, two-inch frame. Undoubtedly, this posture—arms crossed over his chest, intense eyes pinning me to the glass from across the room—intimidates most people.

I'm not most people.

I cock my head to the side, begging him to argue with me. Fight with me. *Let me tell you just how much I hate you, Holden Knight.*

Of course he doesn't.

"We'll be working side by side going forward," he says, his voice icy. "Late nights. Long hours. I'd suggest that you get your emotions in check. I would hate to have to let you go."

I push away from the wall, my head pounding. "You can't do that. I'm the one who—"

"Oh, I can," he says, dropping his arms to his sides. "And I will without hesitation."

My mind races to find something to grab on to—something to level out the playing field in some way. "That would be a grave mistake on your part." I walk across the room slowly, keeping my gaze glued to his. "Rhett? Chad? They're the reason we're in this mess, and it seems I'm the only one who sees that."

He lifts his eyebrows and gives me the slightest of nods as if to tell me his interest is piqued and for me to continue.

"I'm the one who knows everything that goes on in this company." *Aside from the fact that they were selling it.* "I do more around here than play golf and pretend to be an executive. I work. I've taught myself the ins and outs of this business, of this industry. I know it like the back of my hand, and you, sir, do not. I'm the one you need. Not them." I stop a few feet in front of him.

He squares his shoulders to mine. Despite his best effort to remain stoic, there's a flicker of something, the tiniest crack in his veneer, hidden in the depth of his eyes.

"I'm impressed. Truly. How many times did you practice that in the mirror?"

"It's the truth." I refuse to back down. To let him disregard me.

His smile is faint but there. "Did you ever think that there's a reason you're in my office right now and they're not?"

"What?" I ask, head tilting, eyes narrowing.

"You've all but said it yourself. Everyone here discounts you." He runs a finger over his bottom lip, and I hate that my eyes linger there. "Maybe I'm the only one who doesn't."

I feel like I'm wading through a minefield. One wrong step and this could all blow up. Is he playing me? Mocking me? Or is he being serious?

I don't dare to lean too heavily one way or the other because his Jekyll and Hyde performance from the charity auction to the boardroom a few weeks later is fresh in my mind.

"I'm not following you," I say.

"No? Then I guess I was wrong."

Wait. I scream the word in my head but don't utter it. My mind spins as I try to figure out what game he is playing now. Pitting me against my brother? Making me think I'm helping him while he's scheming against me?

"What are you playing at, Knight?"

He angles his head to the side and studies me. "The question is why are you here, Rowan? Why stay? Your brother disrespects you, your parents disregard anything other than your looks, and the whole damn town thinks you should be barefoot and pregnant— well, in heels and pregnant because that's more Westmore, right? So why are you standing here fighting for something that clearly doesn't want you?"

Because I can't walk away.

Because this is where I've always belonged.

Because I promised Gran I would fight.

"What would it take to get you to tear the letter of intent up and walk away?" I ask, completely disregarding his question and suppositions.

That toying smile of his returns full force. "There are only two reasons someone stays in a toxic relationship. They don't have the money to leave, or they're afraid of the ramifications. Which one is it for you, Sunshine?" He just quirks a brow in suggestion that has me turning my back to him and looking out the window.

I don't know how this conversation was supposed to go, but *this* wasn't it.

"Rowan?" His voice is a hushed murmur from right behind me, intimate almost, that causes chills to chase over my skin. I draw in a deep breath, steeling myself for his proximity and the scent of his cologne.

I turn around, standing mere inches from him. His breathing is measured, his expressions calculated. I study the lines of his face.

He doesn't look the thirty-two years that the online stats give him. He's younger somehow, yet comes off as wise and experienced. And damn it if he isn't attractive in all the right kinds of ways. His build. The intensity of his blue eyes. The purse of his full lips framed by his strong jaw.

He studies me too, making me shift from one foot to the other.

"What more do you want from me?"

"Don't ask questions you don't want answers to," he says, and there is something in his tone that says there are many different meanings behind that comment.

"Great. Perfect. I won't." *Fuck this.* I move toward the door. "Next time you want someone to spar with for your amusement, summon someone else. You're wasting my time."

"Rowan." There's something in his tone that has me stopping in the doorway. "You're allowed to look but not touch, right?"

"What?" I turn to face him.

"What if I allowed you to touch? To matter to this company?"

My chuckle is disbelieving. "I'd think you're full of shit just like the rest of them."

He tilts his head to the side and studies me. "No, I think you're scared that I'm not. What if I gave you the chance? What if I let you help me? Then you just might have to prove your worth and the thought freaks you out because maybe you're all show and no substance."

I grit my teeth, refusing to take the bait I think he's throwing my way. The praise was first. Then the backhanded comment. Now the carrot dangled.

He's waiting for me to act with the irrationality everyone in this town expects from a female. *I think.*

I don't know.

"Nothing to say to that?" He chuckles. "Then maybe I *was* right. Maybe you talk a good game but can't back it up."

"This is amusing to you, isn't it?" *Just like every other male in my life.*

"How about you start small and stay in your lane, then?" He quirks an eyebrow. "What if I told you that I wanted to revamp our advertising campaign. The ads—the ones with you in them—are stunning, but they call to *me*. A man. Women drink, do they not? Isn't that a massive demographic we should be courting? When is the last time you walked into a party and saw a man drinking a mixed cocktail out of a can? They don't. We need new slogans. Male models on the beach—with you, of course."

"Alcohol is historically and typically marketed to men," I say while staring at a man who is saying everything I've been espousing for months.

I reject his suggestion out of principle. Off the assumption that he has somehow seen the proposals I gave to Rhett on this and is just using them to try to win me over.

Minefield.

Everywhere I look it's a goddamn minefield.

"And yet you've stated more than once in your online interviews that TinSpirits is anything but typical." He folds his arms over his chest but keeps his eyes focused on me. "I think you'd jump at the chance to change things up. What's wrong, Rowan? Afraid of change?"

"No. I'm afraid of you." The words are out before I can stop them. An honest answer when I should be anything but.

He nods ever so subtly, arrogance brimming in every ounce of his posture. "A little dose now and again is healthy."

We wage a visual war. One I'm more than certain I'm losing as the entirety of this conversation repeats over and over through my mind. As I try to pinpoint what his angle is and his sincerity behind it.

Or if I'm just a pawn in this game of his.

"I don't trust you." The words are barely audible.

"Nor I you," he says casually. "But we have to start somewhere, don't we?"

There's a catch here, and I can't exactly figure what it is yet.

"It takes a lot more than pretty words and flattery to win me over."

"I wouldn't expect any less." He pauses and the silence weighs heavy in the air, almost as if it knows what he's about to offer next. "The way I see it, Rowan, is that you can either work with me on this deal or against me. It's best that I point out that one option is assuredly better for you."

My curiosity is piqued. My reason is skeptical. "Why would I work with you?"

"Your brother isn't acting in your best interest."

"You say that like I should be surprised."

"If you're not then me stating the obvious shouldn't alarm you."

"Ah. So that's what this is." I draw in a frustrated breath as all the pieces of this conversation fall into place. "This is where you attempt to divide and conquer. Ask me to join you so you can make a show that I've turned against Rhett. Or Chad. Try to pit us against each other to make this acquisition easier for you. I may not be Rhett's biggest fan, but I assure you I'm even less of one when it comes to you."

"And just like that you're willing to side with him knowing you might be part of the collateral damage?" Holden gives a measured nod. "After all these grand speeches and defiant comebacks, I was expecting a bit more of a backbone."

"Nice try, Holden," I say, my shoulders squaring and my anger simmering. "I don't give a shit what you think about me."

"Don't be mistaken," he says, his eyes steeled against mine. "I'm not asking you to work with me because I want you to. I prefer to work alone. But you made a solid point earlier—you know the ins and outs of this business. I may very well be an asshole, as you so kindly pointed out . . ."

I glare at him.

"But I'm worth about four hundred million dollars." He lifts his brows in emphasis. "I didn't get here by making poor business decisions, and you, Sunshine, are a business decision."

I have no idea how to take that. It's a compliment and a jab at the same time. My head dizzies from his words, the double-edged opportunity he's offering, his cologne, and the smirk he casts casually across the room.

I need to get out of here.

"Are we done?" I ask.

"Your hostility is blinding you in more ways than one. It's a detriment; don't let it be your downfall."

And with that, Holden Knight sits back down behind his desk and focuses on paperwork, effectively dismissing me.

I stare at him for a beat more before stalking down the hallway, maybe stomping my feet a little harder than I should.

I'm angry. Livid. Furious. At him for asking me. At him for thinking he can put a wedge between my brother and me to use to his advantage.

And at myself for even considering it.

ELEVEN

Holden

Goose bumps on her bare skin.

A hitch in her breath.

The pulse skating in her neck.

Dare I say I admire Rowan Rothschild slightly? There's a grit to her that I didn't expect. That doesn't negate who she is. How she grew up. The things she did or the last name she so proudly wants to represent in owning this business.

Rowan Rothschild played her cards in my office the other day, and she didn't even know it. She's going to say yes to me. She's going to partner up with me to screw over Rhett.

I grin.

And I'm going to fuck her in the process.

A woman with a strong backbone and unapologetic defiance like hers? There's no denying that it's a definite turn-on.

I'm rarely challenged by anyone, let alone an intelligent, stunning woman. To say she's added an element of unknown to this whole venture is an understatement.

To say I need to keep myself in check and not get distracted, even more so.

Make no mistake, she'll say yes, and I'll have her twisted in the sheets beneath me in no time. I can't say I won't enjoy it.

I will.

I'll take so much fucking pleasure in it. Mine. Hers. And because

I'll be taking one more thing away from them. I'll get the company. I'll get the face of it. I'll leave them with nothing.

I'm one step closer to my end game. To getting exactly what I want. I can all but fucking taste it.

"Right?" Rhett asks.

Only assholes hold business meetings in strip clubs.

Assholes or men with small dicks who need someone to make them feel like they're actually bigger.

It's pathetic, really, but no more pathetic than the two men sitting across from me in their expensive suits and holier-than-thou attitudes.

As expected, some things don't change.

For them to think they are held in a higher regard than the rest of the TinSpirits employees and that their one-on-one meetings should take place here of all places. And together.

Entitled, privileged pricks.

"Right?" Rhett repeats.

"Exactly," I say more to myself than to him with no clue what the original question was.

"So if we outsource marketing to a major PR firm, we can dismantle our own department and cut out that cost factor. Fewer salaries, lower insurance costs, fewer benefits. The trade-off will save us in the end."

I chuckle to myself, the sound silenced by the jarring music coming through the speakers overhead.

Somehow the prick never ceases to amaze me.

"So," I say, not hiding my amusement. "Cut your sister out altogether?"

"She'll still remain the spokesperson. Ad campaigns and the like. I mean, let's face it, that's all she's really good for."

"Hmmm," I say, my finger strumming back and forth over my lips.

"I'm talking more about her marketing department. I hate to say it, but our last four ad campaigns missed the mark. We told her they wouldn't work. Some bullshit about changing the demographic.

Pushing more to women. We had to shut her down, and her lack of enthusiasm for what we did approve shows in our sales figures."

Except your sales figures aren't down, golden boy. It's the increased expenses that are lowering profits. And Rowan's denied vision is right.

"Huh." It's all I say so that he keeps talking.

"We could label it more as a restructuring. What I'd call smart business. It's what you're going to do anyway, right?" Rhett asks.

"Last I checked, I can think for myself just fine," I say above the hum of the music.

Bide your time, Knight. Suck it up and only show your cards when you want to.

"Can I get something for you, sugar?" the waitress vying for my attention asks, her eyes wide and her lips in the perfect pout. She doesn't do anything for me. Tits in my face. G-string-clad ass bumping into me every time she serves us.

She's a distraction more than anything, but I don't fault her for working for her tips. She sees expensive suits and designer watches—*wealth.* We all do things we don't like to make money. *Maybe she likes it.* We all put on a show to distract from the truth.

I pull a couple hundred from my wallet, hand it to her, and point to Rhett. "Take him in back for a lap dance?"

Her eyes light up at the overpayment. She can do with it what she wants. Pocket it. Give Rhett a little extra grind. I don't fucking care, so long as he's out of my face for a few minutes.

"Sure thing." She leans forward and pulls on Rhett's tie. "I do believe your friend wants me to show you a good time."

Hesitate. I dare you.

She does a little shimmy with her hips, her free hand *accidentally* bumping against his cock. "Let's go, honey."

Rhett eyes me, and for the first time ever I see distrust. My smile is taunting at best as he walks away, looking over his shoulder several times.

When he disappears into the back room, I shift to stare Chad squarely in the eyes.

"So," he says and takes a long pull on his drink.

I make him nervous. *Good.* Maybe that's why this is the first and only time he's been alone with me.

"So," I repeat back to him and offer another disingenuous smile.

"You're new here," Chad says.

"Can't say I've ever been to this strip club before, no." I glance around at all that the darkened room and red-hued lights hide. The desperate. The dejected. The feckless.

"I meant to Westmore."

"I knew what you meant," I say.

"Don't know the lay of the land quite yet, do you?"

"Why, Chad, are you offering to show it to me?"

"No. I think you're more than capable of figuring it all out for yourself."

"Appreciate the vote of confidence." I lift my glass and take a sip.

"My—uh—family . . ."

"What about them?" *Where is he going with this?*

"They run the sheriff's department. Head the circuit solicitor's office."

The fuck? "Should I be worried that I'm going to be arrested?"

He laughs nervously. "No. That's not what—I mean . . . I just . . . in case you need anything, *they can help.*"

I angle my head to the side and study him. *Why, Chadwick Williams, I do believe you just tried to posture yourself in my favor.*

I grin. He truly has no idea who I am or that I know just how fucking corrupt his family is. *Wow.*

I feign innocence. "Help? Meaning what?"

"Nothing." An anxious smile. A quick look over his shoulder to where Rhett disappeared. "I just thought you should know. Things happen sometimes. Rules need to be bent." He shrugs. "I could possibly get them bent for you or find a way to work around them."

"Ah. Got it." *You know all about bending rules, don't you, you fucker?* "He's still preoccupied," I say when he glances again to the lap dance room. "Is there a reason you're nervous to be alone with me?"

"No. Not at all."

"Hmm." I pause and let him worry about what that sound means. "Tell me, Chad. What are your thoughts on the buyout? It seems you're always standing right beside Rhett so I don't know what your individual opinions are."

"On what?"

"On why the company is bleeding money. You wouldn't have any insight on why that would be, do you?"

Are you going to throw your best buddy under the bus? Save yourself and throw him to the wolves? Is this where the two of you finally turn on each other and point fingers? Or are those secrets you've hidden this long going to follow you to the grave?

Chad shifts in his seat and glances around. "Raw material input costs have risen. Insurance has risen. The labor market is in the employees' favor. We're getting hit with fines in our current distribution center location, which is why we're looking to build and own a new one. It's not just one thing."

Liar.

"And how is Rhett being on the city council going to help with this?"

The flash of shock across his face gives me what I need. There's a purpose to Rhett's sudden desire to serve. Of course there is. Rhett's a man who only does things to serve himself.

"Who s-said it would?"

"C'mon, now. I may be someone who bends the rules every now and again too." I flash a shark's smile. "I know it when I see it."

Chad looks to the back room again then his eyes jump around the club. "Just trying to get around some regulations. Win some favors. Nothing big."

You're hiding something, Williams.

"And your thoughts on Rowan and the marketing department align with Rhett's?"

His slightest hesitation is noticeable. Friend or future wife? Which one will it be? "Not exactly. She takes pride in being a part of the company . . . but . . ." He shrugs.

"But you plan on making an honest woman out of her, so I'd be doing you a favor by doing away with her department. No job means you'd have less of a fight on your hands getting her to quit working. Because that is what you're going for, right? Williams as her last name?"

It's not like their moms don't already have the country club reserved for a wedding reception. Several dates actually. It's always good to have a plan A through G apparently. A few keystrokes gave me access to the online reservation system to show me that.

"She's a strong-willed woman," Chad says.

"As many are." *I bet you hate that, don't you?* "And your point is what?"

"It's her family's company. She deserves some kind of role."

"Like the sex kitten tempting you in the ad campaigns?" I ask.

Does it get you off thinking you're going to marry the woman every man who sees the TinSpirits ads jacks off to?

No. You're more the jealous type who'd be afraid she'd leave you for a real man. One who has his own opinions rather than his friends'.

He blanches, which says I'm right. "Her position, the part she'd get, would be up to you, wouldn't it?"

"But you *do* think she deserves a place or part?"

"Yeah. Sure. Even if it's in name only."

I lean forward. The movement catches him off guard, and he jumps. So damn satisfying. "And is that being said because you believe it or because she's yet to let you fuck her?" My stare is unrelenting as I swirl my drink around so the ice cubes clink against the glass. I watch anger flicker and fade through his expression. Quickest way to the truth sometimes is through shock value. Chad's lack of an answer is telling enough.

"I'd appreciate it if you don't talk about her like that," he finally manages.

Scared? Insecure? Worried she won't have you? Probably a bit of all three.

All I know is if a man said that about my future fiancée, he'd have a lot more than a gentle request to contend with when it came to my wrath.

"You forget, Chad. I'm not from here. I don't have to play by the good ol' boy rules you all do. I can talk about anyone however I want. Rowan. Rhett. The woman you went on a date with last week that you don't want anyone to know about."

Surprise flashes through his eyes but he buries it as quickly as I can glimpse it. "I've known Rowan for years."

"That's not an answer. That sounds more like a pussified excuse for why you let her brother treat her like shit." I shrug as I see Rhett walking back from the lap dance room, his gait a little unsteady from both the booze and perhaps the dance. "But hey, it's no skin off of my back that the three of you are all secretly trying to take each other down," I say.

"What do you mean take each other down?"

"Ever read *Lord of the Flies,* Chad?" I barely have time to get a chuckle out before Rhett slides into his chair at our table.

Rhett's hair is tousled, and his tie is undone and draped around his neck. The smug look on his face says he probably lasted a whole thirty seconds before blowing in his pants.

Rhett emits a satisfied sigh that says everything and nothing. "So . . . what are we talking about?"

"You," I deadpan. "And Piggy." Another *Lord of the Flies* reference that has Chad darting a glance at his best friend before looking back at me with a perplexed expression. His eyes beg for clarification I won't give.

I've gotten in his head. Perfect.

I've planted the seed that Rhett and Rowan are going to screw him. Rhett will soon think the same. And then Rowan will shortly thereafter.

Trust is a funny thing. It's there . . . until it isn't, and it doesn't take much to erode it. A few white lies. A couple of suppositions. A lot of suspicion.

Fucking with them is going to be the fun part.

Watching their house of cards crumble, even more so.

When I look back over to Chad, he's still staring at me. I lift a glass in mock toast and smile.

Let the fucking shell game begin.

TWELVE

Rowan

The room needs a facelift. Its walls are marked with yellow stains where water has leaked slowly and consistently. Its ceiling tiles are broken, if there at all, exposing wires, air ducts, and the ugliness that hides between floors. Its carpet is worn, faded to almost white in some places, and butts against scarred baseboards.

The women in the room look much like the room itself. A little worse for wear. Some with visible bruises while others harbor scars on the inside—between floors—where the damage is unseen but just as brutal.

That's what makes the sight of them all the more jarring as they sit—some with eyes closed, others staring straight at me, a few with tears sliding silently down their cheeks—as they sway or become visibly impacted by the music I create. The cello's melody is deliberately haunting. I've found it's a therapy of sorts, a soundtrack to their pain, that they can get lost in without having to explain a single reason why.

Isn't that what I did after Cassie died? Allowed myself to get lost in music? Allowed it to express the things I couldn't?

The Sanctuary is a battered women's shelter that has been here for over thirty years. Its only rules are simple: you must be sober, and you must be willing to trade something to be here. Chores. Childcare. Job training in whatever field you know. Food service. Anything to help better the place for everyone else who needs it.

In turn it provides a safe, secure place for women and their children who are trying to leave their abusers. It requires individual counseling sessions and group therapy.

The women who sit before me? I don't know their stories. Where they've been. Who has bruised them. What other scars lie beneath that might never be spoken about or shared.

But they know they can count on me to be here once a week. That I'll hold their hand as we talk or sit in silence or as a comfort to them as they cry. And that I'll play music for them. That I'll let them use the sounds to lose themselves for a little bit—whether it's to provide a safe space for them to think more about what they've been through or to shut it out altogether.

My time spent here is not my societal good deed in the Rothschild name.

It's not my way to try to make up for everything that Cassie was that I'm not.

It's not even something I talk about in my circles because I feel like that would cheapen the experience and what it means to the women sitting in this room battling things my friends could only imagine battling.

It's my way to give back. My way to carry on a tradition that Gran started years ago.

She wasn't allowed to work and needed something to do with her time. She saw the humanity in this place, this organization. She saw what it did for other women who weren't able to live the life she did merely because of who they were born to.

I stepped in for Gran in her later years, when her mind was going and she couldn't fulfill her duties. Back then it was about honoring her and her commitment.

Now it's a way to connect with people—real people. My world only cares about money, pride, and egos. None of those things matter here. There's a simple beauty in that.

One that draws me back here week after week. Month after month. Song after song.

I end my song, the last chord still vibrating through the room.

Tears are wiped. Smiles are offered. A few nods are given when I meet their eyes, but I don't allow them to clap for me. My being here has nothing to do with me and everything to do with them.

"Until next week," I say and begin to pack my cello in its case while the ladies in the room shuffle to their feet. Some are off to counseling sessions. Others back to their children who are being watched for them so they can attend my music therapy. A few to meet with the staff lawyers to discuss the status of their pending cases against whoever has caused them to end up here.

A sniffle at the back of the room draws my attention. I look up and offer a soft smile to the woman sitting there. She's new, a face I haven't seen before.

"How are you today?" I ask.

Hollow eyes stare at me for a beat before the slightest smile curls up the corners of her lips. "Hi." She pauses and then gives a quick shake of her head as if I interrupted her thoughts. "Sorry. I don't mean to still be here. I'm—I'm just trying to take everything in."

Never having been in any of these women's shoes, I hesitate to give anything remotely close to advice. "No apologies needed. Ever. I'm glad you're here. I hope you find whatever it is you need."

She angles her head and just looks at me. "Me too."

My heart aches for her. A woman I don't know in a situation I could never imagine.

With a nod of encouragement, I exit the room and head toward the reception area.

"Heading out?" Mei-Ling asks from the door of her office. She's the director of the Sanctuary, and a survivor herself who I've gotten to know over the years I've been volunteering here.

"I am."

"Can I talk to you for a minute?" She lifts her chin so I follow her into her office for some privacy.

"Sure. What's up?" I ask and set my cello case down.

"We've been hit with an unexpected blow, and I hate even asking you this." She sighs heavily and now that I'm closer, I can see the lines of worry etched in her face and sense something weighing on her.

"Please. Ask."

"We're losing the building."

"What?" Shock reverberates through me. "What do you mean?"

"The owner has decided to sell it. The area's too run-down now. He's lost tenants in the rest of the building and he can't recoup his costs enough to pay the mortgage. And on and on."

"Oh my god, Mei."

"I know." Tears well in her eyes but she promptly blinks them away. "He's been warning this might happen for the past four years. Apparently, this time, he really means it."

"So what . . . I mean . . ." Where is everyone going to go? What happens to this program? What about the women and kids in the rooms upstairs who use this as their protection from whoever forced them here, who need to live here until they can get on their feet again?

"Exactly. There are no words. We're searching for other places as we speak, but our funding most likely won't cover a place sizable enough to house everyone we currently have living here."

"I was hoping you weren't going to say that." I shake my head. "What can I do to help?"

"You're better connected than us—obviously—with your family being a staple in Westmore. If you happen to hear of anyone who has a motel for rent or an apartment block—anything, we'd be more than grateful if you could let us know."

"Of course."

"In the meantime, we're going to try and do some fundraising, hopefully have some of the endowments we've been promised come through. Something. Anything." She emits a defeated laugh. "I can't let these women down."

"And you won't. I know you won't. But yes. Definitely. If I hear of anything or think of any other way, I'll let you know."

"Thank you. I truly appreciate it."

I leave her office feeling defeated when moments ago I was content.

"Need any help with that, Miss Rothschild?" Simon, the facility's security guard, asks like he does every time I leave.

"No, thanks. I've got it."

"One of these days, you're going to say yes."

"One of these days you're going to accept my marriage proposal," I repeat our typical banter. Simon is a burly man with an undying devotion to his wife and a penchant for baking magnificent pastries that he spoils me with often.

"Maybe." He draws the word out and winks. "Maybe."

"I'll be waiting."

"And I'll be watching you head out to your car to make sure you're safe and sound."

"Thanks." I lug my cello case with me down the sidewalk but try to make it look effortless or else Simon will most definitely jog after me to help.

Graffiti mars or *decorates*—depending on who is looking at it— the brick walls as I head to the parking lot at the end of the block. This Fairmont neighborhood is sketchy at best with the inner city and its crime having reached its long, tentacled fingers into what used to be a lower-income neighborhood. Apartment buildings blanket one side of the street with front stoops lined with drying clothes while empty industrial buildings and abandoned lots pepper the opposite side of the street.

I'm lost in thought. In thinking about the generational wealth my family has and wondering how I could use it and the Rothschild reputation to benefit the Sanctuary.

The family trust has to approve all expenses and donations. I highly doubt they'd approve spending it on something like this since it would have to be done without fanfare or the society of Westmore knowing. The Rothschilds don't donate to anyone unless it helps to further cement their status or notoriety. These women don't deserve to get caught up in the dog and pony show my family would ensure.

"What in the hell are you doing here?"

I jolt at the familiar voice, surprised to be so oblivious in a place where I'm usually aware of my surroundings. Holden strides across the empty street toward me without looking, as if there's no such thing as traffic or cars.

It takes my brain a few seconds to shake loose my initial thought—*what a striking image he paints.*

He's a juxtaposition against the destitution surrounding him. His tailored pants and crisp white shirt with a blazer, no doubt custom-made. His jaw is flexed, his hair perfectly in place—he's casually confident in a place that's nothing more than a calamity.

I dislike him. *Intensely.* Unfortunately, almost as much as my body seems to want him.

"Last I checked, I don't have to run where I go or what I do by you."

"Then maybe where you go or what you do shouldn't be here of all places." He lifts his chin toward my Range Rover, parked a few feet behind me. "You're lucky you still have rims and tires."

"Because you—the man who's so new to this town—are the expert on this neighborhood, right?"

He purses his lips and nods. "I know a thing or two about Fairmont, yes."

The comment throws me. What the heck would he know about Fairmont when he's from California? "Where's *your* car?"

"I can take care of myself." It's all he says as he moves toward me with a quick glance of our surroundings before trying to take my cello case out of my hand without asking. "You shouldn't be here."

I pull back on my case. "Thanks, but I can handle it myself."

"Of course you can. Until you can't. I'm the nicest person you're going to meet in these parts and that's saying a lot." He tries to take the case again.

I may find a slight bit of joy when I let go of the case the same time that he tugs, and he stumbles backward. *Oopsie.*

Holden glares at me, impatience emanating off of him like the clean scent of his cologne. "Bass? Cello? Dead body?"

I stare after him, not sure if I enjoy him being chivalrous or despise him more for it. "If it's not yours, does it really matter?"

"Will you just get in your car and do as you're told?" he demands.

"Do as *I'm told*?" I laugh. "Don't look now but Westmore's rubbing off on you. For the record, Knight, I don't take orders from anybody."

"Except from Rhett, right? Or from Chad? Let's not forget your dad too. I mean . . ." He shrugs, his smirk taunting me to refute him.

I want to throttle him. But I stand there like an indecisive pansy and that pisses me off even more.

"Suit yourself then. No skin off my back." He sets the cello case down on the oil-stained asphalt and starts to walk off just as a loud noise—a firecracker? A backfire? A gunshot? Something I don't want to find the source of goes off farther down the block and reverberates its way toward us.

I jolt in fear.

Then freeze from the unknown.

Then try to relax my muscles one by one, all while Holden stares at me with a look that's equal parts annoyance and arrogance. *You scared now?* his eyes ask.

Torn between showing my unease, obeying him, and holding my ground, I blurt out, "It's a cello."

He stops and shakes his head. "Oh, so *now* you want to talk. Got it."

I hit the key fob so my liftgate opens as the two of us wage a battle of wills. I was having a good day—great, in fact—and now he's here like a dark cloud on a sunny day.

"Nope. I'm good. Thanks." I go to pick up my cello case and trip over my own feet.

"Give me the goddamn thing, will you," he mutters and before I can gain my balance, he yanks it from my hand, strides the rest of the distance to my car, and places the cello roughly in the back. A siren wails close by, and Holden gives it a glance before looking back at me with raised eyebrows as if to say, *See?* "There you go.

Now you can get out of here." He points to the road to reinforce his words.

With a clenched jaw, I open my driver's side door but turn to face him. "This thing here." I point from him to me and then back. "It's called a working relationship. When we're not at work, I'm just another person walking down the street who you have no say over. Got it?"

His eyes blaze. "Got it. And when we're in the office, you're another employee walking down the hallway who I couldn't give a shit about. Got it?"

I hate you.

As if he can read my mind, he smirks. "But that could be different, Sunshine."

"Stop calling me that."

"Your irritation with me says you've been considering my proposal."

"Nope. Not once." *It's all I've thought about.* "I'm not interested in your smoke and mirrors. *Look here, Rowan, while I screw you handily over there.*" I roll my eyes.

"And yet the offer intrigues you."

"No, it doesn't."

"You've walked down the hall several times, stood outside my door, but haven't come in. *It does.* The question is, what's holding you back, Rowan?"

"You."

"And for good reason." He looks over my shoulder as someone passes by on the street.

One minute he's telling me to work with him and the next he's agreeing he's the reason I shouldn't. "I don't underst—"

"A cello. *And* the wrong side of town. Not that I care, but I've got enough blood on my hands, and I'd rather not add yours to it."

What the hell does that mean?

Get in your car and leave, Rowan.

But it's not that easy. My curiosity wins.

"Then don't add it. Go back to wherever your car is and leave me to mine."

"Ah yes, to you and your cello because classical music is such a formidable means of protection in these parts."

"Where I go it is," I say. *Shit.*

He nods. Lips pursed. Eyes searching. "And where *do* you go?"

I hesitate. "The Sanctuary."

He gives a subtle nod and his eyes narrow. "The Sanctuary? As in that *Sanctuary*?" He points to the building down the block, and I nod.

"Should I be worried about you?"

"No, I—what do you mean? I don't go there for *me*. It's for others. I play for the women who live there. And—how do you know about the Sanctuary?"

"I know Fairmont," he says with a resolute tone that says, *No more questions.* He narrows his eyes. "What do you mean you *play* for them?"

"The cello. I play it."

"The Westmore Women's League pretends to give back. How touching."

"You're an asshole."

He lifts a lone brow and smirks. "Again. Nothing new."

"And you're wrong. My volunteering has nothing to do with that god-awful organization." I grimace at the thought. "It's called music therapy. Something for the women to get lost in for a bit. To feel without judgment. To . . . I don't know." Why do I feel stupid talking about this with him like it's some misdeed?

"So you come here, play some music, and then post your good deed all over your socials so everyone can see what a good human you are. Rich woman. Poor neighborhood. Don't look now, but your god complex is showing."

"For the record, you don't have to work at it—the me not liking you part. That just comes naturally."

His chuckle is low and even. "There are a lot of things that keep me up at night. Whether I'm liked or not isn't one of them."

"Great. Always such a pleasure, Knight." For a man who wants me out of here, he's sure chatty.

"*Hmpf.*" He nods but I can't read his expression. "So she's a model, a businesswoman, a musician, and charitable with her time. Quite the superficial combo."

"Music is . . . look, I *want* to be here," I snap. *Why do I feel the need to explain myself?* "My intentions are genuine. Not that you have any experience with being that."

"You're going to have to hit me harder than that if you're trying to leave a mark." He smirks.

I'm so fed up with people—*men*—discounting me that I lash back. "What about you? What about you can I pick apart and question and criticize?"

He holds his arms out. "Be my guest."

"On second thought, you're not worth my time."

"You say that, but I'm all you can think about. You can admit it. I'm used to it."

"Hardly."

"And yet you're still standing here."

"And yet you're still standing here," I mimic. "How does it feel knowing you were a person who was born to ruin others' hopes and dreams?"

"No, that part was taught to me." Something flickers in the depths of his eyes—a cold, calculating chill—that I can't read and hate that I actually want to.

"Warning heeded." I reach for the handle of the door to pull it closed but he puts his hand on it to stop me. "This? My being here? It's for me. It's to honor my gran. It's not for social media clout or Westmore society consumption."

The muscle in his jaw flexes like he's fighting the truth in my words. "We all have our reasons, don't we?"

It's the look he gives me, that split second of hesitation before he closes my car door, that gives me pause.

It's the one that says he can't quite figure me out.

And the one I shoot him in return says I don't want him to.

THIRTEEN

Holden

"Ditch the exclusivity contract?" Rhett asks, his voice rising in pitch with each and every syllable. "You're out of your fucking mind if you think Greatland will allow us to renege on our contract without repercussions, legal or otherwise."

"I'm sure Chad has some people who could help us get around those legal loopholes," I say, causing Chad to sit up a little straighter as Rhett glares at him.

Bet you didn't know I knew that, now, did you?

"But there's no need to renege on anything. Greatland's contract is about to expire. I see you've already had your lawyers draw up a new one to be signed. We're going to hold off on that, explore other options and see what that nets us."

"We're not going back on our word. End. Of. Story," Rhett insists, his finger jabbing the table with each word for emphasis.

"Our word isn't binding since the contract will have expired by the time we're set to make a decision. Besides, there's something to be said about diversifying, Rhett. We can have more than one supplier for the same product. It's called not putting all your eggs in one basket. I'm sure you're familiar with the phrase."

"And there's something to be said about being loyal to those who have been loyal to you over the years," Rhett says.

Ah. Yes. The good ol' boys network. How could we forget the "I'll scratch your back if you scratch mine" brigade? How about those boys helping to hide your financial fuckups in the process?

Rowan's been loyal to you, and you've screwed her over. How about you learn how it feels?

With a measured nod, I take a slow look at each of the ten people seated at the conference room table. I wait for one of them to speak up and second Rhett's opinion. Rowan's head is down as she jots something on a piece of paper. Several others sit with their hands clasped on the table in front of them, clearly disassociating from having an opinion.

I don't like indifference. I don't have to like someone's stance, but take a fucking side, one way or the other.

Then there's Chad and his wavering expression as he looks from Rhett to Rowan and then back to me.

Where does your loyalty fall, Chad?

"Loyalty. Right. We wouldn't want you to risk losing all of those kickbacks you've been getting from them, now, would we?" I say as I scribble a signature on a piece of paper Audrey slides in front of me. When I look up, Rhett has risen from his seat and stands across the room, glaring at me. "Please tell me that's not what this is about. I'd like to think we make decisions based on fact and not getting unspoken things in return."

Rhett shakes his head ever so slightly, but his expression says it all. I'm right and I just called him on it in front of everyone. Curiosity fills his eyes, but I know he won't voice the question he's leveling me with in this room: *How do you know that?*

You've made a deal with the devil, Rothschild. There's no turning back now.

The uncomfortable shuffling tells me a few others in this room get kickbacks as well.

Rowan's attention has been piqued. She knows her brother well enough to catch the nuance in his voice declaring that he's not happy about something. In my periphery, I can see her studying her brother with confusion etched across her face.

"Kickbacks? No," Rhett says.

Blowhard.

"No? I don't see lavish vacations and extra cash *perks* to the company CEO—*you*—stated anywhere in our contracts with Greatland. I mean . . . they are our aluminum supplier, not our travel agent, right?" I ask. It's all conjecture at this point—no concrete proof yet—but my accountants are digging, and if it's there like I've seen hints of it in my own data scraping, they'll find it.

That and Rhett's sudden widening of his eyes are enough proof for me.

Yep. Now everyone knows you're on the take. What are you going to do about it, Rhett?

"Fulfilling our agreement with Greatland is about staying loyal to a company who meets every demand that we make. Expedited schedule. Delay in schedule. Change in design," he says, completely glossing over my accusation. "It's about taking care of who caters to us when others won't, and who hasn't let us down in the decades we've been partnered together."

"But if you've never ventured outside of Greatland, then how do you know other contractors won't surpass the expectations you've set . . . or become complacent with?"

"They're a solid supplier," a man in the far corner says.

"Joshua?" I ask. "From purchasing, right?"

He nods, his fingers fidgeting endlessly with the pen in his hand. "Why fix what's not broken?"

And why pay for the product you're taking out of here by the case every night and reselling?

I meet his eyes and offer a tight smile. "You can pick up your final check in the HR department."

His eyes bulge as far open as his mouth falls. "Excuse me?"

I lift my brows. "I don't think I stuttered." The murmurs and shifting around the room cease. I've got their attention. Perfect. "The door's that way."

But I don't lift my head to see his stunned expression. I don't acknowledge the cursed protest on his lips. I don't watch his sorry ass shuffle out of the room.

"Would anybody else like to join *Joshua*?" I ask.

"We're not taking on new suppliers." Rhett's the first to speak as he rises from his seat and begins to pace the room. Agitated.

My point has been made.

"Big words from a man who is selling the keys to his castle," I taunt.

"Then maybe I yank those keys," he threatens.

I chuckle. It's menacing and unforgiving and when I tilt my head, eyes pinning him still, his Adam's apple bobs. "If that's how you make deals—negotiate and then renege the minute things don't go your way—no wonder this company is barely holding on."

"It's not failing."

I lift a lone eyebrow, my smirk taunting. "Is this really the conversation you want to have? Right now? In front of everyone?"

The muscle pulses in his jaw. *How much do you like to play with fire?*

"Porter and I go way back," he says of the owner of Greatland Aluminum. "His father goes way back with my father. And so on and so on. *There's history there.* I don't care who you are or where you come from, but TinSpirits is a family company. We pride ourselves on relationships. And we still will even after you sign on the dotted line."

"Way back." I say the last two words out loud as I write them down and underline them forcefully for showmanship. The sound of my pen on the pad resonates around the room. "Got it. We'll manage and run the company on the 'way back' premise. I mean, why change things, right?" There is no mistaking my sarcasm.

"What's your point, Knight?" he snaps at me.

I lift my eyebrows and lean back in my chair as the rest of the room shifts in their seats. I hold Rhett's glassy-eyed glare, knowing full well my slow-to-respond way infuriates him.

I take even more time to let the silence eat at him.

"Bird's-eye view? Logistics are a nightmare. You're losing money by paying higher taxes where your distribution center is. You're ignoring green energy, which would be an investment up front but would cut costs in the long run. You're disregarding untapped markets because you're stuck in the past. Should I go on?"

"When I win the election—"

"Jesus Christ, Rothschild. Is the election going to guarantee *their* paychecks?" I ask, pointing to everyone around the table. "Clearly it will help you somehow, but no one here cares about you. Got it? Win or lose, we're at the mercy of Greatland. They can screw us over and we wouldn't have a leg to stand on."

"They won't."

"But if they do, that loyalty you've fostered nets you nothing."

"So, *big man,* what's your proposal? That we say 'fuck loyalty' and move from sub to sub every time one of them offers a cheaper price? Use them and abuse them until there are no more left because we've burned every bridge there is?"

"Burning bridges isn't my style."

"Then what is? Because I'm sure as hell trying to figure that out." Rhett leans his ass against the windowsill and crosses his arms over his chest, clearly thinking he has the upper hand in this conversation.

He's played into my hands so easily.

"It sure as fuck isn't the 'way back' style." I smile smugly, enjoying this little back and forth. "Your loyalty is blinding you. Greatland is controlling the cost. We have zero leverage for negotiations."

"You don't know what the hell you're talking about."

"Right. How could I forget. We're using the 'way back' rule when it comes to running this place."

"This is one of those times when you stay in your lane, and I stay in mine."

"Ah. Yes. The lane you cross over like a drunk fuck waiting to crash and burn." I stand up, put my hands in my pockets, and meet him glare for glare. "Can we get a show of hands of who thinks we should veer from the current path?"

Silence permeates the room, everyone afraid to piss Rhett off out of loyalty and me off as the new boss.

Rowan studies me with that quiet, inquisitive stare of hers. She knows I'm right. So does everyone else in this room.

Rhett's stupidity will bring down Porter in the end as well. Can't say I'll lose sleep over that when it happens, though.

"Fine." I hold my hands up. "Have it your way, Rhett. Give Greatland a three-month extension. Keep all our eggs in that basket. But if something happens and we lose Greatland without having any other aluminum suppliers, TinSpirits will come to a standstill. Output will be halted. Shelves will go bare. Jobs might have to be cut. *You know me and my quick trigger finger.* That'll be on you, and everyone in this room will know it."

"It won't," Rhett says and glances at those around us to make sure they all know he just won this battle of wills.

He won because I let him win.

He won because I want to take Porter down too.

"I'll hold you to it," I say while everyone begins to collect their things, more than ready to leave this room that now feels like it has turned into a boxing ring.

"And Rowan?" I ask, giving her pause enough to look up and meet my eyes.

"Hmmm?"

"My door has remained open on purpose and you've yet to walk through it."

She continues to look at me, her expression stoic. She's prim and proper today in her black slacks and cream-colored sweater that hugs her curves. But images of her from the parking lot in Fairmont the other day keep flashing in my mind.

Her blue jeans and plain white shirt. Her hair down in soft waves. The natural pink of her lips and cheeks.

Let it go, Holden.

"I'm talking to you," I say. She rises from her chair, her eyes locked on mine as she gathers her things. The only indication she gives that she heard me is a stilted pause and the lift of one eyebrow. "We need to finish our conversation where we left off."

And then she turns on her heel and walks from the room.

I remain where I stand, each manager having to pass me on their way out. Some meet my eyes. Others don't.

I take note. I always take note.

But it's Rowan I watch walk down the hall.

It's Rowan I'm thinking about long after the last person is gone and I'm alone in the conference room. It's her intelligence and her defiance that are beginning to appeal to me more and more.

I've caught myself toggling back and forth between screens of information and images of her several times this week.

It's Rowan who is talking to a team of her colleagues in the hall, who meets my eyes over their shoulders and smirks. How cute. She thinks she has the upper hand.

She doesn't, goddammit.

The woman is getting under my skin. I want to scratch her out of it.

She can't be there.

I don't want her to be.

And yet I'm still staring at her as she talks, still wondering what the fuck is going through her head.

Look away. Look the fuck away, Holden.

Don't let her know you think about her at all. Because she could—would—use it against you. Just as you're doing to her.

You're too close to ruin everything now.

Too fucking close.

And yet when she finally turns to go into her office, I'm still staring at where she was.

Still thinking about the woman I should put off-limits—but know I won't.

She's part of the game.

And sometimes games have consequences.

FOURTEEN

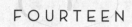

Rowan

He called me out in front of the whole room.

Put a fucking spotlight on me so that every manager in there thinks we have something going on that doesn't exist. *We need to finish our conversation where we left off.* Created doubt in their minds over why he'd make that comment, as if I know something they don't.

Rumors. Rumors. And more rumors.

If he thinks his comment will spark me to act now, he's batshit crazy. Firing Joshua was a nice touch. The fucking prick deserved it, but the subtle threat Holden laid out there to all management was heard. Loud and fucking clear.

And then to sit there like that, like he's fucking king of the castle in the conference room, staring at me as if I owe it to talk to him.

Fuck him.

I stalk into my office, my cell already buzzing in my hand. I'm just about to sit down when I glance down to Chad's text of WTF, Row? I'm out of my office in seconds, not giving a rat's ass if Holden is still there staring, and head straight to Chad's.

"If you have something to say, just come out and say it to me," I snap the minute I've cleared his doorway and have shut the door behind me.

Chad stops mid-motion before slowly sinking into his chair. He has a dark blue shirt on today that makes his eyes stand out more than they normally do. His dirty-blond hair is cropped short but styled, and his skin is tanned from time spent in the sun, most likely playing golf.

He's not a bad guy by any means. He's . . . *he's just Chad*. The guy who has always been around. Rhett's best friend. A guy I used to hunt crayfish with and who taught me how to drive stick shift in my pop's old Ford truck. Someone who has been through way too much with the Rothschild family.

Any spark between us is strictly platonic.

But when Chad glances up and meets my eyes, the look he gives me says he's more than curious about Holden's comment.

"What was that all about?" he asks in that calm, unruffled demeanor of his.

"What was what all about? You two brought the guy in here, not me. Ask yourself that."

But I know exactly what his comment was about.

My door is still open and you've yet to walk through it.

"It just seems like . . ."

"Like I have a less than lukewarm relationship with someone the two of you have forced me to work with? It's not like I was given a say in the matter," I say sarcastically. "You can't have it both ways. You can't tell me I have to get along with him and in the same breath hope I'll remain at odds with him for your own sakes."

"You know what? Forget I asked." He gives that easygoing smile of his. "I'm just being paranoid."

Why? I don't voice the single syllable though. Because isn't that how I've been feeling every second of every day as I resist the urge to tell Holden he's right about both the direction we need to move marketing in and about giving me the chance to get my hands on everything else?

"Don't think I've forgotten what we talked about," he says.

"We've talked about a lot of things, Chad."

Like how much I despise Rhett. Like how unhappy I am with you just going along with this. Like how fucking livid I am that I have to even feel those feelings. So what is it, huh?

He glances to the doorway to make sure no one is there before lowering his voice. "Ways to stop this from happening. I've got an idea or two but I'm not certain how feasible they are in the short time frame we have."

"The question is why now? Why think of these things now instead of before Rhett even agreed to them?"

His Adam's apple bobs, and his eyes glance toward the door and back. "I got caught up in the moment, okay?" he offers, a more than pathetic apology.

I nod, studying him and letting his feckless excuse go in one ear and out the other. But hearing it and seeing how jumpy Chad is also gives me a bit of hope.

I have no qualms playing all sides of this game that I never wanted to be a participant in. And if part of that strategy is exploiting Chad's guilt over screwing me over by having him help me brainstorm ways to stop this bullshit buyout, then I'm all for it.

"Row, you're not saying anything." He scrubs a hand through his hair and sighs. "I'm sorry. I . . . it's a pitiful excuse but it's true. We've been under all this stress trying to find a way out of this financial mess and then in walks the answer with Holden's offer."

"It was too easy," I say to try to get a reaction out of him. The slump of his shoulders and resigned nod are all I need to see to know he agrees.

He lifts his eyes and gives me a halfhearted smile. A smile I buy because of our history but don't completely trust because of what he kept from me. "There have to be some options. We just need to figure out where and how and who we need to help us."

"Agreed, but I have to admit, every day feels a little more hopeless than the one before. Besides, my brother's on board with this. He may have just put on a show in the boardroom—big man on campus—but he's still one hundred percent behind it."

"He wouldn't have agreed to it if he weren't." He looks around the room. "The cash influx and a win in the election will allow us to move forward with finding a new location to build our own distribution center. A cheaper location and cost than what we're spending now. If we bring things in-house, we can control so much more. Holden's purchase gives us the funds to make changes like that, and they'll net us long-term returns."

"Anything can look good on paper," I murmur. "Case in point." I point to an ad sitting on the corner of his desk. It's my body, the side of my face, the newest TinSpirits product—a canned Moscow mule—in my hand. "Airbrushing does me wonders."

Chad's eyes narrow and his expression softens. "You're so full of shit. They haven't retouched a single thing. You're gorgeous, Row. Always have been," he says so quietly that I know it's my cue to exit.

No need to get caught in this emotional quicksand.

"We should talk about it later," Chad continues. If he sees my sudden discomfort, he's oblivious to it. "Over drinks or something. Somewhere private where we can talk more freely." He glances toward the ceiling and then around his office. "For all we know this place is bugged."

He *is* paranoid.

But he probably has cause to be. I wouldn't put anything past Holden Knight. Besides, at this point, Chad knows Holden better than me.

And drinks with Chad? *That's a no-go.* I learned a long time ago not to feed that fire of speculation. One night of drinks leads to squealing phone calls from both our mothers, who literally have our wedding planned and are waiting for the word "go."

That's the last thing I need right now.

"The one thing you can count on around here is not being able to count on anything," I say with a despondent smile.

Chad nods. "It might turn out, you know. This thing with Holden coming in."

Quit playing both sides, Chad.

I rise and head toward the door, turning back to look at him before I walk through it. "For what it's worth, I think Holden's right."

"About Greatland?"

"Yes. About Greatland." Rhett's expression when Holden called him out flashes in my mind. My stomach turned because I know my brother—well enough to know that the look on Rhett's face meant he's getting a whole hell of a lot more back from Porter and Greatland than a few rounds of golf every year. For a man who's loyal to no one, Rhett sure as shit is loyal to them being our sole supplier. "It's basic economics. You know that. Rhett knows that. Holden knows that. What I can't quite figure out is why you guys decided to bring in someone to make changes and fix things, and yet you're fighting the changes."

Chad just looks at me, that muscle ticking in his jaw, but doesn't say a word.

Exactly.

Your silence means you're part of the problem too, Chad.

I leave his office with a simple nod. My stomach wobbles and I draw in a deep breath. *But I was silent too.*

I think back to earlier this morning when I was sitting at my desk, staring at a blinking cursor on an open Word document, when the realization hit me.

Is that what Rhett was expecting—maybe even Chad? That I'll remain silent and not rock the boat? That I'll be so angry with him for this mess that I riot against Holden while my brother maneuvers me out of a job? God knows he'd have the support of my mom to do this too.

The thought sickens me, but it's not one I can afford to overlook. And the more I think about it, dwell on it, obsess over it, the more it makes sense.

A cough down the hall brings me back to the present. I sink back in my chair, close my eyes, and sigh.

A bottle of wine. Watching the sun set from my back porch. My dog, Winnie, chasing bugs around the backyard.

That's what I need right now—to decompress. To get away from this place after a long, hellish week. Besides, it's not like I'm getting any work done anyway.

I gather my things and start to leave but make the mistake of glancing down the hallway. The floor is quiet, office lights are out, and doors are shut. All except for one.

Of course he's still here.

I don't know why, but I head toward his office. It's almost as if I can't figure where my own loyalties lie, and frankly, I'm so sick of thinking about it.

I'm supposed to hate the man out of principle. He's made it more than easy with how much of a dick he's been, and yet there have been glimpses of him—the night at the auction, the parking lot in Fairmont—that make me believe if the buyout weren't involved and I'd met him somewhere random, let's say, I'd be drawn to him.

Not because of his wealth, but more because of his confidence. His defiance. His lack of giving a fuck about who and what he is.

"Yes?" Holden says through the open doorway as I stand there.

I want to be annoyed that he knows I'm here, to tell him to go to hell, but I find myself walking through the doorway. He's sitting with his feet propped up and crossed at the ankles, resting on the corner of his desk. His fingers are laced behind his head. His shirt is rolled up to the elbows showcasing his sculpted forearms and expensive watch. He's ditched the tie he had on earlier and the top two buttons of his dress shirt are undone.

He looks tired.

It's the first time I've seen Holden Knight look anything but perfect, and I hate that it humanizes him. Probably because he looks exactly how I feel right now.

He lifts his eyebrows in response to me standing there and staring at him.

"You came to say you know I'm right. That keeping suppliers in the family, so to speak, isn't good business."

"How did you know all that? About Rhett and the kickbacks?"

He studies me, his lips pursed, his eyes intense. "I know everything, Rowan."

I'm not certain if that's meant as a statement or a warning but I sure as hell don't like the chuckle he emits after saying it. Chills chase up and down my spine and they're only running because there is more going on here. That much I know is true.

"Your game is already getting old," I say.

"You mean the one where I'm trying to pit everyone against each other so I can see who has real integrity?"

I open my mouth and close it, surprised that he just admitted that so blatantly.

"What? You don't expect honesty, Rowan? I do. At all times."

"You love this, don't you? Sowing chaos. Creating confusion. Making us all doubt each other."

He nods unapologetically. "Very much, in fact."

"But why?" I step farther into the room and lean my back against the doorjamb. "You're not making any friends here with your little chest-thumping competitions against Rhett."

He grins. "You say that like you think I care."

"You should. The people standing on the sidelines watching are the ones who are going to implement whatever changes you make. They have to trust you. Look up to you. Respect you."

"And they respect Rhett?" he asks, alert and astute. It's a simple question and yet I find myself hesitating because he knows as well as I do that they most likely don't. Whereas this company is my legacy, for most of them it's simply a paycheck that supports their families. "Employees respect the person who keeps the doors open and the paychecks coming. Every single person in that room knew I was right, and not a single person said so. *Including you.* That gives me pause."

"Meaning?"

His gaze fixes on mine. "You tell me. Would you want someone managing you who's afraid to go against the grain? Who's afraid of making changes for the sake of the company's success?"

He's right. He knows it and worst of all, he knows that I know it.

"Maybe I didn't speak up because I wanted to avoid getting involved in your and Rhett's pissing match."

"And maybe I expected more from you." He angles his head to the side as I bite back the unwelcome feeling of disappointment.

Why do I care what he thinks of me?

But I do, and I *hate* that I do.

"You want to run this company, Sunshine, but you're afraid to speak up and ruffle feathers. That means you're not ready."

"I beg to differ."

"There's a lot more to running a company than understanding how to market a product or look pretty selling it."

Ah, the asshole who pisses me off has made his appearance. That didn't take long. "There you go discounting me. *Again.*"

"Stating facts isn't discounting you. It's calling it like I see it." He shifts, puts his feet on the floor, and sits forward with his hands on his desk.

Energy courses through me, making me stroll around the office like I own the place. Probably because up until two weeks ago, I did—or at least my family did.

"You're standing here because you know you want what I'm offering. The new marketing plans. The ability to matter. All of it . . . but taking me up on my offer fucks up where your loyalty lies, now, doesn't it?"

"Why were you in Fairmont?" I ask, purposely shifting topics and voicing what I've wondered numerous times since last week.

He wants answers from me. Well, I want answers from him.

He pauses and stares at me, fingers steepled, muscle pulsing in his jaw like he's contemplating how much to tell me. "I used to have family who lived there."

I don't know what I expected him to say, but this wasn't it. I never expected him to admit anything outside of business, so it takes me a second to find a response.

"Used to?" I press for more information. The more I know about Holden, the more ammo I have to potentially use against him and even the playing field a bit. "So, what? You were just there on a casual stroll down memory lane?"

"Something like that."

"Were you following me, Holden?"

His dismissive snort is believable, but I have a feeling he's capable of selling anything to anyone. There's a half smirk on his lips. "I have better things to do than follow you."

"Just like I have better things to do than entertain the notion that you're going to be majority owner of this place."

"The sooner you accept it, the easier it will be for you."

I have a feeling that when it comes to Holden Knight, nothing is easy. He gets off on this. The banter. The baiting. The battle.

"You don't own anything yet."

His looks at his watch and flashes a full-force grin at me. "Well, you've got forty-five-ish more days to try and stop me."

"Plenty of time," I lie.

"I welcome the challenge." He lifts his hands. "The offer to work with me still stands though."

"Isn't that what I'm doing already? Working with you?"

"No. You're trying to figure me out. You're figuring how to undermine me at any turn. Hell, you just said it yourself that you're trying to find a way to stop this deal from happening."

I smile. "At least we both know where the other stands."

"True, but you'll see my way soon enough."

I snort.

His face sobers. And just like that, the moment is lost. "Go home, Rowan. I have work to do."

"Oh, I'm dismissed, am I?"

"You are," he says, the playfulness from moments ago suddenly gone when he lowers his head and focuses on the screen of his laptop. "Oh, and don't wear that top again."

"Excuse me?" I stop and look down at my fitted V-neck cashmere sweater.

"It's distracting." He waves me away without looking up. "You make it hard to concentrate."

I stare at him with a disbelieving smile. Did he really just say that?

I should be offended.

I should be livid at being objectified.

I should tell him to eat shit and die.

But as I turn and walk down the hall, I grin, already thinking about the detour I need to make on the way home.

A detour to the boutique where I bought this so I can buy one in every color available.

The surefire way to get me to do something is to tell me not to.

FIFTEEN

Holden

Clank. Click. Clank.

"Hey, Simpson?"

It still takes me a second to hear the name and respond to it. It's weird. But I can still see the look on Mase's face the first time he heard someone call me Holden Simpson. Pride. Joy. Belonging.

The one moment made it all worthwhile, despite what a pain in the ass it's been for me to hear it and respond to it.

The funny part is how easily I was able to make the transition for others to call me it. No one questioned it. No one stopped me to look a little closer.

In this community, people like me are invisible.

Clank. Click. Clank.

"Yo. Simpson. I'm talking to you."

Case in point.

I look up from where I'm bussing a table. I already know the voices, already know the spoiled fucking punks who they belong to.

Their daddies run this town. And their daddies before them did too.

Clank. Click. Clank.

I force the smile on my face and look over to where the three of them sit. Their smiles are smug and there's an air about them—entitlement meets douchebag—that has me gritting my teeth.

"Yeah. Can I help you?" I say, and then look back down to the dirty dishes I'm placing in my bin.

"Ah, where are your manners?" the one—the Williams kid—asks. "Didn't your daddy teach you to speak properly and meet someone's eyes when they're talking to you?"

"Like anyone from that side of town has a daddy. Jesus, Williams. We all know that," the Rothschild asshole says. He grips the silver lighter he carries constantly and jerks his hand so the top opens. *Clank.* He pulls his thumb down on the igniter. *Click.* Then snaps his wrist so the lid drops back down and extinguishes the flame. *Clank.*

Clank. Click. Clank.

It's my alarm bell. The three sounds that tell me the assholes are on the prowl and looking for trouble. Trouble they often find but are never held responsible for.

"Right, Simpson? Do you have a daddy?" Rothschild asks. *Clank. Click. Clank.*

"Can I get you anything?" I repeat, meeting Williams's eyes this time.

"How about some weed? Or maybe something a little stronger?" the prick Porter asks. "No doubt your momma is on the corner selling that nasty pussy of hers for a hit."

My hands fist and jaw clenches.

"Bring us her stash and we'll make sure you get to keep your job," Rothschild says. *Clank. Click. Clank.*

You need this job, Holden.

Out of the corner of my eye, I see my boss walk by the banquet room—where the assholes have helped themselves to a table set for an event later—and assess the situation from afar. "Everything okay, boys?" he calls out.

Their chuckles rumble around the room.

"Yep," Williams says and smirks at me. "We were just asking Simpson here why he was refusing to serve us."

You need this job.

Clank. Click. Clank.

"We know he needs this job so we were just telling him how he should be a little more responsive and respectful to the members here if he wants to keep it," Rothschild says with a bat of his eyes like he's completely innocent.

My boss eyes me, his brows narrowed and chin sharp when he nods. "They're right, Simpson. We've got a wait list a mile long of people waiting to work here. You're replaceable."

Clank. Click. Clank.

Bite your tongue. "Yes, sir," I say and swallow over the bitterness and shame these fuckers are gloating in.

"Good." He walks away and the three assholes burst out laughing.

"See how easy that was?" Porter says, rising from the table and purposefully knocking over the ashtray full of cigar ashes. "Oops. What a mess. Uh, Simpson, it doesn't look like you're doing your job very well."

"Another strike against you," Williams says.

Clank. Click. Clank.

"It's almost tee time," a female voice says that has me looking over to the doorway. She's tall with long legs and blond hair. She's a walking wet dream is what she is. Too bad she's—

"Rowan," Porter says and the four of them laugh at whatever inside joke I'm not catching. She mock curtsies. "Why'd you have to go and spoil our fun?"

"Fun's over," Rhett says as he stands and makes a show of knocking over his iced tea. The brown liquid and ice cubes scatter over the white tablecloth and onto the floor. More laughter rings out. "Would you look at that. You're so clumsy, Simpson. Better get on that."

My hands fist in the tablecloth covering the table I'm clearing. Too many emotions—fury, resentment, bitterness—rage through me. *You. Need. This. Job.*

"Did I hear a 'yes, sir'?" Williams asks. "I don't think I did. Did you, Rhett?"

Rhett Rothschild sets down his lighter as he grabs his clubs and hat. "Nope. Not even a 'please' or 'thank you.'"

"Trash doesn't have manners," Porter says, slapping Rhett on the back. "C'mon, *Rowan*."

"Yeah, *Row*," Williams says as he hangs an arm around her shoulder and they all laugh again.

"Let's go whack our balls around," Porter says.

Laughter erupts around them as they head out the door. My tight shoulders begin to relax the tiniest of fractions.

"What's his first name anyway?" Porter asks as they walk away.

"Simpson," Williams says. "It's Simpson, right?"

"Yeah. Pretty sure, but who fucking cares. He's the help."

I move toward the table where they were to pick up their mess.

Rothschild's lighter is where he left it on the table. I glance over my shoulder to the door before picking it up. It's heavy in my hand. The silver of it is cool to the touch, and the design on its sides—a crest of some sort—is etched into the metal. I run my fingers over it, wondering what it means.

Out of curiosity, I flip the lid open and click the dial so a flame sparks to life. I watch it burn for a few seconds.

Then drop it the second I hear footsteps behind me.

"You'd like to steal that, wouldn't you?" Rhett asks at my back as he all but shoves me aside to grab his lighter. "Definitely worth way more than your mom gets on the street corner." He takes a few steps backward, condescending smirk in full force. "Just admit it, Simpson. You'd give anything to be me. To be us. Sucks for you that'll never happen."

Unclench your fists.

Watch him walk away.

You need this job.

SIXTEEN

Rowan

"Tell me more about that incredibly sexy man who you're working side by side with."

Caroline finally got around to asking. I knew there was a reason for her call other than "just because." "Side by side?" I snort. "Hardly. And his looks? Haven't noticed."

"You're so full of shit you stink, Rothschild."

"Okay, fine. He's handsome. I'll give him that," I say as I throw the ball for Winnie and she bounds after it. "But good looks don't negate all the other reasons I have to dislike him."

"Still tense between you two?"

"Still . . . everything," I say, not exactly wanting to talk more about the man who owns more of my thoughts than I care to give him. "Confusing. Weird. Surreal."

"Ugh. I'm sorry. Should I accidentally trip him the next time I see him?" she teases.

"You've seen him?"

"Yep. He's making his presence known around town."

"I thought he already had."

"Yeah, but it's different now."

"Different how?"

"He's been at the club," she says, referring to the Westmore Country Club. "At Duke's Steakhouse. At the yacht club. He's been seen all of the places where you go to be seen."

"Good for him."

"The question is why?"

"Um . . . because he lives here now and needs to build the relationships my dad and Rhett have to keep the business afloat when he's majority owner."

"*When?* You've resigned yourself to that?"

"No." Winnie jumps after an insect and falls on her back. "Well . . . it's complicated."

"I'm sure it is," she says.

"You have no idea," I groan.

"Wait. You're really not interested in him in the least?"

"No," I lie. "He's . . . arrogant. An asshole. Has a sharp tongue and snarky wit. He thinks he knows everything and lets you know that he does."

"So he's exactly your type, then?" she deadpans.

I draw in a heated breath. "Funny."

She chuckles. "So that means you won't object when I tell you you're busy, not this Friday but the next."

"Caroline," I warn, to which she laughs in response.

"Just remember you love me."

"What did you do?"

"I set you up on a date with a friend of a friend. Someone has to look out for your stagnant sex life."

"I'm not going."

"Yes, you are." Her laugh is deep and rich. "Oh, will you look at that? It's time for me to go."

"Carol—"

"Bye, Row."

The call ends, my protest falling on deaf ears. "Seriously?" I mutter when I know she is. And even worse, I know if I try to dodge the date, she'll send the poor guy to my house on a mission to find me.

I groan and Winnie looks my way. "I know," I say to her. "*I know.*"

With a sigh I lean my head back and take in the view as I silently curse Caroline and her never-ending need to set me up.

The sun is setting slowly in the warm summer evening. The

glass fence that borders the rear part of my backyard blocks the ocean breeze somewhat but allows for killer views of the white sand and blue water of the Atlantic.

Some old classics play from my speaker inside. And the six new short-sleeved sweaters hanging in my closet upstairs are making this glass of wine go down even smoother.

What a day.

Hell, what a fucking few weeks.

Processing what's happening to the company is one thing. Accepting it is a whole other thing I don't think I'm quite ready for.

And then to top it off, I finally ripped the Band-Aid off today. I had a mini meltdown when I picked up a stack of papers from my home office and a picture of me and Gran slipped out. I stared at it through blurred tears for way too long and took it as a sign to finally open the inheritance letter from the estate attorney.

The one that opening means I have to face the fact that she's not coming back.

That she's really gone.

Hence my third—or is it fourth glass of wine? A long phone call with a good friend. And time spent on the porch swing in my backyard, which was Gran's favorite place to just sit and *be* when she visited.

I close my eyes, drop my head back, and let the ocean breeze tickle the loose strands of my hair against my cheeks. It's the most relaxed I've been in some time—no doubt the wine is helping with that.

Memories fire and then float back. Our long conversations. The promises I made her. The sheer and utter devastation of losing the only person who ever truly loved and appreciated the woman I was and the Rothschild norms I bucked.

I miss her. Plain and simple. I love my parents because . . . they are my parents and, despite their shortcomings, are still decent people.

I love Rhett as in, he's my brother and I can talk ill of him as much as I want but my hackles go up when someone else does. At least that's how I've always felt, but recent events have me questioning any defense of him at all.

But my gran, she was my biggest cheerleader, the one I schemed with, and the only person I ever sought approval from.

That's why her death has hit me so hard. It was like I'd lost the real-life angel and devil on my shoulder, encouraging me to do all the things I wasn't supposed to do and praising my determination to do them. I thought I was prepared for her passing. I told myself all the lies one often does—she lived a good life, she's in a better place, it was her time—but they felt like cheap justifications.

It's been a few weeks now and I'm still struggling to gain my footing in a world where she's no longer present. And when I finally felt myself lifting my head above the waterline of grief, I decided I'd open the envelope from Mr. Williams.

Rowan,

Well, if you're getting this, I finally kicked the bucket. Hopefully the bucket was sparkly with the kind of glitter that falls everywhere and sticks to your skin so you can't get it off you. Annoying in the best kind of way. And hopefully said bucket was filled with my favorite gin—the one my grandfather first made—and that Godiva chocolate that I love. You know how I love to make a statement.

Please, don't be sad. I lived a wonderful life. One where I wouldn't change much of anything other than spending more time with the few I loved.

Know that I believe in you. That I trust you'll keep your promise to me. That you'll use your brilliant mind and ingenuity to find a way to keep the company thriving and in Rothschild hands. Stand your ground, kiddo. Fight dirty like your brother would if need be. It should be you who's running it. You have the spark it needs, the tenacity it deserves, and the creativity to look at it through a different lens than Rhett does.

It's his because he was born a male. I love him, but he doesn't have what it takes to make the company endure. He's not you. And because you promised me you'll keep our legacy going for me, I've left you a little something to help with that.

But first, never forget that I'm proud of you. For being everything I ever wanted to be and then some. For your kind heart that you hide from so many others. For going against the grain that was set in stone without women like you in mind.

I've left each of you different inheritances. Rhett . . . well, Rhett no doubt will be unhappy with his, but hasn't he always been given everything? Don't worry, I'll be watching his tantrum over it while drinking that gin.

You on the other hand will be receiving a vast amount more. More about that in a bit along with some instructions on the parameters of claiming that inheritance. It is your prerogative if you want to share what you're getting with Rhett.

I suggest you don't until it's securely in your hands.

You know I grew up in a strict household, in a time where women were supposed to sit quietly, support their husbands, and leave the business to the men. I was before my time in wanting more than that out of life. I bucked against convention but lost in so many respects.

The world is so very different now, Row. Women in the workplace are more accepted. Women wanting more than to be a society lady, even more so. I know you can break the glass ceiling in this damn town, and that is why I'm going to leave you with some wisdom to live by.

1. *Life is nothing without passion. Live yours, whatever it may be. Live your passion.*
2. *Love is a necessity. You deserve someone who makes you feel like you've been struck by lightning. Stop rolling your eyes. Find a man who admires your spirit, who lets you make decisions for yourself, and who fights standing beside you, not in front of you.*
3. *Assess. Adjust. Adapt. Kick ass. You know that was my motto in life. Make it yours.*
4. *Make waves. Don't ever settle.*
5. *Sometimes you have to do what seems wrong, in order to get to what's right. There's a reason I married my first husband. It was so I could appreciate your grandpop even more.*
6. *Give back. Not just with money, but with time. And not to the Westmore community. Find one that really needs it and can benefit from whatever you can bring to them.*
7. *Eat the sugar. Drink the wine. Laugh when it's inappropriate.*

Enough of my Hallmark card wisdom. Now to the good stuff.

I have set up a trust for you, to be set into motion upon my death and take effect on your thirtieth birthday.

You know I hate rules, so this will seem odd that I'm

attaching parameters to your inheritance. I have my reasons. I'll explain below.

My precious Row, I leave you thirty million dollars— but there's a catch.

I know you. You'll get so lost in work, in your drive to succeed, that you'll forget to fall in love. So, listen closely. Thirty million—a lump sum payment—will be yours two years after you marry.

Yes. That means you'd better get on it, because you're not getting any younger, now, are you?

Because you are like me, I'm sure that rule just pissed you off—because no one tells you what to do. Am I right? If that's the case and you choose to overlook the finding love and getting married part, you'll receive one million a year for the next thirty years.

Not bad by any means, but not the same. The lump sum will give you more possibilities.

My opinion? Choose option number one. First, see number two above. And second, that lump sum payment might be enough for you to buy some votes of those on the board. You can outright buy a percentage of the owner- ship or you can persuade a board member and buy their vote at the table. The more clout you have as a board member or owner, the more pull you'll have in one day getting a no-confidence vote of Rhett as the CEO.

(My lawyer has my notes on which members might be for sale, and the dirt I have on them to convince them. Did you expect any less?)

Already thinking of how to get around this? Marry someone, get the money, then divorce them? See? I know you well. That's where my recent addendum to my will comes in: you must remain married for two years before receiving the totality of the inheritance.

In addition, my company, Mirium LLC, is yours. What's that, you ask? It's a company your grandpop set up for me so that I can have a say in my family's business. Your new company nets you a 5 percent stake in TinSpirits, which is a big enough percentage to warrant a board seat. Congratulations, you now have a vote.

It's up to you whether you keep this company's ownership private and vote by proxy or make it known and vote yourself. Private gives you more leverage.

Why am I giving this to you? To give you options and freedom. A chance to use these options to level the playing field if need be. Allow you to work your magic and sell whatever agenda it is you want, just like I know you can.

I love you, Rowan. You have always owned my heart in a way neither Rhett nor Cassie did. I was truly blessed to be your grandmother. Go conquer the world. I'll be watching.

Forever and always,
Gran

It was quintessential Eleanor Rothschild. Quirky, humorous, blunt, and loaded with the tough love I'd come to expect from her. Not to mention a huge *holy shit* in regards to the trust.

The holy shit that prompted me to open the most expensive bottle of wine and down it myself.

The flap of the envelope flutters with the ocean breeze. I stare at it until my eyes blur and my head spins even more than it already has.

I loved it at first. An unexpected treat to *hear* her voice again.

Then I hated it. I read it the one time, followed by all the legal attachments that came with it. Then I tossed it on the table where it sits, mad at it.

At Gran for leaving me.

At the inheritance I'm flabbergasted by but that I don't want all the same.

At the parameters she set on me when she knows that falling in love is the last thing on my mind.

It's like my world has been tipped upside down twice—first with her death and then with the buyout—and she's giving me an unexpected way to try to right it.

But right it at a personal cost I don't exactly want to pay.

Marry and receive an astronomical lump sum that I can possibly use to move mountains. Don't marry and receive a million a year for thirty years.

Net a seat on the board either way.

The clichéd rich kid in me says receive the million a year for thirty years. That's more than anyone needs by far. Gran was crazy if she thought I'd strap my love life to a ticking clock.

Sure, a few dates and some great sex are on my radar—but not falling in love and getting married. Especially the definition of marriage and the role of being a wife here in Westmore.

Will it come in time? Later in life when I'm established, have smashed my goals, and have a more prominent role in the company? Maybe. Maybe not.

All I know is the thought of having to put *me* on hold for the collective of an *us* just doesn't hit me as something I want right now.

My mom calls it selfish. I don't really care.

The lump sum would go a long way to trying to fix the current situation.

Are you out of your mind, Rowan? Who are you going to just pick up and marry? Why would you fuck up your life like that?

I groan and finish the last of my wine.

Leave it to Gran to blackmail me. To make me question everything about myself because of it.

I promised her I'd keep the company in Rothschild hands.

Don't look now, Row, but you're failing at both.

Winnie comes my way when I whistle, and I absently pet the top of her head as she drinks water from the bowl beside me. My mind wanders.

How can I fix this?

How can I stop this?

How can I keep my promise when things are spiraling out of control?

I lift my glass to my lips only to realize it's empty. Shit. What would Gran do if she knew what was happening right now?

Assess. Adjust. Adapt. Kick ass.

Does that motto include bending some rules to reach the end game I promised?

I'm beginning to think that's the only way I can.

SEVENTEEN

Holden

I lean back and stare at the console of screens set up in front of me. There are six in all, curved in an arc around my desk. Each one holds a treasure trove of information I've been coveting for some time.

On Chadwick Williams and the price he's paid and people he's crossed to be where he is.

On Rhett Rothschild, the hasty decisions and all-encompassing greed his last name gave him carte blanche to but that I plan to use to fuck him over.

Both families enabled their sons and wielded their corruption for their own benefit. To keep their power at the cost of so many others.

I'm here to stop it. To harness it. To use it against them as it was once used against me.

The Rothschilds' baby? TinSpirits and its subsidiary products? I'll own it. Then I'll destroy and dismantle it so as to cause maximum collateral damage.

The information is laid out in front of me. I can recite the facts and figures and details without looking at the screens.

But it's the added information I've amassed over the past few days that holds my attention the most. Rowan is an overachiever in all aspects. Graduated magna cum laude from college. A prestigious internship with one of the top entrepreneur programs in the country while getting her master's degree. A rise through the ranks at TinSpirits.

Interesting.

Daddy didn't hand her the VP of marketing position right off the bat like he did for Rhett and his position straight out of school. She had to work for it. Surely she was moved up the ladder faster than most, but she was in fact on the ladder.

And she volunteers at the Sanctuary.

I'm not sure why that one sticks with me the most.

It's also such a major contrast to the pictures I found when I slid past her firewall and into her hard drive. The carefree, wild woman in those images is nothing like the reserved and defiant one who stands outside my office debating what to spar with me over.

The pictures of her in barely there bikinis don't hurt either.

Christ almighty. Brains and beauty are a lethal combination, and she has both.

I startle when my cell rings. A glance at the clock tells me it's late and I've been staring at this for way too long.

"Knight," I say when I pick up.

"Leave Rowan the fuck alone."

The slurred words hit my ear.

"Chad? Hello to you too." I rise from my seat and move to the window of my penthouse so I can look out to the city beyond. To the river that separates who he is and who I used to be.

"You heard me."

"Mm-hmm. I did. I heard 'fuck' and 'Rowan.' Thanks for the approval on what I plan to do. Not that I needed it."

"You motherfucker," he grits out.

My chuckle is a taunt. The closest I'm going to get to plowing a fist in his face. At this point, it'll have to do. Unsatisfying but better than nothing. "Been called worse by better."

"You think this is funny, don't you? Well, don't. It's not." He sniffs. "Leave her alone."

"Now, do you care to tell me what that's supposed to mean?" I can't help my smile. I know exactly what the fuck he means.

The looks I level him as I stand partly in Rowan's office as I talk to her. The purposely placed comments about her as I walk past his office. Anything to fuck with his head.

And . . . it seems to be working.

"You're . . . you're toying with her and I'm not sure why."

"You know why," I bait him but am met with his silence.

"She has nothing to do with it," he says, but I let the comment float and die. *It?* Does he mean the company being run into the ground? The poor financial decisions he and his best buddy have made? The slow demise of their coffers?

Because we all know he's not referring to the real reason I'm here. I was invisible to him then and it seems because I was, he can't see through me now.

"Did you hear me?" he demands on pretty fucking shaky legs.

I don't know what he's referring to and I don't care. But clearly my not answering fucks with his head even more.

"Are you there, Knight?"

"Desperate doesn't sound good on you, Williams."

"I'm warning you."

"I don't have to listen to shit from some drunk wannabe asshole who couldn't find a backbone to save his life."

"Fuck you."

This is more than pathetic.

"That all you got, *Chadwick*?"

"Monarch."

"Monarch?" I ask.

"The reason behind it all."

"Behind what all?"

"Rhett. His carte blanche."

"What the fuck are you talking about?" I demand, confused as fuck.

"Nothing." There's a clink in the background—the neck of a bottle on his glass I presume.

"What's Monarch?" I repeat.

"Rhett. He thinks he's the king of the castle." He waves a hand dismissively. "Ignore me. I'm just drunk."

"Then you shouldn't have picked up the phone." *Keep talking, asshole.*

"We're talking about Rowan here," he asserts. Clearly the fucker is drunk and talking gibberish with his dick in his hand, looking for a contest to prove his is bigger.

He'll lose.

He'll most definitely lose.

"We're not talking about shit here, Williams, but please, be my guest and keep going."

I glance over to my computer screens. To one where emails are populating. To another where an image of Rowan stares back at me.

"You're fucking it all up."

"And yet my money was so enticing to start with."

"Yes. No. *I mean Rowan.*"

"What about her? The part where she's way out of your league and doesn't want you, or the part where you and Rhett disregard everything about her?"

"You're wrong." A slurp of what I assume is his drink. "And I don't disregard her."

"Could've fooled me." I pause on purpose. "The question is why, though. You say I'm to leave her alone, and yet you want more from her than any of us."

"What the fuck does that mean?"

Note to self: alcohol turns Chad into a pussified tough guy.

"It must be hard to want to marry a woman who doesn't want you back."

"You don't know shit."

I chuckle into the phone. That's the only answer I need to give to further the poor man's paranoia.

And he takes the bait. "Like you know what Rowan wants."

No, but after this conversation I have every intention of finding out.

You've made her a pawn in this game, Chad. A piece to position and maneuver and take advantage of in order to use to my advantage.

I'd thought about it.

I'd contemplated it.

I swirled the thought around on my tongue like a nice sip of scotch.

Now you just fucking cemented it.

Thanks for that. Not that I owe you anything.

"It's probably best if you hang up the phone, *Chadwick*."

"Why's that?"

"Because you're threading a very thin needle. You don't want to be on my bad side." *More than you already are, at least.*

"Empty threats don't scare me. I've lived in this town my whole life—do you actually think you can walk in here, throw your money around, and people will respect you over me? We protect what's ours around here. It's best you remember that."

I'm aware. More than you'll ever know, I'm fucking aware.

"You do, until you no longer can. Pretty sure that day is coming sooner than you think."

I end the call before he can respond.

The funny thing about secrets in small towns is once they're out, they not only ruin you, but everything else around you.

That's what I'm banking on. The butterfly effect.

My cell rings again, his name on the screen, and I deny the call.

The fucker saw me hours ago at the office but didn't have the guts to confront me face-to-face.

I expect nothing less from a man like him.

A man who clearly doesn't deserve shit, let alone a woman like Rowan.

A woman like Rowan? Tight sweaters and defiance don't mean you know shit about her, so what the fuck does that mean, Knight?

But I do, don't I? I glance at the computer again. At Rowan's life narrowed down to text on a screen. Emails, texts, social media accounts.

I should feel guilty for invading her privacy. I don't. Knowing everything about each player in this game is a requirement. A necessity. Something I can and will use to my advantage if needed.

And I have no qualms about it. Especially after Chad's call.

Time to kick this game plan into high gear. To adjust it as needed for maximum effect.

Chadwick Williams.

The fucker once took what was mine.

Now it's time to do the same to him.

The end game at all costs, right?

EIGHTEEN

Rowan

There is a low hum that carries up from the floor below the catwalk we are standing on.

The machinery—row upon row that make up the Greatland production line—work in a series of synchronized sequences that Porter explains in excruciating detail.

Almost as if he's trying too hard.

"And from there, the printed aluminum sheets are moved to the press where they are then stamped and molded," Porter says, his chest puffed out like a proud papa.

Either that or Rhett has told him about Holden's plans to diversify suppliers and he's trying to make a point.

By the unamused look on his face, I'd say Holden's thinking the latter.

"And what part of this manufacturing process includes kickback checks to Rhett Rothschild?"

Porter all but chokes on air. He coughs out a laugh as his round belly bounces with the movement and his unshaven face turns red and then pales. "I was warned you were to the point," he says when he regains his composure. And I have to hand it to him, he didn't cower at Holden's question like everyone else that I've seen.

"Subtlety isn't my forte." He lifts his brows. "And you're not answering my question."

"I think it was more of an accusation than a question," Porter says, not backing down.

The smile Holden offers him sends chills down my spine and only reinforces the new information I'm struggling to process and dying to confront him over.

Holden steps closer and lowers his voice, his gaze a laser of distrust. "I'm not from around here, Porter. I don't have to play by whatever fucked-up rules everyone else does. You have one of two choices. Keep going how you're going and see how that ends up. Or step the fuck back and realize you're skating on thin ice." Holden sniffs and his smile turns more than mocking but I think Porter is too busy not pissing his pants to notice. "Either way, it seems you're kind of fucked, so I'd proceed accordingly."

Warning given, Holden nods and then walks off the catwalk toward the exit.

Porter looks at me with wide eyes and a bead of sweat dripping down his temple.

I never much liked him and even less so now that I know there has been some unsavory conduct going on—so I might just take a little glee in seeing him sweat. Literally.

"Rowan? Our driver is waiting," Holden says, eyebrows raised, and tone implying we're leaving and why am I not following.

Which I do, but only because I have no choice. We drove the short distance to Greatland together and in silence—his eyes on mine as I held my ground and didn't cave. Juvenile and petty but so satisfying for him to realize that I don't tremble every time he looks at me.

Plus, I was still processing what I'd uncovered and trying to figure out how to broach it.

He is about five paces ahead of me as we cross the parking lot to the waiting town car. Apparently, Holden Knight is too cool to drive himself anywhere.

"I know what you're doing," I call out to him, the information that has been eating a hole in my gut burning to get out.

"What's that?" he says without stopping.

"What, are you too chickenshit to face me?"

His feet falter, as do mine, until he stops completely. When he turns to face me, he's wearing the same chilled smile he gave Porter. "Hardly. Is whatever this is the reason you've been glaring at me all day? I'm not the Wicked Witch of the West, Sunshine. I don't wither away."

"Unfortunately."

"Has something caused that stick to be shoved farther up your ass or is that just a new accessory I need to get used to? Because . . . you don't scare me, Rowan."

"I should."

"Your confidence is admirable, but you don't exactly know who you're dealing with."

"But I do."

His eyes spark with fire. "Googling me yet again? And here I thought you couldn't stand me."

It's all fun and games with him. It's all quick comebacks and little quips. It's clearly all smoke and mirrors.

"Let me guess, you uncovered the choir boy and Cub Scout shit. *Shhh*." He winks as he jokes. "Don't tell. It'll ruin my image."

"You're buying TinSpirits to dismantle it and sell it off piece by piece, aren't you?" I say, cutting to the chase, my eyes trained on his every motion, waiting to see a flicker of hesitancy to know I'm right.

He raises an eyebrow and laughs—not a stutter anywhere. "You're just a regular Nancy Drew, aren't you? Inventing problems so you can fulfill your god complex and save the day?"

"You didn't answer my question," I grit out.

"Wasn't aware I had to." He moves to the car and opens the door, waiting for me to get in.

I don't move.

The chuckle he emits in response is grating at best and arrogant at worst. "Is this why you had the staring contest with me on the way over here? Trying to map out in your head how to approach me? How to confront me? Did it turn out how you imagined?" I scowl. He smirks. "It never does, does it."

I move toward him and stop right in front of him. "Graden Microchips. Hager Circuit Boards. Prodigy Peripherals." I lift my eyebrows.

"All are companies I've purchased, yes."

"All are companies you've purchased and then dismantled, selling parts to the highest bidders."

"Your point?" He lifts a lone brow, and it takes everything I have not to wipe the smirk off his face.

"Is that what you're planning on doing to my company?"

His smile tilts lopsided. "You mean to *my* company?"

"Answer the goddamn question, Knight."

"Oh, I love it when you talk to me like that." And then in a completely unexpected move, he reaches out and tucks an errant piece of hair behind my ear. His hand lingers on the side of my face, his eyes darkening in the bright sunlight.

I freeze. Mad for wanting the touch and confused that I do all at the same time.

My pulse thunders in my ears and my skin tingles.

And just as quickly as the moment happens, Holden snaps his hand back and clears his throat as if it didn't happen.

Or he's pissed that it did.

His eyes that a moment ago were dark with desire are now guarded and cold. "I'm not buying the company to sell it off."

"I have your word on that?" I ask, my heart still decelerating.

He purses his lips and tilts his head, silent for a beat before saying, "You have my word."

And when I get in the car and he slides in beside me, not another thing is said between us on our trip back to the office.

His thigh presses against mine and I hate that it draws my thoughts back to the feel of his hand on my face. To the look in his eyes.

And then I remember who he is and the threat of what he's doing.

Do I believe him?

I don't believe anybody at this point and for good reason.

But why is he willing to pump so much money into a company he's going to rip apart? That's not good business and if there's one thing I've learned in my searches, it's that Holden Knight is a sharp businessman. So why would this time be any different?

Our conversation replays in my head all day. I analyze every sentence and each exchange. And when I finally leave the office, I come to the conclusion that I need to tell someone what's going on.

I might not need help now, but that doesn't mean I won't need to bounce something off someone in the future.

I slide behind the wheel of my car and dial one of the only people in this town other than Caroline who would remain loyal to me in a crisis. Someone who has zero ties to TinSpirits and the like.

"Holy shit. You are alive," Sloane says in greeting.

"I am."

"You've been missing Wine Wednesday. Like, a lot of Wine Wednesdays," she teases.

"I've been rather busy," I say as I glance up to the light on in Holden's office and then shake the feeling away that he's watching me.

"I've heard." She hums. "I have a feeling that 'busy' of yours is why you're calling me."

"Would you be offended if I said yes?" I ask, hope laced through my tone. I've ditched socializing but then have no problem calling her up and asking for her legal advice. Nothing screams one-sided friendship like that.

"No. Never." I can all but feel her smile through the line. "I'm here to listen. To bounce things off of. And when you want advice, all you have to do is tell me, 'Hey, this is the part I want advice on,'" she says.

"You know I love you, right?" I say, a smile on my lips for the first time in hours.

"Yes. I do. Now start talking. . . ."

NINETEEN

Music blasts through my headphones. The funky beat helps to erase the tension from the kind of day only a Monday can bring. The market analysis I'd worked on all weekend somehow managed to lose all my updates. A graphic designer we've used religiously for the past few years took on a new client and for some reason that I can't get her to explain is dropping us midway through a new campaign. The board—where I technically don't have a seat yet—sent out a letter to me about their displeasure over my new hair color.

Essentially a "blondes have more fun" decree requesting I dye my hair back to its natural color.

Then there's Holden.

In my doorway when I'd look up, shoulder against the jamb, an indecipherable smile on his face. Behind me in the company lunchroom when I was getting coffee so that his crisp, clean scent screwed with my senses. Summoning me to his office time and again for something he could simply ask about over the phone intercom. Then stopping me in the parking lot on the way out, asking me for opinions on things that normally Rhett handles.

And then seeming to be genuinely interested in my responses.

Chaos and confusion.

That's what I've felt since he barged into my life. Especially since that moment at Greatland last week that frequents my mind way more than I'd like to admit to.

For fuck's sake, stop thinking about him, Row. You're here to clear your head, not screw it up more.

I climb down off the elliptical and wipe the sweat from the back of my neck. People mill about, lifting free weights, waiting for machines, or shooting the shit with club employees. When a bench in the free weight area opens up in the far corner of the gym, I quickly move that way before it gets taken.

I mouth the lyrics to the song, maybe even sway my hips to the beat a little, while purposefully choosing to be oblivious to those around me. I'm not here to meet men. I'm here to work out. I've found that keeping my head down and my eyes focused on what I'm doing prevents *most* unwanted advances.

I begin my routine and am on my second time through when I look at my reflection in the mirrored wall and see Holden standing about twenty feet away.

He's in the middle of his own workout. His dark green tank top is loose and showcases tanned, muscular biceps that flex with each curl-up of his arms. His shoulders are broad, his face a furrow of concentration, and the tendons in his neck are taut.

When he finishes his repetitions and sets the dumbbells on the floor, he proceeds to lift the hem of his tank to wipe the sweat from his chin.

It's a casual movement, one you see in the gym all the time, but if I wasn't paying attention before, I sure as hell am now. I'm graced with an array of dips and dents of sculpted abs and the faintest hint of a happy trail that disappears beneath a pair of gray sweatpants that hang low on his hips.

Well, well, well, Holden Knight looks good in a suit, but even more spectacular out of it.

Like there was any doubt.

But Jesus, seeing it and thinking it are two vastly different things.

Why are you thinking about that, Rowan?

I should be working out.

Stop looking.

I should be minding my own business.

Stop gawking.

Yet, I stand there like an idiot admiring a man who is just as beautiful as he is mysterious.

He is the enemy. But what a beautiful enemy he is.

I'm just about to look away when Holden glances up and meets my eyes—like he knew I was standing there staring at him—and a slow, knowing smile crawls over his lips.

My stomach shouldn't flutter. In fact, I'm pissed that it does, and so the only response I allow myself to give is a curt nod before turning back to my own workout.

But I was stupid to think the man who happened to be everywhere I was today is going to be content with a simple nod.

Irritated at myself for my reaction and at him for being here, I slam an extra plate on each side of the barbell and lie down on the bench. Just as I lift it off the rack and lower the bar to my chest, Holden's face appears over me and upside down from mine.

"Sunshine," he says by way of greeting.

I grit my teeth, close my eyes, and push the bar up, trying to ignore him. It's not an easy feat when his cologne is in my nose and if I look back, his crotch is right there.

Maybe he'll just go away.

I'm on my fourth rep when I realize, in my irritation of him being here, I put way too much weight on the bar. I'm strong for my size, but there's no way I'm going to be able to finish this set, let alone lift the bar high enough to get it to the resting bar. A strangled groan escapes my lips as I try to get it there.

"Want me to spot you?" The bar suddenly gets lighter, and as much as I do need the spot, I grip tighter to it so that he can't take it out of my hands.

"No. I'm fine. I don't need your help." I open my eyes to see his hands on either side of mine holding the bar. "Let go."

Holden doesn't release it. "I expected you to be the type who only works out at the country club."

I snort. "No, thanks."

"Meaning?"

"Meaning I'm here to work out. Not to be seen. Not to be gossiped about. Not to be invited to god knows what function I don't give a flying fuck about."

"So you don't like the Westmore Country Club then?" He angles his head to the side as he stares down at me.

"All I want is to work out. Ninety minutes in, out, and done."

He smirks. Only a man would listen to that and hear an innuendo. "In. Out. Done," he repeats with a hint of mischief in his eyes that I can recognize even upside down.

"Can you go away, please?" I mutter as I fight with him over the bar that he's still holding. "You're making it hard to concentrate."

And you're confusing me.

One minute—well, the majority of the time—he's an asshole, and now all of a sudden he's cute and charming. I don't want him to be that. I don't want him to make me smile or want to talk to him.

What in the hell is going on?

"It's the guns, right?" He lifts the bar even higher so that he can flex. "They'd ruin anyone's concentration."

"Go away."

"Oh, the abs, then?"

"Very far away."

He leans farther over so that his face is just over the bar he's holding and whispers, "I'd say it's the quads, but that would require me to pull my pants down to show you. Then we'd have to deal with the whole 'you wouldn't be able to resist me even more than you already do' thing, and it might get messy."

I fight an irritated smile, but it's a smile nonetheless. Holden's words, or rather his demeanor, are so different from what I'm used to. "What is going on here?" I ask more to myself than to him.

"We're talking. Chatting."

"You don't chat."

"No?"

"No. You brood. You plot. You scheme. You attempt to ruin people's lives. You don't chat."

He flashes a grin that would make a lesser woman weak in the knees. "Maybe I'm turning over a new leaf." He shrugs. "Stranger things have happened."

Charming isn't exactly a word I'd use to describe Holden Knight and yet here he is, being just that. And who could have guessed that when he turned it on, it would make him even more devastating than he already was?

"Can I have your asshole nature and my bar back, please?" The tug of war continues, except it seems like I'm the only one that has to put any effort into it.

"Why? I rather like this conversation we're having. You've yet to think I'm an asshole or a prick—at least that's a guess considering I caught you ogling me a few minutes ago. I'd say we should keep this going."

"I wasn't ogling you."

He snorts. "I'll let you think that so you can keep your pride intact. It's better for our working relationship that way."

"Why are you following me?"

"I'm not."

"How did you know I was going to be here?"

"I didn't. Like you, I prefer 'in, out, and done.' Maybe a little more added pleasure in there for good measure between the 'in' and the 'out' parts, but that's just personal preference."

"Are you drunk?"

"While working out? That's counterproductive."

"Then what is wrong with you?"

"Nothing." He grins. "Maybe I'm just finding my footing."

Or maybe you're using reverse psychology on me so that I start to like you.

The problem? *It's working.*

"Are you sure you don't want me to spot you? I mean, this bar is going to feel pretty heavy once I let go."

I hold tight to my anger because I don't want his charm to work. This time when I try to take the bar and say, "I'm fine," Holden lets me.

I struggle under its weight, my arms tired and my head not as focused as it should be. But I am determined not to show it as Holden stands there and watches me struggle through five more reps.

I refuse to let him think I'm weak.

And when I rack the bar and let my arms collapse to my sides, he chuckles. "Great job. Now tell me in the morning when you're unable to move your arms because they're so sore that not accepting help was worth it." He gives a nod and then heads back over to his own workout without another word.

I sit up and stare after him. Annoyed. Irritated. Confused. Needing to look away as he does squats on the rack but finding it hard to.

"Weak woman," I mutter to myself. A great body doesn't negate who he is and what he stands for.

As if on cue, Holden glances my way and flashes yet another grin that has me turning my back to him so I can concentrate.

But there are mirrors. Everywhere there are freaking mirrors to the point that I have to look at the floor to avoid seeing him.

Why does he have to be in my space here too?

I storm through the rest of my lifting regimen with no shortage of huffs and puffs that do nothing to make me less irritated, but I do them nonetheless.

My only saving grace is that when I'm finished and head to the locker room to grab my stuff, Holden Knight is nowhere in sight.

At least there's that.

But my relief is short-lived when I head out to the parking lot and find him leaning against the back of some sporty SUV that's parked next to mine. His legs are crossed at the ankles, and his head is down as he types something out on his phone. But he doesn't miss a beat looking up when he hears my footsteps stop and the unhindered groan fall from my lips.

"Here's what I don't get, Sunshine," he says as if I want to be a participant in this conversation.

"What's that?" I cross my arms over my chest and hate him for being so damn good-looking.

"How you can stand up to me without a second thought, but you don't say a fucking word to your brother when he disrespects or discounts you?"

"What are you talking about?" I ask but know I could name numerous things he could be referring to.

"Today. Yesterday. Last week. Do you really want me to recount the various ways your brother has treated you terribly or is currently trying to fuck you over?"

I roll my shoulders. It's bad enough that Rhett feels entitled to act that way. It's even worse that I've gotten so used to it and know that nothing is going to change, that I let it roll off my back most days. In my master plan, I'd get my ultimate fuck-you to my brother when I take the company from him after convincing the board to pass a no-confidence vote. But for now, it's downright humiliating being called on the carpet by a man I need to think highly of me.

Because that's my dilemma, isn't it? I need Holden to like me enough that should this go through, he decides to keep me around. At the same time, I want him to understand that if I can stop him, I sure as hell will.

It makes every conversation with him feel like walking through a minefield—this one included.

"Your point?" I ask.

"You'd tell me to fuck off and die in a heartbeat. Me, the only person in the company who is holding his hand out to help you, the only man who seems to see you for your worth and intelligence, while you stand steadfast by the side of a man who clearly doesn't give a shit about your place there."

His words hit me like a battering ram. The truth to them. The man speaking them.

Holden pushes off the hood and stands to his full height. "This woman right here," he says, pointing to me. "The one who lifts too much and refuses help. The one who barks back when she thinks I've wronged her in the slightest. The vitriol you seem to reserve only for me? That's the woman I want to see in the boardroom battling things out on our behalf." He moves around the side of his car and opens his door. "I know I've asked you to team up with me, but I take that back. I only want you to if that woman shows up. She's the one I want. She's the one I'm offering a seat at the table to."

And without another word, Holden slides into the seat.

"What do you mean *a seat at the table*?"

He shuts the door.

"Holden. *Wait*."

And backs out of the spot and then out of the lot.

I stare in the direction he went long after his taillights disappear into the distance.

What the hell did that mean?

TWENTY

Holden

"There's potential there, Bob," I say with my cell to my ear as I shuffle through stacks of financials on the corner of my desk. Financials that my accountants have flagged during their due diligence for me to look closer at.

No doubt there's more Rhett Rothschild fuckery all over them.

"Potential? I think moving to the South has fucked with your head."

"If you were here, you'd understand how true that is, but I still want you to pursue it."

I can hear the hesitation in his sigh over the line. His want to refuse me but his knowledge that if he does, I'll just get someone else who'll do what I need. He's seen me cut ties before for less. "I still don't understand what got this wild hair up your ass to go and buy this company. Alcohol? You're a fucking software engineer for god's sake."

"Mmm," I say. "*Was* a software engineer is more accurate."

"You created the program most financial institutions in the world use to protect their customer data."

"Thanks for the biography update," I say wryly.

"My point is, just because you sold the company, that doesn't mean you're no longer a software engineer."

"Noted."

"It just . . . I've seen you invest capital before, but you've never been hands-on like this. Why the change? What are you not telling me?"

Distracted, I watch Rhett and Chad stand in the parking lot below having what appears to be a heated discussion. The sight amuses me.

Way more than this conversation does.

"I have my reasons," I say.

"Great. Holden Knight is being cryptic. Just what the world doesn't need. The last time you were like this, firewalls were breached and money went missing."

"You mean it was *found*."

He snorts. "Whatever you say, Robin Hood."

I shrug, still smug about that one. When one of the richest capital funds in the world tried to pretty up its scandalous reputation by advertising that they'd made sizable donations to Feeding America and their records showed no such contributions. Was it really so bad to give that money a little helping hand to get where it needed to be? To move funds from their account to the charity's? "I have no idea what you're talking about."

At least I provided them with a receipt for their donation so they can write it off against their taxes.

"Of course you don't." He chuckles. "And you're avoiding my questions. Why this random company? Why pump money into something that you plan on piecemealing apart in a leverage buyout until there is nothing left of it?"

"That's between you and me for now."

"It always is. I just don't under—"

"So you'll get me a list then?"

His sigh is as heavy as his frustration with me. Fine by me. "Yes. Sure. I'll start looking for potential buyers. Still doesn't make sense to me."

"It doesn't have to, Bob, so long as it does to me."

"You're the boss with many irons the fire."

I sure am.

"I need updates," I say.

"Potential buyers on the property. You want me still applying pressure to anyone looking for info on it?"

"Yes." There is no room for misinterpretation. Every lead being logged into the real estate agent's database is automatically being rerouted to Bob through a few behind-the-scenes keystrokes. He is then contacting those leads and promptly deterring them.

"Is the land for sale really contaminated?" he asks, questioning the information I've given him to use to spoil any potential buyers.

"Does it matter?" I give him more than I normally do.

"So, what? You just don't want anyone buying it?" He searches for a reason as to why. He'll never figure it out. The less anyone knows, the better.

"Correct." I'm feeling generous today, so I give him another answer.

"Watch out, someone might claim you talk too much," he jokes. When I don't respond, he presses his luck with a third question. "Are you planning on buying that property, then? Scaring people off until they lower the price so then you pull the trigger?"

"No. Just making sure no one else does."

"*Hmpf.*" Judgmental silence he'd never dare put a voice to. He knows where my proverbial bodies are hidden. He knows I wouldn't hesitate to put his there either. "Whatever you say, boss."

"Exactly. Whatever I say."

I wouldn't give Rhett or Chad a dime of my money to bail them out. And I'll make sure no one else does. A loan default. An impending repossession. A life's savings gone.

More like an entire family trust *gone.*

Can't imagine what that would do to the reputation—aside from the private family shitstorm—of two of Westmore's most prestigious families.

"What about the campaign stuff? Am I touching that or leaving it alone?" he asks.

"Keep whoever you have on the staff there. I need to stay in the know on promises made behind the scenes."

"You think he's running to forge shit about the WillowBend property, don't you? Get on the council to fix his fuckup."

"Yes," I say in a quiet, even tone. "I do."

"Last thing," he says. "You saw the attempted firewall breach on your personal server the other night?"

"I did." Someone's fingerprints were all over my firewall. Amateur at best but still fucking there. No doubt it leads back to Rhett somehow. The fucker is rich enough to try to buy an ugly painting, but too broke to hire a good hacker. Fucking par for the course, but it never should have gotten that far in the first place. "You took care of it?"

"I'm sitting back and watching, waiting to see if they leave more of a digital trail."

"If that digital trail makes it past my defenses, Bob, I'm not going to be a happy man."

"So you're telling me to, what—"

"Shut it the fuck down. Plant malware in their hard drive. I don't fucking care but get it stopped."

"Yes, sir."

I end the conversation and steeple my fingers as I watch Chad point a heated finger at Rhett. Then Rhett waves a hand at him before he stalks away and toward one of the warehouses.

Trouble in paradise.

Perfect.

Why are they trying to get into my shit? That was an amusing— and admirable—surprise the other night. But the question is why? Do they doubt me? Was it just a private firm they hired to investigate me and make sure I'm kosher? Were they trying to figure out how someone is ruining their plans at every fucking turn?

Go ahead and look, assholes.

You're not going to find what you're looking for. Only what I want to give you.

I take pride in the slump of Rhett's shoulders as he stares after where Chad just disappeared.

Poor fucking baby.

Time to tackle the first set of notes from my team on the due diligence for the purchase. I expect there to be a whole lot of red flags from shit Rhett's tried to hide. Red flags that most purchasers would use to devalue the company and have a reason to lower the purchase price.

For me on the other hand, they just provide more leverage to hold over the fucker's head. Making his life miserable is my new hobby.

I'm about a quarter of the way through the first report with eyebrows raised and head shaking when a pair of footsteps come through my door.

I glance at my computer and note the time. Thirty minutes since she pulled in the parking lot to come see me. That took longer than expected.

Guess I need to try harder next time.

"Look who's finally back in the office," I murmur without looking up.

"Back in the office?" she asks, her voice riding that fine line of irritation and frustration. "Says the man who hasn't picked up his phone or shown his face in here since last week."

I glance up, a smart quip getting lost on my tongue when it ties itself up.

That damn sweater.

Jesus Christ. How many fucking colors does the woman own it in? My eyes stutter over her cleavage. It's hard not to when her nipples are hard and pressed against the cashmere while her crossed arms only serve to push her breasts up higher.

Images of me clearing off the desk in one swoop of my arm and fucking her on it flash through my head. The soft sigh of her moan. Her pussy tightening around me. The half-hooded eyes as we watch each other. The goddamn rush of emptying myself into her.

It's Rowan I suddenly want.

There's a reason I've made myself scarce in the office this week.

Her presence and my thoughts that suddenly spiral out of control when I think of her. That's one of the major reasons.

"I've been busy." My smile is smug, my expression nonchalant, and my gaze lingers longer than it should on her lips.

You're only prolonging the torture, Knight.

"What the hell did you mean?"

"What the hell did I mean about what?" I say innocently. *How much longer until you're beneath me, Rowan Rothschild?*

Her eyes dart down the hall and then back to me. "In the parking lot. At the gym."

She's talking about a seat at the table, Holden. You set the hook. Now she wants the bait.

Get her fucking out of here.

"I have a long list of shit to do and a conference call waiting for me." I wave dismissively to her as I pick up my cell. "I don't have time for this right now."

She huffs. "Yes, you do."

I push a button on my phone—calling my own voicemail—and pretend. "Yes. Holden Knight calling in for the meeting."

Rowan remains standing there, arms still crossed, jaw still clenched, eyes still glaring.

I point to the door. "Shut it on the way out."

Sometimes playing hard to get makes the other person want it that much more.

Her expression—irritated, impatient, furious—says I'm getting exactly what I want out of this stunt. *Her to want me.*

I lift my eyebrows to her and mouth, *You're still here.*

Our eyes hold, battle, challenge.

She remains a few more seconds before emitting a strangled groan and stomping back out of my office.

I track the exaggerated swish of her hips as she stalks down the hallway. It's not until she enters her office and slams the door shut that I chuckle and drop my phone on my desk.

Mission accomplished.

And as if on cue, Audrey walks right through it with a disapproving *tsk* on her lips. Ever ready with her notepad and pen in hand, she takes a seat opposite me.

"What?" I ask like a kid caught with his hand in the cookie jar.

She levels me with a look. "What are you playing at, Holden?"

"Nothing."

"Bullshit," she says, a rare curse. "I've worked for you for ten years. I know you almost as well as your mother does. In some aspects maybe even better. You've turned on the charm and when you turn on the charm, that, my dear, means you are most definitely up to something."

I laugh. Never can get anything by her. There's a reason Audrey McClain has remained my right hand for so very long. Through owning the software company. After selling it. And now managing my day-to-day among other things.

And she's the only one who knows my reason for being here. The what. The where. The why. *The need.*

She's my conscience when I choose to ignore mine.

I'm never letting her go, and I pay her accordingly.

"I'm innocent as charged." I lift my hands up but emit a mischievous laugh.

"Lord help us," she says as she stands and heads to the door. "Oh, and call your mother. She's probably missing you about now."

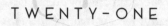

TWENTY-ONE

Holden

FIFTEEN YEARS AGO

"Please?"

I grit my teeth and look over to Mason, who has been nagging me since we got home. He's standing on the other side of the table, skateboard in one hand and his helmet in the other. That poor board has seen better days, but we've done our best to keep the bearings oiled and gliding smoothly.

"Dude. You have to stop asking." I look down to my laptop and my half-written history paper on whether democracy is the best form of government. A bullshit, I-need-to-give-the-class-homework type of assignment if you ask me. But an assignment that's so much easier to do now that I have the computer where I can cut and paste instead of erase and rewrite by hand.

"I've been in a classroom all day. Is it so wrong that I want to get outside for some fresh air? Get some exercise. Have a mental health break."

I level him with a look. "Do you seriously think that's going to work with me when most days you'd prefer to be inside with your butt on the couch watching TV?"

He shrugs, but a shy corner turns up the edges of his lips. "I'm turning over a new leaf."

"You're so full of shit." I sigh and lean back. "What is it? Why are you so desperate to go outside and skate?"

"Mia comes home from soccer practice between four and five."

"Mia?" Christ. When did this happen? Do I need to have "the talk" with him already? He's way too young for this shit. Hell, I'm way too young to have to give it.

"Yeah. She's just a girl. A *friend.* Her parents don't let her hang around the complex after she gets home." He shrugs. "You know why and all."

Yeah, for the same reasons Mom forbids me to let you play outside alone.

"Yeah, I know." I look at the flashing cursor and the stack of other homework I have. Guilt eats at me. It's not Mase's fault Mom's working two jobs. He shouldn't suffer because I've worked three days in a row and am trying to finish a paper I should have done on Sunday night. I scrub a hand through my hair. "My teacher gave me until five to get this done or else he won't accept it for a grade."

"But—"

"I don't have a choice."

"Yeah, you do. I can go outside by myself. You can leave the front door open or whatever."

"Those aren't the rules."

"But Mom's not here, right?" He makes a show of looking around. "It's not like she'd ever know if I went outside by myself for a few minutes."

He's right. I know he's right. He knows he's right. Mom would never know, but . . . still. "Mase . . ."

"C'mon, Hold. I'll stay right outside on the sidewalk. You can leave the door open so you can hear me. I won't talk to strangers." He rolls his eyes on that one. "I know all the stuff."

I sigh. This paper isn't going to write itself and it sure as hell isn't going to get a dent in it with Mason sitting here bugging me every five seconds to go outside with him.

What's it going to hurt?

"Fine—"

Mason whoops and throws his fist in the air that's holding his helmet in the air and we both laugh when the chin strap flails and hits him in the face. "Thank you. Thank you. Thank you."

"But." I hold a finger up. "You can't go past the complex or off the sidewalk. You can't go in anyone's apartment. You can't—"

"Yeah, yeah."

"Mom will have my ass if she—"

"Quit being an old man." He waves a hand at me as he opens the front door.

"Whatever. Leave the door open."

"'Kay," he says as I look back to my screen. "Holden?"

"Mmm?" When he doesn't speak, I look up to see him standing in the open doorway looking at me, his grin wide and eyes bright. "Thanks."

I just nod as he stands on the porch buckling his helmet on and then rides his board down the walkway. I have one brief moment of hesitancy, but . . . a glance at the clock tells me I need to get my ass in gear.

Mase will be fine.

I get lost in trying to grind out my paper, getting up every five or ten minutes to check on my brother when I can't hear the click of his board's wheels going over the cracks in the sidewalk.

I'm making good time and am just starting my conclusion when I hear the screech of brakes, followed shortly thereafter by the squeal of tires. Those sounds are nothing new in this neighborhood—the end of a drug deal, someone taking off after doing something they shouldn't be doing—but it's nothing I want Mason near. I'm out of my seat in seconds and jogging to the front door.

"Mase. It's been long enough. You need to come in, dude. . . ."

Seconds feel like infinity as I take in the white car at an odd angle. As I try to process the faded blue jeans and red sweatshirt collapsed in a lump on the pavement in front of the tires and against the curb.

It all happens so fast.

The passenger door slamming shut.

Someone yelling, "Go. Go. Go."

Another squeal of tires as the car slams into reverse before jerking forward and taking off the opposite way.

It all happens, but I can't focus on it.

All I see is Mason.

His crumpled body.

The skateboard across the street, upside down and wheels still spinning.

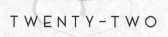

TWENTY-TWO

Holden

It's been a long fucking week. Long days at the office followed by sleepless nights at home or driving around this city I have a love/hate relationship with.

When the insomnia comes—and it always comes—I can't help but wander to the places I used to find comfort in. The places where the ghosts of my past speak the loudest.

All except for one. The cemetery.

I haven't been able to bring myself there just yet.

So that's why tonight's scheduled "how long can you ignore me, Rowan" session isn't a hardship.

The scotch is warm on my tongue, like a welcome friend, as I take in my surroundings. The bar is trendy with a cool atmosphere. The music is good but a bit dated.

And the man sitting across from Rowan is unexpectedly cosmopolitan.

If Chad is the quintessential yuppie, this fucker is the definition of New York with his slicked-back hair, knock-off Rolex, and laugh that's a little too loud because he's trying too hard.

In other words, he's an *asshole*.

It doesn't help that he keeps touching Rowan. Her arm. Her hand. Her shoulder. *For fuck's sake, we all know you're here with her. You couldn't make it more obvious if you held a sign up.*

It shouldn't irritate me, but it does.

What I can't get a read on from my seat at the far end of the bar is Rowan herself. Is this the type of guy she likes, because if so, I'm having a hard time fucking picturing it.

I study her. Take in her polite smile and impassive expression as he drones on, gesticulating wildly as if to impress her. She's gorgeous as usual. Her hair is up, her makeup a little more dramatic than at the office, and her heels hooked in the bottom rung of the barstool are high.

And I'm not going to lie. I'm more than fucking glad she's not wearing one of those sweaters I like.

Those are reserved for me.

But the fire in her eyes when she banters with me? The passion with which she talks about the company? The spark in her glare when she tells me how much she hates me? They're nonexistent.

The question is, who is Rowan Rothschild? I can't quite get a read on her when I can fucking read everyone.

She's loyal to a family who isn't loyal to her.

She struggles with toeing the family line versus doing what's in her best interest.

She's not afraid to play hardball—or at least she says so. I'm waiting to see her do it.

She's a part of this community—the elite of Westmore—and yet I can't exactly gauge how she fits in.

And she plays the cello for fucking strangers to help them stop thinking and allow them to get lost for a bit.

Fucking Rowan.

I started this game of cat and mouse with her. The hard-to-get play I made. Her obstinance in ignoring me right back when I sure as hell know she's curious about what I meant about giving her a seat at the table is cute, admirable even. *A turn-on.*

But it's not helping me in the moment.

I need to focus on the enemy I know—Rhett, Chadwick, the others—without having to look over my shoulder for Rowan sticking the knife in my back.

So I've upped my game, or "turned on my charm," as Audrey claims.

If she wants to ignore me, she's going to have to try a lot fucking harder.

"You good, brother?" the bartender asks me as he wipes his hand on the dish towel tucked in his waistband.

"I'll have another when you get a chance."

"Sure. Not a problem." He leans forward and lowers his voice. "You've got the redhead at the far end trying to get your attention, the brunette two down on your right, and the blonde across. I'd ask if you need help facilitating this, but I have a feeling this is a normal night for you." He laughs and shakes his head.

"I'm not interested, but thanks."

"No? Shit, man, you feeling okay?"

I chuckle. "Yeah, I've got my eye on someone." I glance Rowan's way.

"Oh. Gotcha. Just thought I'd offer to play wingman for you, if needed."

"Thanks," I murmur seconds before Rowan's date steps into the space beside me. He has his phone to his ear, doing that "everyone look at me, I'm cool because I have a cell phone" schtick that was old about twenty years ago.

"Yeah, man. She's more than fuckable," he says with a smarmy chuckle. "Great rack. Killer body. Blow-job lips. I mean, from where I stand, don't be calling me later because I'll be otherwise occupied this evening."

I clench my jaw so hard and my hands so tight around my glass that I'm surprised both don't shatter.

"Another round," the fucker says to the bartender as I debate how my fist would feel plowing into his face. "Just enough to get her frisky."

Rowan's not mine by any means. *Yet.* But his words have my temper itching to be unleashed.

I glance Rowan's way only to find our eyes meet across the

short distance of the dimly lit bar. Shock flickers over her expression followed shortly by confusion. The confusion then morphs to her being pissed off if the narrowing of her eyes and the setting of her jaw are any indication.

Yes, I'm here, Rowan. Same place as you. *Again.*

I smile, lift up my glass, and nod as her date stiffs the bartender a tip and takes the drinks back to their table.

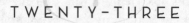

TWENTY-THREE

Rowan

I don't hear a word Gregory Chapman says because I'm too busy fixating on the fact that Holden is sitting at the bar.

Sitting there with his perfectly cavalier attitude and devastating good looks as he blatantly watches me from afar.

"Right?" Gregory asks.

"I'm sorry. What did you say?"

I'm being a horrible date. Distracted. Not participating. Fake.

He's a nice guy. Well educated with a good job, a decent sense of humor if a little dorky, and a good listener, but he has nothing on the man sitting at the bar watching my every move.

Just like he has been for the past week and a half.

If he wants to dangle a carrot and ignore me, then I can do the same. And so far, I've been successful at doing so.

Except for right now.

"I was just saying that with the current state of the economy . . ." Gregory looks at the server who just slid a martini in front of me. "I'm sorry, but I think you have the wrong table. We didn't order this."

The server flashes a quick smile and lifts her chin. "It's compliments of the gentleman at the bar."

Gregory whips his head over toward where she's looking, but I don't have to look. The martini says it all. It's what I was drinking the night of the auction. The first night we met.

"Seriously?" Gregory mutters as he glares in the direction of Holden. "Send it back, please."

I look up just in time to see the smirk in Holden's profile as he lifts his drink to his lips. He finds this amusing. Such an asshole.

The server looks at both of us before reaching for it, but I stop her. "Even better, I'll bring it back to him."

"Rowan. That's not—do you even know the guy? I mean, let me handle—"

"I know him alright," I mutter as I stride over to where Holden is sitting. A very petty part of me wants to upend the martini in his lap. Dirty up his perfection. Holden turns as I approach, a slow smile crawling on his lips.

"Sunshine. What a nice surprise. Except for the *him* part." There is an iciness to his tone, a bit of bite that contradicts the sweetness in his words. But it's the guarded look in his eyes that tells me there is no surprise about it. He knew exactly where I was going to be.

"I don't want your drink."

He angles his head to the side, the muscle pulsing in his jaw. "Always so gracious."

"The door's that way. Isn't that what you said to me the other day?" I ask.

His chuckle rumbles softly. "Good evening to you too."

"Quit stalking me, Knight. What? Do you have my phones tapped? Are you breaking into the company server to read my emails somehow?"

"It's a small town. We're bound to wind up at the same place at the same time every once in a while."

But it hasn't been every once in a while. It's all the freaking time. "You're full of shit. Keep your drink. Quit being rude to my date."

"You mean rude like you're being to him by constantly looking at me?" He lifts his eyebrows as I struggle with a pithy comeback. "Tell me something, Row. Why are you on a date with what's-his-face when you're going to be marrying Chadwick?"

I struggle for a response. Chad has no part of this discussion and the fact that Holden keeps bringing him up frustrates the hell out of me. "I already told you, there is nothing between Chad and me. And even if there were, it's none of your business."

"Ah, yes, but it is my business if two of three of my top managers are to be married."

"You can control a lot of things, Knight, but my life? Who I date? Who I marry? You can't."

"Never put anything past me," he murmurs.

Chills chase over my skin. And I'm not sure if it's because of the huskiness of his voice or the warning in them. Whatever it is, that's more than enough time with him for me.

"I'd say nice talking to you, but it wasn't. I need to get back to my *date* now."

A smile paints the corners of his lips. He shrugs. "Fine. Go ahead. No skin off my back."

"Jealous?"

"I'd have to care to be jealous. I don't. I'm not." He takes a deliberate sip of his drink. "If I wanted you, I'd have you."

I snort. "All talk." The lie rolls off my tongue. The dreams that wake me up panting, with a racing heart and an aching core, prove otherwise.

"Just know that your date is an asshole of epic proportions."

"You don't know shit about him."

"Apparently neither do you."

"What's that supposed to mean?" I stand with my hands on my hips and can all but feel Gregory's stare boring into my back.

"He was just on the phone with his buddy bragging about how he's going to get some tonight. Would you like me to recount all of the things he said about you?" Annoyance tinges his voice, and I can't place if it's directed at me or at Gregory.

"What's it to you?" I ask but wonder if he's telling the truth or just trying to bait me.

"It's nothing."

"Then why do you care?"

His eyes light with amusement. "Like I said, I care about my employees."

"I'm not your employee."

"Sorry. *Soon-to-be* employees." His smile is fast and wicked. "Better?"

"You're incorrigible."

"Thank you."

"Grrrr." I fist my hands at my sides in frustration. "Look, Gregory is—"

"Gregory?" He snorts. "Perfect name for a douchebag."

"He's a nice guy. Leave him out of your games. Out of this." I motion from him to me and back.

"Fine. I will." He stands and puts his hand on the small of my back. "Let's go."

"What?" I sputter out the word and step away from his grasp.

"I said, *let's go.* That way he can be left out of this." He smiles, clearly enjoying this exchange.

"You need to go."

"Oh, I love it when she gets mad," he says to no one in particular and then claps his hands and rubs them together.

"You're everywhere. Then nowhere. You dangle carrots and then when I ask about them, you ignore me," I say, realizing that by me being here, verbally sparring with him, I've giving him exactly what he wants. My time. My energy. My emotions.

He takes a long look at my lips before meeting my eyes and smirking. Something about the combination has me shifting on my feet. "I'm fickle like that."

"Yeah, well, be fickle elsewhere," I say and turn my heel, going back to Gregory.

A part of me half expects him to grab my arm and yank me back against him. That part of me is oddly disappointed that he doesn't.

It only serves to fire the anger that seems to scatter my thoughts every time I'm around him.

"Everything okay?" Gregory asks as I slide into my seat. "You two seemed to be—"

"It's fine. Totally fine. He's just . . ."

"An ex?" Gregory asks.

"No. Never. I—"

"Hm. Could've fooled me."

I try to make my smile as warm as possible and my voice just as placating. "It's nothing. He's nothing." I reach out and squeeze his hand, well aware that Holden is most likely watching. I hope the action pisses him off. But why I want it to piss him off is the even bigger question. To make him jealous? To prove to him I'm a big girl who can do what I want? To push his buttons how he was just pushing mine? "Now, where were we? Something about the status of the economy?" I ask but have absolutely zero interest.

His smile is bright as I focus on him. And it remains that way for the next while as he regales me with his business acumen that he spouts incessantly with a blatant presumption that I know nothing. Why should I be surprised though?

But by the same token, he genuinely is a nice guy. Great manners. A quirky sense of humor. Good-looking in a city-slicker type of way. And while no part of me has the desire to sleep with him tonight, I showed up here. The least I can do is see the night out.

And hopefully in the process piss Holden off in doing so.

That makes you a horrible person, Row. Selfish. Unkind.

And similar, it seems, to the game Holden is playing with me . . . fair *is* fair.

"That's absolutely fascinating." I take a sip of my drink and smile as the server appears again, but this time she has her teeth sunk in her bottom lip and anxiety written all over her jitters.

"This round is on the gentleman. Again," she says as she slides fresh drinks on the table but for both of us this time. "And this is for you." She sets a napkin down in front of me with Holden's phone number scribbled on it.

The arrogant bastard.

I try to stop the smirk that automatically crawls on my lips.

He's persistent. I'll give him that.

"Is that what I think it is?" Gregory asks as I glance up and catch sight of Holden heading toward the men's restroom as I stand from my seat. "His fucking phone number? As if you'd choose him over me. That prick probably doesn't have a decent job and is buried in debt while driving some piece-of-shit car." He puffs his chest out. "I'll go handle this," he says but then startles when he looks toward the bar and Holden isn't there.

"No, please." I put a hand on his arm to stop him. While it's more than chivalrous for him to want to take care of the *situation*, the last thing I want is for him to fight on my behalf. "Just let it go. It's nothing. He's nothing," I repeat again and dart a glance back over to the bathrooms.

Gregory looks at me, jaw clenched and with a scowl on his face as he crumples up the napkin with the phone number already programmed in my phone. "Only dicks do shit like that."

"I know." I offer a strained smile, understanding why he's upset but a little shocked by his reaction. "If you'll excuse me, I'm going to head to the restroom."

"Sure. Yes. Not a problem."

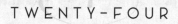

TWENTY-FOUR

Rowan

I head toward the back of the bar, down the hall, and right into the men's restroom without knocking. Holden's standing on the opposite side of the room, back to me, clearly using the urinal.

"You have a lot of fucking nerve," I say before the door even shuts.

"Come on in. I don't mind," Holden says as he turns around, zipping his pants up. "If you wanted to see my dick to measure it up to how small Gregory's is, Sunshine, all you had to do was ask."

My eyes flicker down to where his hands are buttoning his pants and then back up to the grin on his lips.

"The farmers market. The country club. That dreaded fucking polo match. At the gym. In the goddamn warehouse."

"Are you giving me a tour of Westmore?" His tone is wry and his eyebrows are raised.

"No. I'm telling you all of the places you have miraculously popped up at to purposely annoy the fuck out of me."

"You forgot the office. I'm there too."

"Funny."

He angles his head to the side and meets my glare. "Like I said, Rowan, it's a small town. If you give me your schedule, I'll be sure to show up every other place I haven't."

"You have a quip for everything, don't you."

"Only for you," he says as the door opens at my back.

I turn to find a wide-eyed guy looking at me like I'm crazy. Maybe I am. God knows Holden sure makes me feel that way. "Bathroom's occupied," I say, to which I just get a dumbfounded look that has me taking the few steps toward the door, shutting it, and twisting the lock.

"Oh." Holden claps his hands together and rubs them as his cologne drifts through the small space and assaults my senses in the best way. "Things are getting serious."

"You don't get to barge in on my date and make him feel insecure—"

"That's his problem, not mine." He smirks, and I hate that regardless of how angry I am, I'm still drawn to the sight of it.

Of him.

"You don't get to follow me around. Show up where I am. Assume I'll drop everything for you."

"The best part about you is that *you don't.*"

His comment puts a hitch in my stride. The grin he flashes even more so. "Don't. Just don't." I hold my hands up, frustrated with him for continually being charming when I'm mad at him. For what he's doing right now to Gregory—taking me away from him. For having a comeback to every single thing I say. "You don't get to follow me around. You don't get to be everywhere but not talk to me when I approach you."

"I'm talking to you now."

That's a first.

"And you don't get to flaunt a board seat or ownership or *anything* at me one minute and then not explain yourself the next."

He laughs. It's a patronizing sound that echoes off the marble walls of the bathroom.

It infuriates me. It sounds like every laugh Rhett or my father gives to let me know I am less than.

"Fuck you, Holden." I step forward and poke a finger into his chest.

"Right." He grins. "*Fuck me* and the seat at the table I offered and then took back when you refused to work with me."

What? That's what that was all about? How dare he . . . How . . .
The prick.

"Exactly what I said and meant. *Fuck you* and your games and
your half-truths and your innuendos and your—"

From one beat to the next, Holden's hand is fisted in my hair
and his lips are on mine. Ravaging mine. Claiming mine.

It takes a second for the shock to register. For me to realize
what is happening.

I struggle against him. Hands pressed against his chest. Head
trying to move from side to side.

It takes another second for the assault of desire to take over. For
the taste of scotch on his tongue and the dominant demand in his
touch to drag me under and take hold of me. For the groan in the
back of his throat and the hard length of his body pressed against
me to make me feel. For my hands to grab his shirt as the perfect
combination of need and greed and want make my body ache with
a slow, sweet burn that's wicked and wanton all at the same time.

And then I snap to.

To the moment. To who's kissing me. To where we are.

But the draw is just too much. The drug of him too goddamn
sweet that sense and reason get buried in the high of him.

In his hands as they rake over my skin.

In the heat of his mouth as it slides its way down my throat to
the soft spot that has my body jerking in his hands.

In his fingers as they find their way between my thighs.

In his groan as his hand slides beneath my panties and finds me
wet and more than willing for his touch.

In the softening of my body and the widening of my stance as
his fingertips find my clit.

The soft mewl that falls from my lips is met with another jarring knock on the bathroom door followed by "Open the fuck up."

That is what I need to snap to my senses. To realize what I'm
doing and who I'm doing it with. To comprehend that Gregory and
god knows who else is out there assuming what is going on in here.

"It's taken. Use the other one," Holden shouts gruffly at the door as I push back against him with one hand and I reach out to slap him with the other. And the slap isn't because of the kiss but rather the way he's making me feel.

Alive.

On fire.

Desperate and wild when everything else in my life, when everyone else, is dull and stagnant.

It's self-preservation at its worst and embarrassment that it takes him to make me feel this at its best.

He catches my hand mid-swing, his fingers still coated in my arousal, gripping my wrist, and lifts a single brow as he meets my eyes. His chuckle is a low rumble of suggestion and warning.

Both have me aching for him to touch me again.

Both have me struggling to get out of his grip.

"I'll give you that slap once." He brings my hand to his lips and startles me when he licks the inside of my palm. "And only once," he murmurs against my skin so that the vibration of his lips tickles my nerve endings back to life.

"How dare you." I need to say something, anything, and that most definitely isn't it, but it's all I have.

"How dare I?" he asks.

I've never been more aware of someone's presence before.

The scent of his cologne.

The warmth of his body.

The strength in his hands.

His taste still lingering on my tongue.

The effects of all of them on my body.

"You—you can't do that."

"Do what?"

"Kiss me. Touch me . . . like that."

"Like that?" He quirks an eyebrow before he leans in and murmurs in my ear. "I just did. And you liked it every bit as much as I did."

I take a jolting step back. Wanting distance. *Needing* space.

I shake my head, my voice barely a whisper. "This can't happen."

My body says differently. "You're you and I'm me and . . . and it's not good for a business relationship if we . . ."

"You'll find I don't care much about norms. Or rules. I don't like to be boxed in. When I want something, I go after it."

"First my company and now what? Me?"

His shrug is indifferent, his chuckle even more so, making me feel like I'm once again just a pawn in his undisclosed game. The sting of rejection is confusing considering the taste of his kiss still owns my mind.

"It's an interesting world you choose to live in, Rowan Roth-schild. You want to be treated like the strong, independent woman you are, and yet you keep hanging around with people who only see you as an afterthought, who make it your job to soothe, serve, and settle. It seems to me you aren't exactly sure how to break free of that stigma even when you're looking in the eyes of the person who can do that for you." His challenge is there. It's in his words. It's in the lift of his chin and the set of his jaw.

I stare at him, blinking, knowing that he's right and hating him for it. "What does any of that have to do with you forcing yourself on me?" It's a lame comeback but it's easier to focus on the sexual tension vibrating in this small space than it is the truth in his words.

"It doesn't. It's just an observation while we're standing here and you're hating yourself for wanting me to kiss you again. Wanting me to touch you again. Wanting to feel me driving into you. And make no mistake—I will. Most definitely."

"You know what? This is ridiculous. You being at the bar. Me coming in here. You kissing me. You . . . everything." I shake my head and emit a frustrated sigh. "I have to go back. Gregory is waiting. . . ." I speak the words, but my feet don't move, my pulse doesn't stop thundering through my veins, and my want for him to kiss me again doesn't dissipate.

Holden's knowing smile is seductive in and of itself. "Fine. Go back to *Gregory*. But tell me something," he says and steps back into my personal space. "Only go if he makes you feel half of how I just did. But he doesn't and you know it. *I know it.* And that scares the shit out of you, doesn't it?" He reaches out and places his hand on the side of my face so his thumb can brush over my bottom lip. I freeze at the simple but intimate touch. "Go back to him, Rowan. Sit down. Continue that conversation with him that is so stimulating you're looking at me every few seconds."

"Fuck you."

He chuckles. "That's the hope." He walks past me, unlocks the door, and looks back at me. "I'll be waiting in the parking lot when you quit being stubborn and realize I'm right. And Rowan? I don't have to force myself on anybody. Your hands fisted in my shirt and your tongue between my lips? That said as much."

I stare at the door long after he walks out of it, trying to process his words, his actions . . . his kiss. *His touch.* And it's only when the door swings open and I'm met with a wide-eyed customer with a "whoa" on his lips seeing me there that I storm out of the bathroom and back to our table at the bar.

Gregory lights up when he sees me. "Everything okay? You look flushed."

My smile is quick and most likely insincere to Gregory as I take my seat. "I'm fine. There was a line. It was hot. You know how women's restrooms are."

He furrows his brow. "Can't say I've ever been in one, but sure. Yeah." He laughs and I manage to do the same as I glance over to the bar where Holden was sitting.

He's not there.

Good.

I think the thought but I'm sitting taller and looking out the large windows of the bar to see if he's in the parking lot.

"Can we start over now that your stalker is gone?" he jokes.

"Sure. I'd like that."

"I think we were talking about capturing the market and the economy, but when you left, I realized you probably have no interest in that." He takes a sip of his vodka cranberry and offers a placating smile. "I've learned the quickest way to turn a date off is to drone on and on about business. My apologies. Tell me about you. The committees you chair at the club. The things you can't wait to do with your kids one day."

I stare at him, blinking rapidly as if the action is going to help me process the domesticated box he just put me in.

"Who says I'm on any committees?"

"A good Southern woman like you?" He rolls his eyes. "C'mon now. It's okay to brag."

"I'm not on any. I work. A lot. And I—"

"But that's just until you get married, right? After that, what do you hope for?"

. . . You keep hanging around with people who only see you as an afterthought, who make it your job to soothe, serve, and settle. . . .

I lift my chin. "To run my family's company."

Gregory belts out a condescending laugh and reaches out to put a hand on my forearm. I freeze at his touch. It elicits none of the same reactions Holden's did. "That's cute. I'm sure your family has something different to say about it."

Hate to burst your bubble, Gregory Chapman, but you just killed this date.

You and Holden both.

TWENTY-FIVE

Holden

Jesus fucking Christ.

I gulp in the cool night air as I pace back and forth in front of my car.

Rowan's fucking kiss was ... *is* ... electric. The taste of her skin. The heat of her pussy.

All-consuming.

Fucking owning my mind as I stand out here and wait for her.

And she will come.

I scrub a hand through my hair, shake my head, and remind myself Rowan is just the cherry on top of the sundae. Nothing less. Nothing more.

The deep-seated ache in my balls begs to differ.

My attention is pulled to a couple arguing a few rows over. Poor bastard is getting raked over the coals for looking at another woman.

"You're right." Rowan's voice at my back startles me. *She fucking came.* I turn around slowly to find her standing inches from me, hands on her hips, annoyance etched in the lines of her face. Even more gorgeous because of it.

We stand like this for a moment as a car drives by and a flood of sound hits us as the door to the bar opens and closes. And then she fists a hand in my shirt and yanks my mouth down to hers.

There is no hesitation on her part this time. No push and then pull. Rowan Rothschild dives right in with a fervor equal to how the first kiss made me feel. It's heat and hunger. It's fire and ice. It's a battle of wills and a submission of neither.

It's fucking perfection.

And it feels like just as soon as it starts, it ends with Rowan pushing back against my chest and patting it. "There. You happy? *You win.* Now get me out of here." She walks to the passenger side of my SUV and climbs in without me saying a single word.

Alrighty then.

I look back toward the door of the bar, climb into my car, and then head out of the parking lot.

I glance over to her and her pout has me grinning.

She holds a finger up. "Don't fucking gloat, Knight. Not once."

"Or else?"

"Or else I'll jump out of this moving vehicle and the world will blame my death on you. Can't take over my company if you're in jail for murder."

"You can't run said company that I won't be taking over if you're dead."

"Then don't doom the both of us."

I chuckle. If this is how the woman is after she gets kissed, god help me for still wanting to sleep with her.

But I do gloat. Silently. Hell, I could drive her home right now and walk away knowing I won this battle. That I bent her to my will. That she fucking caved. But the feel of her lips and my desire to taste them again has me going anywhere but there.

We drive in silence for a bit, the interior of my SUV feeling small suddenly with the scent of her perfume. Her phone is in her hand, but she never looks at it despite it lighting up every few seconds from incoming texts or notifications.

"Do you want to—"

"No," she says sternly.

I laugh. "Okay then. I'll just keep driving."

"Good idea."

I drive. Through Westmore. Past its outskirts. Into the neighboring city of Hampton West.

I'd like to think I'm driving aimlessly as I do on most nights when I can't sleep, but I know exactly where I'm going.

The question is why, Holden? Why are you bringing her there?

To test her?

To prove she isn't the same person she was back then?

"You're new in town and yet you know this place?" She snorts as I put the SUV in park. "It doesn't fit."

"I wasn't aware I had to *fit* in anywhere."

"You've been seen everywhere one goes to be seen. Westmore Country Club. The Vine . . ." she says and names off a few more restaurants and social spots. Places I've been to play the game that needs to be played while hating every moment of it. "This place doesn't fit that version of the you you're selling."

"Maybe because this person isn't who I want them to see," I say, surprised by my honesty.

She's fucking right, isn't she?

I let one goddamn kiss, one fucking touch of her pussy throw me off so much I came here.

This is not good, Holden.

Fucking Rowan is one thing you've accepted is going to happen. Letting down your guard with her isn't an option.

And you just let it down by coming here.

What are you trying to prove? That she's not like the rest of them?

It doesn't fucking matter.

She's still one of them.

Oblivious to the internal war I'm waging, I see her nod in my periphery. "Why are we here? Why do you want me to see it, then?"

"Good question," I say, wondering the same thing as I look up at the diner's blue neon letters, bright against the dark night sky. The same letters I looked up at as a teen as I waited for my mom to get off work.

How many nights did she have to stay into the early morning

to clean up after the country club kids who looked at her as the hired help?

She wouldn't tell me who they were, but I knew. It was the Rothschild duo, the prick Porter, and the asshole Williams.

How many nights did she have to hitch a ride home with a co-worker because she didn't want me up that late picking her up because I'd be tired for school the next morning?

And how many nights did she swallow her pride and pick up after those spoiled little shits while trying to hide it all from me so I wouldn't react and lose my own job?

Too many to count.

But I never forgot.

I still haven't.

"I come here when I can't sleep," I finally respond as I shake the memory loose. How many times did I sit here in Mrs. Moses's car and watch her clean the counters and mop the floors after closing?

"Does that happen often?" she asks.

"More often than not."

I can feel her staring at me. The questions she wants to ask but don't voice hang in the air. *Why can't you sleep? What busies your mind so that it can't shut down? What haunts you so that you fear your dreams?* To avoid them, I open my car door and get out.

When did you make the decision to let her in? To show her a peek of who you were even though she can't correlate it to now?

Tighten that shit up.

Button it down.

Rowan pushes her door open before I can open it for her.

"This isn't a date, Holden."

I hold my hands up. "No one said it was," I say.

We're seated at a table by the window within minutes, our orders placed, and my head still at war with why I brought her here.

Rowan sits across from me, her arms crossed over her chest, a scowl on her face, and her glare focused on me.

At least one of us is staying true to who we are.

"Do you want to tell me why you're mad at me for wanting to

kiss me? I mean, I'm not complaining, hate kisses are like hate fucks—perfection in every way—but you can at least tell me why you're blaming me for your wants."

She fights a smile as she tries to keep her expression stern. "Do you have hate fucks often enough to have opinions on their perfection?"

I purse my lips and tilt my head from side to side, taking my time giving a response. Fighting a smile but relenting. "From time to time."

"So it's not just me you piss off then."

I chuckle. "No. It's not just you."

"Good. Great. So long as you acknowledge that."

"It's hard to be angry at someone when they're drinking a chocolate milkshake," I say as she sucks on the straw. After the events of the bathroom, the action has my imagination going into overdrive.

She swallows her sip, sets the shake down on the table, and plays with the straw wrapper, clearly lost in her own thoughts and oblivious to mine.

"This place has been here forever," she murmurs.

"Yeah?" I pretend not to know.

She nods and looks around the diner. It hasn't changed much from what I can remember. The booths' upholsteries have been redone, the counters changed out for some type of stone, the light fixtures upgraded, but for the most part, the feel is the same. A '50s diner in the twenty-first century.

"Yeah. It's a big hangout for high schoolers after football games. Or at least it used to be."

"You came here?" I ask, wondering if she was one of the spoiled kids who would trash the place and make my mom stay here for hours after closing trying to clean it all up.

"In the summer usually. With my sister." Something glances through her eyes but it's gone just as quickly as it's there. "But it was typically my sister—Cassie—and Rhett who'd come here."

"You're not a fan of football games?"

She gives me a pseudo shrug. "When you go to an all-girls school a few hundred miles away, it doesn't bode well for hometown football games."

"What do you mean an all-girls school?"

"Just what I said."

I stare at her and question my sanity. But I saw her with my own eyes at the country club when I was working there. I listened to my mom complain about the Rothschild kids after games and the havoc they wreaked in this very diner.

"You didn't go to high school here?"

She gives a slow shake of her head and a partial chuckle. "No, and I was okay with that."

"But . . ." I say the word and then wish I could take it back when her eyebrows furrow. *I saw her here with my own eyes.*

"While all the other girls were ecstatic about their debuts, I was busy trying to figure out how to sabotage mine. My twin—Cassie—was everything my parents expected in a daughter. I refused to be any of it." She shrugs and I'm surprised by her complete indifference in disappointing her parents. "I begged to go away to school. Anything other than the weekend social events, the pageant participation, and the expectations to be a cheerleader."

"And your parents let you?"

"I went to Gilmore. It's prestigious and I sold them on how it would make me more well-rounded—or in their eyes, it might tame me to make me more attractive to marry off someday." She rolls her eyes.

"Clearly the *taming* part worked," I tease, at which she snorts.

"You're lucky I'm tired or you just might have a kick to your shin right now."

I laugh and for the first time a smile widens on her lips.

I stare at her unapologetically.

She's beautiful even with a scowl, but hell if a smile doesn't make her radiant. "Good thing you're tired then." I take a sip of my own milkshake. "So your parents sent you there and not your sister?"

"They wanted to, but she fought them tooth and nail. Sold them as hard on staying here as I did on getting away." She stares back at the straw wrapper she's fiddling with. "We were that odd pair of twins that got along, but who were completely different in every aspect. Did I want her to go to school with me? No. Besides, she liked being the only daughter here. And she liked pretending to be me even more when she thought she was doing something she shouldn't be doing."

"She what?" I ask as thoughts start colliding and truths I should have seen come crashing into me.

"Just what I said. She used to pretend to be me. Whenever she wanted to rebel a little and step out of the perfect role, she'd say she was me, that I'd come home for a visit and . . ."

"Caused trouble."

"Yep." Her smile is bittersweet. "It only served to prove even more why I wanted my own identity away from Westmore and the Rothschild name."

"Yet you came back to claim that reputation anyway."

"I did," she says softly. "Originally it was to figure out how to move forward after Cassie passed."

"I'm so sorry," I offer.

"It was a long time ago. A car accident that was her fault . . ."

I don't ask her for anything more because I know all about the circumstances around her death. Cassie Rothschild died at age seventeen, three days shy of her eighteenth birthday, when she drove her car into a telephone pole while texting and driving.

What I didn't know until now is that the Rowan Rothschild I thought I knew at the club most likely wasn't really Rowan.

It was Cassie.

My head spins but her words pull me back into the conversation before I can spiral too much out of control. "Her . . . being gone. It ruined me for longer than I'd like to admit."

"I understand that. The being ruined and struggling to get over it." I say the words, offering more of myself to this woman when I'm not supposed to be.

"How?"

"A younger brother." It's all I say. As much as I'll admit to when I'm not supposed to be admitting anything to anyone.

"I'm sorry too."

"Like you said, it was a long time ago." I clear my throat and redirect back on her. "So what happened next? You came back?"

"Yeah. For my last semester of high school. That summer. Then off to college."

"And then owning the business pulled you back for a final time?"

"That. And my gran." Her smile is automatic at the mention. "She was just like me but born generations too early to be able to act on it. She's the reason I have the position I have at TinSpirits. My dad was against it. 'It's a male-dominated industry' and all that bullshit. But Gran guilted him into it. The whole 'I never got the chance to because of when I was born,' and she convinced him to let me start at the ground level and work my way up. To learn it from bottom to top while Rhett got to ride the elevator to the top floor."

"Clearly that bugs you—as it should."

"It did. But I also realized I'm better for it. How can Rhett fix an issue six levels below him when he's never had to figure it out on his own?" She sighs. "I don't know. I always wanted to run the company, but the more I worked my way up, the more I saw his gross incompetence and complete arrogance in his entitlement. Then profits started to drop. At first, I thought it was just the downswing of the economy. Then I thought it was something he was doing—taking money out? Making poor purchasing decisions? I don't know. Maybe it's his blatant misunderstanding of how the company is supposed to be run. Perhaps a little of all three."

Perhaps a lot of all three and the flagrant spending on all things Rothschild while he's at it.

"I'll just leave this here," the waitress says as she slips our check onto the table.

"Thanks. We'll be out of your way soon," Rowan says. "I'm sure you want to get out of here and home to your family."

"I do. Thank you. I have a sick kiddo at home." She taps a button on her apron of a little boy in a baseball uniform.

"I hope he feels better soon," Rowan says, and as the waitress walks away I pull out some cash beneath the edge of the table, disguising a few hundred-dollar bills beneath a twenty, and slide it onto the receipt tray.

"No. Let me." Rowan digs in her purse.

"I've got it covered."

"The least I can do is add more of a tip for her. She's working her ass off."

I reach out and put my hand on her wrist. "I assure you, I have it covered."

It's then that Rowan looks down and notices the large bills beneath the twenty, her eyes flashing back to mine, and nods.

She narrows her eyes for a beat, almost as if she can't reconcile the man who just did that with the man she normally sees.

The problem is, right now I'm struggling with making the same damn correlation.

We move on, leaving the discussion about work behind. She tells me about summers spent in the Outer Banks. I give her snippets— benign and generic—of my time in California. We talk about random things, sports teams, favorite vacation spots, the best local places in town to eat—but the whole time I fixate on the notion that none of it matters.

That her caring about the waitress and her sick son and wanting to overcompensate shouldn't affect my opinion of her—*but it does.*

The Westmore elite don't care about anybody else or their struggles. They never have.

And yet Rowan's frequent glances over to our waitress and the sympathetic smiles she gives her say the exact fucking opposite.

She's surprising me at every turn tonight and if she keeps it up, I'll have no choice but to face my own suppositions about her.

"Yes?" she asks with raised eyebrows, pulling me back from thoughts about her.

"I'm sorry. What was that?"

"Ignoring me already, Knight? That's not a good start." She laughs. "All I said was, so computer software, huh?"

I nod. "Yep."

"That's all you're going to give me?"

"What do you want to know?" I ask, my stomach twisting.

You wouldn't like me if you knew.

"Where did you go to college? How did you come up with the software? Why did you sell?" She lifts her eyebrows when I don't respond. "That shouldn't be hard to talk about."

But it is. Every piece of myself that I give her leaves me vulnerable. Opens who I am and what I'm here for up to discovery. That can't be known.

I have a plan. A sequence of events that must occur in my head.

When I want more known about me, there'll be no mistake about it.

And yet, I find myself wanting to tell her some of it. The view of myself from space versus ten feet away.

"College wasn't for me." Besides the fact it was loaded with pretentious pricks like the ones I left behind in Westmore, I couldn't burden my mom with more debt. We were drowning in medical bills, funeral expenses, and our move across the country so we could try to breathe without being reminded every single day of what had happened. And I sure as fuck wasn't in the headspace for any of it.

"No?"

I shake my head. "Taught myself computer science. Enjoyed coding and the software aspect." *Loved breaking into servers behind the scenes even more.* "I had a brief stint as a bank teller and was sick of listening to my boss complain to higher-ups about data security every time it was breached. So I solved the problem for them. It took me years to perfect my original software but when I did, it took off. Won an award at the Consumer Electronics Show.

Things went from there. Ran the company for several years before I received an offer I couldn't refuse. Then sold it."

"And that translates to buying other companies, including mine—"

"You mean mine?" I say.

"—how?" she finishes, completely ignoring me.

"I'm an angel investor in many companies. For some reason, I wanted to be hands-on with this one."

"Why?" she asks.

"Why not?" I shrug and don't back down from her stare. "All of that could have been found out with a simple Google search."

"I'm aware," she murmurs, scrutinizing me with her look. "And yet that's still all you'll give me."

"It's all you need. Life is black. It's white. It's gray. I live in the gray."

She chuckles. "The gray?"

I nod. "A little mystery never hurt anyone."

I sit there with my head angled to the side and study a woman who seems to be so much more than I expected upon that first meeting, and question myself over what to think.

Ruining her family is my end game. She's going to be a pawn in that game. And yet I can't stop wondering what would happen if we'd met at a different time and in a different way.

How would things between us have gone then?

But what-ifs are hard to deal with when you're dealing in what you need to do next.

She meets me stare for stare, her lips a pout and her eyeliner smokey. "Give me time, Knight, and I'll figure you out."

"Thanks for the warning."

"You're welcome."

I lean forward, intrigued. "What about you? The woman who goes on dates with men who don't respect her. Who is said to be marrying a man but tells me she isn't. Who is most likely scheming behind my back on how to take me down. Who exactly are you, Rowan Rothschild?"

She pauses for a moment, glancing away before turning back to me with a mischievous glint in her eye. "I thought a little mystery was a good thing?"

I chuckle, admiring her wit. "Fair enough, Sunshine. Fair enough."

"Hey, Holden?" She smirks and leans in closer so that I have no other place to look besides her lips. Her cleavage. *Her.* "We should probably go."

"Should we?"

"Mmm-hmm." She nods. "The question is *where*." With those words, she stands up and saunters away, leaving me looking after her with a shaking head.

The damn woman was supposed to be a conquest. Collateral fucking damage. I'm not supposed to like her beyond her sex appeal. I'm not supposed to want to know more of her for reasons other than fucking revenge. I'm not supposed to want to fuck her for reasons other than simply fucking her to throw it in Chad's face and to stake my flag in making the face of their company mine.

But she opened up.

She uncovered truths I thought were different. It was her sister here at the diner, not her. It was Cassie who owned the reputation for being a spoiled brat, not Rowan.

How did I not put two and two together? How did I miss that Rowan went to a boarding school?

How can I think I've figured every angle of every goddamn thing when it comes to all of this and then find out I haven't? Are there other holes in my plan? Other things I missed?

Will you look at that? You're fucking human, Knight.

Fuck that.

Where does this leave me?

I don't have to particularly like someone to fuck them. It's just a means to an end with a great orgasm in between.

But I like Rowan and that's an unexpected twist.

I rise from the table, say good night to our server, and head out the door to the woman standing in the moonlight waiting for me.

Fucking complications.

I don't need them.

I don't want them.

And yet it seems I'm about to walk head-fucking-first into them.

TWENTY-SIX

Rowan

The car ride was silent. The music was low and the streetlights made shadows play all over the interior of Holden's SUV.

I questioned my sanity. Why I went with him tonight. Why I initiated the kiss in the parking lot other than to prove the way he made me feel was more than just a one-time thing.

It was.

And having him walk me to the front door of my house, I wonder how I thought this was a good idea. Me. Him. The sex I know we're about to have. And the fallout that's no doubt going to happen afterward.

Because we are about to have sex. Hasn't every single moment between us since the auction been foreplay in one way or another?

And to think we've only kissed twice and our connection, our attraction, our need for one another is so palpable, that us sleeping together is a foregone conclusion.

Hating a man and finding him desirable at the same time is fucking with my head.

I unlock my front door and step through it, ignoring Winnie whimpering in her crate in the back of the house. When I turn back, Holden is standing there, as devastating in appearance as his lips were to mine earlier.

Our eyes hold through the silence. They question. They challenge. *They want.*

"Are you going to invite me in?" he asks, his voice husky and the darkened porch only adding to his allure.

"Tonight was a bad idea all around." I speak the words while every part of my body craves him.

"Probably." He nods, his eyes unwavering.

"It's not in the best interest of . . . everything."

"True." He steps into my house, up to me so that our bodies are all but touching. He reaches out and cups the side of my face, his thumb brushing back over my bottom lip like he did earlier. My breath stutters. My pulse races. Butterflies take flight in my belly. "Do you actually think I give a fuck about right and wrong, Rowan? About precedent or decorum, or that I'll let it stop me from doing what I've thought about since that first night we met?" He brushes his lips against mine. "Do you?"

"No." The single syllable is strained. Desperate.

"Good." The warmth of his breath is on my lips. The heat of his body emanates off of him to mine. "I'm going to kiss you, Rowan. Then I'm going to fuck you. Take that as a warning or a threat, but just know you'll take it. Understood?"

His words, that low, even rumble he speaks them in, do things to me.

"I—"

"Understood?" he cuts me off, his voice a mere whisper now.

"Yes. I mean . . . yes."

His chuckle vibrates around the room as he slides a hand down to the small of my back and splays it there. "Step into the gray with me, Row."

And before I can agree or disagree or overthink what is about to happen, Holden's lips are on mine. They take and claim and possess with the same adeptness as earlier tonight but with a savage desperation that matches the way I feel.

He has one hand under my neck with his thumb and forefinger on each side of my jaw holding my head still as he controls the kiss. A touch of tongues. A tug on my bottom lip. A lick up the line of my throat.

My body convulses as he focuses on the spot just beneath my jaw. Chills chase over my spine with each openmouthed kiss. With each slide of his hand up my side. With every guttural groan he emits in response.

My fingers fumble with the buttons on his shirt until it's open. I run my hands over the hard planes and valleys of his abdomen. The corded muscle beneath tightens from my touch.

"You have way too many clothes on," he murmurs against my collarbone as the stubble on his chin tickles in the best kind of way.

I pull my shirt over my head in response. My bra falls to the floor moments after.

"Fuck." His soft swear echoes around the room as his eyes scrape over every inch of my body while mine begs for his touch. And it doesn't have to beg long as he closes his hand over one breast and then lowers his mouth to suck on the pebbled peak of the other.

His warm mouth. The cool air of my house. The soft pressure of his tongue as he sucks on me.

"Holden," I moan, my hands flying to the button of his pants. To his zipper. To his hard, silky cock constrained within.

His entire body stills at my touch. His hand on my breast tenses as every part of me readies for the feel of him. Teasing me. Pleasuring me. *Owning me.*

"Does that make you wet?" he murmurs against my skin. "If I felt beneath your skirt right now, would that sweet pussy of yours be dripping for me like it was earlier?" He slides a hand beneath the hem of my skirt and his moan of appreciation fills the room. "Oh, it is, isn't it?" His mouth meets mine again. His tongue teases as his fingers rub ever so softly, back and forth over my dampened panties.

The pressure is enough for my nerves to know he's there, but nowhere near what I need or want.

I tighten my hand on his cock in reflex. In need. In desire. It's the only leverage I have to make him give me what I want. *Him.* I try to stroke him, to free him from the confines of his jeans. He emits a quick hiss of breath that's followed moments later by his hand clamping down over my wrist and guiding it to let go.

"Bedroom?" The two syllables are a strained demand as he grabs my ass, and I wrap one leg around his hip. The motion adds to the pressure I need, the friction I want, by rubbing my center against the bulge of his erection.

"Down the hall." With utter ease and total finesse, he picks me up so I can wrap my legs around his waist. My breasts press against the bareness of his chest where his shirt is open. I clasp my hands at the back of his neck and pull him to me so our tongues can meet again.

We can taunt and tease with the sweet promise of what comes next as he moves slowly down the hallway.

"Where? Or the hall floor is about as far as we're going to get," he says, his lips moving against mine with each syllable.

"Last door." The words are panted against the warm skin of his neck. Then they're forgotten as I press openmouthed kisses down the open collar of his shirt. His hands tighten on my ass with each scrape of my teeth. His breathing grows heavier with each nip of his shoulder blade.

The next time I take notice, we're in my bedroom and Holden is setting my ass on my dresser. He stands between my spread legs, his mouth going right back to my breasts and his hands running up and down my thighs. Each run up, the pad of his thumb runs ever so gently against the outside of my panties.

Sensations. They're everywhere. In the touch of his hands. In the brush of his lips. In the warmth of his tongue. In the ache that burns so bright I can't wait for him to light me on fire.

"Holden." My fingers thread through his hair. "Please." My teeth sink into my bottom lip. "The bed." My fingernails scrape down his abdomen to the jeans now slung low on his hips. "Now."

His chuckle is a rumble among panted breaths as he stands to full height and puts his hand like a necklace on my throat. I try to shake my head free of his hold, but he just presses my back against the wall, tightens his grip ever so slightly, and leans in. His eyes are on mine, his breath is hitting my face, and his hips are pressing against the V of my thighs.

"*Don't* tell me what to do, Rowan." He licks the seam of my lips but when I part them, when I welcome his in, he shakes his head, that chuckle returning. "In the boardroom, you can spar with me. Question me. *Try* to tell me what to do." His lips meet mine in a searing kiss that dizzies my head before he pulls back, and his eyes meet mine again. "In here? In the bedroom? I'm in control. Of your pleasure. Of your orgasms. Of—"

"But—"

"It's cute that you think you can argue with me on this." He reaches down with his free hand and slides it between my thighs. His thumb adds pressure to where I want it and my mewl for more is embarrassingly desperate. I need the panties gone. I need his skin on my slick flesh. I need to feel more. "That you think you can tell me what to do." He tugs on my bottom lip and then licks over the sting. "But you can't. Understood?"

He looks up at me from beneath dark lashes, his eyebrows raised, his hand still pressing against my throat letting me know who's in charge, and his eyes begging me to say yes.

"Yes."

"Good girl." He hooks my panties to the side with a dexterity I don't pretend to understand and tucks two fingers inside of me.

I cry out as every part of me tightens around him. Wanting a release. Needing one. Mentally begging for him to keep going.

"Christ, baby, you're a goddamn mess for me." He leans forward, his lips at my ear, his fingers pushing farther into me with the motion. "See how I reward you when you do what I say? I give you what you want."

"Uh-huh." I feel vulnerable. Alive. Overwhelmed. Controlled. A quad of emotions I've never had intermingle. They feel foreign, much like his hand on my throat does. They feel wickedly seductive like his fingers currently sliding in and out of me do. "Yes."

"Good." He takes a step back, his fingers pulling out of me before he pats me soundly so that the reverberations of the motion against my clit ricochet throughout me. "Now take off your clothes, lie on the bed, and spread your legs so I can admire what it is I'm going to fuck."

His words are an aphrodisiac all in themselves. The look he gives me as he says them is enough to turn anyone on.

He helps me off the dresser and in the darkness of my room, I do exactly what he says. It's only after I discard my shoes and step out of my skirt and panties that I hesitate.

Since when do I obey? Since when do I take orders from a man?

But there's something about the dark promise of his words that turns me on more. There's something—

"Rowan?" Holden is against my back, clearly naked, his cock evidently free of his pants as it presses salaciously against my ass. I still as he trails a row of kisses down the curve of my shoulder. "Are we hesitating?" He rubs his five-o'clock shadow over the skin there. "It's hard to give up control. To let someone own your sensations, your feelings, your orgasms." He lifts his two fingers up to my lips. "*Suck.*"

I obey. I suck the sweet tang of myself off of him. My mind spinning and my body burning from the heat of his body against mine.

"If that's what giving up control tastes like," he says in that low tenor of his, "just think what it's going to feel like. Now, on your back on the edge of the bed like the good girl I know you are." His hand grabs my ass and squeezes. "*I'm waiting and I don't like to wait.*"

With a breath that's shaky from equal parts nerves and anticipation, I move to my bed and do as he asks—on my back, legs spread, eyes on him.

I don't even have time for modesty to hit me because Holden moves to the edge of the bed in all his naked glory.

He's hard lines and cut dents. He's broad shoulders and strong thighs. He has a trimmed waist and an incredibly gorgeous cock that's a little above average in length and more than ample in girth. He's strong forearms and big hands. Hands that are currently occupied—one slowly stroking his cock up and down. The other holding my crumpled panties to his nose where he's making a show of breathing them in.

Simply put, the man is gorgeous. Sexy. Commanding. And that smirk he gives as he lowers the scrap of lace and looks at them before meeting my eyes adds an element of danger to him.

"Did you wear these for him? For Gregory?" Holden asks as he brings them to his nose again and sniffs them. "Is this—you on them—from him, Rowan? Or did you put them on thinking of me? Hoping for me? Did you soak them only when you kissed me?"

My breath quickens. My pulse races. My nipples harden. *My body craves.*

"That's what I thought." He chuckles. "It was for me." He drops the panties, runs his hands up my calves, and then pulls me so that my calves are hanging over the bed. "Don't be shy to admit it. It turns me on knowing you were sitting with another man but dripping for me." He lifts my leg up and kisses the inside of my ankle, but his eyes continue to remain on me, creating a kind of intimacy I'm not used to.

Like I'm the center of this man's world and everything that happens from here on out is dependent on my responses.

It's heady.

It's overwhelming.

"You've touched yourself thinking about me, haven't you?" He stands before me, rolling a condom on his cock before taking its entirety in his hand, his lips parting as he slowly strokes himself. Down. Up. A twist of his wrist over his crest. Then the mesmerizing process starts all over again. "Come on, now. Don't be shy. I'm about to do a lot more than ask questions. The least you can do is give me the answer I deserve."

I close my eyes, sink my teeth in my bottom lip, and die of embarrassment as I nod.

I yelp and my eyes fly open at the warm, wet heat of Holden

sliding his tongue up the seam between my thighs without warning. My breath hitches. My hips lift. My legs open wider. My hands reach out to grip his hair but he's standing up with an arrogant grin on his lips before I can.

"Show me what you did."

"Holden." His name is part sigh, part mortification, part rejection. I'm not a prude by any means, but I'm also not used to being put on display like Holden is doing right now.

He raises his eyebrows. "Show me and I'll show you." He continues his slow, steady stroke. "Just like this. In my shower. In my bed. In . . ." His groan replaces his words as I slide my hands down my abdomen, part myself with one hand, and rub lazy circles over my clit with the other. "Just like that, baby."

I'm self-conscious at first. Sure, I've done this with lovers before, but not someone on our first time. Not like this. But I force myself to keep my eyes on Holden. On the taut tendons in his neck. In the flex of his bicep with each pump. On the way he squeezes the base and then tightens it again at his crest. On his face pulling tight and his eyelids growing heavy.

"Keep going. Show me what the thought of me does to you."

I dip my fingers down below to wet them before sliding them back up and moving faster this time.

"Fucking perfection." He steps forward so that with each stroke of his cock, each rock of his hips into his hands, his tip brushes where I want it desperately. *In me.*

The burn becomes an ache.

The ache becomes a need I have to reach.

A tsunami I need to take the ride on.

I lose myself in the sensations. In the way he watches me. In the anticipation of what's to come. In the orgasm I can feel is slowly building brick by brick, row by row.

"Fucking hell," Holden groans, pulling me from my haze of pleasure as he pushes his way into me, his hips bucking involuntarily.

It's the slightest of slips of his control, but it's incredibly empowering knowing I made him lose it.

I moan until my breath is robbed from the feel of my body stretching around him. Of him pushing into me. Of my nerve endings being assaulted in the most sensual of ways.

"Take it all for me, baby." His free hand presses my thighs wider. "C'mon." His head falls back momentarily as the same pleasure swamping me claims him. "I know you can." He focuses back on where we're joined. "Can you take any more?"

I sink my teeth into my bottom lip, my hands suddenly losing their dexterity, but my body sings from his touch now. I meet his eyes and am about to say something but the words get lost in a choked-out breath as Holden begins to move.

He's slow at first. Long, deliberate strokes that hit each and every nerve within. He has one hand on the side of my waist holding me still, the other is under my ass holding my hips up at an angle.

He leans over and kisses me. Our tongues tangle much like our bodies do. His chest pushing against mine, teasing my sensitive nipples with each push in and then separating with the next pull out.

Desire fuels each kiss.

Want drives every touch.

Need pushes us not to think and just feel.

And greed, greed has him pick up the pace. Has him grunt in my ear and my nails score his skin. Has me lifting my hips and opening as far as I can for him. Has me struggling to breathe, to think, to speak—I can only feel.

Oh my god.

Yes.

Right there.

Take it, baby.

Harder.

Come for me.

Faster.

Show me what I do to you.

I know the orgasm is coming. I can feel it in the tingling of my fingers and the tightening of my lower belly, but knowing it does nothing to prepare me for its overwhelming onslaught of sensations.

My legs tense.

My hands grip.

My back arches.

My hips buck.

I look up; my last thought when I see Holden is he's a coil of restraint about to snap and take me with him when he does.

And then I'm gone. Fuse lit. Body detonated. Sensations overloaded.

Pleasure washes over me. It drags me under its pull. It drowns me in its bliss. It owns my breath, my thoughts, my reactions, and the two syllables I moan out. *Holden.*

It doesn't stop after the first wave of it crests and tumbles against the sensations. It ebbs and flows as Holden holds my hips still—fingertips bruising my soft flesh there—as he pistons his hips against mine.

My body is his to use right now. To sate while he steals pleasure. To overwhelm while he is pulled into the undertow. To own while he captures his own climax.

His guttural groan is low and desperate as he throws his head back and absorbs the sensations rocking him.

His hips jerk. His body tenses. He's a sight to behold with a stream of moonlight across his body, a mist of sweat on his chest, and his hair mussed and falling onto his forehead.

TWENTY-SEVEN

Rowan

I stare at myself in my bathroom mirror.

At my flushed cheeks and swollen lips. At the red marking my skin from where Holden's hands held me in place. At the fire in my eyes and disbelief in my expression.

I could ask myself how I let this happen. How Holden Knight is on the other side of this door, in my bed . . . *naked*.

But I know damn well how it did. I willed it to happen, didn't I? I told myself that never in a million years would I sleep with the man who's taking over my company, and in the process I lost sight of the sexual tension that kept thickening between us.

But I wanted it to happen. Hell, I even dreamt of us breathless and tangled in sheets. I just never thought we actually would. I never thought I'd cross that line.

I never thought I'd allow myself to "live in the gray" with him. Shit.

The plus side? Reality was way better than dream-ville.

Drawing in a deep breath, I realize the bravado I had when I walked up and kissed him earlier tonight is gone. Vanished right along with my sense, so it seems.

Panic has surfaced. Hell, it set in the minute the orgasms faded and reality prevailed.

How are we to work together after I just *obeyed* him? How am I supposed to pass him in the hallway at work and not hear that rumble of his voice telling me what a good girl I am? How am I to face him in a boardroom and not envision him standing before me with his cock in his hand, looking at me like he wants to devour me?

First-time sex is awkward enough. Throw in the fact that it was *with him* and that just complicates matters more.

A little too late to wonder these things now, right, Row?

And even later to realize I didn't think through my escape to the bathroom to clean up very well. I don't have any clothes in here to put on. My towels that I could use to wrap around myself are still in the dryer where I loaded them this morning. So now I'm naked, having regrets, and needing to go out to face Holden and set things straight.

Talk about splashing water on a burning fire.

With a fortifying breath, I open the door and move back into my room. I don't know why I expected the lights to still be off. Even worse, I don't know why I thought Holden might be dressed and getting ready to leave. Maybe because he's efficient and professional when it comes to all other matters.

Not this time.

When I step into my room, Holden is lying in my bed, arm propped behind his head on the pillow, bicep bulging from the position and a reflective smile on his face as he studies me.

Jesus. The man is . . . something else. Usually, you have sex and the allure is altered some—lessened. *Not with him.* Not even a little bit.

"Look," I say, preparing to lay it all out there.

"Uh-oh, here comes *all-business* Rowan."

"Stop. Just let me—"

"You know she turns me on too, right? With her tight sweaters, her no-nonsense attitude, and how she sways her hips really hard when she stalks away after I piss her off? Why do you think I enjoy making you mad at me?"

I sigh and walk to the foot of the bed. He shifts to show me I have his undivided attention—eyes roaming over my naked body—and in the process, the sheet slides off some and bares his hip and stomach.

The dents. The dips. The perfection.

If I didn't see it happen with my own eyes, I would have sworn he did it on purpose. A distraction from the sendoff I'm about to give him. His grin when I meet his eyes says that he notices that I noticed.

Needing a distraction, I pick up the first thing on the floor I find to put on—of the mind that he'll take me more seriously if I have clothes on. Of course, it's his dress shirt, but that doesn't stop me from slipping my arms through it and wearing it like a suit of armor.

"This happened. *Tonight* happened. It was . . . a mistake of epic proportions on both our parts," I say, getting more than flustered. "It can't happen again."

"Epic?" He twists his lips and bobs his head from side to side, completely ignoring the last part. "I think that's a good way to describe it. Phenomenal. The best you've ever had. *Sexsational* works too. I mean, those would all be more appropriate adjectives."

"You're not cute."

He lifts the sheet so he can see his cock beneath and scrunches his nose up as he shrugs. "It is kind of cute. But this is where we can get *hung* up on adjectives again."

I shake my head and fight a laugh. How can he be this relaxed? This okay with everything? It seems sex brings out a side to Holden that I was thoroughly unprepared for.

Aren't guys like him supposed to be cold and aloof after? Treat sex like a transaction?

But here he is with a sexy smile and an incredible body, cracking jokes and looking relaxed and comfortable.

I have to get this back on track.

"This isn't a joke, Holden. This—us—tonight—can have serious implications for us professionally. *For me professionally.*" I think of the board, of our managers, of my family. What they'd all think if they found out. How I basically proved every stereotype placed on me right with what just happened—that I let my emotions rule rather than my common sense. *Just like women do.* "This can't happen again. It was just sex. It was a moment of weakness on both of our parts."

He snorts. "Speak for yourself because I beg to differ. There was nothing weak about that performance. I knew exactly what I was doing."

"I know but that's just it. I—"

"Did you go hide in the bathroom so you could make up some kind of Venn diagram to explain to yourself why this can't happen? Did you make sure that 'Rowan's pleasure' and 'Rowan working with Holden' didn't intersect so that you can control the narrative? So that you can deny how I just made you feel?"

"You're making me sound like an idiot."

"For the record, Row. No one controls me. Not a diagram. Not your type A personality. Not the fucking norm. Nothing." He runs a hand through his hair and the ruffled look of it only makes him sexier—if that's even possible. "And 'just sex'? Were those your words? Someone only says that when they want more. Do you want more, Rowan?"

"God. No," I sputter.

"I'm taking offense to that. Grave offense."

"I told you. This was a mistake. It can't happen ag—"

"*Again.* Yes. I heard you. If I can't take offense, can I be insulted, then?" He chuckles and the sound has me thinking of what it felt like when he laughed with my nipple in his mouth. The shockwaves the sensation sent through my system. "I'm thinking I should be insulted."

"No. I—I'm not doing a very good job explaining myself."

"I'm all ears." His smile is slow and mischievous . . . and reignites the spark in my lower belly.

"This. You and me. It was just sex. Just the physical. Only one time. Only tonight to get each other out of our systems."

"Is that so?"

"It is. I—I still loathe you."

"Yes. Uh-huh. You sounded like you hated me as you begged me to make you come harder."

"See, that right there." I point my finger at him. "You can't say shit like that. No one gave you permission to."

"Right." He nods but doesn't fight his grin. Clearly, he finds this conversation more than amusing.

"I've got to get out of here."

"Good. You should. I mean, why would I want to lie here and watch your nipples poking through the fabric of my shirt?" His eyes wander down the narrow strip of his shirt where my bare skin shows. I yank it closed and cross my arms over my chest.

"Yes. I will."

"You're forgetting one thing."

"What's that?" I ask, distracted, as I look for my clothes.

"This is your house."

"*For fuck's sake,*" I mutter and just hang my head and laugh. I'm never flustered by a man and yet here I am, flustered and acting like an airhead.

"Was the sex that good that you forgot? Because one minute you're telling me I have to go and the next you're—"

"You just don't get it."

"Clearly." He scoots up in bed so that he's resting against the headboard, one knee bent, and the sheet dipping dangerously low so I can see the outline of his cock beneath it. "Explain it to me."

"What if someone saw us tonight?"

"I kissed you in a locked bathroom. You kissed me in a public parking lot. That one's on you." He angles his head to the side and studies me. "What does it matter if someone saw us?"

He knows why, but he's going to make me explain it, and I'm not sure if that makes me like him or hate him more for it.

"It's hard enough for me as it is—"

"Thank you." His grin returns right along with his ego as he cups a hand over his cock on the sheet.

"No . . . Jesus." I roll my eyes. "Being a woman in Westmore— one who has aspirations beyond being married and meeting all

the societal goals—isn't easy. It's taken me forever to earn the respect of the board, of my colleagues, of our suppliers. If someone
saw us, if they knew I slept with you, you know any upward mo-
bility on my part will be met with the assumption that I slept my
way to the top. Men get praised for sleeping with bosses. Women
get slammed for it."

He gives a measured nod. "When I'm running the place, your
position is earned by doing the work."

"Or by sleeping with the boss."

"No." The word is curt and unforgiving as he rises from the
bed, no shame as he stands there in all his naked glory. "Is all of
this about how other people perceive you, or about how you perceive yourself? One I'll accept. The other I don't give a flying fuck
about."

"You . . . you just have to go."

"So you've said, but you still haven't answered my question and
I think that's what you're struggling with. You slept with me. You
wanted to. I wanted to. That doesn't make you a bad person. Not
in my book. It makes you *you*. Human. A woman. Someone with
needs. What happens in this bedroom has no bearing on what
happens outside of it."

*I slept with the man trying to ruin my dreams. That says a whole
shit ton about me. A whole lot I'm not proud of.*

I nod, my words caught in my throat, my voice barely a whisper. "We can't do this again."

He chuckles, clearly not believing me. "So you're telling me the
sex was so mediocre that resisting me—resisting there being a
next time—will be easy."

"I didn't say anything about the sex."

"So that part was good?"

Incredible. Phenomenal. Everything.

I shrug and nod.

"And the resisting me part?"

Our eyes meet, and I turn to find my discarded clothes. Anything to do with my hands so that I don't have to face him. So that

I don't show him denying or resisting him will be anything but easy.

"You're a fucking liar," he says as his laugh rumbles around the room.

Yes. I am.

I jolt when Holden's hand touches my neck and moves my hair to the side. I never even heard him cross the room. "Don't worry, Sunshine." He presses his lips there and murmurs as he slides his hand inside his shirt I have on. His touch against the bare skin of my abdomen detonates little earthquakes everywhere. "Your secret's safe with me. The gray is a lot of fucking fun sometimes. It's addicting. You'll step into it again with me regardless of what you say."

I close my eyes and try not to be affected by his words, by his touch, by the feel of his lips on my skin, but I am.

I know I am.

I don't know what to say.

How to respond.

Because he's right.

But I don't need to say anything because suddenly Holden isn't behind me. The heat of his body is gone. I turn to see him pulling his pants up over his hips, tucking his cock inside of them, grabbing his shoes in his hand, and then walking out of the house without another word.

I stare at the bedroom door, at the empty bed, and question my own damn sanity because hell if I don't already want him again.

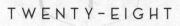

TWENTY-EIGHT

Holden

You're a fucking liar.

Was that meant about you or about her, Knight?

Huh?

Who's the one sitting in his car staring at her house long after he left? Watching the lights go on and off with her perfume still clinging to his skin and the scent of her pussy still on his hand?

This is not supposed to be anything.

She is nothing more than a way to dig the knife deeper into their backs. To stake a flag on a mountain because you laid claim to her like she is a piece of property.

But tonight happened. The bar where I was supposed to simply annoy. The bathroom that she came charging after me in. The diner where I shouldn't have taken her.

Her bed where I was supposed to fuck her but feel absolutely nothing in turn.

This was a game. This *is* a game. One where there can only be one winner. *Me.*

Then why can't I get her eyes out of my mind? Why did I want to stay when I should have been gone the minute she hit the bathroom? Why am I already planning on proving how she can't resist me?

Because fuck if I can't resist her.

Not after earlier.

Not after just now.

Lock it down, Knight. Fuck her to fuck her. Fuck her for the plea-sure. Fuck her for the revenge.

Nothing more.

Nothing less.

And yet I still sit here in the early morning hours staring at a house because a woman is inside it. A woman I can still feel be-neath me and wrapped around me.

It's the hard-to-get thing, right? No woman has ever kicked me out of her bed. That has to be it.

But lies are only good if you're telling them to someone else.

Jesus fucking Christ.

Talk about complicating fucking matters.

Talk about making the gray the darkest fucking shade it can be.

TWENTY-NINE

Holden

FIFTEEN YEARS AGO

"Mason! Help!"

I hear the words yelled.

Over and over.

Again and again.

I can't register that it's my own voice, that they're my own screams as I run to him.

Oh my god.

There's blood. It's everywhere. Coming out of his ears. Out of his nose. On the asphalt.

"Help."

I don't know what to do. His eyes are closed. His breathing unsteady.

"Please."

I go to pick him up but stop. Broken bones. Spinal injuries. His brain.

Don't move him.

Don't move him.

Don't move him.

"Call nine-one-one," I scream. "I'm here, Mase. I'm here. Help is coming. I'm here."

I lie down in the street with him, a mirror image on my side so that we can be face-to-face, so that he can hear me.

"Somebody call nine-one-one," I shout again as the sounds of people around me start to register.

"They're coming," someone says as footsteps run beside me.

"C'mon, buddy. Stay awake. Help's coming." Tears streak down my cheeks as I squeeze my brother's hand.

Please. Please. Please.

There are voices around me.

"Where's the fucking ambulance?"

"We're the last on the list. You know how it is here."

"Did anyone see anything?"

"Hang in there, buddy. Help is on the way."

It's all white noise to me. White noise and the thundering of my heartbeat and the rattle of his breath.

"Help him. Please help him." I can barely get the words out as I look up to the crowd of eyes gazing down at us. But that's all they're doing. No one is touching. No one is helping. No one is fixing.

I need a car. I need to drive him to help myself. I look from person to person. "I need a car. Your keys. I need to take him myself." From my knees I try to gather Mason up myself, but someone pulls me back.

"Stop. No. You might hurt him more," a voice behind me says as hands pull me back.

I struggle against them. "He needs help," I plead. "He needs help and they're not coming. I need to get him to the hospital."

"Let him go," someone says in front of me. There's a clank as he kicks something but I'm so busy fighting against the person at my back that I almost miss the subtle shake of his head and knowing look.

"*No!*" I scream the word out and fight everyone off of me. I drop to my knees and gather my little brother in my arms. I hold him tight and try to squeeze my life into him. I try to make him hold on. I barter with the universe and every fucking thing in it to

trade me for him. "Mase." My lips are against his hair. "Hold on."
My heart is beating against his, willing it to do the same. "I love
you." I rock him back and forth. "I'm so sorry."

There's a strangled sob.

It's mine. It has to be mine. But I can't remember making it.

I hold on to my little brother.

It feels like forever.

Murmurs around.

If I had a car, I could get him help faster.

Sirens in the distance.

If I hadn't wanted a computer, we would have one.

Medics prying him from my arms.

If I hadn't caved and told him to go outside.

The finality in the slam of the ambulance doors.

I had one job to do.

The sound of sirens again.

Keep my brother safe.

The silence as the sirens fade, and the crowd staring at me standing in my brother's blood.

And I couldn't even do that right.

THIRTY

Rowan

"I don't understand."

I look up from my laptop and the various maps spread all over the conference room table. My brother is standing on one side of the table, brow furrowed, face more than impassive . . . but fidgety.

"Nothing for you to understand," I say and go back to the spreadsheet on my laptop. The last thing I owe Rhett is an explanation for anything.

"What is all of this?"

I shrug. "To be honest, I'm not one hundred percent sure. I came into the office today and Audrey had all of these on my desk. She said Holden wants me to look for property and land for sale in neighboring counties."

"Why?" he snaps.

What's your problem? I bite back the retort. The last thing I want right now is to fight with my brother.

"Like I already said once, I'm not really sure. All I was given was a set of maps, a blank spreadsheet to fill in, and some parameters around what to look for."

"But that's not your job."

"Just like marketing isn't your job but you stick your nose into it all the time." My smile is insincere at best.

"I'm the CEO. I have the right to stick my nose in anything I want." He crosses his arms over his chest and leans over to study the various maps.

"Sure. Yeah. Whatever. Why are you acting so weird?"

"I'm not acting any way. I just think it's crap that Holden is asking you to do his grunt work for something that obviously has nothing to do with the company."

"One, I have no idea if it's for him, and two, Holden didn't ask me. Audrey did," I say, just to be a pain in the ass.

Rhett snorts. "He's too important to ask you himself, I take it."

I stare at my brother and blink. *No, he's not too important. He's simply respecting my wishes and all but avoiding me today because of what happened this weekend.*

In fact, I haven't even spoken to him or made eye contact with him. When he walked in the office this morning, he called out a general "good morning" as he walked down the hall, cell to his ear, discussion in full swing. Since then, he's been behind closed doors doing whatever it is that Holden Knight does behind those closed doors.

Disappointed. Pleased. Confused. All three are the emotions that have swirled through me today. He's doing what I asked, so why does part of me think I deserve a decent greeting?

A greeting that would most likely have my resolve and my insides collapsing like a house of cards.

"Not too important. I'm assuming he's busy—like you are."

"So, you're looking for property you know nothing about for some reason that hasn't been explained. Got it," Rhett says sarcastically.

"Not everything has a grand scheme behind it," I say, but I had many of the same questions my brother does. "There could be a dozen reasons. A location for a new warehouse. A place to bring our outside manufacturing in-house. Who knows." All things I would do if I were running it. It would increase cost in the short term, but not having to pay the middleman markup would net a significant profit in the long run.

"Maybe he's doing something shady."

"Says the man who was going to do the same thing before Holden came into the picture. A new distribution center, was it? A run for city council to grease some palms to ensure it? I mean . . . c'mon, Rhett. What's good for the goose is good for the gander."

"Just weird is all."

"So is this situation on the whole, but I'm doing my best with it." I lean back in my chair and watch my brother as he shuffles through the maps on the table, taking note of the red circles I've placed around the locations of the properties I've found that meet the criteria given.

Rhett keeps studying the maps, way more engrossed in them than I expected him to be. If he's looking for a pattern, rhyme or reason, it's not there. I know because I've already looked.

The upside? Maybe while I'm doing this, I'll come across a place that's reasonable to rent or buy for the Sanctuary.

It's a long shot, but I'm still checking.

"You seem quite chummy with him," Rhett says.

"So doing my job is being chummy now? You're the one who made a deal with the devil. Not me," I say.

He snorts in response and then looks at me, our gazes holding while I do everything I can to seem normal. "Are you still happy with your decision to sell?" I ask.

"Happy isn't exactly the word I'd use. Resigned is probably a better one. For the company as a whole. For us as partial owners. For our family name."

I nod. That's the first time I've noted any kind of doubt from my brother. Or is it regret? Is it finally hitting him, finally breaking through that ginormous ego of his that he screwed over our family business somehow?

Or is he just bullshitting me to get sympathy since he's not getting the attention he's used to—in the office and in Westmore in general—with Holden now in the picture.

And just as quickly as the thought comes, as the notion of my brother's humility hits, it flies right out the door when he continues, "I did nothing wrong as the CEO. Chad did nothing wrong as the COO. Things happen sometimes. That's it and this is the best way to see the company through."

"Got it." Good to see the ego is still there.

"You could be a little less hostile." Hypocritical advice from the man who has no business giving it.

"Yes. I could. Just like you could be less of a prick. Telling people that I'm the reason for the company's current situation? I mean, *really*?"

He stutters in motion. *Ah, you didn't think I knew that you were saying that, now, did you?*

"For all you know, Holden may be your saving grace here," he says in response.

"What's that supposed to mean?"

"Well, once you and Chad married, you were going to have to step down here," he says, to which I stare at him dumbfounded.

"Chad and I, married?"

"Yeah. It would be a conflict of interest having a married couple in two of the top positions here. It wouldn't look good. That was the plan."

My laugh drips with sarcasm. "So nice to know you had a plan for me."

He flashes a condescending smile and then riffles through more pages on the desk. "You know me, I'm always looking out for your best interest."

"Prick," I mutter under my breath.

"C'mon, Row. Chad's an incredible guy. He's always treated you great. He's clearly in love with you. You wouldn't have to worry about our families getting along. And . . ."

"And what?"

"And I don't know. It just feels like the two of you were meant to be."

"That's comical."

"Is it so bad that you marry Chadwick and take whatever it is that Gran left you and start something of your own?"

Ah, so that's why you came in here. He's desperate to know what

Gran may or may not have left me since I've yet to say a word about it. My silence on the matter has to be killing him.

"Why would you say that?" I ask.

He shrugs, but the way he's fidgeting with the paper in his hands tells me he is in fact dying to know. "Just an assumption. I want the best for you. Chad's a good guy . . . and whatever with Gran."

Whatever with Gran?

I'm about to make his fishing expedition even more painful than it already is.

"I don't know what Gran left me yet," I lie.

"What do you mean? The will. She specifically says in there that she left you a private letter to explain what she left you."

"Huh."

"Stop bullshitting me. What did the letter say?"

I shrug. "Not sure."

"What do you mean you're not sure? C'mon, Row."

"I haven't opened it yet. I don't want to. Once I do, it means she's not here anymore."

"You can't seriously believe that, can you? You know she's not here. Open the damn letter."

I shrug again and only because I know it pisses him off. "I'll open her letter when I'm ready to open it. End of discussion."

Rhett stares at me dumbfounded—eyes wide, jaw lax, shock evident in his posture. "You're being fucking ridiculous." He shifts on his feet, impatience emanating from him.

"You see it your way. I see it mine." And if I'd put my head down and got back to work, I never would have caught the blood suddenly draining from his face. I glance down to the map that has his attention but it's too far away for me to see what it is. "What's wrong with you? You look like you've seen a ghost."

"I'm fine. Nothing's wrong. I don't know what you're talking about," he says and reshuffles the papers again before taking a quick step back like the table is lava. "It's stress. That's all. Stress'll do that to you."

"It will," Holden says from the doorway. We both turn to look his way, and I swear to god my stomach flips when our eyes meet. The connection is brief and meaningless followed by a quick nod before he waltzes farther into the room, but it does stupid things to my insides.

Things I don't want it to do.

Scratch that. Things I'm fine with it doing but that only serve to complicate a situation I spent the better part of the weekend telling myself I don't want to happen when I actually do.

"Knight," my brother says in a cursory greeting as Holden stops at the table and glances at the array of maps before looking back at him.

"Why're you stressed, Rhett? I thought I was here to take care of everything for you," Holden says, yet I hear a mocking undertone and wonder if Rhett does too.

"Land? Property? What's this all about? We didn't discuss anything about this."

"*We* don't have to discuss anything when it comes to what *I'm* doing. Only when it pertains to what *you're* doing." His flash of a smile is anything but warm.

There is a visual game of chicken that makes no sense to me as tension fills the room. Both are standing with their hands on the chair in front of them, both staring at each other across the table.

My brother blinks first.

"Isn't Rowan's time better spent doing things for TinSpirits than for you personally? I mean, if we're looking to turn things around and all, then maybe we should focus on the business and not your personal affairs."

"Exactly my thoughts. Just like your time is better spent here on-site and in the office than out playing eighteen holes with Chad. There can't be much you have to talk about that can't be discussed here." He knocks his knuckles on the table to emphasize his point. "And I'm pretty sure your sister can speak up for herself. You've never done so before, so why start now?"

I worry my bottom lip between my teeth, not exactly thrilled to be talked about like I'm not in the room.

"Just being a good big brother."

The last thing I need is these two fighting over me. "You guys—"

"You didn't answer my question though," Holden says. "You seem a little pale. Panicked. Not sure why a bunch of maps would do that to you. Or is it the numbers that just came in? I was a little surprised to see our margin had fallen again for last month. I think you really need to get Greatland and their pricing under control. Ironic considering they've been a recent topic of discussion."

"No, I didn't see the numbers," my brother says quietly.

"*Hmpf.* Seems Chad's holding out on you, then, and coming straight to me. Good to hear." A muscle ticks in Holden's jaw, his expression impassive. "But I can't have the CEO not in the loop. That doesn't fly with me. Guess that's another reason why you should be here and not out on the links. Right?" he asks.

"Chad sent them to me. I just haven't had time to go over them," Rhett says, and he's so full of shit. I know my brother and he's silently freaking out.

"Right. Yes." Holden knows he's lying too. "Well, since you and Porter seem to be buddy-buddy, I'll leave it up to you to address with him why costs rose and the product stayed the same. Doesn't compute, but I'm sure you'll get to the bottom of it. And if you don't . . ." He flashes a shark's smile. "Well, that would be a problem."

Rhett forces a swallow down his throat as he fidgets with the top of the chair. "Sure. Not a problem."

"Great. I'll want answers on that in a comprehensive breakdown by Friday."

"Uh-huh."

"Don't sound so enthused, Rhett." Holden chuckles. "This is the drawback to doing business with friends. It's hard not to pull punches when you have to see the bruises they leave on your off days at the country club."

Rhett's glare in response doesn't seem to faze Holden and so he continues telling my brother about what he expects in his breakdown of Greatland.

I look back and forth between the two, only to find myself staring at Holden's hands. Or rather, his forearms and his hands. The cuffs of his dress shirt are folded up to just below his elbows and the ceiling lights glint off the silver of his watch, but it's the corded muscles in his forearms and his large, capable hands that capture my attention.

Flashbacks hit me from the other night. Him standing between my thighs, his hand on his cock, and his forearms and biceps bulging as he stroked himself.

"Rowan?"

My name breaks through my thoughts and I find Holden looking at me with eyebrows raised and the slightest knowing smirk on his lips.

He knows exactly what I'm thinking about.

Shit.

"I'm sorry, what?" I give the slightest shake of my head and lie. "I was distracted by an email that just popped up on my computer. I apologize. Where were we?"

Holden's gaze holds mine and there's amusement in his eyes. "I asked if I should assume Audrey gave you the rundown of what I'm looking for?"

I nod. "Yes. I'm compiling the spreadsheets."

"With owners and contacts?" he asks.

"Yes. Many are LLCs who are using real estate brokers."

"If there is a property that looks worthwhile, we'll do a deep dive on the LLCs and their history. I don't like going into business or buying something substantial without knowing every deep, dark secret that might come to light later."

I stare at Holden and chuckle uncomfortably. "Should I be worried that you did the same to us? I promise my deep, dark secrets are rather benign."

"I know. I've seen them," he says and then laughs, but the thought lingers.

"Funny."

"I try." He flashes a smile that holds warmth for the first time since he walked into this room. Our eyes hold a beat too long before he turns to my brother. "Should I be worried about your secrets, Rhett?"

My brother chuckles, but there's a strain to it.

Here go the games again, and as if perfectly on cue to get me out of their uncomfortable tension, my cell rings. "I've got to take this," I say, holding up my phone and ducking out of the room without waiting for a response.

I welcome the distraction of a simple question from my new graphic designer and hesitate to go back into the conference room until they're both gone. It's hard enough to concentrate in this place lately, and it's even harder to do so when you're worried that your brother is going to pick up on some ridiculously subtle nuance that you slept with your soon-to-be boss.

So when the call comes in about an issue down in the warehouse, I know it's out of my realm, but I gladly go to take it.

A little fresh air and a quick walk across the grounds from the office building to our warehouse across the street will give me a break from all this testosterone.

I step into the elevator and seconds after I push the button for the ground floor, I hear, "Rothschild. Hold up."

I momentarily debate pushing the doors-open button but think better of it. Me. Holden. Alone in a small space like an elevator?

Not the best decision for my sanity.

But of course, just as the doors begin to shut, Holden slips between them. "You're not trying to avoid me, are you, Sunshine?"

I keep my back against the wall and don't turn to face him or even give him a welcoming vibe. "Nope. Not at all. Just heading down to the warehouse. Justin needed someone to sign off on something so I volunteered to go."

"I wasn't aware 'signing off' on warehouse things is part of your job description."

"Neither is looking for property to buy, but I'm doing it, right?"

Our eyes hold as the elevator begins to make its descent. I can't decipher what his are saying but when he reaches out to push the stop button on the elevator, it jolts. We're face-to-face, body to body.

I suck in a quick hiss of a breath. My body is already imagining leaning in and taking another taste of his lips. My mind is saying otherwise.

"Oh, I'm sorry. Excuse me," Holden says with a mischievous glint to his eyes. To his smile. To the tone of his voice. "I didn't mean to bump into you . . . but that's completely okay because us touching doesn't make you feel anything. Want anything. Resisting me is easy, right?"

"I can. It is," I say with a nod, trying to look anywhere but his eyes, and that's pretty hard when he's standing right in front of me.

"Right. Yes. That's why when I was talking to your brother you kept staring at my hands."

"No, I didn't."

"You were imagining my palms running over you, my fingers pushing into you, my tongue . . . doing tongue things to you."

"Tongue things?" My own tongue feels thick in my mouth despite my chuckle.

"Would you like me to elaborate? *Tongue things.* Like what mine plans on doing next time. Licking that sweet pussy of yours. Sucking those pink nipples. If you're more of a show-and-not-tell kind of girl, I can show you what I mean right here."

"No. Oh my god. You're insane." I push against his chest, but he doesn't budge and neither does the ache that's burning sweetly between my thighs.

Holden leans in and whispers in that deep tenor of his that has chills chasing over my skin, "Fear of getting caught heightens the intensity of orgasms."

"Good. Great. I don't want to know how you know that."

"You're sexy when you're flustered."

"Right now I don't want to be sexy, I just want . . ."

"*Me?*" He stands back and mock bows. "At your service."

I close my eyes for a beat and that's a mistake because when I do I see him standing like an Adonis at the foot of my bed with his chiseled abs and gorgeous body. I open them just as quickly as I shut them—hating myself for remembering so vividly.

I emit a frustrated huff. "I—"

"Go out with me. Tonight. Tomorrow. This weekend. I'm not picky."

His words stagger me, and I welcome the disruption to my salacious thoughts. "No. Absolutely not. I said this couldn't happen again."

"No, you said we couldn't sleep together again. You didn't say we couldn't go on a date again."

"A date would lead to sex."

"Correct. The date's a ruse to get you under me again. Or on top. I'm not picky." The grin he flashes is knee bending. "But I forgot. You can resist me. Easily."

"Look. We discussed this in detail, Knight."

"I love that you think calling me by my last name is going to make your panties less wet."

"This has nothing to do with my panties," I say. "And everything to do with what we talked about."

"Which part? The one where it's not against the law to be aroused at work?" he asks.

"How about the 'we can't talk about this at work' part."

"We're not talking about anything," he says and offers me a choirboy expression that is less than believable with his dark looks and dangerous grin.

"I beg to differ. We *are* at work."

He laughs. "Nope. We're between floors, Sunshine. Or we're more on the third floor than the fourth floor, so technically we're on Quest's property," he says of the company that rents the third and fourth floors of the building from us.

"If you think renters mean we still don't own the building, then I need to be seriously worried about your business acumen," I say while fervidly trying to deny every damn way my body reacts to his.

"And here I thought you were good with playing along." He

quirks a brow that has me looking down at his lips and then back up to his eyes. *"Don't you want to play with me, Sunshine?"*

"Seriously?" I can't help but laugh in exasperation. "You're . . ."

"I know I am," he says like it's a badge of honor. "So where were we?" He leans in, his breath at my ear, his hardened cock against my thigh, his arms caging me against the wall.

I clear my throat. My first thought is to avoid his gaze but then realize that will only let him know he's getting to me. So I meet him stare for stare. "We were talking about how *this* isn't happening."

He chuckles. *"This* is all I've thought about since Friday night. *You*. Christ, woman . . . you know how to make a man replay every single second. Over. And over. And . . ." He groans.

"Really?" I'm flattered. I'm aroused. I'm . . . this is *not* happening.

"My cock in my hand and you on my mind is *nowhere* near the real thing, but according to you, it's all I'm going to get, so I'll take it."

"You did not." *But didn't I do the same?*

"Would you like me to show you what I did as I thought of you?" He starts unbuckling his belt with one very skilled hand.

"No. My god. *No*."

He leans forward and tugs on my bottom lip with his teeth but doesn't touch me in any other way. And that's almost worse. Feeling the heat of his body but not touching it. Smelling the mint on his breath but not tasting it. I fight back an involuntary groan.

"What's wrong? I'm only following your rules."

"Rules?" I whisper.

"No touching. No dirty talk from office to office on the phone while everyone else thinks we're diligently working away at our desks. No foreplay beneath the desk despite the very naughty thoughts I had today of crawling beneath yours and licking you until you came. How hard would it be for you to remain silent? To not draw attention to yourself while I licked and sucked and fucked you with my tongue. Do you think you could be quiet? Do you think someone would figure it out? Hmm. Food for thought."

"I don't believe we discussed any of that." I try to sound unaffected, professional, but hell if my body isn't reacting to his words.

"Oh, so we can do all of the above then?"

"No," I bark out.

"Tell me. Did you think of me? Did you touch yourself as you did? Did you get mad at yourself for doing both?"

My pulse races wildly and it beats so loud I swear he can hear it.

Desperate and embarrassingly needy, I duck under his arm and slam my hand against the stop button so that the elevator starts again.

Holden's laugh rings out, and it takes only seconds before the car stops at the next floor. And when it opens, I don't care what floor it's on, I'm getting off.

No pun intended.

The car dings and I walk off as others walk on. I turn to face Holden, standing in the back of the elevator, his head above almost everyone else's and his eyes fixed on me.

Just as the doors begin to shut, I finally respond to him. "Yes. I did, in fact." I grin. "You were magnificent."

The last thing I see before the doors close is the flare of his nostrils and the widening of his eyes.

Jesus.

It's only been two days and that's how he greets me? Hungry. Flirty. Devastating.

How's it going to be after more days have passed?

THIRTY-ONE

Rowan

"You said yes. We were shocked and made bets that you still wouldn't show. So cheers to you actually coming out with us and socializing for a bit." Caroline lifts her glass of wine, as do Sloane and the fourth friend in our quartet, Victoria.

I level all three of them with a look before I join my glass to theirs. When I do, a cheer goes up that has me rolling my eyes.

"C'mon. I'm not that bad," I say. They all glance at each other and burst out laughing. "Well, maybe I am."

"Quick. Someone write that down," Caroline says loudly, motioning generally to the bar's crowd.

And it is crowded for a weeknight. Country music plays and the after-work crowd chatters animatedly. The line at the bar is a few people thick and there isn't an open seat at any of the tables.

"Excuse me, ladies," our waiter says.

"Yes?" Sloane asks.

"This round has been paid for," he says as we all glance at each other, confused. He sets fresh drinks in front of us and I look up, searching the crowd for Holden, half expecting him to be sitting at the bar, much like he was when I was on my date with Gregory.

But he's nowhere to be found. Just as I'm about to give up, I meet Chad's eyes. He smiles and tips his glass to me as my own smile falters.

"Compliments of that gentleman over there," he says, nodding in Chad's direction.

Everyone at the table turns as Chad approaches, grin wide, swagger on full display. "Ladies," he says and holds his hands up. "I have no intention of interrupting you, but I saw you here and wanted to help you celebrate whatever it is you're celebrating."

"We're not celebrating—"

"Yes, we are. We're celebrating Rowan having a new man," Caroline says, cutting me off.

I sputter, and my own expression probably matches Chad's. "There is no new man," I finally get out and roll my eyes. "Caroline has an overactive imagination." If I could reach her under the table, I'd kick her.

"Well. Okay. Um . . ." Chad looks crestfallen, and I hate the sight. "Enjoy your drinks."

"Chad. Wait." I rise from the table and jog the few feet toward him.

He stops and gives me a puppy-dog smile. "Have a good night."

"Don't be like that," I say. "She was joking. There's no new man. Life's too busy in general to have a relationship. You of all people know how crazy work is."

Why do I feel the need to fix things? To lie? To not hurt his feelings when me having a serious boyfriend might do the trick and stop him thinking we're going to get married someday.

"I know." He gives a nod, but his smile doesn't match his eyes. "I'm not giving up hope, Row. We make a good team at the office. We'd make an even better team outside of it."

I force a swallow over the guilt lumped in my throat. "Chad . . ." I sigh, wishing there was something I could say that would deter his interest without hurting his feelings.

"It's okay." He takes a step back. "No need to explain." Then he looks over my shoulder and waves to my friends. "Have a good time."

He walks off, and I return to my table with a stern look for Caroline. "Seriously?" I ask.

"What? You've let trusty Chad down seven ways from Sunday and he's still not getting the hint," she says.

"He's such a nice guy though," Victoria pipes in. "Kind and sweet and clearly head over heels for you."

My mind immediately thinks of a different man who is exactly the opposite. Calculating. Dominant. Arrogant.

"Who knows when it comes to Chad?" Sloane asks and I roll my eyes. "I said I'd never date or fall in love with Jeremy and now we're taking about what kind of engagement rings I like. Stranger things have happened." Her grin is huge, and I couldn't be happier for her.

But this is the last conversation I want to be having so I'm grateful when Caroline says, "So . . ." The mischief in her eyes has me on edge. "Talking about strange things . . ."

"What?" Victoria asks.

"Do you care to tell us about the bathroom of The Local last week?" Caroline asks, her eyes on mine and her eyebrows raised right along with the taunting corners of her mouth.

"I haven't been to The Local in . . . *oh*," Sloane says as she realizes Caroline is talking to me. "The bathroom, Row? *Really?*"

I put my hands up and laugh. "Nothing happened in any bathroom. I swear." I make the statement as my mind dizzies.

"Really? Because Gregory said one minute you were arguing with some guy who bought you a drink. The next you went to the bathroom. The same bathroom that he overheard a guest complain to the server about that a man and a woman were arguing in. And a short while later, you come out, sit for a few minutes, and then say you have to leave." She folds her arms over her chest. "The only reason I'll accept that you bailed on Greg was because Holden fucked you good and hard in the bathroom."

I almost spit out my wine. I think we all do.

"Um. Wow." *Oh Jesus. Who else did Gregory tell this to?*

"That's all you have to say for yourself?" Caroline asks. "Oh, did I mention the guy Gregory described? He sounded a lot like someone who looked like *Holden Knight*."

Shit. "Can we not say that so loud, please?" I ask and hold my hands up. "I plead the fifth."

"So it's true then?" Caroline lifts her brows.

"We were arguing," I confess, which gets a round of whoops from our table along with people looking our way.

"In the bathroom," Sloane states.

"Yes, in the bathroom."

"Men's or women's?" Victoria asks.

"Men's," I say.

Caroline just gives me a knowing smile. "So you were in the men's bathroom. Door locked. Arguing."

"Yes. It was—"

"Arguing with your tongues, no doubt," Victoria snorts.

When I look at my wineglass and don't respond, Sloane points a finger at me. "Aha. I knew it."

"It was—we were—" *What do I even say?*

"He's fucking hot," Caroline says and the other two nod emphatically.

"So . . ." I say.

"*So,* you should act on it." Sloane shrugs. "Well, more than I'm pretty sure you already have."

"Whatever you say here stays between us, you know," Victoria says. "Like it always has."

I look from Sloane to Victoria to Caroline, close my eyes, and sigh. "It just kind of *happened.*"

Why does it feel so good getting that off my shoulders?

I appreciate the fact that as much as the three of them want to gloat, they bite back their grins.

"Of course it did," Sloane says, keeping her focus on her wineglass as she twists her lips.

"We were arguing. He grabbed me and kissed me to shut me up. I fought against it. *Wholeheartedly.*"

"Even better," Victoria says.

"Make sure you add that 'wholeheartedly' in there so we know there was absolutely zero enjoyment on your part," Sloane says.

"Exactly," I deadpan.

"Angry kissing leads to hate fucking." Caroline mock shivers and I hold back on rolling my eyes. Clearly she and Holden should be best buds with their hate-kissing and hate-fucking thoughts. "It's just a given, and girl, *that* is the best, especially with a man who looks as dark and dangerous as he does."

Am I lying to my best friends? Of course. But honesty isn't something I'm ready for yet. Why? Because I haven't wrapped my brain around this myself.

The problem? When I'm not thinking about Holden or wanting him again, my stomach is twisted in knots. I'm confused. My head is messed up. I'm starting to feel valued by the one person who is trying to actively ruin my life. And possibly ruin it in more ways than one.

"You do realize the man is taking my company from me."

Sloane shrugs. "Rowan, darling?"

"He's the enemy," I assert . . . *and yet I still want him.*

"Exactly," Caroline says. "Ever heard the phrase 'sleeping with the enemy'?"

"We are *not* going to sleep together," I lie and avert my eyes. If this keeps up, I'm going to need another glass of wine.

"You want the man. He wants you. Why not?" Caroline asks.

"It's not that easy," I say.

"Actually, *it is*," Victoria says.

"Jesus, Rowan. Sleep with the man. Enjoy him," Caroline says. "If you so happen to get a leg up on Rhett while you're at it, so be it."

"So long as that leg up is because it's up on Holden's shoulders," Sloane says and snorts.

"True. So true," Caroline continues. "The leg up on Rhett isn't the reason you're doing it, so it's a moot point. Besides, Rhett wouldn't hesitate if the shoe were on the other foot."

"But you have to keep it on the down-low. No more scenes in bar bathrooms," Victoria says.

"And just make sure you part ways amicably," Sloane adds. "There's nothing worse than office tension with an ex. Knowing what the other looks like naked can either be super hot or completely devastating when it comes to an office spat."

"Wow. Your suggestion to sleep with him just keeps sounding better and better by the second," I say sarcastically and lift my glass of wine to our waiter, asking for another.

"The sex'll be worth it. I promise."

If they only knew how right they were . . .

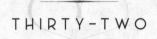

THIRTY-TWO

Rowan

The sex'll be worth it. I promise.

Caroline's words are on repeat in my mind as I head up my pathway with Winnie from her evening walk.

"Excuse me. Are you Miss Rothschild?"

I yelp at the man's voice walking out of the shadows on my porch. I immediately jump and start walking backward cautiously, glancing over my shoulder to see if any neighbors are out and about should I need help.

He must realize what I'm thinking because he puts his hands up, a package in one. "I'm just delivering something. A delivery man. I'm not here to hurt you."

I look up and down the block. Am I being served over something I have no idea about? People don't knock on doors at this time of night for nothing.

"Should I be worried if I am her?" I ask.

He laughs. "Only if you don't want this." He holds the package out to me. "This is for you."

I eye it and him cautiously. What he's offering most definitely does not look like legal documents.

"Oh. Thanks. I think." I take the package and make a show of holding it up to my ear. "No ticking. I guess that's a good sign."

"Bombs these days don't tick. So I wouldn't exactly base it on that," he teases.

"Gee. Thanks." I stare at him. "Do I need to sign something saying it was delivered?"

He smiles. "No. Not this time. It's a personal delivery."

I stare at him as he nods and jogs down my front path, leaving me to look at a box about six inches by six inches in size and wrapped in blue.

"What the hell is this, Win?" I ask her as we unlock the front door and go inside.

Within seconds, the sound of her lapping up water accompanies the sound of me tearing the paper off the box, curiosity owning me.

Inside the big box is a smaller box with a mini card on top. I open the card and stare at the words written there. "Time to change the dress." The five words float vaguely through my mind, registering but not in the way that I can place where they're from.

But when I open the next box, a black velvet case, to find a set of stunning sapphire pendant earrings inside, the context slams into me like a battering ram.

"And I'd opt for sapphires over rubies when it comes to you. They're powerful. Regal. Confident."
"They'd clash with my dress."
"Then change the dress."

"You son of a bitch," I murmur, then let out a chuckled sigh as I pick up one of the earrings and admire it. The sapphires are a deep blue, haloed by a row of diamonds that are small enough not to overpower the center stones. They're feminine with the perfect balance of sharpness and softness.

All I can do is shake my head. He can't seriously think I'll accept these, can he?

I place the earring back in its case and pick up my cell. Holden picks up on the second ring. There's a brief moment of background noise before it falls silent.

And then Holden answers with, "You haven't been talking to me."

"This is not the way to get me to talk to you."

"No? Because it seems to have worked." I can hear the hint of a smile in his tone.

"Holden, I can't accept these." I say the words, but my smile remains. He remembered. He thought of me. He sent me something to make a statement.

"What do you mean by 'these'?"

I roll my eyes. "The sapphires."

"The sapphires? There were just random sapphires floating around in a box that was delivered to your house?"

"You know what I mean. The earrings."

"You don't like them?"

Is that the slightest tinge of hurt in his voice? And why is my reaction to that sound in his voice so very different from when I hear it in Chad's?

"I didn't say that. They're stunning in every sense of the word, but I can't accept them."

"There is no accepting, Rowan. They just are. I told you that the first night we met."

"Things were different then."

"No, they weren't."

I pinch the bridge of my nose and lean against the back of my couch. "You can't send something like this to me. I'm not a whore who needs to be paid. I'm—"

"I know you didn't just say that to me."

"What am I supposed to think? What happened, happened—"

"You mean the sex part."

I sigh. "Yes, the sex part."

"How quickly you forget. Should I show you again—"

"Holden. I'm trying to be serious here. Think of how this would look to someone on the outside."

"When are you going to understand that I don't care about how things look to anyone? And for the record, I've had them for a month."

"You're so full of shit."

"Would you like to see the receipt? The date's on there. I can screenshot it for you, if you'd like."

I don't even know what to say to him. He's making no sense. These earrings make no sense.

"This is not the way to win a date with me."

"No?"

"No."

"That's okay because I don't want a date with you."

"You did the other day." The elevator day. The moments that live rent free in my head.

"And now I don't. *I'm fickle like that.*"

My laugh is a chortle of disbelief. This man is . . . exasperating. Amusing. Unpredictable. Consuming. "Why would you buy these for someone you barely even know?" I ask.

"Barely know?" His chuckle is a deep rumble. "I'm pretty sure I know more about you than most."

"That's not what I mean." I huff in frustration. "I mean—"

"For the same reason I'm buying TinSpirits. *Because I want to.*"

This conversation is getting nowhere. I'll find a way to give them back to him. To return them.

"What does your note mean? 'Maybe it's time to change the dress'?" I ask the question but I'm pretty sure I already know.

"That's for you to figure out."

Time to step into a new role.

Time to agree to partner up with him.

Time to be the woman I am to him to everyone freaking else.

"I can't accept these," I repeat for what feels like the tenth time.

"You can and you will."

"No, it's not right. It feels dirty."

"I thought you liked dirty."

"You're not playing fair."

"I never do, and Rowan, don't get any ideas about how to give them back to me. If I find them in my desk somewhere, if you somehow become a mind reader and figure out where I bought them to return them, *if, if, if* . . . then I'll give them back to you at the Monday morning managers meeting in front of everyone. That sure as shit would cause a lot of rumors to fly."

"You wouldn't dare."

His laugh says he'd do exactly that. "Now accept them like a good girl, Rowan, and say thank you."

I refuse to obey him this time. To do what he says. And as much as I should thank him, as much as the manners ingrained in me know that I should, I don't out of principle.

Silence smothers the line, a battle of wills waging between us.

"Sometimes I do nice things." Holden's voice is low. Even. Mesmerizing. "It's a rarity so take it for what it is. A gift. A reminder that some people look at you and see strength. Power. A force to be reckoned with. Enjoy the rest of your night."

The call ends on those poignant words. Words that replay in my mind over and over as I stare at sparkling diamonds and sapphires.

How did this happen?

How did I begin to like Holden Knight—well, more than like him—when every single part of me should hate him?

How did each interaction—the banter, the verbal sparring, the professional discussions, the dirty talking—build a bridge of mutual respect? The attraction was there from that first night. There was no mistaking it then or now. But now, it's fueled by a desire of knowing what his kiss tastes like. What his hands feel like. The type of lover he is.

I groan in frustration, making Winnie angle her head to the side and stare at me.

I don't catch feelings for people. I don't like to. I don't want to. I'm too damn busy and have too many things to accomplish before deciding that it's okay to start focusing on someone else. To prioritize another person.

We haven't even been on a date yet, and I don't want to. That's just a setup for a fall over a cliff.

We have office banter. We have bathroom kisses. We have diner conversations over milkshakes. We have elevator seductions.

That's it.

That's all.

Yet . . . it feels like Holden is suddenly everywhere in my life. My office, my gym, my thoughts, my space. And even with all of that, I still like *him,* a man who knows way too much about me and doesn't give much away about himself.

Sleeping with the enemy.

Isn't that what my friends called it earlier?

With a shake of my head, I walk over to the earrings, snap the box shut, and make the decision to indulge in a bit more wine.

It's not every day I throw caution to the wind and contemplate going for it.

I raise my glass to nobody.

Here's to having fun.

To some good sex with a wickedly handsome man.

To jumping feetfirst into the gray.

Nothing less.

Nothing more.

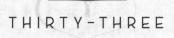

THIRTY-THREE

I stare at the expanse of land. Tall grass stretches for as far as the eye can see while clumps of trees dot it in several locations.

"You're taking care of yourself then?" my mom asks, her voice booming around me on the car Bluetooth, pulling my back to the present.

"Of course I am. Everything is fine."

"No, it's not," she says. "You've been avoiding my calls. That's how I know."

"I haven't been avoiding them, I've just been busy."

"I still don't understand why you up and decided to buy a company there, of all places."

I give a nod she can't see. Her knowledge of my plans is limited, as I prefer it to be until all is said and done. "You know me. Nothing I do makes sense until it does."

"I'm not your employee nor your corporate enemy, Hold." She laughs it off, but I can tell it bugs her that I've been so vague. She didn't want me coming back here. She didn't want me reopening old wounds. "It's not like you have to keep secrets from me."

"Is it hot there?"

Her laugh, deep and rich, comes through the line. To this day the sound of it still makes me stop and listen. It had vanished for so long after *everything* that it was almost like she'd forgotten how to use it.

But she didn't.

And as she warmed up to using it again, to living again, I grew cold inside. Cold with a promise I'm now here to follow through with.

"It has been warm, yes. I'm your mother. Do you think I don't know when you're changing the subject?"

"That's why I wasn't being subtle."

"Yes is the answer to your question. It's gotten considerably warmer. I've had to put shade over some of my roses to protect them from getting burned. Tank won't stay out of the damn pool and his fur keeps clogging up the skimmer." She acts annoyed but I can hear the love in her voice.

"And Graham is good?" I ask of her husband. A good guy all around who treats her how she deserves to be treated and makes her smile even more.

"He's wonderful. He's at the museum today. A lot of field trips before school gets out." She chuckles. "Such is the life of a volunteer art docent, right?"

"Too many kids," I mutter.

"Says the man who was the best big brother in the world." Her voice grows softer with each word, and when the entire sentence is out, we both fall silent as memories collide with the pain that's buried just below the surface.

I clear my throat in response and focus on the hummingbird that's hovering near the hood of my SUV.

"Have you been to see him yet?"

I close my eyes for a beat and try to find my voice. "Not yet. I've driven past numerous times, but it's almost easier to keep going than to stop."

"You'll go when the time is right. If you want to go at all. It's also okay not to."

"I know. I just . . . I don't know."

It's not like I don't know that Mason is buried beneath the slab of stone. It's not like I've ignored it for all these years and I'm just realizing he's dead. But there's something about being back here as an adult, as a man who has accomplished everything but still failed at keeping him safe, that makes it harder than hell to see him like that.

To know that one decision, one exception to the rule, one self-ish moment, changed our lives forever.

For the worse.

And no matter how much I accomplish or how much money I have, nothing will ever bring him back.

There are no amends to be made.

No second chances.

There's just fate's cruel hand and a guilt that has rested on my shoulders for what feels like a lifetime.

"Being back there was bound to churn stuff up, honey. I just wish I was there to help you."

"Thanks. I'm fine. Really."

"Mm-hmm," she murmurs in that way of hers that tells me she doesn't exactly believe me. "You're always *fine*, Hold. It's okay not to be."

"Yep." I run a hand through my hair. "Look, I have to go. A meeting."

"Of course. There's always a meeting when things get too real."

"Mmm. I know. It's easier that way."

"To avoid talking about it? Yes. But . . . at some point, you have to forgive yourself."

"Gotta go," I say with a laugh that follows. A laugh she can see through.

Her silence tells me she knows I'm lying. "Take care of your-self."

"Always. Love you."

"Love you too."

My sigh is heavy as the call ends and silence smothers the car once again. The million things I have to do are forgotten for a bit as I relive memories and reapply the guilt that has clung to me like superglue my entire life.

The guilt that will follow me to the grave.

I jump when the truck pulls up beside me sometime later, scattering the ghosts in the car back into their hiding places.

It took a little longer than I thought for him to show. From the reports I've gotten, he's being paid for every approach of prospective buyers he sees sitting out here.

I glance over as the older gentleman gets out of his truck. His well-worn cowboy hat sits high on his forehead, revealing a mop of shaggy white hair that's tinged yellow. His nose and cheeks are reddened by rosacea, but his blue eyes are wide and his grin is sincere as he tips his hat at me and waits for me to roll down my window.

I do just that. And the minute it's down, he steps closer. "Can I help you with something?" he asks, his big belly leading the way and his eyes taking in my Rolex, my luxury SUV, and judging.

"Tell me about the land for sale."

"WillowBend is what we call it. I'm just the neighbor giving a helping hand to its owner trying to sell. I can call the real estate agent and set up a meeting for you, if you'd like."

"No need." I climb out of my car and shut the door. His eyes roam over my dress shirt and slacks. They say he's not sure what brand they are, but he knows they're expensive. "They'll try to sell me and talk in fancy terms I don't understand. Major turnoff."

"Yes. I know. I get it. Same thing happens to me. The owners . . . I could call them direct for you if you'd like."

"Really? What a kind neighbor you are. I sure hope you're getting some kind of commission for your good deeds."

He chokes out a cough. "No commission." His smile is quick and masks the lie.

"No? But if they can sell this land then your land goes up in value, no doubt."

He twists his lips as he stares at me, realizing I won't buy the bullshit he's selling. "Something like that." He looks out toward the land and then back to me. "You looking to buy property?"

I follow his gaze and shrug. "It depends on the property."

"What about this one here?"

I make a noncommittal sound. "Not sure. It's a nice piece, just curious why it hasn't sold."

His eyelids flutter as he nods. "Not sure either, but I know they're eager to offload it."

"Hm. I'll keep that in mind. I heard rumors that there are problems here with the land."

"Who would say such a thing? Lived here my whole life. Nothing wrong here," he says.

"Sure would be devastating to be suckered into buying a piece of land like this thinking you're going to make a pretty penny developing it and reselling it . . . only to realize you can't."

"I don't see no reason why you wouldn't be able to develop and resell. Not sure what you're talking about."

"Methane is what I'm talking about." I look for a reaction. His eyes widen momentarily. His nostrils flare. "High levels of it. So much so that once you churn this soil up with excavators to, say . . . develop it—cut it up into lots to resell to a developer and turn a quick buck—you're looking at toxic levels. So toxic that the cost to mitigate it with soil barriers and such would price you right out of the resale market."

He looks at me from beneath the brim of his hat, eyes narrowing. "That's a downright lie. Ain't no reports say nothing of the sort." But his gaze says he knows differently. *Good.* That means Bob is doing his job properly. Letting everyone know this land is shit. That the owners are selling damaged goods.

At least there's that.

"Good to know. Hmm. Wonder why I heard that, then?"

"Land is a cutthroat business in these parts," he mutters the line I know to be bullshit. "Lies are a part of it."

"Hmm. I'll keep that in mind."

"You mind telling me who gave you that load of crap? Gotta get that info over to the owners. Let them know so they can take care of it."

I offer a loaded smile. "Don't remember." I shrug and lie, "I was in a bar. People were talking. Kind of overheard it."

"Christ," he mutters before pasting another smile on his lips. "You sure you don't want me to call them owners for you? Set up a meeting so they can tell you different?"

"No, thanks. I can find their number if I need them," I say as I climb into my SUV. "Thanks for your time."

He eyes me, his curiosity piqued now. "I didn't catch your name."

Exactly.

"I didn't give one."

I start the car, roll the window up, and head back where I came from without another word.

How long before the owners of WillowBend LLC, a Delaware corporation with confidential owners, get a phone call from their neighbor letting them know of my little visit? Of some random stranger talking about how the land is tainted? About how they're fucking screwed?

Pressure will either turn you into dust or a diamond.

I know which one I'm rooting for.

My phone buzzes with a text and when I glance over at it, I almost run my car off the road. By the time I pull over to the side, I've properly processed the text. Or at least my cock has as it hardens in my pants.

My grin is victorious.

> Rowan: Leather or lace? Preference?

> Me: I thought you said no sexting

> Rowan: I did

> Me: And yet you're texting me and I know it's not about what material I want for the curtains in my office

> Rowan: You mean MY office

> Me: I don't care so long as I'm fucking you on its
> desk.

> Rowan: Promise?

Fucking hell. I check my text again and try not to question her sudden about-face.

Yes. It really says that.

I groan as I adjust myself, fantasies flying through my head. The ones I've had more times than I care to count will soon become a reality.

> Me: Promise. Looks like I might need you to stay
> after hours, Miss Rothschild. There are a few things
> we need to go over.

Like my desk.

Like my knee.

Like straddling my lap.

THIRTY-FOUR

Rowan

No.

Just fucking no.

Tears threaten. Burn behind my eyes and in my throat.

I don't bother to knock. I simply barge into Holden's office without warning and slam the door at my back. And, of course, he's sitting behind his desk with a broad grin on his face and an arrogant glint in his eyes.

"How dare you?"

"How dare I what?" He chuckles, dismissing my anger. "Take too long to get back here? Sunshine, if you were that desperate for me we could have met offsite and—"

My laugh sounds on the verge of hysterical. "This was all a game to you, wasn't it? Occupy my time, my head, my bed," I whisper yell, "to distract me while you were professionally fucking me over. Congrats, it worked. You just played me. Lesson learned. I won't make the mistake again." I can't stand still. I move, pace, too restless, too angry to do anything else.

"Rowan. What are you—"

"Whatever we had is done. Over. Fucking finished."

"Enough." His voice thunders around the space but falls dead on my ears.

"My whole department?" I shriek. "Every single one of them?"

It's the first time Holden's expression falters as he rises from his seat and moves across the room to me. "I like a riddle as much as the next guy, but you've got to give better clues because I'm sitting here thinking I'm going to get laid one minute and now I'm fucking lost."

"Laid? After the backhanded shit you just pulled?"

He reaches out to put his hands on my biceps, but I immediately jerk my arms from his grasp. "Don't touch me." I glare, my chest heaving and heart hurting. "Just when I started to really like you. Just when I thought you were a decent human being—"

"The two aren't mutually exclusive."

"Go to hell."

"Watch your step, Rowan."

"Watch my step? You're the one who sabotaged my long-term graphic designer. You're the one who just fired the four people in my department. You're the one—"

"The one who has *no fucking clue* what you're talking about."

For the first time his words register through my anger. His lost expression finishes selling the point.

"Rowan." The force with which he says my name breaks through my haze of fury. "Start from the beginning. Explain. Now."

"I came back from a meeting to find my department empty. Not just empty but desks packed up, personal belongings taken, employees gone. Like, never coming back, *gone.*"

The disbelief is still fresh and shocking. The high I was riding after our sexy text exchange, then my very productive meeting offsite vanished when I walked in and was blindsided by the news. The emptiness.

"*What?*" he all but shouts.

"Don't act so fucking shocked. According to Alicia, she said Rhett's explanation was that orders came from the top. That we were making cuts and my department was the first to get hit." I glare at him, my arms crossed over my chest, and my stomach twisted in knots.

Marjorie is eight months pregnant. Michele works her ass off all day to run home and take care of her sick mother. Ralph just bought a house. They all need their paychecks and benefits. They all did a phenomenal job.

Holden stands there with the muscle pulsing in his jaw and his teeth gritting. His eyes flash dangerously dark, and his tone, when he speaks, has me drawing back. "And you believe Alicia?" he asks. "You think I'd go back on my word from that first meeting when I said the day-to-day staff is safe?"

"I don't know what to think anymore," I whisper.

"I had nothing to do with this," he states.

I study him and worry if I've convinced myself Holden Knight is the man I want him to be and not the man he really is. That I'm jaded by the good sex and softening feelings toward him.

I want to believe him.

I'm scared to.

"You don't believe me, do you?" he asks as he moves back to his desk and hits the intercom.

"You're back," Audrey says through the speaker.

"Only been here a few minutes. We had four employees let go today in error. Can you get with HR and let me know why they were let go and by whom?"

"Mr. Rothschild let them go. His reasoning was a downsizing of the marketing department," she says as the dormant knife in my back twists.

"Son of a bitch." Holden's hands curl into fists. "Audrey?"

"Yes?"

"Have HR call them back. Tell them there was a mistake made and we understand if they'd like to not return, but that we'd love to have them as they are valued employees. That for their troubles, we'd like to offer them a signing bonus with an employment contract."

"Okay."

"Please have legal then draw up some kind of agreement that by taking the bonus it clears us of any pain and suffering, etcetera, etcetera, lawsuit."

"Will do. Anything else?"

"Is Mr. Rothschild still in the building?"

"I believe so."

The smile he gives the phone is chilling. "Let him know not to go anywhere. That I need to speak with him. I'll come to him when I'm ready."

"Of course."

He pushes the button to end the call and his low rumble of a chuckle fills the room. If I didn't know him any better than I do, the sound would be a warning alarm to steer clear.

He stares at the pen in his hand for way too long before lifting his eyes to meet mine. "Believe me now?"

We stand feet apart, staring at each other as my heart decelerates, and my head acknowledges what is the right next step to take.

"What is it you want from me?" I ask.

A purely male expression fleets over his face and in his eyes. "That's a very open-ended question. Care to narrow it down for me because I can answer that in a myriad of ways."

I swallow and draw in a deep breath, hating that his comment causes nerves to rattle around inside of me. He's laid the offer to work with him out there for me, he's teased me with it, and he just protected my staff . . . there is more to his offer to team up with him than meets the eye, and I'm walking on broken glass trying to figure out what it is.

Time to just go for it, right?

"Obviously you're a smart businessman—"

"Watch it. In case you didn't realize it, you just complimented me." A crooked grin lights up the darkness his call to Audrey caused.

"I'm asking what it is you want, Holden. Why do you want me to work with you?"

His nod is slow and measured, the calculating expression of Holden Knight reappearing. "Because while I don't think you're ready to run this place, I think you want to learn how. And because . . ."

"And because you want to stick it to my brother. Right? You want to put value in the one thing that he hasn't. Me."

"The face of the company. And I'm beginning to think the underused brains too." His voice is quiet, reserved, when I would expect it to be more triumphant.

"You want to use me to get under his skin. That's part of this, right?" I ask, everything tumbling together to make sense all of a sudden.

"Correct."

I release the breath I was holding, my assumption confirmed. "You don't like him and yet you're still buying the company and letting him be CEO."

"I believe I said that management were the only ones in jeopardy. That means everyone. You. Chad. Rhett. The others. So Rhett's status remains to be seen."

"Okay." I move to the window to look out to the warehouses across the street. To my family's legacy. To the dream I still hold. I make the next statement not 100 percent sure what I'm agreeing to, but knowing I trust the man standing in front of me way more than the man a few offices down who I share a last name with. Both options are harrowing, but he's the only one of the two here who it seems hasn't tried to sabotage me. "Fine. Yes. I'll work with you."

Guilt hits me instantly. I'm aligning myself with the enemy—going against my family. But I shove down the feelings to process at another time.

Everyone in my family seems to be looking out for themselves. Isn't it time I do the same?

Then again, maybe this is why I haven't before—I have a conscience, when clearly they don't.

If I expected Holden to gloat, I'm more than happy that he doesn't. He's silent and when I turn to look at him, his eyes lock on mine and he gives a stoic nod, almost as if he respects how difficult this decision was for me.

"This has nothing to do with . . . what happened between us."

With what's happening between us. The words and thoughts are hard to get out. I don't like blurred lines. I like clear-cut ones. Ones with definition and set consequences.

"I never assumed it did, Rowan."

"Your marketing campaign. The new idea? That's something I've been trying to get Rhett to agree to for the past year. It's a good idea. A necessary shift."

"I'm glad we're on the same page."

"I'll start on that, *and* I'll bring you the suppliers you want," I say, almost feeling like I have to prove to him that I am ready to run this place. That I'm so much more than the marketing department. "Three for each product. We'll diversify so that we have a leg to stand on when it comes to bargaining."

He lifts his eyebrows and murmurs, "Okay."

"It's the best business decision, and if no one else is going to step up to the plate to do it, I will. I don't have ties that I'll sever by looking outside the country club members," I ramble, suddenly nervous.

"Why?"

"To prove to you I can."

"I wouldn't have asked you if I didn't think you could. But why now? Because of what Rhett did? Because . . . ?"

"Because of you." The words aren't easy for me to say, but they're true. His actions with my employees, his suggestions as far as our suppliers, the way he sees through Rhett's bullshit, dare I say, I've come to trust him? "I've put my faith in my family for so long and I net nothing in return. *It's time for me to change the dress.*"

He gives the subtlest of nods. His lack of reaction is frustrating at best, but then again, what is he supposed to say?

"This—me agreeing to work with you instead of against you—"

His *tsk* cuts me off. "I wasn't born yesterday, Sunshine. You may be working with me, but I know you're going to fight this right up until the ink dries."

"So?" I raise my eyebrows in challenge.

"I'd expect nothing less."

"Good. Now let's talk about what I get in return."

A slow smile crawls across his lips. "You act like you're in a position to negotiate."

"I am."

"Oh really?" He leans his ass against the back credenza of his desk, crosses his arms over his chest, and studies me with an intensity that has both my adrenaline and pulse racing.

"There's always room for negotiations."

"And what is it that we're negotiating, because I have plenty of ideas that come to mind." His eyes scrape over the curves of my body before coming back to mine.

"A board seat."

"What about it?"

"You asked me to work with you. I've accepted that offer because we both know I'm a valuable asset for you. Both in my knowledge of the company and the trust that the employees have in me."

"A seat isn't going to give you what you want. Your one vote won't allow you to overpower your brother's, dad's, and Chad's votes all pooled together."

"Correct, but I'll have a voice there for the first time, and it's more than I've ever had."

"It still doesn't change the amount of power you have."

"I'm well aware of that. I have my reasons." The seat he gives me and the seat my gran is giving me mean two votes. My persuasion skills are on point. If I were to convince Holden and Chad to vote with me—and maybe sway a few others with the dirt Gran left me to use—I could manage to get the things for the company it needs.

It's a long shot but it's the best shot I've ever had, and that is everything.

"I want it written in the parameters of your purchase. A seat that is irrevocable."

"The terms of the purchase are set already."

"Then un-*set* them," I counter.

"A seat is enough of a dig for you? That seems so very un-Rothschild of you."

"I'll take a percentage of ownership too."

He coughs out a laugh. "Give a girl an inch—"

"Bet your ass I'm going to take a mile," I say. "So?"

"You're asking me to give up some of my ownership?" He tilts his head to the side and studies me, his finger rubbing back and forth over his lips.

"I am." He'll never give it to me. Never.

"One percent."

"One percent?" I ask, startled that he's even contemplating it.

"Yes. It's all I can part with or majority numbers get tricky, and I like mine clear fucking cut."

"I'll pay for the percentage. For the ownership."

He waves a hand dismissively. "Think of it as an investment in this company."

"Also known as an extra twist of the knife in my brother's back."

He toggles his head from side to side as if he's contemplating it. "You can look at it that way, yes."

My heart races and my head spins. I own a minute percentage of the family company. Rhett owns the majority, our shareholders hold a bit, and the family trust owns the rest. The trust that I get disbursements from, but that Rhett otherwise manages. I get my paycheck, I get my trust checks, but Rhett holds so much more in his hands.

Until now.

Until Holden.

I'll have my small existing portion, another 1 percent from Holden, and then Gran's percentage of ownership.

Holy shit.

I'll now have so much more than a leg to stand on.

Get your head on straight. Think about this without emotion attached. What are the next steps? How do you protect this deal?

"I prefer to pay for my ownership. I'll figure out how," I say, thinking of Gran's inheritance, "but I'll pay for what is mine."

He nods. "We'll talk about it when we get there."

I swallow nervously. "You'll have to rewrite the parameters of the deal to include this."

"I think I know what to do, Rowan." He winks and it eases everything a bit. "But I suggest we present these changes at the last minute. Rhett'll be eager to seal the deal then and might not bat an eye at the new parameters. It'll be easier for me to trade it out with something else to soften the blow."

"I want to see the new paperwork when it's drawn up."

"Of course you would."

"That's not a problem, I presume?"

"Not a problem at all."

I walk toward him and hold out my hand. "I'm trusting you at your word, Holden Knight. That's not the easiest thing for me."

He takes my hand, and my body reacts viscerally to his touch. The flare of his nostrils says his does too. "Trust isn't easy, is it? I don't take it lightly that you're putting yours in me."

A knock on Holden's office door startles us both and has us jerking our hands back as if Audrey can't already see us through the glass wall of his office.

He motions for her to come in.

"Sorry for the interruption," she says, "but Rowan, your four o'clock is here. They were shown to conference room A and told you'll be with them momentarily."

"Thank you," I say.

She offers me a courteous smile and then looks to Holden. "The phone calls have been made and Rhett's on standby to talk to you."

"Thanks." He checks his watch. "I'll wait a bit yet. He deserves to sweat it out some."

THIRTY-FIVE

Holden

"I figured if she has so much free time she can look at property for you like she's your personal assistant, then clearly her workload is light enough that she could offload some salaries."

"And that was your decision to make?" I ask nonchalantly as I stare at the fucking prick. Ever since I walked into his office—or rather his *new* office—he's sat there with a smarmy look on his face and a fuck-you lift to his chin.

"As the CEO of the company, yes, it was."

"Keep making moves like that and you won't be one for much longer."

Rhett chuckles, clearly not taking me seriously. "Technically you don't own shit yet, Holden, so I'm pretty sure I can do as I please."

"Technically you're wrong, considering our letter of intent is a binding agreement, but we'll let that slide." I shove my hands in my pockets and walk to the other side of the room, staring out at the facility below where our employees are coming and going. "Being drunk on power can be a dangerous thing."

"Whatever. You live in that zone so who are you to fucking lecture me?"

Clank. Click. Clank.

The sound jolts me to the past. To fifteen years ago and the last place I saw that goddamn lighter.

I clench my jaw and turn to face him as he flips open the lighter again, clicks the flame, and then snaps his wrist so the lid closes and extinguishes the light.

Forcing myself to look at anything but that fucking reminder, I meet his eyes. "I can lecture whoever the fuck I want."

"The question is, what are your plans for this place, because nowhere in our discussion did you talk about buying property and moving the company."

"Never said I was going to."

That property thing really got to you, didn't it? Don't want your sister to start researching the LLCs and find your name sitting as the president of one? You don't want her questioning how exactly you got the money to do that, do you? Questions are a dangerous thing when you have something to hide.

"Is this about building our own distribution center, then? I know that was part of the discussions."

It was? I don't quite remember that but go ahead, Rhett, shift the gears so I chase another lead instead.

"What about it?" The less I say, the better. Let Rhett talk himself into whatever corner he's going to talk himself into.

"I already have things figured for that."

"You do?" *He's going to fucking try to sell me the WillowBend land, isn't he?*

"Yep." He nods emphatically, as if he sees the light here. "We were scouting places. Properties. If we build a distribution center—our own—we can cut costs and produce a quicker finished product."

"So why have you waited to do this till now?"

"Red tape. A shit ton of red tape. That's why I'm running for city council. To help cut through it and get shit pushed through." He smirks. "We have the perfect place picked out to buy too."

"You do?" I say, face in mock surprise. "Planned and prepared. Where is this property? Maybe I should take a look at it. Pull the trigger and get it purchased." God, this is fun.

"That's a great idea. Chad and I have it all figured out. We pay some guys to cause some problems—maybe even spread some rumors about the property. Devalue it—but it's not like it can get much lower. Once I'm on the council, I'll pull some strings and get the permits approved to raze the whole fucking place to the ground so we can build new. The place is a fucking eyesore. The town will be so goddamn grateful to us for taking out the trash for them."

Build new? Raze what to the ground? I purse my lips and narrow my eyes, trying to figure out how he's going to do that to barren land. "It's a solid plan," I say, confused but curious. He's not talking about WillowBend, is he? "Where is this you're talking about?"

"The dregs of the earth. It's a place across the river. You might not know it yet. Lucky you."

Dread tickles at the base of my spine.

"Try me."

"Fairmont," Rhett says, smug smile in place, oblivious to the fury that just ignited in me.

But I hold it in.

I yank it back.

My Adam's apple bobs, and I have to force my fingers to relax out of my fists, one by one.

"Huh." I play it off. Or try to.

"You can't miss it. It's over the Roosevelt Bridge. It's where losers go to lose. Trust me. Everyone I've ever known from there is just . . . trash."

Steady, Knight.

"So buy the land, push shit through the council with some favors in return, raze it to the ground, and build a distribution center there?" I ask and he nods. "What about the people who will be displaced?"

"Why would we fucking care? The place is a shithole. I'd be doing them all a favor by demolishing their shanties." *Clank. Click. Clank.* "Besides, we can drown out their moaning by saying we're delivering jobs to the community like we're their saviors."

"They can't work a job if they can no longer live there," I say.

"Not our fucking problem, is it? Besides, we're the ones cleaning shit up for the rest of us, right?" His chuckle burns a hole in my gut and fires every goddamn vein in my body.

Over my dead body.

"You're speechless," Rhett teases. "See? I have good ideas."

Hell the fuck no.

"Hmm. There are possibilities there," I murmur, each word like acid on my tongue.

"We should brainstorm it all out—"

"What's going on here?" Chad walks in without asking. Of course the fucking prick does.

It's going to take everything I fucking have to rein in my anger. To control my disgust. To not show my fucking cards when all I want to do is grab their throats and pin them to the fucking wall with my hands until they know what it feels like to be gasping for their last breath of air.

You've practiced for this moment, Holden.

Keep your shit together. You can rage later.

I meet Chad's inquisitive eyes and then look over at Rhett.

Breathe.

Tweedledee and Tweedledum.

Smile.

Pretend.

"What's going on here? Is that what you asked? Saw me in here and had to run in to play the protector?" I ask.

Chad's eyes narrow. "Why would I have to play protector?"

"Because I was just telling Rhett that I've hired back the people he erroneously fired today. And that the signing bonuses I've offered them and increase in salaries we'll be giving them to compensate for their distress—and so they don't sue our asses for wrongful termination—will be coming out of your two salaries."

"What?" Rhett barks out as I rise from my seat.

"Only seems fair to me." I shrug and have so much joy in pissing them off.

"You can't do that," Chad says. "That's absolute bullshit."

I whip around and show them a fucking tenth of the rage I have inside of me. "Fucking watch me."

THIRTY-SIX

Holden

I stew over the conversation for the next few hours. Over Rhett's arrogance. Over the fact that every time I think of Rowan's employees, I see my mom struggling to make ends meet and remember the cruelty some of her employers showed her. Over his plan to fuck over the invisible members of society—the kind of person I used to be—just so he can turn a quicker buck.

The fucking prick.

But as employees shout out their good nights one by one, as the elevator dings time and again, my mind steers back to Rowan.

To her text earlier.

To how goddamn sexy she was as she stood there and negotiated with me in that tight fucking sweater.

To the handshake we shared that's going to complicate matters more than I'd like but now might take so much more pleasure in—because fuck Rhett.

To the goddamn things I've been craving to do to that body of hers.

My phone vibrates and when I see Rowan's name I groan. She better not be blowing me off. Unless of course the blowing me off has to do with her being on her knees with her lips wrapped around my cock.

"Rowan."

"The office is empty. The lock on the elevator doors has been activated with the master key. The cameras have been turned off."

My cock twitches as I stand from my desk. "Someone's trying to earn the merit badge for preparedness tonight."

"Someone has to take control."

"Is that what this is called? You taking control?"

Her laugh is deep and throaty. "It's called *come* and find me."

Most definitely.

"Care to give me a hint?"

"I'm somewhere where you can sit and eat."

"*My face.*"

Another laugh that has my balls drawing up. "Sounds promising," she murmurs and then the line goes dead.

I'm out of the office and walking down the hall, hands already undoing the buttons on my shirt cuffs as I go. The lunchroom is empty, and I stand there staring at the beige wonderland of tables and chairs.

Where else do people eat in this place?

The outdoor patio. I'm on the move to the other side of the floor and push open the doors. No one is there, but I do find a rather sexy pair of black leather panties draped across the middle of the table.

The vision of her wearing nothing but those and heels has me grabbing my cock and adjusting it through my pants. My phone vibrates in my hand. "You left something behind," I say.

"Mmm-hmm. It's okay to have to work hard for what you want, Holden." Her voice is seduction and silk. It owns me in the best kind of way.

"Another clue," I demand.

"Be resourceful."

The line ends as I rush to the human resources department. Going past one cubicle after another, checking under the desks as I go. My shirt front is unbuttoned. My belt is hanging loose. When I hit the last desk, a red lacy bra is hanging from the exit sign over the door.

I snatch it down and run the fabric through my fingers.

My cell rings.

"Red. Black. Leather. Lace. What's your preference, *Mr. Knight*?" she purrs in greeting.

Mr. Knight. I'd love to hear her say that when her mouth is wrapped around my cock and it's hitting the back of her throat.

"You." I grate the word out. "My preference is you."

"Then you're going to have to work a little harder to find me."

"It's all fun and games, Rowan. . . ."

Another throaty chuckle. "And then what? And then Rowan gets fucked?"

"You're goddamn right she does," I mumble as the call ends, and I move down the main corridor like a policeman, clearing each room as I go.

Another pair of panties—crotchless I might add—greets me outside of her office door. A place I covered on my way to the lunchroom so I know she's on the move.

"Rowan," I call out to her, the desperation thick in my voice.

My phone alerts a text. Warmer.

I move into her office and when I do, I hear a pair of feet pad down the hallway, but by the time I get back out there she's nowhere to be found.

I chuckle. Even my laugh is strained with need as I move from office to office. From space to space. The sound of footsteps catching my ear every couple of minutes.

She's going to end up in my office.

Wasn't that the gist of all our texts earlier? Her. My desk. Fucking her on it.

I quietly move toward it and am surprised when I step inside and find it empty. More than surprised. I'm fucking desperate.

I pick up my phone and text. Another hint?

But my text goes unanswered as I head to the conference room to double-check its many places to hide. And I'm just about to head in there when movement catches the corner of my eye through the crack in the door.

Rowan is slinking down the hallway and coming straight for

the conference room. I stand behind the door and wait for her. She pushes the door open, slowly, quietly, and from one beat to the next, I have her body pinned against the wall.

She yelps out a laugh, but her chest is heaving and her eyes are wide, lids half-hooded with desire. Her pulse jumps erratically from where my hand rests like a necklace around her throat.

"Olly olly oxen free," I whisper.

"You found me. Now what are you going to do with me?" Her warm breath hits my lips, each word adding gasoline on the fire.

"Oh, Sunshine, there's a lot of things I want to do with you. To you. In you." I dart my tongue out to wet my lips, and it's only then that I take her in. All of her. The jacket she had on that I didn't question has now fallen open to reveal the fucking sexiest bra and garter set I've ever seen. There are straps and lace and a mix of leather, and her nipples are spilling over the bra's edge while her pussy is bare beneath the garters that are hanging down her thighs.

Jesus. Fucking. Christ.

This woman is going to be my undoing.

My fucking demise.

Her outfit. Her body. The pout of her parted lips. The seductive look in her eyes. Her panted-out laugh.

Fuck waiting.

I want.

And so, I take.

I slant my lips over hers and steal every fucking breath of hers in a no-holds-barred kiss.

It's angry and hungry and she tastes as fucking desperate as I feel. There are no thoughts. No choreographed moves. We're a mess of hands and lips and groans and pleas.

Her jacket falls. My pants are shoved down. We shuffle toward the conference room table, where chairs are shoved aside and her ass is lifted onto the wood table.

"You're a fucking cock tease," I say against her lips as she reaches out and wraps her fingers around my dick.

I hiss out a breath. Then moan out a groan.

"And what a nice cock it is." She lifts her eyebrows in a taunt as I fight the urge to fuck her hand.

"I thought you said we couldn't do this again."

"I changed my mind." She squeezes her hand tighter and my eyes all but roll back in my head. Does she not realize how fucking hard it is to have a conversation when your cock is being stroked by a woman who is dressed like she is?

"You changed your mind?"

"I'm fickle like that," she murmurs and leans in for a kiss that causes me to grow harder—if that's even possible.

"I'll take fickle. I'll take angry. I'll take fucking all of you."

"I think it's supposed to be me taking all of you."

"You will be. Make no mistake about that." I run my hand through her hair and tug it back to force her to look up at me and to expose that sexy line of her neck. Her smirk taunts as much as her body tempts. "I haven't stopped wanting you since that first night we met."

"I know. It's hard to want you as much as I do when I'm supposed to hate you."

I lick the line of her neck and love that her body jerks from the sensations it evokes. "And now you hate that you want me so much." I gently pinch her nipples between my fingers and her back arches, shoving them forcefully into my hands.

"I do."

Our mouths meet again. With more hunger. With more desperation. With the words fueling our need until it burns so bright I swear to fucking god we're going to combust.

"Holden," she murmurs between kisses. "*Hold?*"

I love that her voice sounds as close to snapping as I feel.

"Hmm?"

She pushes her hands against my chest, our lips breaking apart and our bodies separating. She makes a show of standing from the edge of the desk. Because my legs are between her thighs, as she stands her arousal slides over my skin.

Fucking hell.

The thought. The feeling. The knowledge that I did that to her.

Every part of me wants to push her back down and drive into her. Fuck her good and hard until we're both lost in oblivion.

"Sunshine." It's a strained two syllables as she steps into me.

Her eyes flicker down the length of my body before scraping back up to meet my eyes. "Take me from behind." She reaches down and strokes my cock as if her words aren't fucking enough. "That way I can feel every fucking inch of you."

She leans in and kisses me like it's her last breath before turning around, my hands sliding over her torso as she does, and then bends painstakingly slowly over the edge of the conference room table.

I take in the sight. The lingerie. The curve of her ass. The pink of her pussy. The chills chasing over her skin. The moisture glistening for me. Because of me. It's a goddamn concentrated effort to look up to her face when she turns and looks over her shoulder, saying my name.

"Yeah." I grunt the word out, my gaze immediately going back to my hand sliding between her legs and testing to make sure she's ready for me. She's more than ready, begging for me in the way her muscles tighten around me when I push three fingers in and fuck her with them.

The way she pushes back on my hand. How she moans. The feel of my hands squeezing her ass. The way she smells—her perfume mixed with arousal.

"*Please, Mr. Knight,*" she whispers.

And the way she fucking sounds saying that.

I line my cock up at her entrance and drive into her without warning. The sensation of her gripping around me consumes my thoughts. Snaps all control. Between the game and her outfit and her requests, I know once I'm fully seated, once I let her adjust to me, there will be no turning back.

I grit my teeth as I bottom out in her. Her sharp gasp of pleasure mirrors my groan of bliss. I squeeze the sides of her hips and when she pushes back on my cock, I begin to move.

It's fast and desperate. I drive into her over and over, my mind lost and my body alive with every fucking sensation.

Her pussy is the heaven I want to get lost in and the hell I can't resist. It makes me want to take my time and at the same time drive into her until I can't go any more.

It's her panted moan. It's the tight, wet grip of her pussy. It's the jolt of her ass as I slam against it. It's her hands reaching back and gripping the edge of the table.

It's the pressure building, stroke after stroke, moan after mewl. Spreading from my lower back to my balls to goddamn everywhere.

It's her calling out my name as her muscles tighten around me over and over as her orgasm slams into her.

It's me losing all sense of reality as mine follows shortly thereafter.

I buckle under its intensity. My hips jerking as I lean forward and press my forehead to her back.

Exhausted.

Sated.

Consumed.

It's sex.

Just mind-blowing, incredibly awesome sex.

Not my finest work to date. Not even fucking close.

But hell if it's not something I'll forget anytime soon.

"Olly olly oxen free," Rowan says and then we both laugh.

THIRTY-SEVEN

Rowan

I sit in my car in the parking lot and stare up at the light on in Holden's office. I replay the events of the last few hours.

The decision to pursue Holden that opened a box I sure as hell hope isn't Pandora's.

My brother's betrayal.

My partnership with the enemy.

The incredibly erotic game of hide-and-seek sex that I'm rather proud of myself for making up with said enemy.

How many more emotions can one person face in a six-hour period and not need serious therapy?

I sure as hell don't know, but what I do know is that there's a soft smile on my lips and a giddy sensation in my more than sated body.

I stare at the light and know he's up there still working. Still plotting out how to take over the world. Still being the enigma he is.

And I'm down here trying to separate the physical from the emotional. The personal from the business. My sanity from my reality.

The man does things to me. Physically. Mentally. Emotionally. Things that no one else ever has before, and I'm not quite sure what to make of it.

You deserve someone who makes you feel like you've been struck by lightning.

Gran's voice floats in my head.

Her words.

Her wisdom.

"You're crazy, Gran. I love you to death, but you're batshit crazy if you think that someone is Holden."

I mutter the words into my empty car and yet my eyes are still on the window. Still waiting for one more glimpse of the man that I'm supposed to hate but suddenly desperately want.

And the irony in all of it is that when I finally pull away from the lot and head home, heat lightning flashes in the distance, lighting up the sky and the clouds all around it.

THIRTY-EIGHT

Holden

FIFTEEN YEARS AGO

Numb.

Shoes squeak by on the floors. Machines beep constantly. Voices say terms I can't even comprehend right now.

But I can't feel anything.

Not how cold the room is.

Not his dried blood on my hands cracking as I grip the arm of the chair so tight my knuckles are white.

Not the tears that are sliding down my cheeks.

Not the beating of my own fucking heart.

Images flash through my mind. Images that will forever be burned there.

Mason on the pavement.

The back doors of the ambulance and watching through the window as the paramedic on top of the gurney pumped Mason's chest as it drove away.

My mom's rushed footsteps and worried face as she ran into the waiting room to find me. Her frantic words. How cold her hands were as they pulled me against her and just held on as if a hug could make everything better. Could fix how broken Mase was.

My mom crumpling to her knees when the doctor walked out,

when he told us Mase was gone. That there was nothing they could do.

The sound. It was a guttural scream that sounded like someone had ripped my mom's heart out and handed it to her. It's burned into my brain. I keep hearing it over and over.

The dead weight. How heavy my mom was as I tried to lift her back up. As I tried to help her when I was dying inside myself.

Mason. All the tubes and leads in his little body. All the medical stuff—instruments, rubber gloves, gauze, blood—dropped everywhere from them frantically trying to save him. His cold hands. His one shoe on, the other shoe off, and his big toe sticking through a hole in his sock. His wrist—the stupid blue-and-black friendship bracelet that I used to make fun of—looks so dark against his pale skin.

I fixated on that bracelet. On the specks of blood on it. On its frayed ends. On the fact that I'll never be able to make fun of him again.

I repeat the words over and over in my mind. My one last promise to my little brother. To my best friend. To my shadow. *Whoever did this to you will pay.*

It all replays in my mind as I sit in the waiting room.

Over.

This is my fault.

And over.

If I had gone outside with him, he wouldn't have been hit.

And over again.

I killed my little brother.

"Mr. Simpson?" a deep voice calls into the waiting room. It takes a second for it to register that he's talking to me.

"Yes. That's me. But I'm not . . ." *Not a Simpson.*

"Father of Mason Simpson?" the man asks.

I shake my head. Even now there's shame in the stupid response. "No father." I swallow over the lump in my throat and the tears burning. "Brother. I'm his brother."

He makes his way over to me. His button-up shirt is strained over his stomach so that the spaces between the buttons are separated and show a white undershirt beneath. There's a coffee stain on his right sleeve and a badge hooked on his belt.

"Mother?" he asks, stopping before me and pulling out a small pad of paper from the breast pocket on his shirt.

"She's back there." I motion toward the closed doors. "They had to give her a sedative to calm her down. She's . . . I don't know what she's doing. They—the doctor or nurse or someone . . . told me I had to stay out here."

"I'm Detective Martin."

"Holden." I choke over my own name.

"Do you mind if I sit down?" he asks, and I shrug as he does so. "I'm sorry, son. About your brother. That you had to go through that. All of it."

He reaches out and squeezes my shoulder. All I can do is nod and stare at my hands as I run them up and down my thighs.

"Yeah. Thanks," I whisper. "Do you know who did it?" When I lift my eyes to meet his, I already know the answer. *No.*

He gives a subtle shake of his head. "Not yet. We have some leads. A partial plate number—a person thinks. Possibly a white car."

"It was a white car. A Mercedes," I say. "Two people in it."

"Thank you. That will help narrow down the license plate numbers starting with the vehicle. We're also looking to see if there were any cameras in the area that caught anything." He shifts and reaches into his front pocket. "This was at the scene. It belong to you?"

My breath catches when he holds out the square silver lighter and places it in my hand. The weight of it makes my hand dip as I run my thumb over the engraved crest, the etching now stained with my brother's blood.

"No," I whisper.

Clank. Click. Clank.

"It's—I've seen it before." Was it Rhett in the car? Was he the passenger who got out?

Think, Holden. Fucking think.

"Where?" the detective asks.

I try to churn up the rage that roars through me, but I can't. I'm numb. Empty.

"Son?"

"At the country club. Where I work."

"Which one, son?"

"Westmore Country Club," I say as he winces at the three words. A wince I'll later remember. "It—Rhett Rothschild. It's his."

He nods very slowly, his pen poised, as if he's afraid to take down the name. "It *looks* like his," he says.

"Shouldn't this be in a bag? My fingerprints." I push it back toward him but he just meets my eyes.

"I'm sure there are plenty out there that look like this. It's best you don't jump to any conclusions. Let me investigate before we accuse anyone of anything."

"It's his," I murmur, relieved when he finally takes it back and pockets it.

"I just told you not to say that. The last thing we want is someone getting themselves in trouble making false accusations when it's clear your mom needs you here instead of in a jail cell for something silly like that."

I stare at him, eyes blinking, heart pounding, every sensation just . . . dulled. His threat falls on deaf ears.

Dead.

Mason.

I choke back a sob.

"We're chasing everything we have," he says, patting my knee and clearly uncomfortable with my sudden show of emotion.

"My little brother is dead"—I struggle to use the word—"do something. Please."

"It's early in the investigation still. Do you want to tell me what happened?"

The tears come. No matter how hard I try to stop them, they come as I explain about Mase going outside. About getting distracted until I heard the screech of tires. About the person getting out, seeing Mase there, and getting back in the car. About them screeching away and leaving my little brother like a heap of clothes on the asphalt.

The detective keeps his head down, writing on his notepad. "So, you didn't see anything leading up to the event? You weren't outside watching him?"

If I'd been outside, I would have.

If I'd followed my mom's rules, I would have.

"No." That's the hardest answer I've ever had to give. I know it has nothing on how hard it's going to be when I have to explain it to my mom.

"Okay." He simply nods and closes his notebook. "Again, I'm sorry for your loss."

Sorry doesn't fix anything. In fact, it makes it feel ten times worse.

"Yeah," I say, looking for the lighter that he's completely removed from sight, before giving him all our contact information when he asks.

I don't look up when he stands. I don't meet his eyes when he hands me his business card. I don't give a response when he says, "We'll be in touch."

Instead, I keep picturing the thread-made bracelet on Mason's wrist.

Clank. Click. Clank.

Instead, I keep repeating the promise I made to my little brother.

Whoever did this to you will pay.

THIRTY-NINE

Rowan

"Sweet tea and sunshine. What could be better than that?"

My mind immediately flashes to Holden, and I offer my mother a smile that has nothing to do with sweet tea or sunshine. "Nothing," I lie as I glance around the outdoor patio of the Westmore Country Club. It's packed as usual on a warm Saturday afternoon. The members mill about under teal umbrellas and sip drinks that are way too expensive on a tab that's probably overrun.

"I'm sure the Vandeveres will be pleased that you decided to come today," she says as she waves at Muffy Johnson, who is sitting at a table across from us.

"I promised Caroline that I'd be here, so I'm here," I murmur. This whole trying-to-be-a-great-friend thing is harder than it looks. Mostly because I loathe shit like this but also because I've been busting my ass finding suppliers who will work with us. Ones that my brother and father haven't burned bridges with in the past.

"That's lovely, dear." She smiles and then straightens some, prompting me to look over my shoulder. "Caroline is becoming quite the party planner. I bet you they'll task her with organizing and planning the Christmas party this year. What a huge accomplishment that would be for them to put their baby in her hands."

"It's *just* a party, Mom."

"Be happy for your friend. She's doing well."

"I am. More than," I say as I raise my wineglass to Caroline where she stands over by the bar, immersed in a group of people. She raises hers as well and grins.

"Chadwick. What a pleasure to see you," my mom says as Chad walks up and offers her a kiss on her cheek. "Rowan and I were just discussing how beautiful this setting would be for your reception."

"We were not," I exclaim. She's lost her ever-loving mind.

Chad just laughs and gives me a look that's laden with apology before taking the empty seat between my mother and me. "Emmaline, did you and my mother coordinate this ambush beforehand? I promise you I just got the exact same comment minutes ago from her."

"Great minds think alike," she says. Sensing her cue to leave us alone so that who knows . . . we might decide to get married tomorrow, she grabs her sweet tea and excuses herself.

"Will it ever end?" Chad chuckles.

"I don't think so. Not ever," I say as Chad casually drapes his arm across the back of my chair. I don't think twice about his hand accidentally brushing over my bare shoulder. This is the boy I shared my first kiss with. A man who has known me my whole life. There is a comfort level between us that has come with years of knowing each other.

"Fuck it. Maybe we should just get married to shut them up and then when we get it annulled a few months later, they'll stop all of this."

"What would we cite as the reason?" I play along. Maybe it's the wine. Maybe it's a good mood.

"You can say that I snore too loud, and I'll divulge that you're a horrible cook. I mean, there are worse things, right?"

I laugh and tap my wineglass against his. "It could work."

"It could." He sighs and shakes his head. "I mean, we should just stand on the table, tap our forks, and announce it right now."

"Go right ahead," I joke but when Chad stands up and puts one foot up to stand on the chair, my eyes bug out of my head. "No." I grab his arm. "Oh my god, no."

He looks at me and bursts out laughing as he puts his foot back down. "C'mon. I wouldn't do that to you."

I hit him playfully. "You gave me a heart attack."

He leans in close and murmurs in my ear, "Don't look now, but our moms are watching."

Great. Perfect. More fuel for their fire.

"Then we should have a huge fight. A public display. Something to prove to them that we're not right for each other." I say the words but then notice his grimace.

"You know I think differently." His voice is soft, sincere, the playfulness gone.

"I know," I say, looking toward the crowd milling around us, not wanting to see the hurt in his eyes.

"But it *would* be funny," he says, trying to recoup the lightheartedness we just had. "You could throw a glass. I could flip a table. We'd end up falling into the fountain."

"We'd be the talk of Westmore." I smile at him softly and nod. It feels like it's been forever since we've talked like this. Since we've joked like this. I forgot how easy it was to be around Chad outside of the office setting. How well the two of us mesh together.

"We would, wouldn't we?" he murmurs as he reaches over and pats my knee. "Also, not to talk shop, but . . ." He casually looks around us. "I've been talking to my cousin. The corporate lawyer."

"Who's not a lawyer in your family? And I know who Henry is."

"I know." He chuckles. "But he might have a few ways to help us out. Ideas on how we can stop the deal."

"Really?" It's the first sign of hope that I've had since this whole thing started, and my voice reflects it.

"Mm-hmm. Do you still have a bad feeling about it all?"

I study Chad and wonder how to play this with him. As it is, I've agreed to a deal with the devil. I'm working with Holden in return for a piece of the pie and a seat at the table.

But I'm still in a conundrum. Two votes and a small percentage of ownership don't give me the leverage I need and the long-term return that I want. I need to own more of the company. And after spending hours reviewing Gran's "dirt notes" and riffing with Sloane over it, I think I know where I can get it. Two members are on the decline health wise and might welcome an inflow of cash to buy their shares.

The problem?

How do I get the money to do that without the lump sum payment from Gran?

You do realize that you're actually considering whoring yourself out—so to speak—to make dreams become more tangible realities, right, Row?

Do you still have a bad feeling about it all?

I contemplate how to answer Chad's question as I lift my wine to my lips.

Do I play the damsel in distress, worried about my family's legacy with the new owner who is the big, bad wolf? Or do I play "I have the right to own this company and I'm going to fight for it"?

As if this could get any more complicated. At this point, I don't trust anyone, and as for tanking the deal . . . as the days tick by, the reality is setting in that this plan isn't going to happen. My only option is to put myself in the best position I can within the company as the second largest shareholder of TinSpirits. That way my votes will hold more weight than theirs combined. At least that's my plan.

Rhett will know that when they go to sign the sale papers and they're revised. Little will they know Gran's holdings will be mine soon too.

"Hello?" He waves his hands in front of my face. "Where'd you go?"

"I'm sorry. Just thinking. What was the question again?"

He studies me for a beat but then replies, "Do you still have a bad feeling about this?"

I sigh to buy time. "It's complicated." My smile is half-assed as I toe the line between black and white. "I think keeping all options open at this time is the safest bet."

"Agreed." He nods.

"Says the man who has had more hush-hush closed-door meetings with my brother in the last month than ever before." When he just looks at me doe-eyed, I continue. "Yes. I've noticed. Early in the morning. Late at night. Even thirty minutes ago here. You two looked like stress cases talking about whatever it is you were talking about."

"We're just under a lot of pressure." His smile isn't believable. "Holden has us doing some things and we want to get them right."

"Oh." I give a startled jostle to my head. "I didn't . . ."

"You don't think you're the only one he gave special projects to, do you? You have property searches, and we have . . . other things."

"Okay." I draw the word out.

"Look. We'll see what my cousin has to say. Maybe there's something there. Maybe there isn't. 'Kay?"

"Okay."

It's then, when Chad glances down to answer a text on his phone, that I look up and jolt, seeing Holden across the opposite side of the patio. He's wearing a pair of sunglasses, but despite the dark tint of the lenses, I know he's looking straight at me. I can feel it as clear as I can see the muscle pulsing in his jaw and the taut tendons of his neck.

I take him in. Him in his normal Holden-dark attire, while everyone else is dressed in white or bright spring colors—or boring khaki for the men. He's surrounded by a group of men, all clearly vying for his attention while anyone who knows anything about him can tell he couldn't care less.

And it's clear that they don't hold his interest.

I do.

But the smile I offer him isn't returned.

In fact, there isn't any reaction I can get out of him at all.

"Okay?" Chad asks with raised brows. Clearly, I didn't hear whatever he said.

"Sure. Okay."

"I need to talk to Porter. He's over there." He chuckles when I look at him with a furrowed brow. "I just told you that. You didn't hear me."

My smile is quick, apologetic. "You're right, I didn't. Sorry."

"It's okay. I know how you get when you're thinking too much. Have another glass of wine. Relax. Stop thinking about work," he says and leans in to press a kiss to my cheek as a goodbye.

The minute he moves out of my line of sight, I'm met with Holden's implacable stare once again. He offers the men surrounding him a comment, but his focus is back on me.

"He is something to look at. I'll give you that," my mom says, following my gaze as she steps up beside me.

I pull my attention to her immediately and cough over a response. If she only knew how my insides were reacting to him right now. "Looking nice and being nice are two different things," I murmur.

But isn't that part of what I find attractive about him—besides the fact that he's incredible at sex? That I can't quite figure him out? That there is an edge beneath that pretty exterior? An edge that is so fine, I'm not always certain which side I'm on or if I want to be cut by it.

It's thrilling.

It's unpredictable.

It makes me feel alive and desired while at the same time challenged and on my toes.

"I think we need to invite that man to one of our family functions. Maybe our annual summer barbecue we have coming up. It's important that he understands what we are about. How important this family is to this town. The jobs we provide. The money we infuse into this economy. The legacy we must continue. Maybe then he can fathom what we're giving him the keys to and how he needs to protect and preserve the company as best as he can."

"I'm not exactly sure he cares, Mom." And when I look up this time, Holden is gone. The circle of men is still there, but he's not.

How stupid is it that my shoulders sag at his sudden absence.

With him here, at least there was something to look at. To look forward to.

"Let me at him." She winks. "I'll make sure he cares. No one can resist Emmaline Rothschild's charms."

FORTY

Rowan

It's dark by the time I pull into my driveway.

I'm tired from the exhaustive conversations over nothing that apparently were deemed necessary at Caroline's deck party. I'm drained from the nonstop prodding from my mother about Chad and my future. I decide that if I never go to another function again, I could die a happy woman.

Walking up my path to my house, my only thought is how I want to climb into bed with a good book and get lost in it. Anything to stop my head from thinking. About my conversation with Chad. About the pressure from our moms. About seeing Holden there and how it made me feel. About—

"I'd expect you to wear sapphire earrings to an event like that."

I yelp at the sound of Holden's voice and the sight of him as he steps out of the shadows on my front porch. "Jesus, you scared me," I say.

But he doesn't even react to my yelp with a smile. "They'd match your dress."

And be complete overkill for a sundress.

"I told you, I can't accept them."

He chews the inside of his cheek as he tilts his head and narrows his eyes. That stare I felt from beneath his sunglasses earlier is back, but this time I can feel the singe of its heat.

"Is something wrong?" I ask as other questions I don't put words to play rapid-fire through my mind.

Why are you here?

What's going on?

Why do you seem so angry?

"Mmm," is all he gives me as he reaches out and rubs my bare earlobe between his thumb and forefinger. It's incredibly intimate in the weirdest of ways and causes chills to chase down my spine and stoke the ache lighting between the apex of my thighs.

"Mmm? That's all you're going to give me?"

He chuckles but it's short and daunting. "He had his hands on you, Rowan."

"Who?" And the second the word is out, I know exactly who he's talking about—Chad. "Why, Holden Knight, are you jealous?"

"I don't share." Three words. Three syllables. Absolutely no mistaking the threat behind them.

My breath catches as he moves his hand down to rest on the curve of my shoulder. He rubs his thumb back and forth over my collarbone.

"I'm thinking I should be insulted by your insinuation."

"I don't care what you think." The way his eyes flit down to my lips and then back up to my eyes has my nipples pebbling against the lace of my bra.

"That makes two of us."

"Are you really going to marry him, Rowan?"

I run my tongue over my bottom lip this time when he looks at my mouth. His nostrils flare ever so slightly. "Maybe. Someday."

It's a total lie.

A complete taunt.

A challenge to get him to react.

And react he does.

He puts his hand on the small of my back and yanks my body against his. It's impossible not to feel every hard, sculpted line of him as he slants his mouth over mine and takes.

It's a commanding kiss. One that dominates and demands and possesses.

"He's not allowed to touch you," he says as he uses the fist he has in my hair to pull my head back so I'm forced to look at him. So there is no mistaking his words. "No one is."

My only response is to grin. A jealous Holden Knight is a wickedly sexy thing to behold. The darkening of his eyes. The clenching of his jaw. The desperation in his touch.

"Open the front door, Rowan."

"Why? So you can tell me what I can and can't do?" It's hard to be sarcastic when my body is begging for more of his touch. "I don't think so."

"Open your door or your neighbors are going to get to watch me fuck his touch right off your skin."

FORTY-ONE

Holden

I needed a break. Away from the office. Away from the mind games. Something to remind me why I'm doing what I'm doing—as if Mason not being here isn't enough.

So I sit in my SUV, hand on the wheel, eyes slowly taking in everything around me, my elbow resting on the rolled-down window. I let the memories come.

The good.

The bad.

The ones scarred into my memory.

The ones I wish never happened.

I haven't been able to stay away from Fairmont since I've been back. It doesn't matter how busy I am, I find myself driving these streets. To work things out in my mind. To occupy myself when I can't sleep—which is often. To pull me back and force me to re-member the why for all of this.

I've spent years trying to forget this fucking place, and now I'm letting it consume me.

The cemetery. The one I've driven to at least a dozen times only to pull into the parking lot and never get out. I tell myself I need to visit him. That it's about time I see the elaborate headstone I had made to replace the basic marker on Mase's grave.

But every time I think of Mason, I see my mother, lying on top of the freshly piled dirt in her finest clothes. I hear her sobbing and saying she *had* to sleep there with him. That she couldn't let her baby be alone on his first night in this strange, scary place.

The diner. It makes me think of the late nights my mom worked. Her aching feet and mustered smile. The sacrifices she made so that I could be where I am today.

The apartment. The one about a hundred feet from where I'm parked with its broken wrought iron gate, its sagging sidewalk, and its faded brick exterior stained with years of graffiti and despair.

The spot. That place over near the telephone pole with its crumbling asphalt and cracked surface. The strip of street that has been driven over countless times, drivers oblivious to what happened at that corner. To my brother's life lost and the lives irrevocably changed forever.

This street. The one that holds more memories than I can bear. More moments that I wish I could forget. And the one that's coincidentally a block down from the Sanctuary.

My two fucking worlds colliding.

Colliding when I don't believe in coincidence at all.

"Hey, man. You lost?"

I glance over to the young kid standing on the sidewalk looking in my passenger window. He's about twelve or thirteen with big brown eyes and a head of shaggy dark hair. His green shirt is worn enough that I can see his shoulder through the stretched seams of the fabric.

"Not lost, no."

His eyes roam around the inside of my car. To my hands. Stutter on the Rolex on my wrist. To my wallet visible in the cupholder. To the black gym bag on the front seat.

"Sorry, man. We don't want any. If you go four blocks down and take a left, that's where people go to buy whatever it is you're selling."

I bark out a laugh. The little shit thinks I'm slangin' dope. That's fucking comical. "I'm not selling shit, son."

"Do you need directions, then?"

"Nope. I know where I am." I stare at him for a beat before exiting the car. Those big brown eyes of his track my every movement as I walk around the hood of the SUV to lean my ass against its fender.

I take in his oversized jeans. Notice the two cans of spray paint in his back pockets. See the stain of its colors on his fingers.

He studies me too, looking me up and down, thinking his puffed-chest bravado masks his wariness. But I see it. I used to be the same way. "You don't look like you know where you are because if you did, you wouldn't be here."

"What's your name?" I ask.

"Why? I don't want nothing to do with whatever it is you're here to do."

"Good. I'm glad you're thinking like that. It'll keep you out of trouble. Your name?"

His look says he doesn't trust me, but his answer says he does. "Leo."

"Nice to meet you, Leo. I'm Holden." I hold my hand out and he stares at it for a beat before shaking it reluctantly. "And how old are you?"

"Thirteen."

"Do you live here?" I ask, lifting my chin to the apartment complex at his back.

"Close to here," he says, and if it weren't for the dart of his eyes to the green bike lying on its side on the porch behind him, I'd believe him. But you don't leave bikes on porches in this neighborhood unless you want them stolen or you're nearby to watch them. "Why all the fucking questions?"

I shrug, my eyes constantly surveying what's going on around us. Knowing your surroundings around here is a matter of life and death in some instances. It's amazing how that habit comes back without it being a conscious decision. "Just curious is all."

"What-the-fuck-ever, man."

"Just a word of advice. You might want to chill out on saying 'fuck' so much." When he goes to argue, I lift a hand to stop him. "You seem like a smart kid. You keep dropping f-bombs when talking to adults, they're going to immediately look at where you live, where you go to school, and write you off. Give you a label you don't deserve."

Fuck you, Rhett.

He angles his head to the side and stares at me. "Let's be real. No one fucking cares about me. Don't act like some three-piece-suit-wearing motherfucker like you does."

Guess he means me.

"No one?" I ask. "Mom? Dad? Grandma?"

"Dad's who the fuck knows where. Gotta chase the next high, you know." He shrugs but I know that look. I still *feel* that look some days. "Mom's at work. Always at work."

"Isn't that because she does care? Her working so much? Trying to give you every opportunity she can?"

"Yeah. I guess."

"You an artist?" I ask and love the startled look on his face.

"Fuck no, man."

"But you carry paint in your pocket."

He rolls his eyes in response. "Yeah. So?"

"I'll tell you what. Instead of tagging whatever it is you're planning on tagging next, why don't you spray over the shit on those walls," I say, lifting my chin toward the building.

"What the fuck—" He catches himself. "What would I do that for?"

"Because just like you don't want dealers out in front of your house—you shouldn't want that shit where you live."

"You're whacked, Three-Piece."

"I guess you don't want to get paid then."

That got his attention. "You gonna pay me to spray over someone's tag?" He snorts. "You're outta your mind if you think I'm going to believe you. *Why?*"

And why do I care if he does believe me?

"I used to live here."

"You tripping if you think I believe that."

"I don't give a fuck if you believe me or not. I did. That corner unit right there." I look at it and can all but see Mason sitting on the front porch with me, oiling the bearings of his skateboard. His laugh—one thing I can still hear all these years later—rings in my ears.

"You're trying to tell me you got out of here. That you're driving that and wearing a Rolly—and you didn't sell dope to get there?"

"I am."

"Yeah. Right."

"The only difference between you and me, Leo, is that luck met determination at the right time."

"Yeah, well, in case you didn't notice, the only luck you get around here these days is that the bullet misses you when it's fired."

"You get good grades?"

His eyes narrow at me. "Bs mostly."

I nod. "Do drugs?"

"Nah, man. Not my thing."

"Play sports?" I ask and see his face fall a fraction before he covers it back up.

"Baseball, but it's expensive and my mom can't always get me there because of work."

I look at Leo and see Mase. See me. I'm not sure why the fuck I do, but I do. He seems to be a good kid in a shitty situation by no fault of his own.

I question myself before I even open my mouth. "Back to my offer."

"To spray over tags?"

"Yeah. The deal just changed."

"Of course it fucking did," he says, clearly used to being let down. "Nice meeting you, man, but you're just like—"

"Hold up. Hear me out," I say and reach into the open passenger-side window and grab one of Audrey's nondescript cards without a company name on it. They often come in handy. She can't be googled. I can. "I want you to work for me." He snorts again and I just keep talking. "To make this front building look nice. Repaint the gates. The porches. Paint over the tags."

"Why? You own this place or something?"

"No."

"Then why?"

Because pride is a real thing. So is shame. The shame of having friends come and see the place you live when it looks like this. The having friends drop you off on a corner a few blocks down so no one knows where you live.

"Because I want to."

"Like I said, you tripping, man."

I hold up Audrey's card. "Call this number tomorrow. You can give her your name and address. She'll have supplies sent here for you to get started." He eyes me. "But only after your homework is done."

"So you want me to do all this work and for what?"

I open my wallet and take out a crisp one-hundred-dollar bill. His eyes widen. "This is a down payment on your work."

He glances left and right and I'm not sure if it's because he's afraid someone will see it or if he wants someone else to see it so he believes it. "A down payment? I'm supposed to believe you'll be back?"

"I'll be back to check on the progress and to pay you." I hold out the bill, and he stares at it for a few seconds before accepting. "I'm also going to have Audrey—the woman on the card—buy you a bus pass. That way you can get to and from practice."

"How do you know where practice is?"

"I told you, I used to live here. The bus stop is down there." I lift my chin down toward the Sanctuary. "And it drops you off a block from the fields, right?"

"Yeah."

"You do a good job, we'll work on getting you some new gear too, but you have to earn my trust first."

"How do I do that?"

"You do what you say you're going to do. A man's word is sometimes all he has."

Leo stands there with his hands shoved in his pockets, one hand clearly fisted around the one-hundred-dollar bill, and continues to stare at me with a look that says he's doubting every single thing

I've said. Not many people make promises and keep them when you're in his shoes.

I get it.

I used to be him.

"What if I run out of . . . stuff."

"Call that number and tell her."

"You'll come back?"

"I gave you my word."

"Why?" he finally asks. Eyes searching, almost as if he's afraid to hope.

I shrug. "Fuck if I know," I say.

The refrain repeats in my head as I pull away from the curb and drive through Fairmont again. On streets I walked as a kid. Through memories I'm trying to hold on to. To the curb by Mason's plot. Close enough to see it but far enough that I can't really make anything out.

To all the places I refuse to let Rhett Rothschild demolish and ruin.

And I end up right back on the same street I was on a bit ago, but this time a little farther down the block.

Right in front of the Sanctuary.

It shouldn't surprise me. Being here. Waiting for her.

Wanting to see her again.

I have so much work to do. So much planning to complete. So much fucking over other people's lives to accomplish.

But I know she is here.

And when she walks out in her white linen pants and light blue shirt looking like the personification of spring, I breathe a little easier.

She startles when she sees me, shifting her cello case in her hand as I jog across the street to her.

"Why are you here?" she asks.

Because I needed someone.

Because I wanted to see you.

Because . . . *it's you.*

FORTY-TWO

Rowan

Because I wanted to be.

Five words in response to me asking, *Why are you here?* Five words that hit me right in the heart and muddied waters I need to stay clear.

But then I added my own mud to the water when he asked if I wanted to *take a drive* with him and I said yes.

I study his profile as he drives. The defined lines and strong features. The styled hair and thick lashes.

"You're staring at me," he says with a quick glance my way.

"I am."

"And what do you see?"

A man I can't quite figure out but want to. A person who knows way too much about me but not the other way around. A lover who is incredible in bed but an enigma outside of it.

"I was just thinking that I bet you don't play hooky from work very often."

He gives a crooked smile with his glance this time. "I can't remember the last time I did."

"I figured as much."

"And you? When was the last time you did?" he asks as he makes a turn toward the coast.

"I just did when I went to the Sanctuary."

"That's not playing hooky. That's volunteering. Hooky is when you do something for yourself."

"That is doing something for myself," I say.

"What do you mean?"

"Have you ever heard of Clayton Seaburn?" I ask.

"No, but if you tell me it's the name of a Kentucky Derby horse, I wouldn't be surprised."

I burst out laughing. "You have a valid point there. But no, he's not a horse. He's one of the most acclaimed cello players in the world. He was knighted by the Queen of England and has won every award under the sun. That kind of thing."

"Okay. What does he have to do with you being at the Sanctuary?"

"He doesn't. He has to do with me." I shift in my seat so I can face him some. "The boarding school I went to had a phenomenal music program. I'd always played, but it was there that I fell in love with the sounds it could make and the feelings those sounds could evoke. Then Cass died, and I came back home to try and figure life out without her."

"It's a horrible feeling."

"It is. Days and nights ran together. Time felt like it crawled, but I remember one night in particular when I was at a super low point. I was sick of everyone telling me it would get better. Sick of being told how I should feel. I put my headphones in and on a random shuffle, heard a piece by Clayton Seaburn for the first time. His notes, the way he strung them together, sounded how *I* felt. His work became my therapy. It helped me get through one of the hardest times in my life."

"And now you offer that same light in the darkness to others."

I study him as emotion wells in my throat at the poignancy of his comment. "Something like that," I murmur.

"What did you play for them today? One of his?" he asks as the ocean comes into view off to the left of us.

"I wouldn't even attempt to play one of his pieces," I say.

"You've been playing for longer than half your life. You can't be *that* bad," he teases.

"If I told you what I played, would you even know what I was talking about?"

"Not unless it's classic rock, no."

"It's doable on a cello, but doesn't sound quite the same. You really don't like classical music of any kind?"

The look he gives me says it all.

"Is that look more along the lines of you tolerate it but it's not your jam, or you'd rather stab your own eyes out with a fork than be forced to listen to it?"

"Fork is a bit harsh. Maybe something more along the lines of a spoon."

"A spoon?" I laugh. "Is it that bad?"

"Is this where I reserve the right not to answer in the interest of self-preservation?" A text alerts from his phone sitting in the console and he laughs. "Saved by the text."

"Lucky you."

"Don't I know it," he says as he glances down at the text. "That's Audrey. Your car is back at the office."

"That was kind of you to arrange for it to get back there."

"Of course. If we left it there, who knows what we'd come back to. No car. No wheels. A new paint job done by spray paint."

"I'm sure it would have been fine, but I appreciate you taking care of it for me. You sound like you know firsthand about it," I joke.

"I do."

That's all he says. He doesn't elaborate, and the way those two words are spoken tells me the conversation is over.

An awkward silence falls over the car. It's something that hasn't really happened before between us. Other than the one night at the diner, we've never really spent any time together outside of work or sleeping together. Sure, we talk after a round of toe-curling sex, but not about anything meaningful. Not our pasts. Not our present. Not what this even is between us besides the joking reminder that this is "just sex" every so often.

And at the office, some of our late-night "work" sessions have ended up with the elevators locked again, takeout food cold and forgotten as the two of us *somehow* end up losing a few items of clothing.

To say this fling between us has been fun is an understatement. I've never done something like this. There's a thrill in its secrecy. A high in doing something others wouldn't approve of. An adrenaline rush in looking across the room at a man who everyone else thinks is calculating the risks of major decisions while I know he's actually cursing me for wearing one of his favorite sweaters and texting me exactly what he wants to do to me while I'm wearing nothing but it later.

"What about you, Holden Knight?" I ask.

"What about me?"

"It's kind of weird to me that we pretty much know every inch of each other's bodies and yet I don't know much about you other than that."

"Sure you do."

"What you like to eat isn't one of them."

His grin is lightning quick and dirty as hell. "Am I supposed to be ignoring that door you just opened about what I like to eat?"

I squirm in my seat, my body reacting viscerally to the memory of the skill of his tongue that last time we were in bed.

"Yes. You are supposed to ignore it." But my grin matches his and the look we share says I wouldn't mind if he did it again. "I mean things about you. Growing up. College. Broken hearts. The kind of things that build character and make you."

He glances my way for a beat before giving a quick shrug. "Grew up with little. My mom, brother, and me. Then it was just my mom and me. Tried college. It wasn't for me. I'm not good with structure or being told what box I need to stay in. Taught myself coding. Then software. Got lucky being at the right place, the right time, with the right product."

"Pretty sure it was more than that," I say and get a shrug in response. "Where in California did you grow up?"

He looks over his shoulder to change lanes, causing a pause in his response. "Northern."

"Silicon Valley?" I ask because that's what I read.

He nods.

"Are you close with your mom?"

"Very. There was a long time where it was just the two of us. Now she has Graham—her husband of five years. He's good to her. Makes her laugh. I would say he takes care of her, but she'd be mad if I did. She firmly believes she doesn't need a man and can do everything herself."

"I like her already," I say.

"You probably would. What about you and your parents?"

I twist my lips as I watch the world pass by. "It's complicated."

"As I figured."

"I love my parents to death, not just because they're my parents but for who they are. I can respect them for that. At the same time there's resentment there. For the longest time, I thought they wished I was the one who died that day instead of Cassie."

"Rowan." He sighs out my name.

My smile is sullen. "I was young, but that's where my thoughts went."

"But why?"

"Because she was everything they—and the society they try to impress—wanted her to be. Content with the part she was supposed to play while I bucked against it. Still do. She was happy being known as Rhett Rothschild's sister—"

"The golden child."

"Mmm-hmm. And I didn't want to be the person propping him up on the pedestal. I thought he should have to earn it rather than have it handed to him solely because he was the boy of the family."

"From what I've seen of Westmore, they're the norm. You're the—"

"Outsider? Unconventional? The rebel?" I laugh and wave a hand. "I've heard it all before and am one hundred percent fine with all of the labels. Good, bad, and patronizing. Hell, if it weren't for my gran putting her foot down, I wouldn't even have been allowed to work at the company."

"Good thing for Gran."

"You don't know the half of it," I say as he makes another turn. For wanting to "go for a drive" we sure are driving. "Are we going anywhere in particular?"

"No, but I'll know when I find it," he says when he takes another turn down the main drag of a quaint beach town.

"Don't think I didn't notice you ignoring the heartbreak question," I tease as we stop at a stoplight.

Holden stares at me with an intensity I wish I could understand. "No heartbreak."

"By choice or because you're the one breaking them?"

The muscles in his jaw tick. "If you're asking if I've had lovers, clearly by my skill level—"

"Oh, please."

"The answer is yes," he says and I suddenly wonder why I even asked the question seeing as how hearing those words makes me sick to my stomach. "But that's all they were, Rowan. I'm a busy man. I have things I want to accomplish and I'm too selfish to compromise those things." Something glances through his eyes that I can't read but want to and before I can, he looks away.

"I understand that." More than he may ever know. The difference is society makes it okay for a man to say that, but not a woman.

"And relationships mean feelings, and I don't have time to manage someone else's feelings when I hurt them. Because I'm bound to do just that—hurt the person," he says unapologetically with a brutal honesty I've come to expect from him. "That and . . ."

"And what?" I ask as the light turns and he begins to drive.

"Nothing." He says the word but there is something in his expression that says there is more. "Never mind."

"That and because people you love leave," I all but whisper, revealing my own fear out loud. Then I wince, embarrassed I let that slip, but when Holden glances my way, when he reaches out and squeezes the top of my thigh, when he gives the slightest of nods, I know my words resonate with him too.

We fall silent as we drive down the main street. Past souvenir shops, tourist traps, and little cafes. Past families struggling to wrangle their children, their skin pink from the sun but their smiles wide.

I get lost in thought. Replaying Holden's words over in my head—*I don't have time to manage someone else's feelings when I hurt them. Because I'm bound to do just that—hurt the person—* and wondering why they affect me when I've lived my life much the same way.

It's because you're on the flip side of it this time.

It's because you're catching feelings when you don't catch feelings.

It's because you know how this is going to turn out—he just told you without telling you.

FORTY-THREE

Rowan

"If your phone buzzes one more time, I think it's going to implode," I say as it vibrates again on the table.

Holden gives a quick shake of his head as he picks up his phone and makes a show of turning it off. "That should take care of it," he laughs as he tosses it back down.

That's something I've noticed about Holden. As busy as he is, when we're together, he ignores his phone. He rarely picks it up to look at a text. He never takes a phone call. It's not something I'm used to, but it makes me feel like he knows my time matters.

Silly, really. But isn't this whole thing silly if you look at it?

I'm screwing my soon-to-be boss.

But when I look at him over the rim of my wineglass with the ocean at his back and his eyes on me, it doesn't feel very silly. Far, far from it.

The restaurant he brought us to is small in size but huge in ambience. Private tables on a balcony overlooking the beach. Expensive wine and delicious food. Great service and a beautiful sunset.

"This was unexpected. You being at the Sanctuary. The drive. The drinks and appetizers."

He shrugs. His smile soft. His fingers reaching out to play with a lock of my hair. "We've both been working hard. I overheard you on the phone say you were heading there and . . . thought it might be a much-deserved break."

"Well, thank you. I really think you'll be happy with the suppliers I'm nailing down. Brownstone has been a difficult one to figure out. . . ." I drift off as Holden shakes his head.

"No."

"No, what?"

"No more talking about work. I just want to sit here and enjoy the rest of our wine with a beautiful view and a gorgeous woman."

"Oh."

He leans forward. "Yes. *Oh*," he mimics me moments before he presses his lips to mine.

"We can't." I press against his chest. "Someone might see—"

"There's a reason I drove so far away, Sunshine. Why I scoped out this restaurant. No one knows us here." His eyes meet mine as he runs a thumb over my bottom lip. "Why I wanted to take you here."

This time when he presses his lips to mine, I welcome it. The slow seduction of his tongue dancing with mine. The feel of his strong hands framing my face. The taste of wine. The muted sound he emits that tells me this kiss is affecting him just as much as it is me.

It's a kiss without a forgone conclusion. There isn't a place where we can rip each other's clothes off and go at it. There is no urgency along with it.

It's a kiss simply to kiss. A soft, slow reminder that whatever is between us is there without the promise of sex.

It's intimate when we've seen each other naked.

It's tender when we've always been in a frenzy.

It's . . . it's *wow*.

And the kiss sticks with me long after he pays the tab. It stays front and center in my mind while we stroll up and down the main street without a purpose. It's as if we know when we leave, the feeling that kiss gave us—contentment, intimacy—will remain.

We dig our toes into the sand. He looks funny in his slacks and bare feet, shoes in hand, but he obliges me when I ask to go closer to the water. We walk in a comfortable silence, soaking up the atmosphere, the break from work, and each other's company.

Cloaked in the moonlit darkness, we slowly make our way back to where his SUV is parked. Music starts up somewhere. It's a pop song with a funky beat that I start dancing to, causing Holden to shake his head and laugh.

"C'mon. Dance with me," I say.

"I don't dance." But he watches me. His eyes on my hips as they sway. His lips pursing as I spin around like a teenager who doesn't care who's watching.

He's a stoic figure that I try to cajole and tempt but fail at convincing.

The song ends and he claps as I bow dramatically, before grabbing my hand and pulling me into him.

I land against his chest, out of breath, and suddenly become fully aware of the emotion brimming in his eyes.

Desire and something else I can't place.

The song changes. Someone's laugh floats toward us. The waves crash on the beach behind me.

But he's the only thing I see. The one who has my undivided attention.

I lean up on my toes and kiss him.

I get lost in the sensations. The warm sand on my feet and the cool ocean breeze. The heat of his body against mine and the softness of his lips. The strength in his hands as they hold me against him and the ache burning in every single place we touch.

"Don't look now, Mr. Knight," I murmur against his lips as we sway ever so subtly, "but you're dancing."

CHAPTER FORTY-FOUR

Holden

To say I was surprised to see our floor's lights turned on when we pulled into the parking lot well after 9 P.M. is an understatement.

My first thought? *Fuck. There goes my chance to kiss Rowan one more time before sending her home.*

My second? *What the fuck is going on?* No one stays here this late except for me. Except for Rowan. So why do I see lights on from my parking spot in the lot? And why is my fucking light on in particular?

So when I walk into my office and see Audrey sitting behind my desk, arms crossed, eyebrows raised, and a mouth pulled tight, I'm more than a little surprised.

"Why are you still here?" I ask, glancing over my shoulder when I hear other voices down the hall, but then back to her.

She chuckles but it holds no humor. *Why do I feel like I'm about to get my ass handed to me?*

"Well, it was either stay and cover for you in your meeting with Allied Industrial or leave like you did and hang you out to dry."

Oh. Shit.

The meeting. I forgot all about the fucking meeting. Between Leo and . . . and then taking Rowan to the coast.

The wine.

The moonlight.

Her kiss.

"Why didn't you call me? Why didn't—"

"Kind of hard to do that when your phone is off, now, isn't it?"

And the hits just keep on coming.

"It's a long story. The phone I mean." I try to explain away like a teenager in trouble. My pride has me biting back the excuse, but the fact that this woman can see right through me has me putting it out there regardless.

"I'm sure it is. Long and full of bullshit."

"I'm human, Audrey. I forgot."

"But that's the thing. Holden Knight never forgets a thing. So that begs the question: What is it that has you so distracted?"

I stare at Audrey. Big eyes. Clenched jaw. This is as close as she gets to reprimanding me, and that's happened fewer times than I can count on one hand.

My chest constricts in my chest, but I don't give her question an answer.

"Like I said, it slipped my mind."

"Uh-huh." She's not buying it.

I snort. "I apologize. I deserve whatever shit you're about to hand me."

"I'm not handing you anything, Holden," she says like a true mother, a master at guilt. "I've worked for you for many years. Hell, I even picked up my life to come here with you while you're doing whatever it is that you're doing here." She knows what it is that I'm doing, but her glance down the hallway tells me she's choosing her words wisely. "But in all that time, I've never seen you turn your phone off, let alone miss a meeting. Not once."

I scrub a hand through my hair. She's right. She's fucking right. "Stuff happened."

"Stuff?" She lifts her eyebrows, clearly not buying my story. "I'm sure *stuff* happened."

"What? Just come out and fucking say it. You're going to in the end anyway."

She rises from my seat and stops as she passes me. Her voice is soft, stern, when she speaks. "I understand why this project has you rattled a bit. There are a lot of moving parts and even more history behind why they're moving. But the Holden Knight I know doesn't fuck up like he did tonight. He's meticulous. He's calculating. He puts the end game before all else."

A nod is my only response.

"If you want this to all go down like you've planned, then I suggest you figure out why you fucked up tonight, what distracted you, and fix it fast." She lifts an eyebrow with a glance toward Rowan's office. I don't dignify the supposition with a response. "Figure out how to *undistract* yourself. You're only going to get one shot at this."

"Noted." I clear my throat and move to take back my seat. Audrey's lecture time is now over, and as irritated as I am that she just read me her riot act, her words eat at me more than they should. "A kid named Leo will be calling you tomorrow," I call after her just as she's about to leave my office.

She turns and meets my eye. "He already did. Hours ago. Said he wanted to make sure your word was good, whatever that means."

"Great. He was part of the reas—"

"Don't try to blame some kid for your fuckup." She gives me major side-eye that has me laughing and holding up my hands in surrender. "There's more to the story. Just don't get so lost in its chapters you forget about the ending you want."

I watch her walk toward the elevator, purse over her shoulder, and pinch the bridge of my nose.

Well . . . *fuck*.

But I don't have much time to dwell on her or chastise myself for it because the minute the elevator doors shut, Tweedledee and Tweedledum are walking down the hall toward my office.

Huh. Guess we weren't here alone after all.

Audrey's right. You're losing your edge, Knight.

"Where were you?" Rhett asks like he has a right to know.

"Excuse me?" I ask.

"You heard me," Rhett says. He's clearly irritated and more than wrong if he thinks I'm going to tell him shit.

"I was out. What I was doing is none of your business."

"You were with Rowan," he says as he strides in front of my desk. "You had Audrey bring her car back so that means she was with you. Are we taking secret field trips now? Should I worry about the lengths you'll go to get inside information on me? On us?"

Touchy. Touchy. Someone is most definitely getting paranoid.

"Now, why would I need inside information?" I ask. "What good will that do me if everything is on the up-and-up like you say it is? Is there something you want to share with me?"

They exchange a look. *Ah. Definitely paranoid.*

Gotcha.

"Rowan. Were you with her?"

"I was. Yes." I lean back and contemplate the million answers I could give. The thoughts alone leave a half-assed smirk on my lips.

Rhett catches it. So does Chad. *Perfect.*

"Looking at property," I say.

"Where?"

I chuckle; the sound hits like a *fuck you if you think I'm telling you,* but then I decide to play with them some. "There are a few across state lines we checked out. A few within state lines."

"You still haven't said why you're looking at property," Chad says.

"I wasn't aware I had to, but you can never go wrong with property, right? It's always deemed a surefire investment." Haven't we had this conversation before? "It's tangible. The interest is a write-off. I could go on, but I'm sure you guys know all the reasons."

Rhett nods. "Rowan doesn't know shit about real estate."

"Perfect. All the more reason to have her tag along so I can teach her." *What else you got, Rothschild?*

"Great, fine. But can't it wait? This is a huge transition—you coming in. Taking over. Probably changing things up. Maybe we should all just stick to what we know for now and rattle the cages in six months when everyone is more comfortable."

I hold his stare and love that he's trying to make demands of me. I decide to carry on the conversation as if he asked. "We were looking at a piece of land off of Grafton Road. Another on Highway 43.

And, shit, where was the other one?" I shuffle through the papers on my desk as if I can't recall and stop when I find some random map. "Oh, right. Another out on WillowBend and Greenmill."

The forced swallow.

The fleeting glance between them.

"Grafton Road is a shit area," Chad says.

"Well, that depends on what you want the land for, right?" I ask, knowing damn well why he's steering me elsewhere.

"True, but you haven't lived here for long. That area has decreased in value a lot over the past few years," he says.

"Perfect. Buy cheap, sell high, right?" I say.

"Yeah, but it won't hold its value. What about the others?" Rhett asks, his eyes glancing down at the notes I have on the map. Notes that mean shit but I cover them up as if there is some big secret there.

"Indifferent to the one on Highway 43. Really loved the one on Willow whatever, but then wasn't thrilled to find out it's sitting on contaminated soil."

You gonna take the bait, motherfuckers?

Rhett clears his throat. "Contaminated? What are you talking about?"

"Yeah, got an earful about how the ground has high methane levels that make the land fucking useless. I mean, you can mitigate it coming up through the soil with barriers and shit, but that's a huge investment over and above purchasing the land." I watch them closely. The pulse in Chad's throat. The tapping of Rhett's fingers.

"Who told you that? The owner? The real estate agent?" Rhett laughs and glances at Chad. "Not very smart if they're trying to sell the land."

"A concerned citizen apparently," I say. "Not sure. The message came through to my broker."

"Out on WillowBend, you said?" Chad asks.

"Mmm-hmm. It's a fucking pity though. Nice piece of property. Perfect for what I needed it for," I say.

"There's no methane in the land out there. Christ," Rhett swears. "We had a friend—"

"Nathan?" Chad asks.

"Yeah, Nathan." Rhett nods. "He had to deal with these Greenpeace-loving motherfuckers when he was trying to develop some land last year. They went around sabotaging every contract, contractor, even when he tried to buy the land. Tried to scare off buyers with the whole methane spiel."

"It was all about 'save the land, don't develop,' and shit like that," Chad says.

"So you think that's who contacted us?" I ask.

Rhett shrugs. "Sounds par for the course."

"So you think these activists—"

"Tree huggers," Rhett snorts.

"You think they are trying to discourage someone from buying the land and developing it by saying it's contaminated?"

"Yep. That's what happened to Nathan's company."

"Too much hassle. No, thanks," I say and wait for the reaction.

Three.

Two.

One.

"I disagree. That makes it the perfect time to buy in my opinion. The property has been slandered. No doubt your broker sees in the MLS listing that the price has been dropped several times to mitigate the hassle. Buy cheap, isn't that what you said?"

"Yes, but the methane—"

"The lie can be proven baseless with an independent consultant, Holden. Have someone go out there. Do some tests, give you a reading to prove that the land is fine. Problem solved," Rhett says.

An independent consultant? That's your fucking sales pitch? How much are you paying that consultant to lie for you? No wonder you're drowning and taking your company down with you.

"Aren't you the solver of all problems?" I say.

"What can I say?" He holds his hands up. "Whatever I can do to help. I can even get you the consultant that Nathan used if you want. He's familiar with the land in that area and is knowledge-able in methane since he dealt with this shit for him. Once you have that report in hand, you'd be able to breathe easier about buying the land."

"Problem solver and referral artist. A regular jack of all trades," I say. *How does he keep a straight fucking face?* "But, question, why doesn't the current owner do that in the first place? Hand out the report debunking the crazies so they can keep their valuation as is?"

"Beats the hell out of me," Rhett says with a look to Chad. "Maybe they've already washed their hands of it."

"Their stupidity could be your gain," Chad adds in.

You'd like that, wouldn't you? Me to buy it? To save your asses? Maybe if you two read the fine print you could do that yourselves.

Then again, maybe not.

The two of them stare at me. "Was there something else besides your need to know where I was?"

Rhett straightens his spine. "Just wanted to make sure we're still on track with buttoning everything up on this deal in the next few weeks."

You want your money, don't you, Rhett Rothschild?

I nod. "We are. There will be a few changes based on some of the issues I've found."

"Like?" Rhett asks. I give a glance to Chad and then back to him. "You can say it in front of him."

"Some things don't add up in the ledgers. Why we've picked up payments to Greatland when units are the same. Why we're pay-ing consulting fees when we don't need consulting. Two and two isn't equaling four in some aspects."

"Yeah, we're still unraveling the damage our controller did. She screwed a lot up," Rhett explains.

Sure. Blame it on the controller. Fucking spineless prick.

"So, what's changing in the deal, then?" Chad asks.

"Just a few more commands and controls set into place. The fine print is always important," I say.

"Agreed," Rhett says. "But we're still going through with it, money to be transferred and all that jazz?"

"Yes, all that jazz," I say wryly. "My lawyers have been in touch with your lawyers on all of this."

"Great. Perfect." He fidgets some. "Some of the board members were asking is all," he explains.

I nod. *You have payments coming due, Rhett, and no way to pay them. There's not much more you can shift and then reshift to cover all your bases, is there?*

"Anything else?" I ask.

"No. I think that's it," Rhett says.

"Make sure it is." I shift my focus to my laptop and start typing to dismiss them.

They hesitate before leaving.

But it's only when both of them enter the elevator and the doors shut that I let my guard down.

Fuck, Knight. Just . . . fuck. I scrub a hand through my hair and lean back in my chair, staring at the cursor on my laptop taunting me to work, but my mind is lost somewhere else.

To her. To moonlight in her hair. To her carefree laugh. To her dancing in the sand.

To Leo. His wary eyes. His hopeful smile. His reminding me of a little brother I never got to see reach that age.

To Rhett. His bullshit lies. To the freight train barreling down on him. To the warm, fuzzy feeling I have deep down inside knowing I'm the conductor on it.

To one hell of a fucking day that really had nothing to do with work.

I don't know how exactly to think about that.

I'm not slipping.

I haven't lost my edge.

Fuck that Audrey thinks differently.

Fuck that my solution to a weird day is wanting to go to Rowan's house instead of my own.

And fuck that my personal life is most likely going to crumble—

when Rowan figures out the lies—at the same time everything else I've dreamt of doing for so long comes true.

Fuck, man.

Maybe I do need to pull on the reins a bit.

Maybe I do need to mitigate expectations no matter how much I don't want to.

FORTY-FIVE

Rowan

"I need an update," Caroline says the minute I answer the phone.

"I'm at work. I can't talk now," I say and strain my neck to look down the hallway to see if Holden is in his office.

"You're always at work," she snorts. "I have a feeling it's because you're doing more than *banging* out contracts at the office these days."

"Oh my god."

"I'm sure you've yelled that a few times too."

"Caroline," I warn.

"What?" she asks, the voice of an angel. "I'm just saying what you're thinking."

I roll my eyes but don't speak.

"It must be good if you're not talking. Like, mind-blowing, back-breaking, multiple-orgasm-inducing good."

"Perhaps," I murmur.

"AHA. I knew it. I knew your silence meant you were getting busy."

"I really have been busy at work trying to onboard some new suppliers."

"Suppliers, uh-huh. Someone to fill up that empty warehouse of yours."

All I can do is hang my head and bark out a laugh. "Whatever."

"So . . ." she says.

"So?"

"Is there more going on here than just 'supplying the warehouse'?"

"No. *God no*," I say quicker than I should. If I can hear the panic in my own voice, I know Caroline can too.

"Uh-huh," she murmurs. "Well, if supplying the warehouse should turn into . . . I don't know, something more, that's more than okay."

"Caro—"

"Don't *Caroline* me. I know you have to keep this quiet because you have your reasons, but sometimes when there is no public pressure or bright spotlight on you, it's easier to figure things out."

"Things?"

"Feelings. You know, the thing you never talk about."

"Noted."

"And she's all business, once again," she mutters.

"She is. And she has to go because someone is heading this way."

"Desk sex is fun. Just saying," she says seconds before I end the call and Holden strides into my office with a definite purpose.

He has on a light gray shirt today and black pants. His sleeves are rolled up and the top two buttons of his shirt are undone when he usually is wearing a tie.

I have only seconds to act on the fantasy that just popped into my mind before he sets the black velvet box down on my desk with force.

Guess he found them.

"I warned you about this," he says, eyes meeting mine, hands bracing on the front edge of my desk so we are face-to-face.

"Holden." I hesitate because the look on his face is intense. Irritated. "I can't accept them."

His smile is quick, disarming and disconcerting at the same time. "And I told you what I'd do if you tried to return them."

"You're being ridiculous."

His eyes drift down to my cleavage, which I'm sure he has a

great view of from his vantage point. They linger for longer than is appropriate. Good thing I know how incredible Holden's inappropriate is.

"I gave you a gift. End of story." He drags his eyes back up to mine. "That's your one and only warning or else Monday's meeting next week is going to be awfully enlightening about what we've done on the table we'll all be sitting at."

My eyes shock open wider and I reach my hand out and slowly drag the box toward me and put it in my drawer.

"That's a smart decision, Sunshine," he murmurs in that low, husky voice of his that has me biting my lower lip in reflex.

"Yes, Mr. Knight," I murmur. Two can play this game.

And I get the reaction I want. The flare of his nostrils. The twitch of his fingers as if he's itching to touch. The clench of his jaw followed by the slow, seductive crawl of a smile onto his lips.

"Should I be worried that your mother called me today?"

That statement is enough to knock me out of my lust-induced haze. "She what?"

"Yep." He helps himself to a seat at my desk. Something I don't think he's ever done before. "Surprised the hell out of me too."

"She invited you to the barbecue, didn't she?" *Damn it.* My two worlds outside of work are going to collide. I mean, they have at the country club, but not at my family home. Not with the people who know me better than anyone watching the two of us interact.

"She did." He nods. "Invited me and offered for me to bring a plus-one. Any suggestions on who that might be?"

We haven't had any discussions about exclusivity when it comes to whatever it is that we're doing here. At the same time, his whole "I don't share" routine pretty much said that's what we are— exclusive . . . and yet even the idea of him bringing someone else has me rolling my shoulders in irritation.

"If you were a smart man—and I happen to know for a fact that *you are*—you won't be bringing anyone."

"No?" He lifts a single brow and offers me a lopsided, taunting smirk. "Why not? It might be a nice time for a good society lady. An event where she can step out and let Westmore know she snagged the new eligible bachelor." I snort. "God knows I've had plenty of open invitations from them."

"I don't think that would be a wise decision." I lean back in my chair and fold my arms over my chest, raising one eyebrow to match his.

"And why's that?"

"Because I'm more than certain by the"—I look back and forth down the hallway through my office window and then lower my voice—"way you were fucking my mouth last night, that you know exactly where your bread is buttered."

His laugh is low and rich. "Sunshine, I do believe you are trying to get a reaction out of me." He looks down at his lap, grunts, and then back up to me. "For the record, it's working."

I shake my head but the grin—god, the grin is automatic. It always is around him. "Then again, maybe you should bring someone." I shrug and play along. "A Junior League chair who likes her mint juleps strong, her picket fences white, and who would probably accept a pair of sapphire earrings and wear them to a run-of-the-mill barbecue without batting an eye."

"Probably," he says as Audrey calls him from down the hall. He rises from his seat, his eyes still locked on mine. "But I prefer a woman who argues with me over accepting said sapphires and chooses to wear them with nothing else on."

FORTY-SIX

Holden

She's been avoiding me since I stepped foot into this backyard.

A cursory hello. A polite smile. An absent glance my way.

But that's about it.

I don't like it one bit. It's total bullshit.

And it's fucking killing me.

Her short sundress. Her sun-kissed legs. The strappy sandals.

The dirty things running through my mind are endless.

Her hair is pulled up. The curve of her neck exposed. Her lips a pale pink.

Does the need for her ever wane? Her mouth? Her body? Her mind?

"So it seems like things are going well. On track," Rupert Rothschild says, pulling my attention back to him.

I give a measured nod. During my dive into the Rothschild digital footprint, I didn't find much and that's almost as telling as finding a treasure trove. Dear old Dad doesn't know his son has bargained away both the business and the family trust.

Doesn't have a fucking clue. Duped bank statements can go a long way.

I look at Rupert and smile. "It is. Coming right along."

"Good. Good." He pats me on the back, and I grit my teeth. *I'm not one of your good ol' boys. Far fucking from it.* "My retirement thanks you. My family thanks you."

My smile is sharp and fleeting. "Of course."

This will be the third time Rupert has brought up the purchase of TinSpirits during the party. The third time he's sought me out and woven it into our conversation.

He's curious.

Rhett's not telling him shit and for good reason. Daddy can't know the family company is bleeding money—among *other* things.

And so, he's coming to me for answers on whether his return is coming. Do I detect a hint of doubt in his golden child?

"Your date. She's stunning. I had no idea you were . . . *taken*. The Westmore women will be crying in their pillows tonight."

"Hmm," I say as I take a sip of my scotch. I have no interest in responding.

And maybe because I'm not 100 percent thrilled with that development either.

I glance over to where Mallory stands amid a circle of other Westmore women. She's the exact opposite of what Rowan looks like—or rather, she's exactly what Rowan used to look like, the TinSpirits spokesmodel Rowan. All blond hair and wide, innocent eyes.

By design of course. No doubt Audrey thought of that when she surprised me with a date for today's event.

To get rid of the distraction said her text.

Mallory looks over to me and smiles a smile any man would appreciate.

And any other time, there is absolutely no fucking doubt I'd act on it. On her. On the opportunity that she's put out there.

"I know it's none of my business even though it is technically my business," Rupert says, pulling me back to him as he chortles at the pun. My face remains impassive. "When it comes to the deal, are there any sticking points that might cause a delay or a problem?"

"You'll have to excuse me for saying this, Rupert, but I can't discuss the specifics of the deal with anyone. Rhett and I are under a nondisclosure agreement, and I take those very seriously."

In other words, no, you can't know anything other than the memos the board members get—and those are scant on details.

"Yes. Of course. Ever the consummate professional."

My smile is there but disingenuous. "Always."

He continues to stare at me as if he thinks that will make me talk even when his questions don't. It's awkward for him. A shift of his feet. A clearing of his throat. I just continue to stare back, waiting for him to get the hint that nothing more will be said.

"Well, it was great talking to you," he finally says. "So great. If you'll excuse me."

"Of course," I say with a nod.

You'll be back. You'll rephrase the questions. You're Rupert Rothschild. You're used to people doing what you ask.

Not me.

Not when it comes to them.

Fuck that.

I lift my beer to my lips and look around the Rothschilds' lavish backyard. People I've come to learn are the who's who of Westmore society stroll about. It's old money—subtle and unassuming with classic style—beside new money—loud and obvious with everything on trend. Regardless, the guests are decked out as extravagantly as the yard.

Massive trees provide a canopy of shade over the perfectly manicured lawn. The patio furniture is abundant and placed around the patio area, white with turquoise cushions, much like at the country club. Servers mill about with food and drink. An acoustic guitar player is in the corner providing background music.

Just a "quaint, friendly backyard barbecue," read the invitation.

That's how far removed the Rothschilds are from reality.

Caterers? Servers? A musician?

This is a place where they're used to hiring the help. Is this what my mom saw every day—the lavishness, the waste, the excessiveness—as she cleaned their houses before coming home to us every night? Is this disparity what drove her to not give up so we could have the same opportunities?

I saw it in my job at the Westmore Country Club back then—but what was on display there more than anything was a sense of entitlement. She saw *this*—an embarrassment of wasted food—while we could barely feed ourselves, often eating the same thing over and over because the ten for $10 deals on canned goods were our staple at the end of most months when the money ran out. People complaining about the hired help not doing this or that when she was the hired help. The inability to pick up after yourself because you're so used to someone else doing it for you.

My gaze drifts toward the pool area, and that's when I find Rowan again. She's standing among a group of people. Her smile is wide, the glass of wine in her hand almost empty.

She's a part of this world. I have a habit of forgetting that. She might not say the things they say or act the way they do, but she's still a part of the culture and the privilege.

That she fits in here is without question.

I put the image I have of Rowan at the diner, concerned about the waitress, side by side with the one I see right now. Diamonds glinting, hand reaching out for a fresh glass of wine from a server with barely a nod, and more than comfortable with how over-the-top this party is.

Rowan leans her head on her mom's shoulder as she laughs at something being said. It's normal to be at odds with someone in your family—their ideals, their whatever—and still want to be around them. And still love them.

I get that. Everyone gets that.

And yet it's hard to reconcile the things Rowan says about her family, the way she feels, with seeing her like this. Hard to believe she truly means those things.

When the world falls down around them, when I make it tumble, what will happen to her?

It doesn't matter, does it, Knight? She's just a good lay for the time being. A way to twist the knife a little deeper.

Nothing fucking matters but the end game.

And yet still I stare. Still I wonder. Still I justify.

"They make a handsome couple, don't they?"

I glance over to the woman who has just walked up and taken Rupert's place beside me. She's tall with blond hair and an imposing presence. Pearls around her neck, a French manicure on her nails, and a purse to her lips that says she uses it when she's passing judgment on someone.

"I'm sorry. Who are you talking ab—" But I see exactly who she's talking about when I follow her gaze back to where I had been looking moments before. Back to Rowan . . . and *Chad,* who is now standing beside her with puppy eyes and a pathetic smile.

He's regaling the group with some animated story and every time he wants to add emphasis, his hand goes somewhere on Rowan. Her shoulder. The small of her back. Her arm.

It creates a visceral reaction from me that no matter how hard I try to ignore, it doesn't go away.

Yeah. A good-looking couple if you're into pretentious, sackless pricks.

"See, they take your breath away too," she says and holds her hand out. "Florence Williams. So nice to formally meet, although I've already heard so much about you from my son."

Ah yes. Of course. *Chad's mother.*

I temper the sarcasm of the response I'd really like to give. "Nice to meet you."

She offers me a warm, searching smile before turning back to watch the topic of conversation. "Their wedding is going to be the talk of the town, you know. She'll be such a stunning bride in tulle and taffeta. And he's always dashing in a tux."

Tulle and taffeta? That's the last thing I'd picture Rowan in. *Not that I think of her in a wedding dress by any means.*

"I wasn't aware they were engaged." The last word is like broken glass on my tongue. "Apparently I need to pay closer attention to my soon-to-be employees."

She bats a hand at me and laughs the fakest fucking laugh I've ever heard. "No need to pay any closer attention to anything. Some things were just meant to be, you know. She and Chad have played cat and mouse since high school. They were even a thing way back when. First kiss, first . . . *all that*."

I grit my teeth and exhale, slow and measured. There's no fucking way she lost her virginity to *him*.

"I'm sure she'd be thrilled that you're telling everyone her personal business." I don't hold back on the sarcasm this time.

"Oh honey, I'm going to be her mother-in-law. I get to say whatever I want. All of us go so far back we're probably connected on some family tree somewhere." She laughs like a hyena and bats my arm again. "Not really, but it feels like it."

"Charming." This woman is a nightmare. An absolute fucking nightmare.

"It is, isn't it? The wedding's planned." She sucks heavily on her straw. "I mean, the flowers, the venue, the caterer, the colors—every single last detail. All we need is for Rowan to finish sowing her wild oats and come to her senses."

"Is that so?"

"It is, yes. Chad is crushed every time she rejects him—but we understand it's simply because she's scared. Cold feet are a real thing. But the chief—"

"The chief?" *The fucker.*

"Yes, my husband. The chief of police of Westmore proper. Has been for over thirty years." She wobbles her head on her shoulders like it's something I should already know.

Don't worry, *Flo.* I *do* know.

"Thirty years? No shit."

"Yes, indeedy. Oh look," she all but squeals as Chad does something I clearly don't catch by the time I look back over at them. *Maybe that's a good thing.* "See? They *are* perfect together."

"Mmm." Fucking *perfect.*

"I made a special request to the department to have a police salute caravan parade thingy for them on the ride from the church to the reception. And you *know* it'll get approved." She winks.

"Last I checked, Chad wasn't on the police force."

"Honey, haven't you figured it out yet? Westmore might as well be called Williamsmore or Rothschildmore. We're as much a part of this town as the soil itself. Born and bred. Tried and true." She smiles but all I see is her smugness, and the corruption she wears like a second skin. "With the Williamses being the law side and the Rothschilds being the captains of industry, this town would do anything for our families."

I know. Believe me, I fucking know.

"Chief's dad was a chief and his grandaddy was too. My daddy and his daddy before him have been the circuit solicitor. That's why everyone is silently rooting for these two to get married sooner rather than later. That way, Rowan can quit that silly company and get to work on what she was born to do—give me grandchildren." She laughs and her chest bounces with the motion. "We need a chief or another solicitor in training to be born, and fast."

Jesus fucking Christ, this place is backward.

I'm not exactly sure how Chad's dad being the chief has anything to do with why people are silently rooting for them but I've heard enough.

"And what does Rowan think about that?" I ask.

She squeals again, but this time I catch what she sees. Chad lifting an appetizer to Rowan's mouth for her to take a bite. My hands clench.

"There you are," Mallory says as she slides a hand around my waist and presses a kiss to my cheek.

I smile politely. "Haven't moved," I say, fighting the urge to look back at where Rowan and Chad are.

"We could get out of here," she murmurs, her eyes lighting up as they meet mine. "There are plenty of other things we could be doing?"

My smile is as automatic as any man's would be when a gorgeous woman suggests something like that, but fuck if I have any desire to leave a barbecue I was dreading coming to in the first place.

And no doubt it has to do with the woman Florence is still stalking with her eyes.

"And who is this?" Florence asks when she realizes someone is beside me.

"Florence Williams, this is Mallory Sanders," I offer but don't give any more of a description of who she is to me, because fuck if I know.

This is me heeding Audrey's warning.

This is me trying to mitigate distractions.

This is me standing beside Mallory while only wanting to talk to Rowan.

The Rowan who literally locked eyes with me when I walked in, and then froze when she saw the woman on my arm. I've had enough scotch to dull how the hurt glancing through her eyes made me feel.

But not nearly enough to forget it.

"The pleasure is all mine," Mallory says, her hand extended and her sultry smile as much a part of her as the air she breathes.

"I wasn't aware you had a girlfriend," Florence says.

"Didn't think there was a need for a memo," I state, not answering her question. But as my hand rests on Mallory's lower back, my eyes flick back over to Rowan.

"It just melts my heart to see them like this," Florence says, following my gaze as she puts a hand to her chest and coos. Fucking coos. "To watch the yarns of *like* start to weave themselves into a blanket of *love*."

"Stop badgering the man, Florence," Emmaline says as she walks up to us.

Saved by yet another overbearing mother who raised another entitled, pretentious prick.

"Mrs. Rothschild, you have a lovely home," I say.

"Please, Holden. I told you both to call me Emmaline. And I do hope you are enjoying yourselves. What's ours is yours."

You have no fucking idea how true that is, Emmaline.

Your daughter. Your company. Your fucking future.

"Thank you. I'll make sure to handle with care."

FORTY-SEVEN

Rowan

I've about had my fill.

Of the fakeness.

Of the boring conversations.

Of watching Holden from across the yard with his hand on *that* woman's back. Of the churning in my stomach when I see them and the lump the size of Texas in my throat.

It doesn't matter how many times I've repeated in my head *it doesn't matter . . .* because it does.

Here I thought the biggest problem about today was going to be keeping my distance from Holden to prevent everybody from seeing right through me. To keep our friends and the board members who are milling around from knowing that we're sleeping together.

But it wasn't by a long goddamn mile.

Instead, it was a game of charades. Of pretending like I don't care where Holden is or what he's doing. Of fighting back the tears that would threaten at random times when I'd catch sight of them interacting. Of throwing myself into any and all interactions with Chad as my only means of a "fuck you" to Holden.

I brace my hands on the bathroom counter and emit a fortifying sigh. The fake smile I've had plastered on my face all freaking day looks back at me. Mocks me. Tells me I'm crazy for thinking what this was with Holden was . . . something to be upset over.

"You said it was just sex," I mutter to myself.

When I showed up today, I had thoughts that maybe I'd be rewarded for this punishment later. That I'd find Holden sitting on my porch when I got home, and we could . . . entertain ourselves after a long day full of pretention and monotony.

A knock on the bathroom door startles me.

"Just a minute," I call out, more than irritated. This is a bathroom in the back of the house. Guests are supposed to use the front ones. There's a reason I came back to this one.

Knock. Knock. Knock.

Jesus. Impatient, much?

Knock. Knock. Knock.

"What?" I snap as I yank the door open only to yelp as Holden pushes me back inside the same moment his lips claim mine.

"Get off me—" I attempt to get out, but my words are lost as our tongues touch and bodies meet.

Pent-up desperation overrides sense.

"Holden—"

Blatant desire erases all semblance of rationality and obliterates all thoughts of that carbon copy of me.

"It's not what you think."

There's just me.

"Who is she?"

Just him.

"No one."

Just this bathroom.

"Liar," I say when I tear my mouth from his.

Just a finite amount of time and a hunger that never seems to get sated.

"I'm in here with you, aren't I?"

Just our hands fumbling—mine with my panties beneath my dress and him with his pants until his cock is free.

Our eyes hold in a suspended state. It's a split second—anger meets jealousy, hurt joins confusion, lust fuels need—and then we crash into each other again.

Bodies against one another's.

Mouths taking.

Fingers roaming.

Need escalating.

Moments flash. His hands on my ass, lifting me onto the shallow counter. My hands in his hair. His taste on my tongue. His fingers parting me and finding me wet. His appreciative moan.

He enters me without warning. There's a sting of pain chased by a rush of pleasure as he seats himself with a feral grunt.

"Fucking take it, Sunshine. Take the whole goddamn thing." Another low growl as my fingernails score his neck, prompting him to lift me up so that I have no choice but to take every deliciously hard inch of him.

"I hate you," I groan out.

"No, you don't." A chuckled moan.

"You're a prick."

"Mmm-hmm," he lets out as he thrusts into me. "Just like that," he praises, my legs falling farther open. "Just. Like. That."

His restraint is snapped, his control lost as he presses my back against the wall—pinning me there with his body against mine as leverage—and begins to move.

It's all rushed and euphoric. We're harsh pants and unrefined movements. Our only thought is chasing the high. Our only need is to make sure we reach it.

"Holden," I moan his name out and then catch myself when reality seeps momentarily in to remind me where we are.

"No. Don't stop," he murmurs roughly against my ear. Each word said between a thrust up. "Ride it. Just like that. God, you ride my cock like a goddamn pro, baby."

His every action is my reaction.

His every exhale, my next inhale.

It's not soft.

It's not tender.

It never has been between us. But there's something about this time. Maybe it's the moment, the seeing and not touching, the hiding from the outside world and reveling in our sexy secret, the knowing if we get caught there's hell to pay . . . whatever it is, it's violent desire mixed with desperate need.

It's about being wrong but feeling so goddamn right.

It's about his date being out there while he's here inside of me.

It's about his murmured praises and his gruff commands.

It's about the orgasm that hits like a lightning strike—I knew it was coming but when it strikes, I succumb to its fire. My skin. My nerves. My breath. My pulse.

I sink my teeth into his shoulder to muffle my moan.

But he doesn't stop. Can't. My back slams against the wall with each deep stroke, his arm holding me still while he drives into me.

Again.

And again.

Until it's my name on his lips as his whole body wracks with tension as his own climax slams into him.

We're still against the wall, our hearts beating as frantically as our breaths are labored. His forehead on my shoulder as one hand still holds me against his and the other is on my ass.

"Let me go," I say as my sense seeps in through the haze. As I realize he brought a date and I fucked him anyway.

"No," he grunts and tightens his grip on me.

"Who is she?" I ask, his cock softening slowly.

"This right here." He ignores my questions and licks a line up the side of my throat. "It's all I've thought about all goddamn afternoon. Tasting your skin. Feeling your pussy. Owning this body. Having you stand at the party after this, when everyone is looking at you, and still feel me in you."

"Holden," I murmur in simple, satisfied appreciation. It's without thought. An effortless reaction when I should be rioting against him.

At the sound of his name, Holden slowly lowers my feet to the ground, but instead of letting me go, he slides his hands up until they are framing my face.

And when he leans in to kiss me this time, it reminds me of the night at the beach. It's tender. It's quiet but so damn powerful. It's the exact opposite of what we just did.

He leans back, his eyes on mine, and his thumb now brushing over my bottom lip. There's something in the look he's giving me that has chills chasing over my already overstimulated skin. His guard slips in that split second, but it's not long enough for me to place the unnamed emotion before it's pushed back down.

He opens his mouth to say something, hesitates, and then leans in for one more brush of his lips, almost as if to make up for the pause. And then he murmurs, "I fucking hate being ignored, Sunshine."

If that's what this is about, then I'm going to ignore him constantly. Holy hell, was that . . . intense, hot, erotic, *something I want to do all over again.*

And so very fucking wrong.

But he's here. Not with her.

It's me. Not her.

I look at him, swallow my pride, and act like she doesn't exist.

In this moment, she doesn't.

"Then I guess you should have brought the girl who would've worn the sapphires."

He belts out a low chuckle and shakes his head. "I guess so."

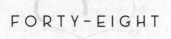

FORTY-EIGHT

Holden

"Another, please," I say to the bartender.

He eyes me cautiously. "You take a wrong turn or are you looking for trouble?"

"Does it matter? My money's good all the same, right?"

He nods. "Yeah, but guys like you don't come into places like this."

I look around the hole in the wall. It smells of stale liquor and years of cigarette smoke that has seeped into the walls. The customers have a familiarity with each other that says this is their daily haunt.

And a guy like me, with clothes like this, sticks out like a sore thumb.

"Sometimes it's good to remember where you came from."

He lifts his brows and purses his lips as he nods, clearly surprised by the comment. "Or to punish yourself for making it."

"That too."

But I'm grateful that he accepts my response and serves me up another cheap scotch that tastes like shit but whets the palate nonetheless.

I wanted to go to her house tonight. To sit on her porch and wait for her. To explain who Mallory was and the why behind me bringing her to the barbecue.

But isn't that the whole reason Audrey invited her to be my

date? Because I do want to explain? Because it's obvious to the person who knows me best that Rowan is getting closer than I've let someone get before?

It was Audrey's shot over the bow. A shot I understood, that I needed to see, but I'm not liking the taste it left in my mouth.

My cell rings.

I look at it.

I debate answering.

"Knight here."

I'm met with Rowan's silence. Silence that oozes emotion—if that's even possible.

"The 'no touching what's mine' thing? That goes both ways," she says resolutely. "I don't know what stunt you tried to pull today, but if you plan to keep doing whatever it is the two of us are doing, it won't be happening again."

"Is that so?" My grin widens. Christ, she's sexy when she's assertive.

"That's so," she says. "I can't have a conversation with Chad without you going all caveman on me, but you can bring a fucking date to my family barbecue? Not cool, Knight. Not fucking cool."

"What are you saying, Sunshine?"

"You're a smart man."

"Yes but you're making me fucking hard talking to me like this with all that authority."

"Let's get something straight. I'm not a doormat."

"No one would ever claim that about you."

"I'm not sleeping with you because I can't get someone else. I'm with you because I want to be. Because it's great fucking sex. So don't let whatever it was today fucking happen again. Understood?"

I chuckle. I can't fucking help it.

"I'm waiting for an answer."

"Understood."

"Good," she says and hangs up the phone.

Fucking hell. This woman is something else in the best kind of ways.

Most women would have called me up and whined. Asked a million questions. Thrown a fit and demanded answers.

Not Rowan.

No.

She stood her ground. She put us back where we are supposed to be—just sex. And left me without having to answer a damn thing.

And fuck if I don't like her more because of it.

It backfired, Audrey.

Fucking backfired.

FORTY-NINE

Rowan

Days are ticking by.

One after another after another.

At the start of this whole takeover, I had figured I'd have a game plan by now. No, it wouldn't be finding some poor sap to marry so that I could meet my gran's impending timeline. Although, yes, that would prove handy and allow me to eventually gain the money needed to buy out other minority owners (after the two-year "stay married" statute took hold), it would do nothing for me in the immediate future.

I can't buy out other people's holdings and add to my growing majority if I don't have the kind of cash it takes to do that. A cool thirty mil would solve a lot of problems, problems I never envisioned I'd ever have, but that's not going to happen.

But I'll take the board seat and the 1 percent that Holden is granting me. That percentage, added to mine and the amount Gran has, will make me the second largest shareholder of TinSpirits. With Holden on my side, Rhett will have no other option but to kowtow on decisions or be overruled.

Both scenarios will bruise his fragile, entitled, unchecked ego. And I'm all for it.

The name on my screen when my cell rings brings a smile to my face. I hastily rise from my desk and shut my office door before answering it.

"Rowan here," I answer in my most businesslike voice.

Holden's rumbling chuckle over the connection has goosebumps on my skin. "God, I love when you talk to me in that professional, prissy tone, Sunshine."

"Good morning . . . or I guess it's afternoon where you are," I say, looking at the clock and realizing the time difference in London, where he's currently off conquering the world.

"It is. I'm jet-lagged as fuck though."

"Poor baby," I coo.

"I'm not complaining in the least," he murmurs. And I know what he's thinking about. The night before last. My Jacuzzi. Then his mouth driving me insane as I lay out on the pool deck until the stars I was seeing outshone the ones in the sky.

A little pre-trip pussy were his words.

I called it another day in his make-up-to-Rowan tour.

"Good. You shouldn't be." I smile.

"The office is good? No one is going off the rails?"

"You already know the answer to that. Audrey's anywhere and everywhere."

"That's what I like to hear." He pauses. "And the paperwork? Your lawyer received it?"

"She did, and she's made a few changes to it," I say.

"Of course she has."

I can't tell if he's irritated or not by what my lawyer redlined. Just seeing the legal documents naming him as the majority owner of TinSpirits—even when I knew it was coming—was hard enough. The newly added addendum naming me as a recipient of a board seat and an allocated percent of ownership when the deal closes even more so.

My dream of being the CEO one day now feels nearly impossible.

I shove down the emotions, blink away the tears, and nod in resolve.

It may not be exactly what I've always dreamt of, but I'm at least securing a better position for myself.

"Someone has to look out for my interests."

"There are a lot of your interests that I'm looking out for. Just in *other* respects," he teases.

"So when will Rhett see this? Just want to be prepared for the fallout."

"When we close the deal. Like I said, I'm sure there will be some last-minute bargaining on each side. I've found that to be a normal part of the process. It's a game of chess. Each move has a countermove that will eventually lead to a checkmate."

"And the timeline? A week? A month? More? I'm sure you have to have a guestimate."

"Not sure yet. Due diligence is still happening."

"But you'll let me know when it's getting close."

Holden chuckles. "Don't worry. You'll have plenty of time to gloat."

"Good." I cross my arms over my chest and lean back in my chair.

"Good," he mocks me.

"You never answered my question the other night." And one that I've been thinking too much about lately.

"Which question was that?"

I glance out the window of my office, hesitant, as if I'm afraid that someone might be there to hear my next question. A question I shouldn't even be asking while I'm here but am going to anyway. "Why it is that we never go to your place?"

"Ah. Yes. That question. I believe I got distracted with my face buried between your thighs. I found pleasuring you to be a way more pressing matter than talking." Another chuckle. Another subtle pause that leaves us both thinking back.

And leaves me suddenly feeling ridiculous for bringing it up again. Like some clingy, needy woman—the type of woman that makes me cringe—when this is supposed to be sex. Just exclusive, monogamous sex.

"I wasn't complaining. I was just curious is all."

"Let's see. My answer is that I live in a very populated area in the heart of downtown. An area frequented by many of your lovely

Westmore Country Club members who pay way too much attention to what I may or may not be doing. No matter if I'm coming or going and regardless of what time of day or night, I almost always run into one of them. And considering your rule on this is that it stays on the down-low to preserve your reputation with the board, I just assumed that it would be best if we use your place since it offers more privacy."

Completely logical. So why did my mind make more of it?

"Why? Is it that important to you?" he asks as my mind overthinks.

"No. Yes." *It's just sex, Row. Just physical.* "Your answer makes perfect sense."

"You can stop overthinking it now." He chuckles, and I startle at his comment and how right he is. I guess we're starting to get to know each other better than I thought.

Who am I kidding? How can we not know each other as much as we're around each other?

There's some kind of commotion down the hall that has me rising from my seat to open my door and see what it is.

"Everything okay there?" Holden asks, clearly able to hear what sounds to me like Rhett losing his temper over something.

"Uh, not sure. Rhett's upset about something. Talk later?"

"Of course."

I end the call and stride down the hall to the closed conference room door. Employees glance up and then avert their eyes, as if they think they're going to be in trouble for being as curious as I'm being.

But I can't be fired for being nosy.

I open the door without knocking to find Rhett staring out the window. His hands are on his hips and there's clear tension in the set of his shoulders. Chad is sitting at the other end of the conference room, his eyes on my brother before looking over to meet mine.

"Do either of you want to explain why you're making a freaking scene in here so that everyone out there is wondering what in the hell is going on?" I demand.

"Just go away, Row. It's nothing," Rhett says without turning to face me.

"Doesn't sound like nothing. In fact, it sounds like a whole hell of a lot of something."

"Go." He shoves a finger in the direction of the door. His errant dismissal has me gritting my teeth.

I turn to Chad, whose eyes are wide and body is just as tense as my brother's. "What the fuck is going on?"

He shifts in his chair. Clearly uncomfortable. "It's nothing. Just some bad news. Rhett—uh—was trying to make a deal with someone—"

"A deal?" I ask.

"Yes. A fucking deal," Rhett spits out as he turns to face me. "I was trying to do what Holden asked. Make a deal with someone—some new supplier—and it fucking backfired."

Chad blanches at Rhett's explanation and I don't know what to make of it. Not in the least. He seems way too upset over a deal falling through. Then there's the fact that Holden is having me do the same thing. Is he pitting us against each other? Is he playing both sides to see who wins and then will take that person and give them what he's promised—a seat on the board for me or another vote for Rhett?

My stomach churns at the thought. At the worry that I've put my trust in Holden when maybe I shouldn't have.

Jesus. You're sleeping with the man. Now you think you can't trust him?

"Is that all?" Rhett demands. "Because you're standing there looking at me with your jaw on the floor and it's not a very good look for you."

"Fuck you, Rhett," I say with every ounce of disgust that I have. "Fuck you and your mood swings. Whatever this is that you're pissed about, just remember that you brought it on yourself. All of it. So no one in this office should have to hear your tantrum over one thing gone wrong when you're throwing all of their lives in an upheaval with this sale. If they acted like you are right now, you'd fire them. So figure your shit out and grow the fuck up."

I storm out of the conference room and back to my own desk, but I'm too irritated to sit. I pace from one corner to the next, hating the uneasiness churning inside.

When my phones buzzes with a text, I already know who it's going to be.

Holden: Everything okay?

I stare at the text for the longest time, almost as if staring at it will erase the doubt I feel crawling its way up my spine. Might as well just go for it.

Me: Are you playing me against my brother?

Holden: Explain

Me: Did you make a deal with my brother like you did me?

Holden: No. You have the deal in writing. You said your lawyer has it. That's it.

Me: Did you promise Rhett anything other than what's in the documents?

Holden: Why would I do that?

Holden: Rowan? Why are you asking?

Holden: Answer me!

I want to believe him. I stare at the texts, can hear his voice in every single word he types, and I want to believe him.

And is it sad that I do in fact believe him over my own flesh and blood's answer?

My phone begins ringing in my hand. Not surprised he's calling, but I push it to voicemail.

Me: Forget I asked. All is good here.

But it isn't.

Far from it.

Either Rhett's telling the truth, or he's pissed off about something.

And neither is a good thing.

The question is, what's he so upset about?

I hate that the questions still linger long after the last text. So much so that when there's a soft knock on my door, I groan inwardly when I see it's Rhett.

The look I give him says I'm anything but thrilled he's standing there.

"Hey," he says softly and moves to take a seat opposite me. "C'mon, Row. Don't ignore me."

With an exaggerated sigh, I drop my pen and lean back in my chair to meet his eyes. "I have every right to kick you out of my office after the way you've treated me. And I'm not just talking about earlier. I'm talking about the whole fucking situation going on here."

"You're right. You do."

I do a double take. Those were not the words I expected. I stare at my brother and see a glimmer of the boy I used to know and look up to.

"Go on," I say, refusing to give him an inch.

"I apologize—"

"Holy shit." I make a show of looking out my window. "Is hell freezing over?"

"C'mon. Don't be an ass."

I snort. "I'm pretty sure that's your forte."

His sigh is one of frustration. "Look. I apologize. I've been under a lot of stress lately. A lot of things are happening all at once. Coming to fruition all at the same time and—"

"Like what?"

He grimaces. "I can't, Row. There's an NDA and the repercussions if I break it, if any of the board members breach it, are . . . they're fucking terrifying." He runs a hand through his hair. "If you thought we had a good legal department, it's got nothing on Holden's."

I nod. Still not completely comfortable with this conversation and what he's implying. That there are a million more secrets out there that I don't know about.

Games upon games upon games.

"Truth be told, the only person I can count on right now is Chad. It's been . . . fuck, it's been brutal."

"Uh-huh," I say. "Don't expect me to feel sorry for you."

"I don't, it's just, I think we all need to stick together." He sounds defeated and the emotion confuses me. He's getting what he wants. A cash buyout. Responsibility off his back while he gets to retain his cushy title.

"Why do you say that?" I ask.

"No reason in particular. I think Holden's a great businessman but that doesn't mean we don't have to have each other's backs."

"Maybe you should have thought of that before you blindsided me, fired my whole team."

"Blood is thicker than water, Rowan."

"I'm not falling for that bullshit, Rhett. It's admirable but I'm not falling for it." I shrug. "It's perfectly fine to get cold feet and back out of the deal. You'd have more than just my support on that if you did."

"Like whose?" He narrows his eyes.

"It's not my place to say, but just know you would," I bluff.

He stands abruptly, his eyes never leaving mine. "You don't have to accept my apology, but just know I mean it. Truly, I do."

My brother walks out of my office, his shoulders slumped and his head down.

The problem is I'm so jaded, I don't know if I believe him or if this is just another act in his smoke-and-mirrors show.

FIFTY

Holden

"How'd they take it?"

"'The real estate agent? The owners? Who?" Bob asks as noise clatters on in the background.

"How about all of the above?"

"Furious. Livid. Threatening this and that for reneging on the deal. Their agent has called no less than three times a day begging for you to reconsider on his client's behalf."

"Mmm," I murmur, preoccupied with avoiding whatever altercation is happening in the intersection in front of me. People out of cars. Rough characters looking about to fight.

Welcome to Fairmont, where it's an everyday occurrence.

But then I stop myself as Rhett's words ghost through my mind.

It is an everyday occurrence here. Just like it is every-fucking-where.

"You have them where you want them, Holden. They've offered to lower the price some just to close the deal. They're desperate. What about—"

"I just got off the jet. I'll be in the office later. Call me then."

"But what do I tell them in the meantime?"

"Nothing." I proceed through the intersection with caution now that the light has changed.

"Nothing?"

"I believe I made myself clear."

"Yeah. Okay, boss. I just—"

"Stop questioning me, Bob. It's all part of the game. You make a move and then you have to sit and wait for its effects to be known. To take hold." I chuckle. "Then right as they get settled, you make the next one."

"Keep them guessing."

No shit.

"Mm-hm. Make them stew on it for a few days. It just makes the knife a little sharper when it goes in."

I end the call as I pull up to the curb of the old complex. The graffiti is gone on its facade. The rusted wrought iron pickets have been repainted a matte black. The wood on every front porch that faces the street is now a muted brown. The tagging on the cement sidewalks is now covered by crude squares made by gray paint.

He fucking kept his word.

My smile is automatic as I get out of my car and round the hood. I need to see it closer up.

A front door opens a crack at the place where Leo's bike had been last time. It stays slightly ajar for a brief moment before a woman walks out and shuts the door at her back. She eyes me warily, her gaze steadfast on mine as she makes her way over to me.

"You Three-Piece Holden?" she asks, hand over her forehead as if it'll make her see me better.

Three-Piece Holden. I smile. Audrey gave enough information for him to know me but not know who I was.

Perfect.

"I am. Should I assume you're Leo's mom?"

"What do you want with him?" she asks. She's a little over five feet with the same features as Leo. Her hair is a little darker and she's built a bit stockier but there's no doubt in my mind she's his mom. She's wearing a set of worn scrubs with the name of a medical facility embroidered on the top right chest.

"With Leo?"

She nods again. "What are your intentions?"

I shrug. "I used to live here. I used to be him. I don't know. I saw him. I spoke with him. I thought he was a good kid and offered him a chance to earn some extra cash to help out." I hold my hands up. "No strings attached."

"Everything comes with strings around here."

"Not what I have to offer."

"It's the people with the fancy cars and shiny shoes you have to sometimes worry about the most. The flash blinds most from the bad they're doing right beneath their noses."

"Agreed. You have no reason to believe it, but not when it comes to me."

"Then why Leo?"

"From what I can tell, he has a good head on his shoulders. Simple as that. I looked at him and saw me, saw my brother when we lived here years ago, and wanted to give him an opportunity I wish I'd had."

"Mmm," is her only response as she scrutinizes me.

"I know you're busting your ass to provide for him. I didn't mean any offense by the help. It's just . . . if he's sticking to his word, if he's doing the chores, then he'll get paid as promised." I point to the building behind her. "And it looks like he's doing just that."

"Don't fill his head with promises, mister, if you don't intend to fulfill them. He's been hurt enough by all of the men in his life. He's starting not to trust them. I can't have that—can't have you hurting him too—if he's going to succeed in life."

"I understand that more than you know," I say softly. How is it I don't talk about this shit with anyone, and I feel completely comfortable confessing it to her?

Because she understands. She knows. *She is standing in your family's old shoes.*

"Mom!" We both turn to see Leo jogging down the sidewalk toward us from the direction of the bus stop. His backpack is slung over his shoulder, his baseball hat low on his head, but his smile—pure relief—when he sees me, sees that I came back, is everything I didn't know I needed. "Oh my god. I'm sorry, Holden. I fucking begged her not to bug you. I promise—"

"Leo," she warns, I'm assuming for the cursing.

"It's okay. She's just being a good mom, wanting to make sure I'm on the up-and-up."

He stops a few feet before us and looks from her back to me. "You're not mad?" The cautious fear in his voice is fucking brutal. Almost as if he thought his mom questioning me would make me go back on my word.

"It's fine. All good." I point to the work he's done. "I'm impressed. You've done a great job since I was here a few weeks ago."

He bristles with pride. "You think?"

"It looks great." I reach in the window of my car to pull out a small gift bag with tissue fluffed out of the top of it. Cash. Gift cards to the grocery store and Walmart. Another for a sporting goods store. All packaged like a small present from Audrey's swift thinking. "As per my word." I hold up my hand when he goes to dig through the tissue paper and pulls out what's sitting on top, a teddy bear.

"What the—"

"You know there are eyes on us, Leo. Every apartment. Across the street. Curiosity isn't always a good thing. Open it inside. No one needs to see what's in there. For all they know it's a stuffed animal. Let them keep thinking that."

Leo's mom nods subtly. She understands what I mean. That locks on doors can't prevent gunfire through walls or baseball bats through windows in a quest to take what they'd see is in that bag if he opened it now.

"I promise you it's there."

Leo's eyes hold mine, and he nods. "Yes, sir."

"I've got to get going."

"That's it?" he asks and then catches himself and what it sounds like. "I don't mean what's in the bag. I mean . . ."

I smile. Motivation is a strong thing. "More stuff to do?"

"Yeah."

"Give me a few days. I just got back in town. But call Audrey the day after tomorrow and she'll have more work for you." God knows there's endless work that can be done here.

"Okay. I will."

I smile at both of them, and then as I start to walk around the car, Leo says, "Hey," and jogs over to me.

"Yeah?" I ask but when I look at him, he's looking down at his hands fiddling with the handle of the gift bag.

"Just wanted to say thanks for coming back. For keeping your word is all."

"Funny. I was going to say the same thing. Good job, Leo. Thank you for keeping your word to me too."

FIFTY-ONE

Holden

My feet fall heavy as I walk down the office corridor.

There are too many fucking people here. Too many employees. Too many visitors. Just too many obstacles to getting the one thing I've been thinking about for the past five days I've been gone: fucking Rowan.

Figuratively and literally.

Especially with the last text exchange we had before my flight took off. Something about how she gets on her knees for no one. Of course, she was talking off the cuff about work, but fuck if her pause after she said it didn't have me growing hard thinking about her on her knees before me as she takes me to the back of her throat.

The thought makes me pick up the pace a bit more.

And of course, she's nowhere in sight. Not in her office. Not in the lunchroom. Not in the . . . there she is.

I open the conference room door and four sets of eyes whip up to meet mine.

Men. There are three men in the conference room with Rowan.

Three men around her. Talking to her. No doubt distracted by the swell of her tits sitting snugly in her fuchsia sweater.

Fucking hell does she look incredible.

"Holden. You're back," Rowan says, her eyes lighting up and her smile growing a little wider as she tucks a piece of hair behind her ear.

"Straight from the airport." *Why are these assholes here? I'm in serious need of a spontaneous off-site visit where Rowan shows me the lay of her land.*

"Gentlemen, may I introduce you to Holden Knight. He's the incoming—"

"We know who he is," Eager Joe with the mismatching tan suit says. He stands and reaches his hand out. "Akiro Nishikawa with GWA, Don Staley, and Josh Jackson."

"GWA?" I ask as we shake.

"GlassWare America," Akiro responds.

"They're one of the largest glass bottle suppliers on the East Coast," Rowan says. "We've been working through a structural contract and pricing pyramid that will give us mutually exclusive incentives if we decide to onboard them as one of our new suppliers."

There's my girl. Kicking ass and taking names.

My girl?

What the fuck was that, Knight?

"Great." I take a seat, jet-lagged as fuck, but curious as to how Rowan works in these situations. "Don't mind me. Carry on."

Rowan gives me the strangest of looks before taking a deep breath. "Now, where were we?"

The four of them continue their conversation. Price points. Inventory thresholds. Markups. Restocking fees. The give and take. The back and forth. Over and over.

I'm turned on by her all the time now, but Rowan Rothschild negotiating? Now that's fucking hot.

She's firm when she needs to be. Auspiciously compliant when it suits the request. There's a savviness to her that I knew she had but I had yet to see in action.

I'm impressed. More than I expected to be and that's a rarity for me.

Audrey texts me that she needs me. Torn between getting to her and leaving this negotiation, I decide to jump into the conversation.

"Great. Perfect." I rise from my seat and draw the attention of the room. "How about we shave two percent on sticking point one. Offer a referral program under number three. And since we're shaving on one, Akiro, you take what we've offered on point four." All eyes stare at me. "Good? *Good.*" I don't wait for a response. If you leave an inch, the opposition will take a mile. "Great to have met you gentlemen. I look forward to doing business with you. Now if you'll excuse me, I have some pressing matters to get to."

I exit the conference room with a few handshakes and a nod, then spend the next hour catching up on things with Audrey. There's too much to do and not enough fucking time—land deals to squash, buyers to vet, unknowing enemies to reacquaint myself with—but isn't that the best part about all of this?

Being right under their noses and them not knowing it? Shaking hands. Looking them in the eyes. And getting the knife ready for their backs.

"Holden?"

"Mmm?" I don't look up at Audrey's voice as I continue typing my email.

"You're being called down to storage. Something about an issue with the server—a break in the firewall that someone—Harold, I think—wants to show you," Audrey says at my doorway.

"Because that's the last thing I want to do," I grumble.

"I can go for you."

"You, look at firewalls? C'mon now," I tease. Audrey is a self-proclaimed ostrich, purposely keeping her head in the sand when it comes to anything other than the basic tech.

And I'm fine with that for a lot of reasons.

But this? Our IT manager summoning me for something that he should be able to take care of himself is a tad irritating.

Then again, why is someone other than me poking their nose in our firewall? A few keystrokes from my desk could easily find out the answer. But Harold needs to know that I know what I'm talking about.

"I'm going."

"See and be seen, huh?" She raises an eyebrow.

"Exactly." Especially after there was an apparent temper tantrum while I was gone. A very loud, very public freak-out by Rhett.

One that may have had me pouring a glass and toasting my empty hotel room while I gloated after Audrey told me about it.

One that I may have had a small hand in.

"We're at that stage of the purchase already?" she asks because, to everyone besides Rhett and myself, the timeline is unknown.

"We're at that stage of seeing which managers are competent enough to stay onboard."

"Ah. I see."

"Fun times," I say with a sarcastic lift of my eyebrows that she's known me long enough to interpret—someone might be about to get fired—and I rise from my seat. I'm on the elevator and off at the seventh-floor storage room within minutes. The receptionist there, Gina—I think her name is Gina—is on her cell phone and throws it down like it's on fire the minute she sees me. If she was trying to hide that it was a personal call, she needs to learn how to be more subtle. But she's young, biding her time with this job while she gets her degree, and more than intimidated by me.

As I like it to be.

For that reason alone, I let it go.

"Oh. Mr. Knight. Hi. I wasn't—I didn't know you were coming."

My smile is efficient when I offer it. "Harold's office?"

"But he's not—it's back there." She points vaguely over her shoulder. "The last door on the left. I mean—"

I nod. "Last door on the left? I thought his office was on the right."

"It is . . . but servers are on the left."

"Great. Thanks."

I stride past her and down the long hallway, irritated to be called for such a trivial thing, and more than ready at this point to put Harold on notice. Or just fire him.

But when I open the door to the server room, the hulking, six-foot-five meek giant Harold isn't there to greet me.

Not in the least.

It's Rowan and her lips find mine almost as fast as her fingers find the lock on the door at my back.

We're on each other like it's been a year rather than a mere five days. But those five days felt like fucking torture, and it's only intensified now that I have the taste of her kiss and the warmth of her body against mine.

Her hands are on my belt and she's undoing my pants as her tongue teases mine. And without warning, she's dropping to her knees and yanking my slacks down with her as she goes.

Good fucking god. It's my only thought and as it is, the thought is sucked from my mind as Rowan looks up at me and takes me inch by inch between those fucking perfect pouty, pink lips of hers.

My hips buck in reaction and my hand reaches down to the side of her face as I hit the back of her throat.

I fight the guttural groan I want to emit. It's brutal to not let it out—from the sensation her warm, wet mouth evokes and the visual of her before me with her cheeks hollowed out around me.

She may be on her knees, but I'm at her fucking mercy.

She begins to work me over. Her hand twisting and her mouth sucking and tongue expertly applying pressure exactly where it needs to be applied.

My whole fucking body is on fire as the coil in my lower belly and balls begins to tighten. Each lick with another fucking twist in it. Each hit of the back of her throat a fucking euphoria like no goddamn other. Each scrape of her fingernails against my balls an added bonus.

My hand is fisted in her hair as I fuck her mouth. Over and over. Again and again. I beg for it to happen faster at the same time I want it to slow down. To prolong this moment. This goddamn pleasure.

"Yes. Row. *God, yes.*"

My cock swells.

"All the way in. Take it for me."

Hardens.

"You suck cock so fucking good. *Fuck.*"

Hurts with the best kind of pain as she works me toward my orgasm.

And right as I'm on the cusp, about to the point of no return, Rowan releases my cock from her suction with a loud pop and rises to her feet.

A protest is on my lips, my body revolting against her stopping. "Row?" It's a croaked plea. "*Please.*"

She chuckles as she leans into me, her lips inches from mine, her finger pointing into my chest, and her eyes wild with fire.

"How's it feel, Knight?"

"How does *what* feel?" I all but plead with my tone, my cock in my hands and my pants around my ankles.

"Not getting to seal the deal." She takes a step back and smiles.

"*What?*" What the fuck is she talking about?

"I spent weeks on the GWA deal. Endless fucking hours negotiating, bargaining, and putting all the work in all by myself, and then you walk in and close the deal without letting me finish it myself." She glances down to my cock, at the pre-come dripping off its tip before meeting my eyes again. Her smirk is a taunt I'd like to fuck right off her face and would if I weren't preoccupied with being stunned.

"What are you . . . ?"

"It feels kind of like this. Working yourself up, waiting for the release, just on the verge of coming, and then *bam,* having it yanked away. All buildup and no finish."

"Are you fucking serious right now?" I laugh the words out, my head dizzy and my balls aching.

"As a heart attack." She takes another step back and unlocks the door. My eyes all but bug out of my head as she shrugs. "Now if you'll excuse me. I have another meeting to get to."

She opens the door and then shuts it. I stare at the door she just walked out of, hang my head, and just laugh.

That's all I can fucking do because I'm sure as shit not stroking myself off in the server room. Besides, my hand has nothing on Rowan's mouth.

Fucking Rowan Rothschild.

No woman has ever done something like that to me before.

And I kind of like it.

FIFTY-TWO

Holden

"Mom. There's someone at the door." I look into the bedroom of our apartment. To the bed the three of us used to share. To my mother curled in a ball on it with Mason's flannel shirt and pillow bunched up in her arms, her nose buried in it to remember his scent.

She doesn't stir at my words.

She never moves anymore. She lies on the bed with her eyes closed and tears streaming or watching television with a hollow stare. She goes through the motions of living but isn't living. Gets up. Goes to work. Comes home.

She doesn't talk and when she does it's a whisper. It's as if Mason took her voice with him when he died.

She barely eats. In the past month I've learned to get by. I know how to reload the EBT card now. What stores to go to where the food's the cheapest to use it. I've taken over the cooking and the laundry. The bill paying. The living for both of us.

I lost both Mason and my mom that day. I'm just not sure which one is harder to accept. Mason because he's actually gone or my mom because she's here and doesn't see me anymore.

"I think it's the detective." *Move. Respond. Tell me you hear me.* "Okay. I'll speak with him."

I close the bedroom door and pick up a few things on the way to the door. Detective Martin stands on the other side when I open it.

"Holden." His smile is genuine, if a bit sad. It tells me all I need to know before he says another word.

There is no news.

There is nothing to report.

Mason's murderer is still enjoying his life.

"Sir." I clear my throat. "Would you like to come in?"

"It's okay. I don't want to intrude on your time."

"Anything new you can tell us?"

He sighs and then opens his mouth and shuts it. He looks down and then back up before he finally speaks. "You haven't seen the *Times* article yet, then?"

"What are you talking about?" It takes everything I have to stand there and face him rather than run to my computer and search in our local newspaper for whatever he's talking about.

"Good. I'm glad. I wanted you to hear it from me first."

"Hear what?"

"A source leaked information on the case."

"So there is information? What is it?"

"The case has been closed. The powers that be determined that it was all an egregious mistake. Your brother darted out in front of the car. The driver didn't have time to react. He didn't even realize he'd hit anyone until he got home and saw his broken front headlight."

"What do you mean it was all an accident?" My voice rises in pitch, my head shaking as if I didn't hear him correctly.

"Exactly what it sounds like. Sometimes things like this happen—tragic accidents—and there really isn't anyone to blame."

"But there is. The driver. He hit him. He killed him. The passenger got out and looked at him. Then they drove away. Mason never rode in the street. He was on the sidewalk. I know he was on the sidewalk. . . ." My voice cracks as my head spins and tears threaten. "This isn't right."

"I'm sorry. I—"

"You know it's not right. The look on your face says it."

"I wanted you to hear it in person." His smile is sympathetic. "There's nothing more I can do."

He gives a nod.

"What about the lighter?" I think of Rhett Rothschild. "I mean, the owner—"

"The owner has agreed not to press charges against you."

"What?" The word is a shrieked syllable marred with confusion. "What the hell do you mean he's decided not to press charges?"

He eyes me, clearly not thrilled with my outburst, but doesn't reprimand me outright. His voice is soft and placating as I glare at him, demanding answers. "They know you stole it when he accidentally left it in the main dining room."

"And what? Grabbed it when I went out to help save my brother and dropped it? Are you out of your fucking mind?"

This can't be happening.

It can't.

"Other club members saw you with it in the days before the accident."

"This is unbelievable." I shove a hand through my hair and pace back and forth in the small space. My gut churns. "You're serious, aren't you?" My teeth clench and hands fist as my head rages with fury. "He was the passenger of the car."

"There was no passenger. If you read the article, you'll see that."

"And you're just believing them?" My heart feels like it's exploding in my chest. My head feels like it's detached from my body.

"What you should be is arrested for petty theft but considering the situation, the lighter's owner—and the country club itself—have decided not to press charges."

"Big of them."

"You should be more than grateful that they're going to let the matter go, even let you keep your job so long as this doesn't get brought up again."

"Wow. That's . . . so *them*."

Entitled fucking pricks.

Rhett. He wasn't driving but he sure as shit got back in the car and didn't help.

"You believe that bullshit?" I ask.

Detective Martin gives me a placating nod. "Like I said, I'm sorry. Accidents happen sometimes and they're no one's fault."

"I think you need to leave," I say when I finally find my voice again as my body trembles with rage.

He meets my eyes again and then heads back down the sidewalk and toward his car parked near the very spot where Mason died.

The article.

It's only then that it hits me about the damn article. I'm at my computer in seconds, cursing the shitty internet speed for taking its sweet-ass time to load. Once it does, I forge my way past the *Times'* paywall so I can read the article.

The story is short and succinct.

Why waste ink on a poor kid who was killed, right?

*   *   *

No charges have been filed in the hit-and-run death of a twelve-year-old in the Fairmont area last month. Both the chief of police and the circuit solicitor have declined to file charges, citing the accident as just that—an accident. *Witnesses who stated the car jumped the curb have since recanted their statements to say the youth rode his skateboard between parked cars, darting out in front of the white Mercedes driven by seventeen-year-old Chadwick Williams of Westmore.*

*   *   *

Chadwick Williams.

I know that name.

Even worse, I know the prick. Mr. Polo Shirt and Chinos with the shitty jokes about my mom and entitled *everything.*

Rhett's friend was the driver.

Jesus fucking Christ.

I can picture him clearly. His grating laugh. His condescending tone. His arrogant demeanor.

My hands fist as I stare at the words. They blur as anger owns every single cell in my body. *It was him?* I shake my head, as if to make it sink in that the assholes from the club killed my brother.

Accident. No accident. They didn't stop. They didn't help. They killed him.

And now because of who they are, of where they live and the last names they hold, they won't be punished.

* * *

The teen driver "didn't even realize he'd hit anyone" until he got home and saw his broken headlight. Investigators were able to place him in the area at the time of the accident, but there is no footage of the actual event happening to refute or support eyewitness claims.

Williams, a senior at Canyon Academy Prep, is deeply troubled by the turn of events. He and his family have requested privacy at this time.

* * *

Privacy? Deeply troubled? A sound fills the small apartment—a deep, growling bellow—and I don't even realize it comes from me.

I reread the article.

There were no fucking cars parked on the street. No place for Mason to dart out between.

And then I read it again.

He hit Mason. Rhett was with him. I saw him get out of the car. I saw him look at Mase. They knew what they did. They knew they had hit him. Then they reversed and fled. That's what Mr. Bonman from unit 10B said happened. *That's what he said.* The same as my story. Why would we lie?

Total bullshit that Chadwick *didn't know* he'd hit anything.

On the third time through, I stop and research who the chief of police is. I have every intention of banging down the man's door and demanding more for my little brother. And as the chief's picture slowly loads on our shitty internet, as his name beneath it comes clear, it all makes fucking sense. *Chief Edwin Williams.*

"Chief Edwin Williams, loving husband of Florence Daybell-Williams and father of teenage son Chadwick Williams, was born to protect and serve the town of Westmore, just like his father and his grandfather before him have." I mutter his website bio, a fury of disbelief rioting through me.

His fucking father is the chief of police.

I jump to the solicitor's site but have a feeling I already know what's there. Why no charges have been pressed. Everyone in that goddamn country club protects their own.

The current circuit solicitor is Clifford Daybell.

How convenient.

How utterly fucking convenient.

No doubt Clifford Daybell is of some relation to Florence Daybell-Williams.

They rigged this whole fucking thing. If I didn't live here, if I didn't work at the Westmore Country Club and see shit like this every day, I would think it's not possible.

But I do live here.

I do work there.

And I know the truth. Chadwick Williams murdered my brother—and Rhett Rothschild was in the car—and they're getting off because they have friends in high places who fix shit for them.

Just like they do at the club.

Clank. Click. Clank.

I sink back on the couch and close my eyes. I let the tears stream down. I let the grief I've been wading in swallow me whole.

Mason was somebody. A good kid with a bright future. My little brother with a goofy laugh. A somebody who mattered.

But apparently the only people who matter are those with money. Are those in high places. Are those who can fix "mistakes."

Nobody cares about the other people. About us. The people who are merely trying to get by. The ones trying to better themselves despite being dealt a shit hand in life. Those of us who are one bad decision away from being them.

Even our lives don't matter.

There is motion in the doorway to my right and I open my eyes to see my mom standing there. Her once proud shoulders now sag. Her usually styled brown hair has her roots showing and streaks of silver in it. Her gentle smile is lost.

"Anything?" she asks just above that whisper I've grown so used to in the last month.

I stare at her and know the truth will only make her spiral further. "No. Nothing." The lie rolls off my tongue, and I hate myself for it immediately.

I'll tell her the truth soon. I will. But not now.

I need you too, Mom. I've lost him and now I'm losing you too.

She stares at me with hollow eyes and nods—"'Kay"—before shuffling back into the bedroom and returning to her fetal position of rejecting reality.

I stare at the ceiling and prepare for another night of trying to forget.

I've got to get us out of here.

Every day we leave the house we see where he died. Every day we hear the kids playing and we expect him to come in the front door.

Every day we lose him all over again.

And even worse, every time I go to my job that I so desperately need—that I can't lose—I come face-to-face with Mason's killers.

FIFTY-THREE

Rowan

"Your gran was a fucking catty, meticulous genius who knew exactly what she was doing. I mean"—Sloane shuffles papers on the other end of the line—"she has all of this shit line-itemed out."

"I know. It's pretty impressive," I say as I glance once more at my closed office door—just to make sure it didn't miraculously open itself back up.

"Affairs between board members and officials high up the town's chain of command. Loans made to shady people for gambling debts. Illegitimate children who no one knows about. Dirty deals with the wrong crowd."

"She was stockpiling."

"She was giving you blackmail material is what she was doing," she murmurs.

"It's easy to say that, but that doesn't mean anything will pan out." I've looked at it all. I've studied it all. It's not beneath me to use it, but I need the money from Gran to use it.

That's the crux of it all.

"You're learning the playing field. You're seeing who might be a logical person to pressure if need be. Most of them are old. Some might be so old they don't care about a scandal. Others might be so old they don't want the scandal. Rowan? Are you there?"

"Yeah. One sec . . ."

The phone is to my ear, but my feet are moving toward the door so that I can better view the woman who just walked down the hall.

She's tall. Statuesque and svelte. Her pencil skirt is a deep gray and her sweater is tucked into it tight. Her nylons have seams in the back and her heels are higher than high.

She carries herself with an elegance and air that has others in the office peeking their heads out of their offices to take notice.

And she walks right into Holden's office without stopping.

Holden steps into the doorway and meets my eyes from my position down the hall for the briefest of seconds. I hate that I can't read what they say, but before I can figure it out, he shuts the door and the blinds seconds thereafter.

"Rowan?" Sloane says in my ear.

"Yeah. Sure. I'm here."

"No, you're not. What just happened?"

"Nothing," I say.

And it was nothing, wasn't it? Just a business associate of Holden's.

One for whom he shut the blinds and the door.

Much like he does when we're in here alone at night and having sex in some form or another.

My tongue feels thick in my mouth.

"Are you okay?" Sloane continues.

Am I? Of course I am.

I have to be.

Just a business associate.

"Yes." I shake my head to clear it and force myself back to my desk so that I can't see down the hallway.

But that doesn't stop me from wondering.

Is this a payback for the server room stunt?

Is he really that petty?

"I'm here," I say. "Where were we?"

"We were talking about making a short list of people who'd be the easiest to apply pressure to."

"Isn't that illegal?" I ask.

"As your friend and legal advisor," she says in her primmest of tones, "I can make anything look and sound pretty. Lines can be blurred. Threats can be subtle."

"So yes and no?" I laugh.

"How bad do you want it?" she asks.

Fucking bad.

"Now we just need to figure out how I can come up with the money to be able to do this. And no"—I cut her off before she says what she's going to say—"a mail-ordered groom is not the answer."

Her laugh rings through the line and makes me smile.

Our conversation sticks with me as I purposely keep myself more than busy all day. It's easier than wondering what the hour-long, closed-door meeting with the supermodel was about.

Audrey usually sits in on all his meetings. Takes notes for him. Types up a list of actionable items afterward.

She wasn't in that meeting.

The thought repeats as she gives me a cursory smile as she passes me on my way into the break room.

I need caffeine.

And a distraction.

And that distraction isn't in the form of looking up to find Holden standing in the break room doorway, blocking my exit.

"Hi," he says.

I offer a smile. A nod.

And try not to be irritated.

"You're not going to talk?" he asks.

"What was that all about?" I ask.

"What was what about?" He narrows his eyes. "Ahh," he says when he realizes what I'm talking about. The chuckle that follows soon after grates against my nerves.

We hold each other's gazes.

"I have a lot of people come in and out of my office, Rowan. Some conversations are private. Some are not. Nowhere in whatever this is do I have to justify every single person I meet with . . .

and you don't want to be the woman who asks me to. I assure you on that."

He holds my eyes for a second longer before turning on his heel and walking out.

Just when I think Holden Knight's walls are broken down, they go right back up.

Almost as if he, himself, isn't sure where they need to be positioned.

FIFTY-FOUR

Holden

"We signed the papers. The ink is dried. Why hasn't the full amount been fucking transferred?"

"The ink is still drying last I checked, but please, by all means, come on in," I say, glancing up to Rhett and his impatient fucking stare as he stands in my doorway with anxiety radiating off him.

Clank. Click. Clank.

This is for you, Mase. All for you.

He puts the lighter in his pocket, stance wide, shoulders squared like he's ready for a brawl. "I will. I don't need to ask permission to come into my own goddamn office."

Testy. Testy.

I make a show of glancing around the space. I've changed it up a bit since I moved in. The golf memorabilia is gone. So are the plaques praising Rhett as an esteemed member of the Westmore Country Club world. Less is more for me. And I don't have to stare at my accomplishments to know my worth as a man. Apparently, he does.

I offer a pitying smile. "Last I checked the office was mine, but I'll let your mistake slide since it seems you're upset." I fold my hands methodically on the desk blotter in front of me. "Now, how is it that I can help you?"

"The funds were supposed to be in our account by the close of business. It's past then so I don't want to hear shit about missing the bank's wire deadline or something like that. You knew the deal was closing today. The money's not here. It's been less than two hours and you're already defaulting on your promises."

My chuckle is a low, unforgiving rumble as Chad comes into view behind him. *Don't have the balls to confront me yourself, Rhett?*

"Surprise. Surprise. Chad's here," I say. "What's that saying? Two's a crowd, three's a party?"

"Rhett's right. Only a very small portion of the funds is there," Chad says.

"Yeah, like you forgot an extra zero," Rhett spits out.

"First off, I haven't defaulted on shit." My smile is a sarcastic *fuck you.* My hatred for these two runs deep. "Second, the funds are there. I double-checked myself. I'm not quite sure what you're talking about."

"The purchase price was one hundred million," Rhett says.

"I'm aware. I, too, signed the docs," I say.

"Only ten million is in the account," Chad says.

"Yes. I'm aware of that too." I give a measured nod and bite back my smile that wants to gloat. This is what happens when you're so eager robbing Peter to pay Paul that you don't read the fine print.

You had the chance to fix this, Rhett, but you were so goddamn eager, you dismissed your legal counsel's advice during our meeting last week.

> *"I don't fucking care, Kyle. So long as the structure is the same, we're good to sign," Rhett says, pulling the papers from his lawyer's hands and shaking his head.*
>
> *"But—"*
>
> *"But what?" Rhett snaps. "Is the ownership divvied up how we agreed? Are the board members the same? Do I still have four percent more than Rowan in total company holdings? Yada yada yada."*
>
> *"They are," Kyle says.*
>
> *"Is the purchase price the goddamn same?" Rhett barks.*

Kyle nods and meets my eyes across the table. "I still think it's best—"

"I don't need to fucking think," Rhett says, desperation in his voice and sweat on his brow.

"As your attorney, I wouldn't be doing my job if I didn't advise you that it's best if you reread all of the—"

"And as your client who's paying you a hefty sum, I demand to get the goddamn deal closed and the money transferred. That's what I want. I need . . ." He shakes his head as if it'll erase that last sentence.

But I heard it.

I know how it was supposed to end.

You need . . . the fucking money, don't you, Rhett? That land you thought you sold, the land you bought thinking it was a good deal but got snowed on because of your greed. The land you're trying to snow some other unsuspecting sap into buying—that deal? It fell through this week and now you're desperate.

You emptied your family's trust to buy that land and sustain the loan. You siphoned money out of this company to play the shell game, put the money into the trust so no one in your family noticed it was missing. You're banking on this deal to save your ass, to prevent the loan from going into default, before anybody other than a trusted few figure it out.

But you're so goddamn greedy, so focused on the end game, that you're refusing to see the forest for the trees.

Why would a guy like me, the man who shows up out of the blue offering to buy a company that's not for sale, do anything other than be your hero? Why would I try to screw you over when you are banking on me saving you?

The devil was once an angel too, Rhett.

Be careful who you put your faith in—especially when

your back's against the wall and you reek of despera-tion.

"You sure you don't want to take a moment to read things over again?" I offer. "The last thing I'd want you to do is to sign the deal without being one hundred per-cent informed."

Rhett's attention switches to me. His hands fidget. His eyes flicker about. He's so goddamn high on the prospect of finally getting his ass saved that he can't see anything else but the dollar signs. He's jonesing for this final fix.

Exactly what I was planning on.

"No. I'm fine." He grabs a pen from the center of the table. "We've waited too fucking long to get to this point as it is."

"So where's the other ninety million?" he asks.

"In the escrow account like we agreed upon."

"So get it out. Get it transferred," he demands with a frantic look to his business partner. His land deal partner who has emp-tied the family coffers as well.

"I can't."

"What do you mean *you can't?*" His voice breaks.

"Just what it sounds like. *I can't.* That's the point of the escrow account," I say. "Ten percent up front to be dispersed among all the shareholders commensurate with the number of shares they own. The other ninety percent is to remain in an escrow account for a year so long as a set profit margin is retained. After that year fifty percent will be dispersed. Then after the second year the remain-der will be. What exactly is the confusion over?"

Rhett swallows and stares at me with confusion etched in the lines of his face. "That wasn't the deal."

My smile is a slow crawl. "But it was. Your lawyer tried to re-view the terms with you. You told him no."

"Bullshit." But the flicker of fear in his eyes says he's questioning himself.

"Not from where I sit." I roll my chair back and pull the signed contract out of my top drawer. I drop the stack of papers on the desk with a thud before thumbing through it as both Chad and Rhett move closer. "Right here." I point. "Section four. Clause five. It's the payment terms. They're all laid out. Right there. And your signature is a few pages after, agreeing to them."

When I look up, it takes everything I have not to gloat.

"What in the flying fuck. That wasn't in the original terms. That—"

"By the number of hours my lawyer is charging me, I'm more than certain she went back and forth with your lawyer numerous times. It's called negotiating. It's called settling. There's nothing shady in this deal. I assure you."

"But . . . *why*?"

Why are you a greedy fuck who didn't understand the terms of his own deal?

Why do you need a better lawyer?

Why are you so desperate for money that you refused to read the fine print?

"Why?" I chuckle. "It's a standard practice in large deals. It adds a guarantee that you won't try to sabotage your own company. That you can't try and deplete its capital, its staff, its whatever if you suddenly regret making the deal. And it's a guarantee on my end that I can't sabotage it from the inside—unless of course I don't give a 'flying fuck.' That was your term, wasn't it?"

Chad yanks the paper out of my hands. He reads it, his eyes growing wider as each second passes. *So much for being an awesome COO, huh, Chad?*

"You motherfucker," he mutters.

I smile. I dare him to look closer than he's ever looked before. But then again, he never stopped to look into my brother's eyes, he never stopped to help or even acknowledge he killed him even when he was found out, so *how would he know*?

"You slimy piece of shit," Rhett says.

"Wow. I'd think you'd reserve that for the lawyers who worked out the deal, but hey"—I hold up my hands—"who am I to judge?" I chuckle and take the signed paperwork back, sliding it back into the top drawer. "Relax, Rhett. The time for cold feet is over. Besides, your cut of the ten mil should be more than enough to hold you over for the next year, right?"

Rhett looks at me with shell-shocked eyes. "Wait until—"

"Until what? Until *who* finds out?" I ask, knowing exactly where he's going with this. And his glare only confirms it. "One, you signed a nondisclosure as part of the terms of the contract, so no one knows the deal is done until I announce it. And no one knows the terms of it—ever. Two, you complain to others about the deal? It only ends up making you look stupid and people look closer at why you're so upset. Is there a reason you're so upset, Rhett?" I bait him and I fucking love every goddamn second of it. Of this.

"You conned me. Us." He spits the words out.

"I did no such thing. It's in your hands in black and white."

His jaw is clenched so tight it's a miracle his teeth don't crack.

"Is there anything further I can do for you?" I ask. Blank stares meet my amused one.

FIFTY-FIVE

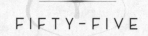

Rowan

"Holden needs your assistance." I look up at my doorway to see Audrey and her ramrod-straight spine standing there.

While I'm getting used to her presence, I'm still not sure what to think of her . . . nor do I exactly know what she thinks of me. She's not the warmest of people—unless you're talking about Holden. When it comes to Holden, Audrey is a completely different person. She's softer, more personal. Her smile is genuine. Her tone gentler.

And for some reason I don't understand, I want to win her approval.

"Oh. Okay. Is he in his office?"

Her smile is tight. "No."

"The conference room?"

"No." This time there is no smile.

"Have I done something to offend you, Audrey?" I ask the question that is on my mind every time I interact with her.

She studies me. Her eyes narrow and her lips pinch momentarily as if she has to think about things. "The last thing Holden needs right now is to be distracted. There is too much at stake for him if he is."

"Good thing the deal will be finalized soon, and he can figure out his own distractions for himself, right?" I ask, more than peeved at her implication that I'm a distraction.

And if she thinks that, then does that mean she knows about the two of us?

The pinched mouth returns. So does the all-business attitude. "He's off-site, evaluating a new asset."

"Oh." Is that why he's been holed up in meetings all day yesterday and nowhere in sight today?

"He sent a car to take you to him."

"Okay. Um . . ." I don't even know what to say. Other than a few comments in passing over the past few days, after the break room incident, we haven't exactly had time to talk much. Sure, we've exchanged a few texts back and forth. Some flirty. Some professional. Neither have addressed that situation and I'm not sure if that's good or bad. Regardless, it's fallen by the wayside since we've both been seriously busy.

Me buttoning up the deal Holden made with GWA—which he has stayed completely out of. And Holden behind a lot of closed doors in meetings during the day, and then at night out entertaining some old clients who are in town.

Besides that, for some reason that I can't put my finger on, there has been a tense undercurrent in the office the past few days. A lot of closed doors and not much of the lighthearted banter we're used to.

Or maybe it's just me. Maybe I've been working too much with not enough downtime.

I'll admit that every time I come home, I'm a tad bummed not to find him sitting in the shadows of my porch waiting for me.

"Should I tell the driver you're on the way down?" she prompts. Clearly in her eyes I'm taking too much time and that's her blunt way of letting me know.

"Yes. Sure." I rise from my chair and look around as if I'm not sure what to bring. Within seconds I have my purse and my phone in hand, head down the elevator, and get into the waiting car.

Curious but not overly distracted by Holden's request, I get lost in answering emails on my phone during the drive. My immediate assumption is that I'm being driven out to meet him at one of the properties he had me researching.

I'd provided a long list. He most likely has narrowed it down and wants my opinion. I don't know why that makes me feel good, but it does.

The assumption is logical enough, but when the car jostles over something and I look up, I'm more than confused.

Why are we at an airport?

Moreover, why are we not just at the airport, but on the tarmac?

What is going on here?

I immediately sit up straighter, my head on a swivel as I look around before landing on the jet we're headed for. It has a matte black exterior, a "KH" logo on the tail that I know stands for Knight Holdings, and a black carpet rolled out beneath a set of airstairs leading up to the open door.

The Rothschilds have always had wealth. We've never done without. We have a huge trust of old family money. Hell, Gran has thirty million sitting somewhere for me alone. So we're not poor by any means . . . but a private jet? And not just one to rent for a trip but one that he owns? That's a whole other level of wealth that I don't think I fully wrapped my head around Holden having until right this moment.

"Here we are, Miss Rothschild," the driver states as he pulls up to the edge of the carpet.

If the logo weren't on the plane, then I'd be questioning if we were in the right place. But it is.

"Thank you," I murmur as I exit the car, nerves suddenly bouncing around inside of me for some odd reason.

Maybe because we're always on my turf and for the first time in whatever this is, we are 100 percent on his.

I take the stairs up to the plane and stick my head in the cabin as if I'm afraid of what I'll find. But that fear is erased instantly when I see Holden sitting at a table on the right side of the plane. His laptop is out, his cell is to his ear, and he's having an animated conversation with whoever is on the other end of the line.

He sees me when I walk in and his face lights up in a way that affects me way more than it should. He waves to me to come in with his free hand.

"Yeah. I get it. But the offer remains off the table. I said to let them stew, so let them stew. Antsy sellers are the best kind." He nods even though the person can't see him. "I have a feeling this owner is a bit more eager than most. Mmm-hmm. I know. But getting fucked over is part of doing business sometimes. Great if you see it coming. It sucks if you don't." He shrugs, his eyes still on me. "No skin off my back. Yeah. I know. Okay. We'll talk later, but for now, don't respond to the agent. Say I'm busy. Yep. Got it. Later."

He gives a nod as he ends the call and tosses his cell on the table in front of him with a clatter. "Sunshine," he says, rising from his seat.

"Hi." I look around and smile at the two flight attendants in the back who are eyeing me subtly while pretending to keep themselves busy.

What are they thinking? Is this normal for Holden to invite women on his jet, or is this new to them?

I'd like to think it's a rarity but I'm not that naive.

I take a polite step to the right of Holden, turning my face so the kiss he plants hits my cheek to let him know we are being watched.

His laugh is bombastic as he grabs my face and kisses me directly on the lips. I freeze. "I can't kiss you on my private jet, but you'll suck my dick in the server room?" he murmurs quietly against my lips. "You can do better than that, Row." He brushes a lock of hair off my forehead as he studies me. "Besides, they are all bound by strict confidentiality agreements. They won't break them. I make sure of it. The consequences are too dire."

"So you do things on your jet often enough that you need confidentiality agreements?" I ask.

"Business deals. Meetings. Private conversations. If that's what you're talking about, then yes," he taunts, almost as if he can see my mind spinning tales of him having sordid sex with someone at thirty thousand feet. "But I have a feeling you're asking something entirely different."

"Perhaps," I whisper.

"Don't let your imagination run too wild, Sunshine. Save some of that wild for me." And this time when he goes in for the kiss, I don't fight his tender brush of lips against mine. I don't dodge the quick delve of his tongue to touch mine. He emits a soft groan that has my body reacting viscerally. His fingers loosen on my chin as our lips meet softly again. "Promise?"

I nod. "Promise," I whisper.

When he takes a step back, there is a wickedly mischievous glint to his eyes and widening of his grin.

"What?" I ask, surprised over the shift from sweet and soft to suddenly mysterious.

"Nothing." He lifts his brows and points to the seat across from his as he sits. "Take a seat. If we want to stay on schedule, we need to get taxiing."

"What do you mean *stay on schedule*?"

"We are on a jet, Rowan." He winks. "Flight plans aren't the easiest to change."

"I—but—*why* are we on a jet? Are you going to look at property? Are we meeting with a potential client? Audrey said you needed my help on something. Why am I here?"

He angles his head to the side, staring at me in that way of his that makes me feel seen and undressed at the same time. "How about all of the above?"

"That's not giving me much to go on."

"Little Miss Always-in-Control Sunshine doesn't always need to know everything." He flashes a grin that I hate to admit makes me melt.

I glare at him in response as a small part of me—the romantic part of me that I'll swear to any and everyone else doesn't exist— might silently sag, realizing this is *just* a business trip.

My mind goes back to our dinner on the beach. To being free to kiss him in public and just be normal with him.

The part of me who holds tight to that night, who sticks her head in the sand instead of acknowledging that the "more than sex" part about that night meant something to me, deflates a little.

"Is something wrong?" Holden asks.

"No. Of course not." I muster a smile.

"You sure?"

I nod. "Yep. Everything is fine," I say as one of the flight attendants approaches to inform us that we need to put our seatbelts on as we've gotten clearance from the tower.

Her eyes linger on Holden longer than they should. Her smile is fake; her cleavage in a conservative uniform is somehow pronounced.

"Thank you," Holden says to her.

"You're so very welcome, Mr. Knight."

Gag. She couldn't be any more obvious if she tried. I watch her as she walks toward the back of the plane to take her own jump seat. Maybe that seatbelt will get locked, and she'll be stuck there for the rest of the flight so she can't come over here and drool all over Holden.

"What's that look for?" Holden asks, bringing my eyes back to his.

"Nothing."

"You're not good at hiding your emotions, Rowan." He glances over his shoulder and then grins when he looks back at me. "What?"

"She wants you."

He snorts. "Sweet little Rhonda?"

"She may be sweet, but that doesn't make her want you any less."

He shrugs, amusement lighting up his eyes as he narrows them. "And that bugs you?"

"No," I say stone-faced, even though every bone in my body is rife with jealousy.

"No?" He smiles, clearly seeing the unwelcome emotional response in my eyes. "And here I was turned on by the thought of you being jealous over me."

"I'm not."

"You are." He leans forward. "But we'll let that slide. If you're going to take her down when we order drinks, just let me know ahead of time though. I might want to record it on my phone."

He thinks this is hilarious.

"Is that why you summoned me here? To get back at me for the server room stunt by making me watch your gorgeous flight attendant drool over you?"

"And here I thought you thought better of me."

"You don't seem like a man who's challenged very often. It wouldn't surprise me if what I did pissed you off."

His smile is a slow, crooked crawl. "Is that why you think I brought you here? For me to get back at you?"

I shrug, suddenly feeling juvenile but still needing validation. "We've barely talked at all. A few texts. Some meetings in the conference room. A lot of closed-door meetings. You've been busy at night. It seems a logical assumption." I say the words but with each one, I feel more ridiculous by the syllable.

"Part of the reason I asked you to come with me—to take this little trip—is because I owe you an apology." I open my mouth to speak, and he shakes his head as if to tell me to let him finish. "You were right. I may not have liked the way you did it. Scratch that. My dick didn't like it, but hell if the rest of me didn't admire the fuck out of you for having the balls to do it."

"It was stupid. I didn't—"

"Don't go all soft on me now, Sunshine." He laughs. "It takes a lot to make me speechless. That did. Let's just not make a habit of it." He reaches out and touches my hand. There's something about the action that startles me. Holden's not one for casual touching, but then again, we're never really in the situation to be able to. "I butted in when I shouldn't have. I asked you to do a job because I knew you could do it and then I overstepped."

"You don't have to apologize."

"When I'm wrong, I say I'm wrong. I was wrong."

"Thank you." Those are big words from him and appreciated more than he'll ever know. I'm so used to my brother stepping all over everything and never caring. "I appreciate it. I truly do. But that doesn't explain why I'm here. An apology could have been done in the office."

Holden leans back as the jet begins to taxi. "It's killing you not knowing, isn't it?" His grin taunts.

"It is."

"Good." He leans back in his chair as if this topic is over with. "Now, tell me about the other suppliers you've been in contact with."

I stare at him for a beat, hating that he's not giving in to me, but then again, I don't expect any less from him. If he thinks I'm a control freak, he's one ten times over.

He lifts his eyebrows as he waits.

I relent.

We talk shop for the next two hours. I lay out the ideas I've been culminating over the years. Markets I feel like we've left untapped. Revenue streams I think we've been so shortsighted on that we're missing possible gold mines. Current suppliers who I think are screwing us—Porter and Greatland included.

I take advantage of his undivided attention to prove I have a head for more than just marketing, as my title denotes.

"And so Horner's coming to the office to meet with you on Monday?" he asks in regards to a raw materials supplier I'm trying to onboard. "May I ask if I can sit in?"

I smile. He did get my point. They're my clients. They're my deals to seal. "Sure, if you plan on coming to Georgia with me to meet them."

"So now you're meeting them on their turf to avoid me butting in. Got it," he teases.

"Maybe. And maybe because that's where their distribution center is set up and I asked to oversee their operation logistics for a few days so I can make a better decision on terms."

"How long are you gone for?"

"Three days plus travel, and with all the canceled flights these days, who knows how long that will take."

"Take the jet."

"Hilarious." I roll my eyes.

"I'm serious. Take the jet. Besides, then you'll have time for you and Rhonda to compare notes about my skills."

I connect with his shin beneath the table. "Ow," he belts out but then laughs. "There are no notes, Sunshine. But see, you are jealous. Now I'm definitely turned on."

I blow out an exasperated sigh and shake my head. "Funny."

We banter back and forth between business discussions, laughing and teasing as we do so.

"And your brother," Holden asks eventually. The sky is dark outside the windows of the jet with dots of light below us wherever we are. "Where do you think he stands in all of this? Gut instinct."

"I think he's to blame for the company failing. Yes, the economy plays a factor, and the interest rates affect our loans, our price points, but that doesn't account for the loss in capital."

"And where do you think that capital has gone?" There's an intensity in his eyes. An expression that says he might know more.

"That's the million-dollar question, isn't it?"

"Excuse me, Mr. Knight," Rhonda interrupts, her voice even more sultry this time around.

Holden looks at me and grins before turning to her. "Yes?"

"We've been cleared for landing. I need to collect your drinks and plates."

"Of course," he says, chewing the inside of his cheek to fight the grin that acknowledges my jealousy.

"You're still not going to tell me where we're going?" I ask to distract once she's left us.

"Not yet, no."

"Can you give me a hint?"

He twists his lips for a moment and then nods. "We're celebrating."

"What are we celebrating?"

"Whatever it is you want to. Closing a deal. Getting out of the office. Finally doing something you've promised yourself you're going to do forever." He shrugs playfully. "Make of it what you will. You don't always have to have a specific reason to celebrate."

"Yes, you do."

"You don't get to make the celebration rules, Sunshine."

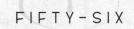

FIFTY-SIX

Rowan

"Manhattan?" I ask, eyes wide as I stare at him, excitement bubbling up. "Why are we in Manhattan? We have clients—"

Holden's lips meet mine to shut me up as the limo heads toward the city's lights. Our tongues touch and our bodies heat up as I thread my fingers through the hair at the base of his neck and his splay across my back. "No more talking about work. We're off the clock." Another brush of his lips. "We have plans."

"Plans?" I ask and then silently freak out at the clothes I have on and my makeup bag being back in the office. *Hold up, Row. You're in New York City. The man just whisked you away in his private jet. This is when you sit back, stop trying to control shit, and enjoy the ride.* "What kind of plans?"

He just gives me a shy smile and shrugs, but then wraps his arm around my shoulder, pulls me into his side, and presses a kiss to the crown of my head. "You'll just have to wait and see."

But the waiting and seeing doesn't take long—the car soon pulls up in front of the Ritz-Carlton. We bypass the front desk and step directly into a waiting, private elevator. Holden nods at the elevator attendant and within moments he is opening the door to the royal penthouse suite without breaking stride.

I follow him in and am surprised to find a team of women waiting there. "Holden?" So many questions in those two syllables of his name.

He leans over and presses a kiss to my lips. "Can't have you going out for a night on the town without having someone help you get ready."

"Are you . . ."

"Serious?" He smiles. "Yes, I'm serious. I'll be taking these from you because no working is allowed," he says, removing my phone from my hand and my bag from my arm before turning to the team of ladies waiting for me. "I'll be over here working. Ladies, she's all yours."

Our eyes hold for a beat, so many things I want to say but don't know how to voice so I try to put them in the one, single look. *Thank you.*

For making me feel special.

For taking time out to do something.

For whatever this is.

Over the next two and a half hours I am pampered within an inch of my life. A relaxing massage at a glass window with the world around me. A quick shower and then a mani-pedi. My hair done. My makeup done. Several sets of lingerie to pick from followed by a rack of ridiculously expensive dresses.

"That man's got it bad if he's going through all this trouble for you," the lead stylist, Anissa, murmurs softly so that Holden can't hear.

I laugh. "No. We're not like that. We work together. We . . ."

"Sleep together," she finishes for me with a chuckle and a knowing look. "It's obvious in the way he keeps looking at you. Like he wants to eat you up and then come back for more. Girl, you can tell yourself all you want that you're just having a sexy little fling, but this"—she points to the entire room set up solely for getting me ready—"says a lot more than that."

"He's just an over-the-top guy."

But that's the thing. Holden isn't. He's stoic. Not flashy . . . and yet he hired a team of women to pamper me.

"Uh-huh." She nods to the five boxes of Christian Louboutin heels set on the table in front of me. All in my size, all apparently mine to keep. "You just keep telling yourself that." She looks me up and down and whistles. "I do think you made the right decision going with this dress," she says as she adjusts my bra strap.

It's a deep, dark blue. The cleavage is low and the drape at the curve of my ass even lower. It's sophisticated and classy with just enough sexy. And I feel incredible in it.

Anissa is fixing the hem some as I stand looking at my reflection in the mirror. Holden comes into view over my shoulder. He's wearing a tuxedo that's clearly custom tailored and only adds to how handsome he is. Our eyes meet and he smiles in a way that I don't think I'll ever forget. Mesmerized. Taken with me. Pleased.

How did we go from me being lethally jealous a few weeks back to this? Just . . . how?

I turn to face him. "You like?"

Anissa somehow fades away like the true professional she is as he moves the short distance to me and presses a kiss to my cheek. "Breathtaking," he murmurs in my ear. "I'm one lucky man to have you on my arm tonight. But I do think these might complement the dress a bit more."

I laugh when he pulls the sapphire earrings out of his pocket. "Breaking into my house these days?" I tease.

"You left them in the top drawer of your desk. Not a very safe place to keep something so very important." He stares at them and then back up to me. "Will you wear them for me tonight? Just this once?"

With my eyes on his, I take the first sapphire earring from the velvet case and put it on. Then the next. He turns me around so I can look in the mirror. He's behind me like a second skin and as much as the earrings are stunning and complete the entire look, he does even more so.

There's a contrast between us.

He's dark while I'm light. He's unreadable while my emotions are on my sleeve. He's the bolt of lightning and I'm feeling blinded by its force.

He leans forward and presses a kiss to my bare neck without

breaking our connection in the mirror. Desire fires in his eyes despite the room full of women suddenly trying to act small so as to not interrupt this moment.

"Do I get to know yet where we're going?" I ask yet again.

My guess is we're going to some charity function. Some place where Holden Knight needs to see and be seen, which then poses a problem for me and our platonic-in-the-eyes-of-everyone-else situation.

"Our first stop of the evening will be dinner."

"And then?"

His chuckle is a low rumble. "*And then?* Is dinner with me not enough for you? Greedy girl."

"That's not what I meant." I laugh.

He puts his hands on my shoulders, turns me around, and steps into me. "Then what did you mean, woman I want to kiss but whose freshly applied lipstick I don't want to mess up?"

"You said *first,* so that implies there is a second part. That's why I asked," I say as I run my hands up the lapel of his tuxedo. I love the soft hiss he emits. It tells me he's just as affected by my presence as I am by his. Then I lean in and whisper in his ear, "Always mess the lipstick up. *Always.*"

I feel the rumble of his chuckle the same time as I hear it. "Good to know we're on the same page."

He runs the back of his hand down my cheek. "Hmm."

His response piques my curiosity. Before I can think too much about it, he leans in and brushes his lips ever so slightly against mine.

"Time to go."

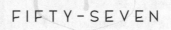

FIFTY-SEVEN

The evening has been magical.

And that's coming from a woman who isn't keen on romance and flips the channel anytime a Hallmark movie comes on.

But it has been.

The surprise trip to Manhattan. The pamper team waiting for me at the hotel. The way Holden looked at me when he saw me wearing my new dress and his sapphires.

Then there was our private dinner on the top floor of a skyscraper with nothing but a wall of windows separating us from the city beyond. The food was delicious—and *real*. Not the fancy-looking morsels that food magazines post images of that look like art and diners go home hungry from. It was paired with a fine wine and an incredibly cozy atmosphere. But more important than the meal was my time with Holden.

It was like we were back at the rooftop restaurant on the coast and then some. We talked about anything and everything but work. We laughed about silly stories. We cringed at embarrassing moments.

We were normal, everyday people—just *Holden and Rowan*—on a date. Not bazillionaire Holden Knight who is poised to take over my company, and not determined Rowan Rothschild struggling to figure out who this new version of her is who sleeps with the enemy and enjoys it.

And now we're here, standing outside on a street in New York

City. My hand is in Holden's, and I'm beginning to think my heart might be too.

The distance between "think" and "know" is short. And I'm trying not to focus on it.

I shake the thought away and force a smile when I notice him scrutinizing me.

"What was that look for?" he asks, ever the observer.

"What look?"

He narrows his eyes. "The one you were just giving me when you were looking at me but not really seeing me."

I was seeing you all right. In fact I was seeing you so much I was trying to put all of these emotions you create in me in check. The problem? It's getting harder and harder to do that the more time we spend together. The more we get to know each other.

I shrug. "I was just wondering what you did with the painting."

He barks out a laugh that makes his shoulders shake and his eyes fire to life more than they already are. "How about I haven't done anything with it yet?"

"Oh?" I ask and he nods. "I thought that you had destructive plans for it," I tease.

"I do. I'm taking my time with it, enjoying its ugliness for a bit before I have fun destroying it." His eyes meet mine and narrow as the muscle in his jaw pulses.

I don't know why that sentence has goose bumps clawing their way up my spine, but it does.

And just as quick as the feeling comes, it passes. So does the somberness of his expression. I watch as he flips a switch, his smile lightening the shadows that were just there.

"We both know that's not what you were wondering. Lay it on me, Sunshine."

I laugh, welcoming the shift. "Maybe I was simply wondering where we are and what we are doing . . . which in all fairness has been an ongoing theme tonight."

"Perfect. That's exactly what I was going for." He squeezes my hand and brings it to his lips. "Good to know I succeeded." He looks at the door. It's as nondescript as the building itself. There is a plaque next to it that is all blacked out and offers no clues to what it holds inside. "Are you ready?"

"For?"

"You asked me why I *summoned* you to the jet today. I said part of the reason was to apologize, and the other part was this."

"This?" I laugh nervously.

"Yes," he says and opens the door for me to go through. It's a lobby of some sort with high ceilings and a huge chandelier. It feels new but looks old with its décor and lighting. "*This.* An early birthday present."

"What? It's not for two months. How did you even know?"

Now that we're alone, Holden leans forward and kisses me. It's gentle yet urgent. Tender but laden with desire. When it ends, he rests his forehead against mine. "You forget, I know everything."

And before I can respond, he grabs my hand and leads me farther into the building. But when we go through the next set of doors, I realize this is anything but a building, it's a theater of some sort.

I look around. At the ceilings. At the walls. At the stage. The small area is ornate in the best way possible with appliquéd walls and thick velvet drapes framing the stage. Polished wood sits on its floor and oversized theater seats are spread out and luxuriously spaced rather than being right on top of each other.

"Holden." His name sounds like how I feel—in awe. "This place is incredible. Look at the attention to detail on everything."

I look back to him and find him smiling at me. And there's something in his smile that has me only wanting to look solely at him when I'm in a room where everything is beautiful.

"It's an incredible place. Built in the early 1900s. Purchased by a private buyer who restored it to its original state and has kept it that way."

"How did you find this? I mean"—I look back up and turn my face up to the ceiling—"it's stunning."

"Mmm-hmm. It is. Now this? This is where I'm going to need you to trust me, Sunshine."

"What? Why?" What does he have up his sleeve?

"Please, take a seat." He motions to a seat in the middle of the front row.

"Why? Why am I getting a feeling I'm not going to like this?" I chuckle nervously.

"Why? Because I asked you to and this is where you stop trying to control the situation and let me handle things."

I fight my inherent response to tell him I can handle things myself. But I'm able to staunch it. "Has anyone told you that I don't do well with surprises?"

"You seemed to do perfectly well with the surprise I threw at you today, now, didn't you?"

Shit. I guess I can't use that excuse.

He leans in and kisses me, hands cupping my face and lips coaxing me to relax. "Trust me." There's a tenderness in his voice, in his eyes, that has emotion lumping in my throat.

It's like something has suddenly shifted. What is it? I can't put my finger on it, but it has.

I trust him. And that's not an easy thing for me.

"C'mon, Sunshine. Sit down for me and close your eyes."

I do as he asks. It's incredibly hard for me to not sneak a peek but after everything he's done tonight, the least I can do is not ruin whatever surprise he has planned.

"You good?" he murmurs as our joined hands lower as he takes a seat beside me.

"I'm good."

There is shuffling. Some footsteps. A cleared throat.

And then the music begins to play. It's the slow, melodic sound of a cello. It's deep and melancholic and when my eyes flash open, the gasp that falls from my shocked lips is as reflexive as breathing.

I stare at the man on stage. He's imposing in his black tuxedo and absolute confidence. In the way he runs the bow back and forth over the strings. In the way he commands the instrument like the world-class musician he is.

I'm mesmerized. Stunned. Overwhelmed.

"Holden." Tears well in my eyes but I'm afraid to take my eyes off of the man in front of me. I'm afraid if I do, he'll disappear, and this will all be a dream. "It's—it's . . ."

"Clayton Seaburn," he murmurs.

FIFTY-EIGHT

Holden

I may not understand or appreciate the music the man before us is creating, but I know Rowan's expression and that's all that matters.

Every penny it took to get him here was worth it when I saw the look on her face during those first notes.

The flash open of her eyes. The shocked O of her lips. The way she said my name as she looked at me fleetingly, as if she were afraid if she took her eyes off him that he'd disappear.

And then there were her reactions during the hour he played for us.

For some pieces, a smile was wide on her face.

For others, tears slid silently down her cheeks.

At times, she moved her hands along with his as if she were playing the notes with him.

At others, she closed her eyes, swaying to its melody like she could feel the music weaving deep down in her soul.

I didn't feel fucking shit.

I take that back. The music didn't make me feel fucking shit but the woman I still can't take my eyes off—even an hour after we parted ways with a man she idolizes—sure as shit does.

"You despise classical music—hell, you even made me change the song on my playlist in the jet today when a piece came on—and yet you did that for me?"

I nod. "Mmm-hmm."

"*And* you sat through the entire performance without falling asleep?" she asks. That smile hasn't left her face once since we left the theater.

Not fucking once.

"I feel privileged." She holds her arms out and twirls on the sidewalk. "I feel loved. I feel . . ." She stops and looks at me, her eyes alive with fire and her smile burning bright as she steps into me and whispers, "*Incredible.*" She brushes her lips against mine. The kiss is soft at first. Simple. "You make me feel that way." Another brush of lips. Then a tug of her teeth on my bottom lip before she looks back at me with tears welling in her eyes. "Thank you. That's the nicest thing anyone has ever done for me."

"It was nothing," I say gruffly, hating the ball of whatever it is lumping in my throat.

It was just a good deed.

It was just . . . *what, Holden?* A way to ease the guilt? A way to show you care when you're not capable of voicing it? A way to prove to yourself you're not the bastard you know you are?

A way to leave her with something good from you when you detonate the world all around her?

What the fuck was it? Because those are four very contrasting things.

"It wasn't nothing," she says. "It was . . . you hearing and really listening. It was you understanding something about me that no one else does."

"I'm glad you enjoyed it." I itch to put my hands on her. To run them up and down her abdomen. But I know if I touch her, I'm not going to want to stop, and standing on the sidewalk of Central Park South isn't exactly the place to do it.

As it is, I've had to deter her from running barefoot in Central Park like she wanted to do five minutes ago.

"Happy early birthday, Sunshine."

FIFTY-NINE

Rowan

I study Holden through the darkened penthouse where he sits on the outdoor patio. Its glass walls are slid open, allowing the night breeze to blow in right along with the muted sounds of the city far below.

He paints a striking picture sitting there with his shirt unbuttoned at the collar, his bow tie hanging undone around it, and a glass of scotch in his hand that's resting on the armrest.

He's looking out into the darkness beyond as if he's contemplating how he's going to complete his world domination . . . and still he somehow looks relaxed. More relaxed than I think I've ever seen him before. He's content. Sexy.

My heart swells in my chest in a way I've never felt before. It's getting harder and harder to ignore. And if I'm honest with myself, I'm not sure that I want to.

But I don't know what the alternative is. I don't know where to go from here when it comes to a man it can't go anywhere with.

He takes a sip of his scotch and absently swirls the remainder around in the glass. I can't take my eyes off of him. Nor do I want to as I replay every uniquely incredible thing that he's made happen for me in the last ten hours.

Clayton fucking Seaburn.

My mind is still blown over how he made that happen. How he

got the world's most decorated cellist to fly in from London for a private performance for me. *Me!*

Moreover, how the idea ever crossed his mind in the first place. I mean . . . I'm still in complete and utter shock.

I move out to the patio and stand there studying him until he notices me. "Mmmm," he murmurs, holding his hand out to motion me to come over to him. "You tired?" he asks.

I shrug. "Not really. I'm still on a high from everything. You?"

"I rarely sleep."

I nod as my phone lights up on the table beside him once again. Holden frowns as he picks it up. "Does the guy ever stop fucking calling you?" he mutters as he makes a show of turning off my phone. "Bye-bye, Chad." Clearly irritated, he tosses my phone but only when he looks back up does he take notice of me.

I've let my dress slide down my body and pool at my feet so that I'm standing in front of Holden in nothing but lacy underthings, my very expensive high heels, and his sapphires.

"Don't be jealous of Chad. He gets a phone call. You get *this*."

"Good god," he groans as I move forward, straddle his thighs, and lower myself to sit on his lap. "Good fucking god." His eyes roam over the parts of me he can see, and his cock hardens instantly beneath me.

I lean in so my lips are a breath from his. "Hey, Holden?"

"Hmm?" He runs his hands down my back, his touch electric.

"Mess my lipstick up."

Our lips meet. It's slow and taunting at first. Our breaths melding and tongues dancing in the moonlit night. There's an undercurrent of desperation, but it stays just that. Beneath the surface—an indisputable constant—that takes second to our need to savor.

Our hands on each other's skin. Our tongues in each other's mouths. Our breaths shared as one. Our nerves tingling from each point we are touching.

He cups my breast that's barely contained in my demi cup and

then flicks his tongue over it as I grind over his cock still con-
stricted by his slacks. It feels incredible. *He* feels incredible.

The warmth of his mouth on my skin as he laces openmouthed
kisses everywhere he can. The strength in his hands as they move
constantly over my skin. The hardness of his cock as I rub my clit
over it with each rotation of my hips.

We move slowly. My fingers getting enough buttons undone so
that he can get rid of his shirt. Me rising up so that he can push
down his pants, his cock now free, thick and heavy against my
parted thighs.

We kiss like this. With him ready and me soaking him. We kiss
like there is no tomorrow to think about. Like the sun won't rise
for another twenty-four hours. Like we have no life to go back to
where we can't exist like this. Together. Out in public. Just us.

A man I still can't figure completely out and a woman who is
admittedly falling for him.

My breath hitches at the thought, but at the same time he pulls
my panties to the side, and I lower myself ever so slowly down
onto him so the sound gets lost and misplaced with the action.

"Look at me, Sunshine," he murmurs as he fills me to capacity.

It takes a moment for me to hear him because I'm so busy riding the waves of pleasure that come with him filling me. But when
I do, when my breath returns and mind clears, I find his eyes. His
own are having trouble focusing as I purposely squeeze myself
around him before forcing him to abide by his own command
and meet mine. Our gazes hold and the softest of smiles turns up
his lips before he pulls my face closer and his lips close over mine.

I begin to move like that. To rock my hips with our mouths
met, our tongues touching, and our hands on the other's heads.
His framing my face and my fingers threaded through the hair at
the back of his neck.

We're hushed murmurs and sated sighs.

We're rocked hips and grinding pelvises.

We're slow and steady when all we've ever been before is fast
and furious.

It's different this time around. The movements are the same—us both bringing pleasure to the same table—but this time it feels like a five-course meal instead of fast food. Just so damn different.

We savor the connection. The feel of his cock rubbing over every nerve I have within again and again. The rumble of his groan against my tongue when he emits it. The possession in his fingers as they touch me.

We can't get enough of each other. It's like we're ravenous for more but our actions are painstakingly deliberate, intentionally slow as I ride him, as if we fear we're going to overpower the myriad of sensations pulling us under.

As if we fear what happens when this ends.

"You feel so goddamn good," he moans against my lips, his hands still in my hair, his lips lifting to meet mine as I grind once again over him. "So wet. So tight. So fucking good."

"This. You," I pant out, my own thoughts so scattered by the pleasure surging through me that I can't finish them.

"Ride me." The tendons in his neck pull taut. "Take every fucking inch and ride me."

We soak up the moment. Our bodies. Our pleasure. The moonlight on our skin. The words that we say.

The pace stays the same but the pressure builds. One layer of pleasure upon another. One high chased after the other. One snap of a live wire against another.

"Holden," I mewl as my body tenses and tightens seconds before I lose all sense of reality and reason.

Before my orgasm swells into a huge crescendo that crashes down all around me until there is only him. Just Holden. Just me. Just our bodies. Just my feelings. Just everything I thought I wanted that now suddenly feels different.

"Row," he pants out. "Look at me." My breath stutters and my body shudders. "Look. At. Me."

It takes everything I have to respond. To meet those sex-drugged eyes of his that hold so much more emotion than lust in them.

But I do.

And I'm so fucking grateful I do because watching him crash over the edge is an incredible sight. To see what I do to him. To see how I make his body react. To see the same damn emotions in his eyes that are confusing the fuck out of me.

I press my lips to his.

It's easier to get lost in the kiss as he loses himself to his orgasm.

Because this—the kiss, the pleasure, the physical—is so much easier to comprehend than why this just felt so different.

Why the sex between us was different.

Why things just shifted without warning.

Why I fell for Holden Knight.

Why being with him feels like I've been struck by lightning.

SIXTY

Holden

I scrub a hand over my face when I lift my phone and see the time.

Eight in the morning.

Jesus.

I slept.

For the first time in forever I slept a solid five fucking hours. I'd like to think it was because I was equally exhausted and sated, but when I shift a bit, I'm pretty fucking sure it has everything to do with the woman currently twisted in the sheets with me.

Her warm skin.

Her even breathing.

Her face on my shoulder and hand resting over my chest.

I freeze and try to clear the cobwebs from my head but nothing shakes loose. They're not cobwebs, it's Rowan.

Simply put, it's fucking Rowan.

What is happening, Knight?

You don't spend nights with women. You have a good time. You mess up the sheets or the counter or wherever the fuck we find ourselves landing . . . then you leave. And even when you find yourself going back to the woman, over and over, you sure as shit know better than to blur the lines.

But lying here with Rowan on my chest and no desire to bolt the fuck out the door, I know I blurred the lines. But fuck if I'm struggling to find where the problem is?

But there is a problem.

A huge one.

One that has nothing to do with the scent of her skin and the feel of her body against mine and everything to do with the confusion in my head and pressure in my chest waking up to her. With her.

Fucking complications, man.

I didn't want them and I'm walking head-fucking-first into them.

Rowan shifts in her sleep and rolls off of me. It's my chance to escape. To distance myself. To put myself in check.

And yet when I sit up in bed, I can't take my eyes off of her. The soft lips. Her thick lashes. The pink of her nipples peeking just above the sheet.

What if we'd met under different circumstances? What if she weren't a Rothschild?

Would that make any difference?

No. It doesn't change who or what you are, Knight. It only adds a weak spot you can't risk. An Achilles' heel when you're a mere mortal.

But still I sit and watch her. Still I wonder. Still I want.

Get out of the bed, Holden. Get out of the fucking bed.

*   *   *

Rowan shifts against me. Her legs are curled up and her back is against my side, my arm wrapped around the front of her chest. We're both staring out the jet's window as we taxi down the runway and prepare for takeoff. Prepare to get back to a different reality.

We've both been quiet this morning.

I'd like to think it's because we had a late night and we're both exhausted. I may be clueless when it comes to a lot of things, but I'm well aware our quiet comfort has little to do with being tired and a lot more to do with last night.

The dinner. The concert. The sex on the patio. The sex in the bed. Rowan curling up against me and falling asleep, me with the scent of her hair in my nose and the feel of her hand on my heart. Waking up with someone.

I tried to step out of the bedroom. To busy myself with my phone, with work, but I was drawn to her.

Sleepy yawns, pillow-creased cheeks, and crazy bedhead. Morning coffee overlooking Central Park led to another round of sex. Another bout of confusion for me.

Her eyes on mine. My cock buried in her. My fucking cold heart beating when it shouldn't be.

I spooked. Spooked to the point that I lied about an unexpected business matter I needed to take care of to create a needed distance.

She went shopping for a bit. I stared at the fucking door she left through.

She came back. I still had no answers as to why my head was so fucked up.

But I can guess. I'm a man who likes to take risks and anything beyond just sex with Rowan is one I can't take.

So why am I fighting that realization like my life fucking depends on it?

Absently, I go to press a kiss to the top of her head and then stop myself.

What the fuck are you doing, Holden? You've spent your whole fucking life to get to this point, creating opportunities to fulfill the promise you made to Mase.

You've just completed the first step. You have several more to go.

And now you're, what? What even is this that you're doing? That you're allowing to happen?

This can't happen.

And yet aren't I the one who made it happen? The one who planned this. Who wanted to do this. Who chose to stay the night when the jet was fueled and waiting on the tarmac for us after the performance last night.

I scrub a hand over my face and sigh.

"You okay?" Rowan murmurs, lifting her head up and against mine.

"Yeah. Fine. I just . . ."

"Just what?"

"Nothing." I do in fact press a kiss to her head this time and keep my lips there when I answer. "It's nothing."

"Dreading going back to reality?" she teases.

"Mmm." If she only knew what that reality was. "Something like that."

She reaches out for her cell phone across the table. "Maybe I should turn it back on just in case—"

"No." I take it from her and toss it out of reach as my other hand slides around the front of her neck and prompts her head to lean all the way back. "Not yet." I press my lips to hers in an upside-down kiss. "Can we just forget the world for a few more hours until we land?"

That's not going to fix shit, Knight.

Her lips spread in a smile against mine before she kisses me back again, but this time our tongues touch and a soft moan falls from between her lips. "No complaints here."

"That's what I thought."

But when she snuggles back up against me and falls asleep as we ascend, all I can do is lean my head back and stare at the ceiling.

The thoughts and plans that constantly shift and meld when I can't sleep are there like always.

But now there is something new mixed in.

Now there's Rowan.

And I'm not fucking sure how she fits.

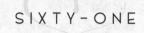

SIXTY-ONE

Rowan

The jet is fueled and ready when you are.

I reread the text from Holden as I pull into the TinSpirits' parking lot. My smile is automatic. Just like it has been every time I think of the past forty-eight hours. The magic of it. The settling into the notion that I've fallen for him. The realization that I'm pretty sure it's mutual, and what exactly do I think about that? Even worse, what if it is mutual and he refuses to accept it?

Because if there's one thing I know about Holden Knight, it's that I don't know him.

But whatever it is, it feels good.

Isn't that all I need to know for now?

And isn't that why I'm here, making a quick stop before I head to the airport for my meetings with the GWA representatives at their site?

To give him something back—a little token of my appreciation—for all the effort (and money) that he put into this weekend.

I bypass my personal parking spot and pull right up to the front doors. It's a Sunday so the place is a ghost town, which is exactly what I was hoping for. I grab my master key and head inside.

My cell rings when I'm in the elevator. It's Chad. *Again.*

I sigh and roll my eyes. We need to put a moratorium on our mothers getting together—which lately seems like it's every fucking weekend. Because them spending time together means more plotting, more planning, more pushing Chad to win me over.

I haven't returned his calls—or even listened to his voicemails—from the last few days, and that's why.

Our floor is empty as I make my way through it, detouring at my office for my spare set of keys that will open Holden's office.

There's no way he'd mind me being in here for the sole purpose of dropping off a surprise.

I unlock and open his door and set my purse down, pulling my present out of it. I open the velvet box and smile at the cuff links nestled inside. They're brushed platinum, round with a sunburst design engraved in their centers like rays of sunshine. I saw them nestled in a jeweler's case when I was shopping in New York and I had to have them. I had to thank him in some way other than words—and really good sex—and I thought these were perfect.

But rather than have them delivered by courier as he did mine, I figured I'd beat him at his own game. He went into my drawer and got my sapphires. I'm going to go into his drawer and leave his cuff links.

I close the lid and move behind the desk, opening the top drawer without really thinking. It didn't bug me that he went into my top drawer, so I really don't think twice about doing the same to his. But when I open it up and am greeted by a stack of papers, I simply stand there and stare, my brain working to register what I'm seeing.

Why does the top of this contract look different from the one he showed me?

It's the old contract. The one without my seat on the board.

It has to be.

But then why is the date on the top of its cover page from this past Thursday?

I hate the unsteady way my pulse beats and my breath rasps as I try to rationalize away my sudden, irrational fear.

Curiosity piqued and privacy be damned, I pick up the binder-clipped stack of papers, cuff links forgotten.

I flip through to the section I'd memorized. The addendum that added a transfer of shares over to me, Rowan Olivia Rothschild, upon the completion of the sale. But that page, which was in the papers Holden gave me, isn't in this set. There is no Addendum A on page thirty-three.

"It's an old contract," I mutter, but my heart thunders in my chest as I flip to the last page. As I see inked signatures by Holden Knight of Knight Holdings, LLC, and Rhett Rothschild, CEO of Rothschild Enterprises, aka TinSpirits. As I take in the date signed.

My hands tremble as adrenaline surges through my body. As disbelief courses through me faster than my pulse pounds.

He lied to me.

I put my faith in Holden Knight, and he fucking lied to me.

He never intended to give me the board seat or the ownership. He never planned on having me be on equal footing with him. He simply conned me into thinking I was so he could keep an eye on me.

So he could control me.

So he could ensure the safety of his precious fucking deal.

And then he slid into my bed when he realized he couldn't.

He slid into it and made me feel when I didn't want to feel. He made me believe when I'd never thought to before. He made me hope when I had never put much faith in that emotion to begin with.

He used me in every sense of the word.

And when all was said and done, when the deal was signed and I'd been thoroughly screwed, he gave me the most thoughtful gift anyone had ever given me solely as a means of distraction.

Not because he genuinely wanted to.

But because guilt is a powerful emotion.

Because he had to try to salvage our working relationship somehow.

Because he felt bad.

The taste of salt hits my lips. My own tears streaming down my face. My own heart lodged in my throat.

I need to get out of here. I can't breathe. I can't think. I can't process.

I don't know how I manage it, but I straighten the stack of papers and put them back in the drawer how I found them. I shut it, then stand there and look at the closed drawer.

Oh. My. God.

This is so much worse than I could have imagined. He betrayed me. He looked me in the eyes, he let me be vulnerable with him, all while sharpening the knife to stab me in the back.

I rush from the office, locking the door behind me, and get on the elevator as fast as I can. It's only when I'm tearing out of the parking lot that I think about the cuff links I left on the top of his desk.

He'll know I was there.

He'll know I left them.

But will he know that I know about everything else?

I pound the heel of my hand against the steering wheel, the tears coming harder now.

When was he going to tell me?

Or maybe he wasn't. Maybe he was going to string me along, have me get everything done he wanted, and then let me know that *oopsie,* he wasn't going to uphold his end of the bargain.

I don't know where to go. I don't know what to do. I sure as hell don't want to go to the airport and hop on his private jet bound for Georgia.

But if I stay here, he'll seek me out. He'll demand to know what's wrong.

If I go, I'll have a few days away from him. A few days where I can truly process the heartbreak—because yes, fuck it, this is heartbreak in so many ways—before I have to face him again and . . . and what?

Act like nothing happened?

Confront him and let him know I was in his desk?

The pain in my chest is crushing. The memories of this weekend are more than soured. The tears on my cheeks are like acid.

I don't know.

I just don't know.

But I head to the airport.

Ring. Ring. Ring.

I need the reprieve.

Ring. Ring. Ring.

The distance.

Ring. Ring. Ring.

The time to think and plan and process.

Ring. Ring. Ring.

I ignore the constant ringing of my cell, the bombardment of Chadwick Williams and all that he is.

I park my car.

I walk to the hangar.

I walk up the airstairs and onto the plane.

I plaster a fake smile on my lips for Rhonda and her judgmental looks.

I buckle myself in.

And when the plane takes off my chest hurts so fucking bad. All I want to do is cry. Is rage. Is throw this glass in my hand against the wall.

But I don't. Won't. I refuse to give him the satisfaction of getting to me regardless of how much I loathe him right now.

Ring. Ring. Ring.

"*What,*" I snap, sick of the sound and needing it to stop. Needing everyone to just let me fucking be. "Leave me alone, Chad. Just leave me alone."

"Rowan. I need to talk to you. *It's important.*"

SIXTY-TWO

Holden

This is the last place I want to fucking be.

The Westmore Country Club. The bane of my existence and the place that holds some of my sourest memories.

But I'm playing the game.

I'm kissing the babies and shaking the hands and hating every fucking second of it. But when Audrey calls and says I need to be somewhere, I need to be somewhere.

The question is why do I fucking need to be here?

I get you're working from home for a few days, but isn't that supposed to make you happier? More relaxed? Quit being such a surly asshole because I'm sick of it.

Weren't those Audrey's words?

And why are you being a fucker, huh, Knight?

Why haven't you slept for longer than two hours at a time in days and why are you checking your phone every few goddamn seconds?

It comes down to one thing—Rowan.

She left on the fishing expedition to Georgia to try to reel in a new supplier. I know she got there because the fucking jet is mine . . . but I've heard little from her since.

Her texts are short. My unanswered phone calls are met with a quick responding text that she's busy with clients. My late-night calls are replied to the following morning that she had fallen asleep.

It's fucking maddening.

It's been three days and I'm about to get on the jet and head there myself.

And now, of course, I'm here. At the teal-and-white hell that seems to be where every fucking business meeting is preferably held.

And Rowan's new client, GWA, the one she left my dick high and dry on, has requested just that. A meeting. Here. With me.

The only explanation they gave Audrey is that they want to go over everything with me. They'd better watch where they step, or I might squash the deal altogether if they think that going over Rowan's head and coming to me without her knowing is a good decision. Or if they hint in any way possible that they don't think she's capable because she's a woman.

"Yes?" I answer my phone as I enter the outdoor patio and bar area where people come and relax after a long, *taxing* day at golf. Like they know anything about taxing work here.

"Akiro just called," Audrey says. "He's running about ten minutes late. He apologizes profusely."

I nod as I look around. "Good. That'll give me time to have a drink or two."

"To what? Take the edge off? Yeah, you might want to make that three."

"Funny."

"It's not funny when it's true." She snorts.

"Put in a call to James," I say of my pilot. "Have him on standby in case I need to get to Georgia when I'm done here."

"Why would you need to go to Georgia?" she asks in that knowing tone of hers.

"Audrey," I warn. "I appreciate you trying to keep me on track, but I'm a grown man who can manage his own distractions."

"Just like I'm a long-term employee who knows when her boss is losing his grip on things. You pay me to keep you on track."

Fuck.

Am I pissed because she's right, or am I pissed because I don't want to admit to her being right?

"Right now I'm paying you to back the fuck off," I state, irritated with not being able to reach Rowan and pissed that I'm irritated about it.

"Noted." Her voice is clipped, the reprimand not sitting well with her. "I'll get in touch with James, but I believe the jet's having regular maintenance being done to it. I had to authorize the work yesterday."

"Fuck," I mutter.

"Whatever holds your interest in Georgia can probably handle herself." Considering she helped me with accommodations in Manhattan, I know she knows something is going on. But in true Audrey fashion, she'll only hint at it.

And in true Holden fashion, I won't confirm shit.

"Goodbye, Audrey."

"Goodbye, grumpy."

I make my way across the patio to the bar and startle when an arm is sloppily hung over my shoulder. "Holden. My man. My boss. The asshole who is fucking us over," Chad slurs as he weaves back and forth on his feet.

I grit my teeth and try to politely step aside, but Chad just holds on tighter.

"That's okay. You can fuck me over all you want because I won't feel a single goddamn thing."

"Clearly," I say, finally extricating myself from his hold, now needing a drink more than fucking ever.

"I'm celebrating. Did you know that?" he asks, grin goofy and eyes glazed. "Finally fucking celebrating."

"Good for you," I mutter and hold my finger up to get the bartender's attention for when he has a moment.

"We're finally going to fix this. Finally going to say check-fucking-mate. Finally . . . finally getting what's mine."

That's a lot of fucking finallys.

"A scotch, please," I order all while taking in my surroundings. I see the Rothschilds at a table with the Williamses. Or at least I can presume the round-bellied motherfucker in the police uniform is his dad.

"C'mon, Knight. Don't be such a hard-ass. Toast with us."

The scotch is slid across the bar. My first sip can't come soon enough. "What are we toasting?" I ask, completely disinterested.

"To Mr. and Mrs. Williams."

"Great. Perfect." I glance at his parents as the chief slips his arms around Florence's shoulders and presses a kiss to her cheek. An anniversary? The Westmore elite will find any excuse to celebrate around here. "Congrats to them."

"We are in fact talking about me."

"You?"

"Yep. Me."

"And why's that?" Not like I really fucking care.

"It's finally happening." He sways but his grin grows wider. "I'm finally getting married."

Now there's a bright spot in my fucking day. Chad married means he'll leave Rowan the fuck alone. No more touching. No more sharing appetizers. No more anything.

"No shit? Congrats." I tap my glass against his simply to go through the motions. "And who's the lucky lady?"

Chad throws his head back and laughs before looking me straight in the eye and saying, "Rowan."

What.

The.

Fuck.

"Didn't she tell you? She finally said yes. We're getting married."

I choke on my sip.

This is a joke.

It has to be a fucking joke—a revenge prank for them getting screwed out of the cash they think is theirs that's still in escrow.

I don't respond to Chad.

Can't.

All I can think about is getting the fuck out of here. Is getting ahold of Rowan.

I'm off the patio and into a back room of the clubhouse without responding to Chad. My heart is pounding and fuck if my hands aren't sweaty as I try to pull my phone out of my fucking pocket.

The phone rings. "Pick up the fucking phone, Rowan," I order.

Her voicemail picks up. My hand fists. The need to punch something owns me.

Goddamn it.

I call again.

Same fucking result.

My throat feels like it's collapsing in on itself. My heart feels like it's trying to squeeze its way through the space that's left.

When my phone rings in my hand I all but jump. I can't answer it fast enough.

"Rowan?" Her name sounds as breathless and desperate as I feel.

"What? I'm busy."

This is not the same woman I kissed goodbye after Manhattan.

"I just talked to Chad. Tell me he's wrong, Rowan." My demand is met with her absolute silence. "Tell me he's fucking wrong."

Silence stretches.

Eats up the distance.

Weaves into my chest and squeezes my lungs until there is no fucking air left.

"It's time to change the dress, Holden."

And then the line goes dead.

ACKNOWLEDGMENTS

Thank you so very much for taking a chance on Rowan and Holden's story. I'm more than excited for you to see where their journey takes them.

I'd like to acknowledge a few people who made *Twisted Knight* possible. First and foremost, you, the reader. It's you who inspire me to bring stories to life. Thank you for your support over the last decade and the love you have for the characters in my head.

Thank you to Alison Manning, Chrisstine Pearce, and Stephanie Gibson for keeping some kind of semblance and consistency for me over the years. To my VP Pit Crew—you've been there since day one, and I couldn't do this without you guys.

Lauren Blakely, Christine Reiss, and Laurelin Paige—our weekly Wednesday check-ins might seem trivial but have been such a welcome constant in this author world of uncertainty. Thank you for that.

Nina Grinstead, Meagan Reynoso, Christine Miller, Kim Czermak, and the rest of the Valentine PR crew—your time, advice, honesty, and effort to keep me visible is always appreciated.

Kimberly Brower—we've come a long way since *Driven*. Thank you for your representation, your honesty, and fighting for me on all fronts.

To my team at Tor—thank you for taking Rowan and Holden and helping to make them shine. I appreciate your efforts.

And last but not least . . . thank you to my family that puts up with me when I'm on deadline and through the endless mumblings when I have writer's block. I couldn't do this without you.

ABOUT THE AUTHOR

New York Times bestselling author K. Bromberg writes contemporary romance novels that contain a mixture of sweetness, emotions, a whole lot of sex, and a little bit of realness. She likes to write strong heroines and damaged heroes, who we love to hate but can't help but love.

Since publishing her first book on a whim in 2013, Bromberg has sold more than two million copies of her books across twenty different countries and has landed on the *New York Times, USA Today,* and *Wall Street Journal* bestseller lists more than thirty times. (She still wakes up and asks herself how she got so lucky for all this to happen.)

A mom of three, Bromberg finds the only thing harder than finishing the book she's writing is navigating parenthood during the teenage years (send more wine!). She loves dogs, sports, a good book, and is an expert procrastinator. She lives in Southern California with her family and their dogs.

kbromberg.com
Facebook.com/AuthorKBromberg
Twitter: @KBrombergDriven
Instagram: @kbromberg